MURDER CAN SPOOK YOUR CAT

A DESIREE SHAPIRO MYSTERY

Selma Eichler

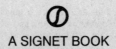

A SIGNET BOOK

SIGNET
Published by New American Library, a division of
Penguin Putnam Inc., 375 Hudson Street,
New York, New York 10014, U.S.A.
Penguin Books Ltd, 27 Wrights Lane,
London W8 5TZ, England
Penguin Books Australia Ltd, Ringwood,
Victoria, Australia
Penguin Books Canada Ltd, 10 Alcorn Avenue,
Toronto, Ontario, Canada M4V 3B2
Penguin Books (N.Z.) Ltd, 182–190 Wairau Road,
Auckland 10, New Zealand

Penguin Books Ltd, Registered Offices:
Harmondsworth, Middlesex, England

First published by Signet, an imprint of New American Library,
a division of Penguin Putnam Inc.

First Printing, January 1998
10 9 8 7 6

Copyright © Selma Eichler, 1998
All rights reserved

 REGISTERED TRADEMARK—MARCA REGISTRADA

Printed in the United States of America

PUBLISHER'S NOTE
This is a work of fiction. Names, characters, places, and incidents either are the product of the author's imagination or are used fictitiously, and any resemblance to actual persons, living or dead, events, or locales is entirely coincidental.

To Puck

ACKNOWLEDGMENTS

My thanks to—

Dr. Ilene Betman, of Riverside Care, Inc., whose input on mental illness was truly invaluable

Captain Alan G. Martin, of the New York State Police, who, once again, so patiently helped me out on law enforcement matters

Martin Turkish, M.D., who—also patiently and also once again—assisted with medical facts

My agent and personal cat authority, Luna Carne-Ross

My astute editor, Danielle Perez

Joseph Todaro, who supplied lengthy, step-by-step telephone instructions (speaking of patience!) on how to deglitch my Mac when it went berserk at a critical point in the manuscript

Judy Todaro, who introduced me to butternut bisque—one of the stars of Connie's delicious lunch

And Nikki and Julian Scott, who are always so ready to help

Chapter 1

The first time I met him was in November 1990, in the victim's town house. Only she wasn't the victim then. She was a vibrant and talented woman—exceptionally pretty, too—with a successful career, a beautiful home, and a wonderful new husband who was completely loopy about her. She seemed to have all sorts of great things to look forward to in those days. I remember that I even felt a little envious of her. Which I suppose doesn't say too much for me. But life did seem to have heaped an awful lot of goodies on her plate, don't you think?

I'm digressing, though. I wanted to tell you about *him*. . . .

When I came into the room, he was sitting there placidly—in the most comfortable chair, naturally—gazing at me intently. He was, I decided instantly, quite handsome. Dark hair—black, really—and lively gray-green eyes that I guess you could say kind of danced. At least, that's how I heard them described once. "He has dancing eyes" is how it was put to me.

But let's set aside how he looked. His personality was, if anything, even more attractive than his appearance.

He had absolutely the best disposition: warm and accepting and friendly. Although not *too* friendly, you understand. Not overbearing or anything. Just friendly enough to make you glad to be in his company. And he was intelligent, too. Plus he was attentive; he seemed to hang on every word you said to him. And tell me, how often do you come across *that* quality?

The fact is, I found him completely delightful.

But it was more than five years before I saw him again. And I couldn't believe the change in him.

The eyes still danced—but almost maniacally now. And his disposition—well, it was as if an alien being had gained possession of his body. To say he acted strangely would be like saying Einstein was bright. His behavior had become totally bizarre.

Do you know how he greeted me when I walked into the house after all that time?

He spat at me!

I was stunned. Naturally. And more than a little angry—at first, anyway. But then, of course, I realized that it was a reaction to the tragedy. And I ached for him. After all, the poor thing was grieving—*really* grieving. I mean, there were one or two others who took Luella Pressman's death hard.

But I'm convinced that her cat took it hardest of all.

Chapter 2

Kevin Garvey lived down the hall from me for more than two years. For about a month after he moved into the building, our contact was limited to half a dozen or so quick hellos in passing. And then one night I ran into him in the laundry room, and we introduced ourselves to each other. Almost immediately I thought what a lovely man he was, this initial impression becoming nothing less than a conviction when he insisted on carrying my laundry basket upstairs. "That looks a little heavy for you," he told me. "Here. Let me take it."

I protested—although not too strenuously—that there was no problem; I could manage. But he wouldn't hear of it. So really, what could I do?

Up until then, the very little that I knew about Kevin I'd picked up from building talk. (I was living in a much smaller apartment house with much chattier neighbors back then.) According to my elevator sources, he'd been an admiral in the navy—or at least a captain (it was captain, I eventually found out)—and he was now a marketing consultant. And—also according to these same elevator sources—a very well-compensated one.

I suppose if he'd been a little younger, or if I'd been a little older, I might have been bowled over by Kevin's looks. But he was almost sixty at that time, and I was—well, let's just say I was quite a bit his junior. And so his appearance didn't really have an effect on me. Not that I failed to notice what a pleasant smile he had and what nice, even features. And you couldn't help admiring all that wavy silver hair. He was well built, too, and so tall I got a crick in my neck looking up at him. Although being five-two, this is not an uncommon occurrence with me. But the point I'm trying to make is that while I was aware that he was an extremely attractive man, it never went any further than a dispassionate observation.

At any rate, we became pretty friendly, Kevin and I. At first, whenever we bumped into one another doing the wash, we'd sit around and visit until the clothes were out of the dryer—a real change in routine for me. (As a rule, I keep busy running up and down just like almost everyone else I know.) But I really enjoyed talking to this man. Surprisingly, considering how little we actually had in common, our conversations covered a lot of ground, too. We'd discuss the new marketing strategy he was working on, my latest investigation, the government, religion, *L.A. Law*, *Cheers*—all sorts of things. And after a while, our laundry room get-togethers progressed to his sometimes inviting me in for a drink. And from there to my asking him over for dinner every so often. And then to his reciprocating by taking me out to a restaurant—a really *fine* restaurant, I might add.

Like I said, though, it was strictly a friendship. Nothing more. Oh, I don't think I mentioned that Kevin was single, did I? Well, anyway, it seems he had never married—maybe because he was in the navy for much of his life. But whatever the explanation for his status, by the time I got to know him, there was no reason to expect he'd ever change it.

And then one evening, right after dinner, he rang my doorbell. I'd never seen anyone look more sheepish.

"I wanted you to know I'm moving out tomorrow," he said softly.

"Oh," I responded, not terribly thrilled to be hearing this. "How come?"

"I went and got married last week." Following which he turned a very pretty shade of pink.

I hadn't even been aware that he was seeing anyone! But then, it wasn't as if we were confidantes or anything. Of course, when I regained the power of speech (which never eludes me for very long), I hugged him and told him this was wonderful news and wished him all the best.

"Yes, uh, well, thank you," he stammered. "Luella—my wife—has a town house on East Forty-ninth and that's where we'll be living. You'll have to come over as soon as I get settled in and Luella has some free time. I'll give you a call in a few weeks and we'll set something up then," he promised.

But I really didn't expect to hear from him. Not that I didn't think he meant what he said, but here he was, entering his sixth decade and embarking on a whole different kind of existence for the very first time. And I figured with all that was happening in his life now, entertaining an ex-neighbor had to be relegated to about number 324 on his "to do" list.

But I was wrong.

He phoned on a Monday about three weeks later—right after Thanksgiving. And incidentally, it was the same day I'd finally gotten around to sending him a wedding present—a crystal pitcher from Tiffany's—at the new address I'd obtained from the super.

"Luella and I want you to have dinner with us," he told me. "How is Friday?"

Friday was just fine.

"Good. I can't wait for you to meet my bride." You could almost *hear* the blush.

I arrived at the town house at six—exactly on time. The woman who answered the door was, I guessed, in her mid to late forties, about five-three and slim. She had a pleasant face; shiny medium-length brown hair with a few sprinkles of gray here and there, which she wore in a pageboy; and lovely almond-shaped brown eyes. She might have been really attractive except for a much too prominent chin. But in light of the chin, "average" would probably be the best you could give her.

"You must be Desiree." She smiled and held out her hand.

Smiling back, I shook the outstretched hand. "And you must be—"

"Connie Neiman. Luella's sister and Kevin's recently acquired sister-in-law. Come in, please," she invited.

She led the way down a long narrow hall. "Kevin called a few hours ago to let us know he'd be a little late. He'll probably get here before seven, though," she said as I trotted after her.

Suddenly she stopped dead in her tracks. "Damn!" she muttered. We had come to a closed door now, and she spoke to me over her shoulder. "I reminded Luella at lunch that we were having company tonight. But it looks like she's still in her office; the door's usually open otherwise." With this, she knocked softly a couple of times. "I've been in the kitchen fixing dinner for the last hour and a half," she explained irritably, "and I assumed she'd gone upstairs to get dressed. After all, I *did* remind her." She knocked again, louder this time. "I really should have known better. Luella gets so caught up in her work that—" Connie was reaching out for the knob when the door swung open. Facing us was a small, thin woman in stocking feet who was, I presumed, the remiss Luella.

My presumption was confirmed as I focused on the almond-shaped eyes, an exact replica of her sister's.

Luella stood there motionless for a couple of seconds. "I'm so sorry," she told me—not very distinctly, since there was a pencil clamped between her teeth. Removing the pencil now, she added, "I had no idea what time it was. I'd intended to change before you came." And she glanced down regretfully at the baggy light gray sweat suit that matched her short salt and pepper hair—which was mostly salt and looked as if it had just gone through a wind tunnel. I wish you could have seen it! Some of the strands were actually straight on end, while others fell limply into her face, and a whole big section on the crown of her head seemed to be all matted together. I'd finally found a worthy rival to my own absolutely impossible (although gloriously hennaed) hair. And I'm talking about on its most mulish days.

"Anyway, I hope you'll forgive the . . . ah . . . informal attire, Desiree." She shot me a rueful smile—and exhibited the world's biggest, deepest dimples. "You *are* Desiree, I gather." And before I could verify it: "Of course you are. You must be. Who else would you be? And in case you haven't figured it out, I'm Luella Pressman. I kept the name because of the books—I write them; I'm an author." She spoke so rapidly that a couple of the words were swallowed up in her haste to get the next ones out there.

Now that I had a really good look at her, I estimated that Luella, in spite of the almost white hair, was somewhat younger than her sister—early forties, maybe—and a lot younger than her new husband. I could also make a pretty decent guess as to what had attracted Kevin—at least, at first. Let me tell you, not even that wild hair of hers and the naked, unassisted face—I mean, by so much as a smidgen of lipstick—could conceal the fact that this was an exceptionally pretty woman.

"Can I ask a favor?" she said. "Will you come sit with me for a couple of minutes? Kevvie"—(*Kevvie?* I wanted to gag)—"tells me you're very knowledgeable, and I could use a bit of help with my new book." And then she addressed her sister in a beseeching, kind of childlike voice. "Could we have our drinks and hors d'oeuvres in here, Connie, do you think?"

"Well, I—"

Luella broke in, turning to me again. "That is, if you wouldn't mind." And evidently opting to assume that I wouldn't: "What can we get you to drink, Desiree?"

"Red wine, please, if you have it."

"Me, too," she informed Connie, who with a perfunctory nod left to fulfill her charge.

Now Luella took me firmly by the arm and walked me into the room, which was paneled in a rich dark wood and dominated by a massive old oak desk. Propelling me toward the comfort-sized oatmeal tweed chair alongside the desk, she politely advised its current occupant—a sleek, inky-black cat—that he/she (I had no idea of its sex at this point) would be required to vacate. "I'm afraid, my dear, that you'll just have to find someplace else to sit," she said. The cat merely cocked its head and looked up at me with these beautiful, intelligent eyes. I got the feeling it was trying to decide if I was worth relocating for. But I don't think any conclusion was actually reached, because almost immediately Luella added impatiently, "Come on. Vamoose! Amscray! Listen, do you want me to put you out of the room? I know how that ticks you off."

I suppose it was her tone, really, that produced results. After all, the cat couldn't possibly have understood the threat. But anyway, it jumped off the chair then, allowing me to plant my not insubstantial back end on the now-empty seat. And following this, it proceeded to rub against my legs. I took the hint and bent down to scratch behind its ears. Which I was happy to do, being fond of cats in general and immediately taking to this one in particular.

"I haven't quite gotten myself into this book yet," Luella was saying in that mile-a-minute way she had. "Of course, I finished my last one only a few weeks ago, so I'm not that concerned. But still, I would like to start making some progress." Now settled at the desk, she began rummaging around its unbelievably littered surface for something. Her movements were fast and jerky—spasmodic, really. Just watching her made me yearn for a tranquilizer.

While she was busy with her search I had the opportunity to slip in a few words. "What do you write?"

"Children's books," she answered, at that moment coming

up with the something she'd apparently been after: a dog-eared lined yellow pad.

It was truly astonishing to me that she was able to unearth it so quickly. I mean, you have never seen such chaos. Directly in front of her—and taking up a good chunk of space—was an ancient and outsized Royal typewriter (dating back, no doubt, to the Stone Age). The rest of the desktop was covered by a fairly tall stack of blank typewriter sheets, a very short stack of typewritten pages, a lot of crumpled paper, an *American Heritage Dictionary,* a *Roget's Thesaurus,* and at least four other books with titles I couldn't make out. There was also a stapler, two staple removers, Wite-Out—three bottles of it, all lying on their sides—and several boxes of paper clips. Plus scattered over everything were maybe a half-dozen chewed-up pencil stubs—with even more gnawed-up stubs in a white ceramic mug that, incidentally, was painted with a black cat bearing a startling resemblance to the author's feline companion.

"Didn't Kevvie tell you? I'm Aunt Lulu," Luella informed me, a trace of pride in her voice. Just then the flesh and blood cat decided to join its likeness. Leaping up on the desk, it embarked on a thorough sniffing tour of the entire premises before finally settling atop the typewritten stack—which was in the corner farthest from us two-legged creatures—for what I'm sure was a well-deserved nap.

"Aunt Lulu?" I was really embarrassed about having to ask.

"As in *Aunt Lulu and the Twins at the Farm, Aunt Lulu and the Twins at the Movies, Aunt Lulu and the Twins at the Beach,* et cetera and et cetera. You're not familiar with my books? I'm counting on that to mean you don't have any children. Please. Tell me you don't."

"No, I don't," I affirmed.

"Whew! That's a relief! I'd hate to think you had a house-ful of kids and had never heard of me." She laughed when she said this, dimpling again. It was apparent, however, that she couldn't have been more serious. "But anyhow," she went on, "as I mentioned, I recently started working on my latest—*Aunt Lulu and the Twins at Central Park,* it's called—and I have Aunt Lulu schlepping the kids to the zoo there. Only I've never been myself—to the Central Park Zoo, that is. And neither has Kevin. And Connie hasn't been in years. What kind of animals do they have, do you know? Lions? Tigers? Hippopotamuses—or is it *hippopotami*? Gorillas? What? It would be nice if they had a panda, wouldn't it? I'd really love it if they had a panda."

She picked up the yellow pad now and, retrieving the pencil that had only seconds before found its way between her teeth, she sat poised to receive my invaluable input. "So?"

It pained me to admit that I'd never been to the Central Park Zoo, either.

Shrugging, Luella put down the pad and pencil. "Well, that's okay. I should probably take a little trip up there myself anyway—you know, to kind of get the feel of the place. Are they open this time of year?"

But I failed her once again. "I really can't say," I owned up reluctantly. *She'd gotten herself one hell of a resource, hadn't she?*

At this point, the cat rose, yawned, stretched, and marched across the desktop to push its head under her hand. "My muse," Luella told me, smiling indulgently at the animal and running her fingers through the silken fur. And then she began running her spare set of fingers through her own hair. It was now clear to me why she had such a singularly striking coiffure.

I was about to request an introduction to the muse when Connie poked her head into the room. "Ready for a little sustenance?"

"For sure," Luella answered, depositing the cat at her feet and then leaning over to sweep a bunch of crumpled papers off the desk with her forearm.

Connie used the newly available space to set down a small silver tray filled with a variety of tempting canapés. "Help yourselves," she instructed. "I'll be back with the drinks in a minute."

I promptly reached for a little bread round spread with what turned out to be a delicious cucumber mixture, while Luella selected a tiny pumpernickel triangle topped with cheese and sun-dried tomatoes. I noted then that the woman's nails were bitten to about an eighth of an inch of their lives and that her cuticles were all red and practically in shreds.

Regardless of how likable I found the charmingly ditsy Luella Pressman to be, there was no denying that Kevin's wife was also a giant nerve ending.

Kevin arrived a short time later. And while Connie dealt with the last-minute dinner preparations, the three of us sat in the living room sipping wine and making dent after dent in the contents of the canapé tray. The refreshments, of course, didn't prevent Luella from chatting up a storm—or even slow her down to any great extent. But in spite of being a very attentive audience, I did manage to get in a few surreptitious peeks at my surroundings.

The room, which was furnished with handsome—and no doubt costly—traditional pieces, was wonderfully spacious. But the fire blazing in the hearth and the vases of fresh flowers strategically positioned here and there made it seem surprisingly cozy in spite of its size. I suppose the color scheme also contributed to the feeling: A deep chocolate brown predominated, set off by bone walls and carpeting and warmed with soft peach accents. And while my own taste runs to contemporary, I remember thinking that I could probably acclimate myself to a place like this with practically no strain at all.

Anyway, Kevin had just offered me another drink (which I politely declined), when suddenly we three became four—as Luella's cat jumped up next to me on the sofa and then strode purposefully onto my lap, where it lay down with a single contented mew.

"Hello there," I said, stroking it gently. Lifting its head, my lap guest stared at me intently.

"Well, how are you?" I inquired amiably.

The cat opened its mouth, and there was something about the way it was looking at me that—for a split second, anyhow—had me anticipating that something like "fine" would be forthcoming. But all it did was meow. (Which, of course, might have translated to "fine" in cat talk, for as much as I know.)

The cat and I were in the midst of some further conversation and bonding like crazy when I realized I had no idea of its name. "You haven't told me your name, yet," I reminded it.

"Oh, sorry," Luella said. And she proceeded to do the honors. "Desiree, meet Beatrix; Beatrix, Desiree."

Ahh. A lady. (Well with a moniker like Beatrix, wouldn't *you* have assumed that *he* was a *she*?)

"Umm, I do hope you don't mind my not changing for dinner," Luella put to me then. "I didn't get much sleep last night, and I don't have the strength to drag myself upstairs."

"Of course n—"

"But I'm shod now, at least." Extending both feet, toes

pointed upward, she grinned down for a second at the beat-up Nikes. And then to Kevin: "I should probably go in and give Connie a hand with the meal, though, shouldn't I? But I just can't. Besides, I'm too tired to be of any real help to her." And without missing a beat: "Beatrix certainly seems to have taken to you, Desiree. I'm usually the recipient of all that affection—and cat hair. I hope you don't mind about the cat hair. Do you like cats, by the way?"

"I'm—"

"What a stupid question! You must. I can see you do."

Just then, Beatrix rolled over, narrowly escaping a fall to the floor in a bid to induce me to perform a little belly rub. I naturally obliged and was instantly rewarded for my good work with a whole lot of soulful purring. "What a sweet, gorgeous girl you are," I murmured softly—my eyes, obviously, having been focused exclusively on the cat's face.

But anyway, that's when Connie summoned us in to dinner.

I came close to weeping when I saw the dining room. A reaction that at the time I managed to think of not as envy, but as an appreciation of things beautiful. The color scheme here was the same as that in the living room but carried out more or less in reverse, with the walls lacquered a deep brown and this exact shade picked up in a magnificent brown, peach, and cream floral rug. I couldn't even guess at the dimensions of that room; all I can tell you is that it was about the size of a small auditorium. The table, which seated twelve—easily, was covered with a white lace cloth over a peach liner and set with the most elegant china, crystal, and silver. (As a matter of curiosity, I'd have loved to check out the back of one of those gold-trimmed plates when no one was looking, but there always seemed to be someone looking. And anyway, that would have been truly tacky of me, wouldn't it?)

The meal itself was superb: shrimp bisque, a big salad, veal medallions with wild mushrooms, beets in orange sauce, and a mud cake that was to die for. (A crummy choice of words, I suppose, considering the tragedy that was to come.)

Luella did most of the talking at the table—hardly a surprise—while her sister interjected a few phrases here and there and her husband interjected even fewer, appearing content to pretty much sit quietly and beam goofily at her between mouthfuls. Anyway, with Luella prattling on almost nonstop, by the time I demolished the last morsel of mud cake, I'd found out quite a bit about my hosts. For instance, I learned that Kevin and Luella had dated for only two months before they married, having met when Connie brought him home to dinner.

"Kevin and I were both taking this gourmet cooking class," Connie put in at this juncture.

"We became acquainted when she helped me extinguish the first of the three fires I started in that class," Kevin embellished, grinning.

"But in spite of his being a disaster in the kitchen, I knew immediately that he and Lu would hit it off," Connie pronounced. "I didn't tell *him* that, of course—just lured him here with the promise of a home-cooked meal. But you see? I was absolutely right, wasn't I?" she demanded, looking smug.

Kevin smiled shyly. "You certainly were."

Following this exchange, Luella resumed her chattering, telling me, among other things, that she and her sister had been living in the house since they were children. That Connie was a teacher in a private school. And that the two of them were three years apart in age, with Connie the older sibling. And incidentally, I am pleased to report that neither of the women was foolish enough to reveal exactly what ages we were talking about here.

After dinner we returned to the living room, where Connie served refills of a delightfully aromatic blend of Danish coffee, and Beatrix—who had been barred from the dining room—lost no time in taking up residence in my lap again.

"You know, Desiree," Luella said out of nowhere, shaking her head wonderingly, "it's hard to believe you're a private eye."

Well, this is the sort of reaction I'm accustomed to, and most times I can manage to ignore it. But just then, I stiffened. Luella was appraising me thoughtfully, and I knew exactly what it was she saw: someone toting around maybe twice the mileage of those sexy blond make-believe P.I. creatures on TV. Plus cheeks—and not the ones on the face, either—that extended almost all the way across the damn sofa cushion. And legs that were too damn short to reach the damn floor.

"You don't fit my mental picture of a P.I. at all," she said.

"Maybe not, but it's what I am." I hoped that didn't sound as defensive as I was afraid it did.

Luella responded with a flash of dimples. "I know. But it still throws me. The thing is, you're not the type. You're so . . . so *feminine*."

Now, I can't really say if she meant that or not, but I was perfectly willing to go on the premise that she did. *I could really learn to love this woman,* I thought then.

And today, just over five years later, Kevin has come to inform me that she's dead.

Chapter 3

After that night I never set eyes on Luella Pressman again.

I had tried on a number of occasions to reciprocate their invitation and have the three of them over to my place for dinner. But there was invariably a personal appearance Luella was committed to or a manuscript that was past due or else she was just plain exhausted. Could I please call in another couple of weeks, Connie would say (she was always the one to answer the phone)—Luella was almost certain to be available then. And I would agree. But it would turn out to be more or less the same story two weeks later. And two weeks after that. And so eventually I gave up.

But I did run into Kevin one morning about two and a half years ago—in the spring, it was—on Fifth Avenue. Right in front of Saks.

He was striding purposefully down the street, heading in my direction, when I spotted him half a block away. I waited for him to catch up to me, and he stopped long enough to hug me briefly and then tell me he couldn't stop. "I'm late for a client meeting," he hastily explained. "I'm supposed to be semi-retired, only I seem to be busier than ever these days." He said it ruefully; nevertheless, I suspected he was pleased. "Look, I'll phone you soon, and we'll have lunch. Okay?" He was already moving on.

"Okay. Great!" I called out after him.

But that time he didn't keep his word.

And today, on this bleak December afternoon, my old friend was sitting in my living room, his eyes moist and red-rimmed, his mouth set in a thin, tight line, and his hands in almost constant motion, fidgeting with the fabric of his chinos. He looked at least ten years older than he had less than three years before.

"I apologize for not calling first; I should have," he had

said when he rang my doorbell a few minutes earlier, at just past noon. "But I decided to take the chance you'd be home."

And now, after two or three gulps of air, he was apologizing again. "I'm sorry to intrude on your Sunday. I probably should have waited until tomorrow and come to your office to talk to you. But I . . . well, I couldn't get myself to do that."

The second alarm in my head went off at the word "office," the initial alert having sounded the instant I saw his face. "What is it, Kevin? What's wrong?"

"Luella's dead." It came out in a hoarse whisper.

"Your wife?" I responded stupidly. I like to think that was because I was so stunned.

"Ex-wife."

"*Ex*-wife?" I parroted, stunned again.

"Luella and I were divorced a couple of years ago. Not very long after you and I bumped into each other on Fifth Avenue. Do you remember that?"

"Sure I do," I told him, following an unsuccessful attempt to swallow the lump that had formed in my throat.

"But I never stopped caring about her," Kevin said. "We remained very good friends. Maybe even better friends than when we lived together." And reaching hastily into his pants pocket for some tissues now, he produced a fistful and daubed at his eyes.

"I'm so terribly sorry," I murmured while he was ministering to himself.

He mumbled a choked "thank you" before blowing his nose. It took a few moments before he was able to speak again, and then he said in a quiet, even tone, "You know, Desiree? Half the time I can't even believe she's gone."

"She'd been ill?"

"No. Luella was in perfect health."

"Then—"

"She was murdered."

"My God! Who did it? Do you know?"

"That's what I'm hoping you can find out. You will help, won't you?"

"Of course I will. I'll do anything I can. When was she . . . when was she killed?"

"Yesterday."

The next question was obvious. And I was afraid to ask it. I mean, I had these strobe images of poor Luella's terrible fate. I saw her covered in blood, lying on the cold hard pavement with her throat slit as two young punks fled down the street with her handbag. In the next instant I envisioned her sprawled on the bed in this filmy white nightgown, her lovely face purple, a thick silk drapery cord wound tight around her neck. Only a few feet away a black-hooded man was tearing through her dresser drawers, scattering her dainty personal possessions everywhere. I even squeezed in a picture of her squashed body on the subway tracks, a deranged street person (naturally, I made this perpetrator a male, too) looking down from the platform, laughing maniacally.

For a second I shut my eyes to blot out the horrifying tableaux I'd foisted on myself and then, moistening my lips, I forced myself to say the words: "How did it happen?"

"I'm afraid you'll have to wait for the answer to that one," Kevin responded sheepishly. "We both will."

I let out the breath I'd been holding. "I don't understand."

"Hortense—she's the housekeeper who comes in four days a week—well, she found Luella on the floor of her office yesterday afternoon, just before one o'clock."

"She was already dead?"

"Yes. Or, anyway, she was by the time the paramedics arrived. And the police have no idea yet how she died. They're conducting an autopsy."

"Then what makes you think it was murder?"

"I told you. Luella was in excellent health."

"Those things happen, though, Kevin. You hear about it all the time. One day a person appears to be fine, and the next . . ." I left it to him to fill in the rest.

He was shaking his head. "Luella didn't *appear* to be fine; she *was* fine. She had a complete physical not even two weeks ago, and the doctor said she had the constitution of a woman fifteen years younger."

"Still, it could have been a sudden heart attack," I suggested optimistically. "Or a stroke," I added brightly. Not that either alternative would be cause for a celebration, but the way I look at it, they beat having to live with a loved one's murder.

"No," Kevin pronounced firmly.

"But how can you be that positive? You don't even have a suspect in mind."

"That's not precisely right. The truth is, I don't *know* who killed her, not specifically, that is. But I would wager everything I own in this world that one of Luella's stepdaughters had a hand in this. Or maybe all three of them did." And taking a few more tissues from the seemingly limitless supply in his pants pocket, he swiped at his eyes again.

"Luella had three stepdaughters?" I asked, surprised at that for some reason.

"From her first three marriages."

"Her *first three*—"

Kevin broke in before I'd even had ample opportunity to express my astonishment. "That's right. And the girls all continued living with her after their respective fathers died—or in one case, after her father walked out. At any rate, Luella saw to their material needs, but I'm afraid she didn't give them that much attention. Her writing was incredibly time-consuming. It really took an awful lot out of her."

Oh, come now! We aren't talking any War and Peace *kind of epics here. We're talking Aunt Whosis drags those twins of hers to the wherever, for heaven's sake!*

It was as if Kevin had crept into my head. "I realize that *Aunt Lulu and the Twins at the Circus* and *Aunt Lulu and the Twins at the Ice Cream Parlor* don't sound like great literature," he told me, his tone amused and defensive at once. "And they're not, of course. But Luella's books are highly entertaining—much more inventive than most children's stories. And she was a perfectionist; she put herself under an awful lot of pressure. It does seem to have paid off, though. It's an extremely popular series, you know."

And now his voice grew confidential. "But besides the Aunt Lulu books, she was also working in a different genre—somewhat covertly. Had been for more than ten years, off and on. It's a historical novel set in fifteenth-century Spain—the time of the Inquisition. Naturally, something like that requires a great deal of research. And of course, being Luella, she was never satisfied with anything she'd written—I used to tell her she was noodling the thing to death. Anyway, progress was terribly slow, what with the noodling and the research and her Aunt Lulu commitments. Actually, I don't believe she ever even got to page two hundred."

And now Kevin sighed. "But the point it's taking me forever to make is that because of the demands of her career, I'm afraid the girls often got short shrift as youngsters."

Aunt Lulu didn't have time for her own children, I mused. I mean, the irony of it!

"Yes, I know," Kevin said, exactly as if he were poking around in my head again. "But you can appreciate, can't you, that under those circumstances it was even more to her credit that she kept the kids with her? And it isn't as if they were ever neglected," he asserted. "Connie's great with kids, and she served as a sort of surrogate mother to them."

"They're all adults now?"

"Yes, and out on their own. But they stay—stayed—in very close touch with Luella. She insisted on that."

"Why, if she wasn't that fond of them?"

"Oh, but she *was*—in her own way. Especially once they were older. It was kind of a funny thing about Luella. She was really very family-minded." My eyebrows must have shot straight up to my hairline at that one. "It's true," Kevin maintained. "All three of them spoke to her on the phone several times a week, and they came over to dinner frequently. Listen, it was practically on penalty of death or—worse yet—disinheritance that they miss spending a holiday or birthday with her." And chuckling a little: "Particularly when the birthday was hers." And then he added with the slightest, saddest smile, "Hey, I never said Luella wasn't eccentric, did I? That's one of the reasons I lo—I felt the way I did about her. But what I'm trying to make clear is that while these days she and her stepdaughters got along just fine, the fact remains that when the girls were growing up, she kept them at arm's length most of the time. And that can certainly hurt."

"She wasn't abusive to them in any way, was she?"

"Oh, no! Nothing like that." And now Kevin sat there silently, plucking away at his pants leg, and I got the definite impression he was weighing something in his mind. Finally, he said reluctantly: "Uh, well, she did lose her temper once in a while, and so she'd do a bit of screaming sometimes. She used to tell me how bad she felt even now about not having had more patience, more time for them when they were little ones. It wasn't her fault, though," he added quickly. "Luella was just a terribly nervous person, and she *was* busy with her work. But anyway, that could hardly be characterized as abuse."

He seemed to be looking at me for confirmation, so I obliged. "No, of course not."

"Actually, the girls always claimed to be very grateful to her for raising them." He locked his eyes with mine at this point. "But it's not hard to see how one of them could have had some secret resentment toward her that had been festering for years."

"And you think this resentment just boiled over?"

"No, no. But obviously, whoever did this had no great affection for her."

"You mentioned something about disinheritance before. Was Luella a wealthy woman?"

"I was just getting to that. Luella was worth millions. Although for a while I had no idea of that. I was aware she did pretty well with her books—she wrote close to sixty of them. But writing isn't as lucrative as you might imagine. I only found out about the *real* money once we were married."

"The *real* money?" I seemed to be echoing half the things Kevin said to me.

"That's right. Luella's mother came from a fairly well-to-do family. Not exactly *rich* rich, but extremely comfortable. Anyhow, she died when Luella and Connie were young, and their father—who was the executor of the estate—made some pretty shrewd investments with the inheritance she left. He passed away about twenty-five years ago, but before he did, he managed to assure his daughters would be set for life." The next words were spoken slowly, with emphasis. "And their heirs, as well."

"So you think Luella was killed for her money?"

"I'm convinced of it. And I also think that Connie's afraid I could be right. She's always been so close to the girls, though, that she's reluctant to admit it, even to herself. But when we talked yesterday and I told her about my suspicions, she said that it might not be a bad idea to have you look into things. To put my mind at ease is how she phrased it. But I have a feeling she wanted to settle things in her own mind, too. At any rate, I promised her I'd get in touch with you immediately." A fleeting grin now. "Actually, I had already decided to ask for your help. The instant I heard about Luella."

For a brief time after this, neither of us spoke. I was still attempting to absorb the fact of Luella's murder—if it *was* murder, that is—while Kevin was occupied with pressing a couple of fresh tissues into service.

"But why now?" I said to him when I broke the silence.

"Why not kill her years ago? Or years later, for that matter. Unless . . . Was there anything that might have precipitated things?"

"Exactly." And with this, some of Kevin's tension seemed to evaporate—for a couple of minutes, anyway—and he sat back in his chair for the first time. "Luella had begun dating someone about two or three months ago," he explained. "Bud Massi, the man's name is. And it seems Massi's starting up this new company—some kind of educational software thing—and Luella planned to invest in it. I don't know just how much she agreed to lend him, but it was a substantial amount, from what I understand. And what made things even hairier—from the girls' point of view, at any rate—is that there was a good chance he might have become husband number five. And who knows how much money she would have sunk into his company if they'd married? Or how sound a business venture the thing was? Look, she could even have changed her will in his favor."

I wondered then how Luella's taking up with a new man had affected Kevin himself. Just as I wondered what had led to their divorce. But this was hardly the time to try to find out, common decency told me. And I was too fond of Kevin to ignore common decency's dictates.

"Incidentally, Luella and I had dinner just last Sunday and we talked about her relationship with Bud," Kevin added. "She insisted it wasn't serious between them. Only I wouldn't have made book on that. Not from the look on her face whenever she mentioned his name."

"And her stepdaughters might not have believed her, either," I mused, directing that mostly to myself. And then to Kevin: "I suppose you know for a fact they were her beneficiaries."

"Oh, yes. Luella herself told me. And not that long ago, either. The girls get all of it, except for some personal stuff she left to Connie—jewelry, things of that nature. Connie didn't need the money. She was even more well fixed than Luella was. Over the years she'd bought and sold quite a lot of property, making a pretty sizable profit on her investments."

And now he leaned toward me, and there was a new urgency in his voice. "I want you to know, Desiree, that I've always liked those girls, all three of them. And that's God's truth. But I feel in my gut—no, I'm *certain*—that one of them, at least, is responsible for Luella's death." He pressed his case. "Do you really think it's a coincidence that so soon after entering a relationship that could adversely affect her stepdaughters' financial prospects, a healthy woman—one without a single serious physical ailment—suddenly becomes a corpse?"

Well, of all the things I don't believe a P.I. should put any stock in, coincidence is the thing I don't believe most.

"You may very well have something there, Kevin. Let's see what the autopsy report—"

"But according to the police, when the cause of death isn't immediately apparent, it could take weeks—possibly even months—to complete all the testing. And didn't you once tell me that the more time that elapses, the colder the trail gets?"

I couldn't argue with that. Of course, it would have been helpful to know there'd even been a murder before I started hunting for a murderer. Still, I'd gone down this road before, and everything had eventually fallen into place. I was about to agree to begin at once, but Kevin seemed to take my acquiescence for granted.

"I think it might be a good idea for you to pay a shiva call—tomorrow, if you can make it—so you can meet those girls." And now, a little uncertainly: "Uh, you do know what shiva is, don't you?"

Chapter 4

Do I know what shiva is?

Apparently, Kevin wasn't taking into consideration that I come by the Shapiro part of my name legally. I mean, I'd been Mrs. Ed Shapiro for five years, hadn't I?—until a chicken bone lodged in Ed's throat and left me a widow. But I suppose Kevin was concentrating on other things just then.

For the record, though, aside from having made I-don't-know-how-many shiva calls on my own, I'd been baptized (so to speak) by fire right at the start of my very happy, too-brief marriage, which is when two of Ed's elderly uncles, one cranky old aunt, and his cokehead cousin Willie all passed on within a three-month time period.

Anyway, thinking about those things, I didn't answer for a moment. Kevin mistook the brief silence for ignorance.

"I'm surprised you're not familiar with it," he said. "Especially living here in New York. But anyway, as one Catholic to another, let me explain.

"When someone in the Jewish religion dies, after the funeral there's a period—it used to be a week, although nowadays it's usually only two or three days—where the family and friends of the bereaved gather around them to console them."

"And this is called shiva?" (I didn't want him to feel he'd gone to the trouble of explaining for nothing.)

"That's right. Luella's body is being released sometime today, and the funeral's set for tomorrow. So if you could come by tomorrow evening . . ." He looked at me questioningly.

"Of course."

"Good. I was hoping you'd be able to. It seems to me that the sooner you start your investigation, the better chance we have of nailing the perp." He grinned. "See? Now you know I was really paying attention during our laundry-room days.

I even picked up the lingo." He reached for the ballpoint clipped to his shirt pocket. "Here, let me give you the address."

"That's all right. I've already got it," I told him.

"Oh, they're not going to be sitting at the house. Connie couldn't bear to have it there—she's pretty distraught. Everybody will be gathering at Nadine's. She's—she *was*—Luella's youngest stepdaughter." And with that, he took a business card from his wallet and jotted down Nadine's address on the back of it.

As soon as he handed me the card, I had a suggestion. "Look, I think it might help if you could give me some background on who's who before I actually meet all of them—whatever you can think of."

"Good idea. I guess—"

He didn't get the chance to continue. Because just then I realized I'd been so caught up in Kevin's tragic news that I hadn't so much as offered him a glass of water in all this time. (My niece Ellen—the Perle Mesta of West Nineteenth Street—would probably have apoplexy if she ever found out.) "But first, why don't we break for a little lunch?" I interrupted. "I've got a mushroom quiche in the refrigerator. Or I could make us a couple of ham sandwiches. I also have some tuna if you—"

"Thanks, Desiree, but I couldn't eat a thing. You fix a bite for yourself, though."

"I'm not very hungry, either. But how about something to drink? Something hard? Soft? What?"

"Well, I wouldn't mind a cup of coffee, thanks," Kevin said, time apparently having erased from his mind the properties of my coffee.

"Still take it black, no sugar?"

"Still. And you're phenomenal," he pronounced, obviously pleased that I remembered.

I excused myself and came back a couple of minutes later with two cups of what is almost universally regarded as my truly horrendous brew. One sip, and it was obvious that Kevin's memory had been jogged.

"Let's see . . . where do I start?" he said, managing to catch himself in mid-grimace. "I suppose I may as well begin with Enid, since she's the oldest—thirty-three, I believe. Enid's single. And a very intelligent young woman. Also, very ambitious. She's a mergers and acquisitions specialist. Enid's the one you'd have predicted would be working on her second million by now. And until about four and a half years ago, she seemed to be on her way to fulfilling everyone's expectations. She had a job with a top firm, and from all appearances, they regarded her highly there. But then along came this new boss who had some personal plans for her—if you understand me."

Kevin waited for my "I'm sure I do" before going on.

"The situation eventually got so bad for Enid that she wound up filing a sexual harassment suit. But she didn't have any proof against the bum and well . . ." He spread his arms and shook his head. "She's with a much smaller company now and really struggling to get her career on track again."

"Enid's father was husband number one?"

"Right. Walter Pressman. He was a widower and more than twice Luella's age when they married. She was only twenty-four at the time, much too young to be stepmother to a nine-year-old. Especially one who was still pretty shaken up by her mother's death just a couple of years before. From cancer I think it was. Anyhow, Walter and Enid moved into the town house—Connie continued living there, of course—and for a while things were going along fairly well, it seemed, in spite of the fact that everybody more or less went their own way. Luella had just started on her first book, you see, and she was closeted away a good deal of the time. Walter was a business executive of some sort, and he put in a lot of hours at the office. And Connie was busy with her teaching. But right away they hired a full-time nanny to look after Enid. And then on Saturdays and Sundays the family would usually do something together—in those days Luella made it a point to keep her weekends free." Now Kevin gamely took another swig of coffee. After which he threw in the towel and slipped the cup unobtrusively (he thought) onto the end table.

"In retrospect, however," he continued, "Enid probably needed more attention than anyone was willing to give her. Losing a mother—well, that has to be awfully tough on a child. But to my way of thinking, the responsibility for Enid rested primarily with Walter. She was *his* daughter, wasn't she? At any rate, after a time Enid got into a little trouble— she was rebelling, I suppose. Or maybe she just wanted to see if anyone gave a damn. Who can say?"

"What kind of trouble are we talking about?"

"Shoplifting. But Walter straightened things out with the store, and Enid promised it would never happen again. And it didn't. She was, I believe, eleven or twelve years old then."

"How old was she when Walter died?"

"Oh, he didn't die."

"What did happen to him?"

"It was straight out of a movie script. You know, where the husband steps out for a newspaper one day and then keeps right on going. Only in Walter's case, it wasn't a newspaper; it was a can of baked beans. That was when he and Luella had been married five years, so Enid must have been . . . she was fourteen."

"He abandoned his only daughter?" I said shrilly. *The guy deserved to be hung up by his thumbs for deserting his child like that!* Not that I condoned his skipping out on his wife, you understand, but no doubt they'd been having their problems. So as far as his treatment of Luella, well, for once I was willing to reserve judgment.

It didn't take two seconds before I decided judgment had been reserved long enough. *No matter what the problems, the man should have talked things over with his wife instead of just taking a powder. After all, he'd made a commitment to her, hadn't he? Hell. This Walter was scum, plain and simple. In fact, forget the thumbs. He deserved to hang there by a less visible part of his anatomy.*

"How did Enid react to his leaving?" I asked.

"A few weeks after he ran out on them she got arrested for drunk driving."

"Oh, my. At fourteen?"

Kevin nodded. "She and a friend"—he hesitated here—" 'borrowed' a Lincoln town car that belonged to the friend's father. And when the father discovered his car was missing—naturally, he had no idea it was his own daughter who'd taken it—he called the police.

"Well, eventually that little escapade was smoothed over with the authorities, and afterward Luella got Enid some psychological counseling. She also hired a full-time housekeeper to look after the girl—they'd let the nanny go a couple of years before."

"So Luella did all she could to deal with the situation," I said offhandedly.

"Of course." And now Kevin appeared to project an implication into my remark that, believe me, hadn't been intended.

"Listen, Desiree, I think you may have misunderstood me earlier. My fault, really. I'm sure I wasn't as intelligible as I might have been. I want to make it clear to you that Luella was basically a very caring person. She might have been too caught up in her work and I'm not denying she had a temper, but still, whenever it was important for her to be there for those girls, she was, I assure you."

And then it must have occurred to him that in the light of his previous revelations, I could argue this point. "I suppose, though," he conceded, flushing, "that when it came to day-to-day living, you might say she did let them down a little."

"The therapy and the housekeeper—did they do Enid any good?" I asked.

"Well, something did, because gradually she straightened out. Most probably it was a combination of factors. I think Connie played a part in things, too. At the end of the semester she took a leave from school in order to be able to spend more time with Enid. In fact, she didn't go back to teaching until all three of her nieces—that's how she regards them—were out of the house.

"At any rate, at seventeen Enid was off to Princeton. And then when she graduated, she went down to Texas and moved in with Luella, who was married to her third husband, Fred, by then and living in Fort Worth. After maybe a year, though, Enid came back to New York and got a place of her own. But she always flew out to Fort Worth for birthdays and holidays—that sort of thing. Of course," Kevin added with a chuckle, "knowing Luella, poor Enid didn't have much choice."

"Whatever happened to her father?" *(That scuzzy bastard!)*

"Well, for a while there, all anyone knew for sure was that he'd bought a plane ticket to L.A. That was it. But a few years later, after Luella met Ned Murray and they decided they wanted to get married, she hired a private detective to track him down, so she could serve him with divorce papers. The detective located him in some small town in Massachusetts."

"In all that time Walter had never made any attempt to contact Enid?"

"No. And he hasn't to this day. She doesn't even know if he's still alive. And she doesn't much care, either."

And who could blame her? "And this Murray—he became Luella's second husband?" And when Kevin nodded: "What sort of man was he?"

"Ned? He was an airline pilot. They were only married a year before he was killed in a plane crash."

"God, how awful!"

"Don't feel too bad. At least, not for Luella's sake. From what I heard, he was quite a ladies' man. He had something going with one of the flight attendants before he and Luella met, and just a few months after the wedding, he resumed his relationship with the woman. In fact, Luella was certain she would soon have been headed for the divorce court if Ned hadn't died when he did."

"She sure had luck with her men, didn't she?" I murmured. And then I had the good sense—belatedly, of course—to recall who I was talking to. "Oh, I didn't mean . . ." I said, my face hot. "I was referring to—"

Kevin laughed. "Don't worry. I know what you meant."

"Was Ned a widower, too?"

"No, divorced. But his former wife was in a mental institution. She died there about a year after the plane crash."

"And their daughter is who?"

"Nadine."

"Nadine's the youngest, you said before."

"That's right. She was eight when Ned and Luella got married. She's about twenty-four today, I'd say."

"What can you tell me about her?"

"Well, she's smart. Energetic. Extroverted. Attractive, too. And like Enid, she's single. She works for an advertising agency as an assistant producer, which is a very impressive title for someone who functions primarily as a go-fer."

"I don't suppose that's too high-paying a job, then."

Kevin's immediate response was somewhere between a laugh and a snort, after which he said, "No, but she's hoping to make producer in a couple of years. Also, there's quite a bit of travel involved—which she loves."

"And that *does* pay—producer, I mean." Since what I know about advertising agencies wouldn't fill an eye cup, it was actually a question.

"A helluva lot more than she's getting now."

"How did Nadine adjust to living with Luella?"

"All I can tell you is that she drove Luella crazy," Kevin responded, a poignant smile on his handsome face. "The minute the nanny or Connie would turn her back, Nadine would dash into Luella's office and interrupt her work to report on some little incident that had taken place at school or

ask her a silly question or read her a poem she'd written—
anything to get into that office. Luella said she should have
realized it was because the child was so lonely, but at the
time she wasn't that analytical; she was just annoyed. Of
course," he added hastily, "that was before Ned's accident."

"Nadine took her father's death very hard?"

Kevin thought for a moment. "I'm not really certain. As I
understood it, she appeared to cope well enough once the
initial shock wore off a bit. And after the crash, Luella did
spend more time with her than usual for a while. And then
the following year Luella married Fred and moved to Texas—
and Nadine had herself a brand-new sister. One that wasn't
always off at school. She was delighted about that."

"Nadine never got into any trouble or anything?"

"Not that I'm aware of."

"You say that Luella and Fred were married only about a
year after Ned died?" I wasn't able to keep the surprise out
of my voice.

"You didn't know Fred. Of course, neither did I. But the
word is, he was a very dynamic man. He and Luella met
when she was in Fort Worth on a book tour, and he was so
taken with her that he followed her to the rest of the cities on
her itinerary just so they could have dinner together or lunch
or cocktails or whatever it was she had time for. And then
he began flying up here to New York every weekend to
court her.

"Luella was flattered, naturally. He was very good-looking,
very successful. By all accounts, a decent person, too. And
apparently, she couldn't resist him. As much as it pains me to
admit it, of all her husbands—myself included—Fred was the
one she loved best."

I was flustered. "Oh, don't say that," I protested. "I saw
the two of you togeth—"

"It's all right, Desiree. I know Luella loved me. Only not
the way she loved him, that's all. It's something I came to
accept.

"As to the others, though, it appears Walter's appeal was
that he was like a father figure to her. My feeling is she
married him because of her grief at her own father's death—
she'd just lost him earlier that year. Luella thought that
must have been the reason, too, by the way—in retrospect, of
course."

"And Ned?"

"If I were to play amateur psychiatrist—and that's precisely what I seem to be doing," Kevin admitted, grinning, "I'd say she became involved with Ned because he made her feel desirable again. By her own admission, her ego was in shreds when Walter left her.

"Anyhow, Luella was absolutely determined that her marriage to Fred would work. As I said, she even pulled up stakes and moved to Fort Worth, where Fred had his business interests—he was in oil. Of course, you can write in Texas just as easily as you can in New York."

"Connie remained here?"

"Oh, no, they all went. Nadine, and Enid once she graduated, and Connie, too."

"But they kept the house on Forty-ninth Street?"

"Connie insisted on it. She probably wanted to leave her options open. Besides, she really loves that place. And it wasn't as though either of them needed the money," Kevin pointed out.

"What finally became of Fred?"

"His oil wells dried up. It happened about six months after he and Luella got married. The man lost everything, too. Well, as you can imagine, he was despondent over it." A deep sigh. "And then eventually he just went ahead and did it one day."

I waited uneasily for the rest, although I didn't have much doubt about what it was that Fred went ahead and did.

"Killed himself," Kevin confirmed softly. "He got out his revolver and put a bullet in his brain."

"Luella must have been devastated."

"Completely. Even more so, I'm certain, because she blamed herself to a great extent for what happened. The trouble was that in spite of her love for this man and all of her resolve, Luella just couldn't help being Luella. For the first year or so that she and Fred were together, she cut back considerably on her writing in order to devote more time to him and the girls. But then she gradually drifted back into the same old routine: shutting herself away to write for twelve hours at a stretch, running out to meetings of some organization or other, and jetting all over the country on book tours. And that left Fred feeling neglected and resentful. Well, this compounded by his financial losses . . ." Kevin shook his head sadly. "Unfortunately, Luella just hadn't picked up on Fred's pain. Or I should say that she hadn't been aware of

the extent of it. That didn't occur to her until he finally took
his own life." He shook his head again. "Between the grief
and the guilt, Luella was inconsolable for a long while after
Fred's death."

I could have cried then. And not for Luella. Or for poor
Fred, either. But for Kevin who, it was clear, still loved this
woman and whose own marriage to her must have, in many
ways, followed the same unhappy scenario. Although, thank
God, that union had terminated a lot less tragically. Inexplic-
ably, just seeing him sitting across from me alive and well
prompted me to half rise, lean over, and buss his cheek.

He looked to be of the opinion that I'd just misplaced a
few brain cells. Embarrassed, I put in quickly, "How long
were Fred and Luella married before he killed himself?"

"Three or four years. Something like that. And then when
he died, Luella packed up the family again—which now included another stepdaughter—and moved back East."

"And this third stepdaughter is—?"

"Her name is Geena. She just celebrated her twenty-seventh
birthday last month. Fred also had a much older son living in
Vermont someplace who passed away a few years ago. Fred
was quite a bit Luella's senior," Kevin explained. "Actually,
we all were. All except Ned; there was only a five- or six-year
age difference there."

"How old was Geena when her father married Luella?"

"I think she was . . . wait a minute." Scrunching up his
brow, Kevin tapped his finger on his palm in what I took to
be an aid to his calculations. And then he said, "She must
have been thirteen."

"Did she and Luella get on okay?"

" 'Okay' isn't the word. Geena's mother had been killed
in a burglary about five years before, and while Fred tried
his best to fill in for his wife, let's face it, he wasn't a
woman." Kevin smiled fleetingly at this stating of the obvious. "Anyway, when Luella came along, the child was practically ecstatic. From what Connie told me, Geena came
close to worshiping Luella. And the fact is, in her efforts
to please Fred, Luella *was* more of a mother to Geena
than she'd been to the other two girls. Although, actually,
the whole family reaped the benefits of the new, improved
Luella for as long as the metamorphosis lasted. I imagine
that when she resumed her old habits—and she just couldn't
help herself, Desiree—Geena was shattered. I wouldn't be

surprised if she thought it was because of something *she'd* done." Kevin caught himself. "But there I go, playing psychiatrist again," he said sheepishly.

"You're probably right, though. Tell me, how did the three stepsisters get along with one another?"

"Just fine. Enid wasn't around that much, of course, but she seemed to enjoy the role of big sister. And the other two were real buddies, in spite of the fact they were almost polar opposites."

"In what ways?"

"Nadine was a little spark plug—quick and bouncy. Into everything. Geena, on the other hand, was shy, the quiet, reserved type. She still is. And she was also three years older than Nadine. But evidently none of that mattered. From everything I've heard, they hit it off immediately."

"Speaking of older, this brother of Geena's you mentioned— he had no interest in having her come to live with him after their father died?"

"Apparently, that was never a consideration. He and Fred had been estranged for a long time, and he hadn't laid eyes on Geena since she was an infant. And besides, he had four kids of his own at home."

"What are things like for Geena now?"

"Well, she got married last year. Fellow's an artist of some kind—an *undiscovered* artist. They have a small apartment down in SoHo—a fifth-floor walk-up. I visited them there with Luella a couple of times, and it was a toss-up as to whether my heart or these ancient knees of mine would give out first."

"Is she happy?"

"Seems to be. As far as her marriage, anyway. But she sells real estate—a job for which she couldn't be more temperamentally unsuited and which she loathes. And she's not terribly successful at it, either. She needs whatever money it brings in, though, to pay the rent."

"Luella wouldn't help out?"

"She wanted to, but Geena claimed they were managing just fine. Of course, it could be that her husband convinced her to refuse the offer."

"And this husband? What do you think of him?"

"I've always found Andy pleasant enough. I can't tell you if he has any talent, however, because I'm certainly no art connoisseur. But Luella didn't care for him, which was very uncharacteristic. She normally doesn't—didn't—expend her energy on disliking anyone. But what was really so odd about it was that when I'd ask her what bothered her about the man, all she could say was that she just had a funny feeling about him."

I sat there for a minute or two then, going over things in my mind.

"What is it?" Kevin asked, responding to the silence, I guess. Or I might have been wrinkling my brow or something.

"Maybe you can explain to me," I answered, "why a woman like Luella, who was so consumed with her career, would ever have gotten married in the first place—to say nothing of taking a stab at it three times after that. We'll forget about the children for now, which is another issue entirely. Although I find it just as difficult—maybe even *more* difficult—to conceive of her willingness to assume the role of stepmother."

For a few moments Kevin didn't reply, and when he did, it was as if someone had turned down the volume control on his voice. "I don't quite know how to say this," a now beet-red Kevin all but whispered, "but Luella, she was a . . . well, she was a very sexu—that is, she was a very sensual woman. Unfortunately for her, though, she was saddled with old-fashioned morals. Which meant she couldn't just have an affair; she had to be married to her lover."

"I'm surprised she made the time for anything like that," I commented sarcastically. (And then was immediately ashamed of myself for being irritated with a dead woman.)

"That's the one aspect of marriage she did make time for—even if it wasn't *much* time." I wouldn't have thought it possible, but Kevin seemed to turn redder than ever with this.

"And as for marrying men with children," he went on, "that's just the way it worked out. What I mean is that Luella regarded the children as part of the package. And you have to appreciate that she didn't actually *dislike* kids. I honestly don't believe she could have written the stories she did, if that were the case. According to Luella, each time she entered into marriage she was very optimistic about her new relationships, both with her husband and her stepdaughter. She always managed to convince herself that now she'd be able to balance her life more successfully than she had in the past."

"You haven't actually said, but I gather Luella never had any children herself. Any natural children, I'm talking about."

"No, she didn't." And then he added defensively, "Listen,

Desiree, motherhood wasn't something Luella actively sought, but when circumstances put her in that position, no one can say she didn't handle it as best she could." Abruptly Kevin glanced at his watch. "I think I should get going." I had no doubt the last few minutes had left him anxious to make his escape. "The girls are handling all the necessary arrangements," he informed me, "but maybe I can help with something. Anyhow, I'd like to see how Connie is doing. So if you don't have any more questions . . ."

"None I can think of at the moment."

He looked relieved. "I'll give you my phone number in case something should occur to you later on. Just leave a message on the machine if I'm not in yet."

A short while later we were standing at the door.

"By the way, have the police concluded their inspection of the premises?" I inquired.

"Yesterday."

"Would you have any idea whether anyone else has been in either Luella's office or her bedroom since her death?"

"I very much doubt it. Connie slept at Nadine's last night, and as far as I know, no one's even been in the house since then."

"Good. Just see what you can do about making certain nothing's disturbed in either room until I've had a chance to check things out."

"I'll take care of it." Then, his eyes glittering with just-forming tears, he said, "You don't know what it means to me, your agreeing to investigate Luella's murder." And while the response was still on my lips: "And it *is* murder, Desiree. But you needn't take my word for it; you'll be finding that out for yourself."

He bent down and kissed my forehead. "I'm depending on it," he told me.

Chapter 5

I'm a little embarrassed to admit this, but practically the instant the door closed, Luella's death and Kevin's anguish flew out of my mind. I had a more immediate concern just then: Tonight I'd be seeing Bruce.

Now, I had been dating Bruce Simon regularly for some months. (Note: *Regularly* does not mean *frequently*.) And eventually I'd deep-sixed what little sense I'd been born with and allowed our relationship to become an intimate one.

What made it such a bad move, I guess, was that I'd never in my life had casual sex. Actually, never before had I slept with anyone who wasn't, at the very least, a good and trusted friend. And you could hardly call Bruce a friend.

While he was often extremely charming and fun to be with, the man could also, when he was so inclined, be totally obnoxious. Plus, he was far from the most considerate person I've ever met. Very far. And *nerve*? It was this guy's middle name! I'm not through yet, either. Add to this that he kept me at arm's length emotionally. And that he had a real talent for throwing me off balance, too. I mean, whenever we said good night, he left me wondering if I'd ever hear from him again. If you want the genuine, rock-bottom truth, I wasn't at all sure I even *liked* the guy.

So why let him put that well-on-the-road-to-bald head of his on my pillow?

Because in spite of the fact that he angered, irritated, and aggravated me—and wasn't really my type appearance-wise, besides—I was, for some unexplainable reason, extremely attracted to him. Also, as long as I'm putting aside my reticence to talk about anything like this, I may as well admit that it had been so long since there'd been someone special in my life, I was probably more than a little primed for some nice, warm physical interaction. Not to mention that I have a definite tendency toward stupidity—something I was becoming increasingly convinced of with each date I accepted from the man.

Let me tell you about the last time we went out. (Which, by the way, was over two weeks ago.)

Bruce had been invited to a cocktail party downtown in TriBeCa at the home of a woman who worked at the same P.R. firm he did. And she'd mentioned he could bring a date, if he liked. I was so pleased that he'd asked me to go with him, I even bought a new dress for the occasion. A lovely celadon wool A-line that the salesperson at Woman of Substance claimed made me look positively svelte. *Svelte!* Well, stupid I may be, but not quite witless enough to swallow that. Still, the dress did fit beautifully, and it was a great color for me, too. Which is why I spent a lot more for it than I should have and even refused to give myself permission to feel guilty about it.

Anyhow, about an hour after we arrived at the party, Bruce and I were standing around and chatting with a group of maybe eight people, when a waiter stopped right alongside me with a large tray of hors d'oeuvres. He practically shoved the damn thing under my nose. Honestly. So just not to be rude, I helped myself to a couple of these mini crab cakes that I'd already sampled on one or two of his previous rounds. I was happily nibbling away, thinking how tasty they were and wondering exactly what had gone into them, when Bruce made this nasty little joke for the benefit of everybody within hearing distance. "Hard to believe, isn't it?—ha-ha—that Desiree's actually an anorexic in disguise." And he punctuated this with a friendly pat on my rump.

Well, no one knew quite how to react. There was an embarrassed, half-hearted grin or two, but mostly people just sort of pretended they'd suddenly gone deaf. Except for this one woman, that is, whom I'd already pegged as a total lamebrain and who let loose with a shriek of laughter. Sounding exactly like a hyena, I might add. (And she looked like one, too.) As for me, I eked out a brave smile and cast it in Bruce's general direction, just to let everyone know that I wasn't bothered in the least. I think I might have pulled it off, too, except that I have the misfortune to change colors when humiliated.

Nevertheless, for the same reason I smiled, I forced myself to remain at the party for another three quarters of an hour.

By that time, Bruce was off talking to a few of his coworkers, and I had just concluded a conversation with the world's most single-minded and frightening female. (For ten minutes she laid out for me in horribly graphic detail exactly what she'd do to her husband if she ever learned that he wasn't working late at the office that night as he was claiming.)

As soon as I could break away from her, I went over to Bruce and quietly informed him that I had a headache and would have to call it a night. "But there's no point in your coming with me," I said. "I'll take a cab back to my apartment and try to sleep it off."

"Look, why don't we grab an early dinner now," he suggested, actually having the gall to appear concerned. "I'm sure you'll feel a lot better once you've had something substantial to eat."

I shook my head. "No. All I want to do is go home and lie down."

"Don't be silly. Let Dr. Simon—"

"I *said* no." It must have come out more strident than it was supposed to, because I noticed a few heads turning in my direction. "I'm leaving," I told him softly now. And proceeded to do just that.

Quickly retrieving my coat from the hall closet, I slipped out the front door. Bruce, still pulling on his trench coat, caught up with me just after I'd stepped off the curb to hail a cab.

"Hold it a second, will you!" he commanded, grabbing my elbow and joining me in the gutter. (Which, I decided, was exactly where he belonged.) "Are you upset with me for some reason? Is that it?" he asked innocently.

I really had no idea whether he was that insensitive, that obtuse, or that good a performer. And it didn't matter. Feeling under no obligation to answer, I merely glared at him.

"What did I do, for chrissakes?" Just then a taxi catapulted around the corner. Screeching to a stop, it came *this close* to mashing my toes but, sad to say, not quite close enough to damaging any part of Bruce.

Shaking off Bruce's arm, I practically threw myself into the backseat. "Move over, Dez, will you?" he said, attempting to join me. And when I didn't budge: "Come on, don't be such a baby. If I offended you, let's talk it over, at least."

I was struggling to wrench the door from his grasp when the small turbaned cabdriver turned around. "There is some trouble, yes, miss?" he asked anxiously.

"No. No trouble." And then not wanting to cause this nice man any problems, I opted for some ladylike restraint. Reluctantly, I released the door handle and slid over. "There'll be two stops. The first is on East Eighty-second Street, please," I said, giving him my address.

"I'll be getting off there, too, driver," Bruce instructed as he squeezed—with difficulty—into the narrow space I'd allotted him. And then slamming the door shut, he said in a reasonable tone, "Look, Dez, we have to talk about this. Whatever it is."

Whatever it is? In spite of my very recent resolve (re: ladylike restraint), I might have let loose with a few choice epithets at that moment. But I'll never know for sure. Because just then our driver sped off, negotiating the corner on two wheels. And I ended up in Bruce's lap.

"Well, at least you won't have to pay to have my kneecaps broken," he told me, laughing good-naturedly. "I think you've pretty much taken care of that yourself."

I turned to frown at him before resuming my place on the seat. But I couldn't keep this smile from playing around the corners of my mouth. Still, it was dark in the taxi, so I was hoping he hadn't noticed. He had.

"That's better," he pronounced. "Look, whatever it is"— those infuriating words again—"we'll straighten it out."

I didn't respond. But it wasn't easy.

"Let me come upstairs for a few minutes to talk, okay?" he said when we pulled up in front of my building. "You owe me that much."

Well, as far as I was concerned, I didn't owe this man one damn thing. But, I don't know, maybe it *was* some ridiculous sense of fair play. Anyhow, a couple of seconds later, a grudging "Oh, all right" just kind of slipped out.

We were sitting at my kitchen table, eating cheese omelets and drinking coffee. And I found myself thinking that there wasn't a more deserving recipient for that god-awful stuff— my coffee, I mean—than Bruce Simon. And this, in spite of my having agreed only minutes earlier to put tonight's episode behind us.

The fact is, though, even as I'd been telling Bruce that all was forgiven, I was wondering how long it would take me to regret that. But then again, he *had* taken great pains to assure me there was no malice in that joke of his—only poor taste.

"I didn't mean to hurt you, believe me," he'd reiterated a number of times. And finally came two words I'd never heard from him before: "I'm sorry." And so he'd won me over. But only sort of. After all, I *am* a Scorpio.

"You know, I didn't have any idea how sensitive you are," he was saying. And when there was no response, he added kiddingly, "I suppose I'll have to watch my step from here on, won't I?"

"I wouldn't put it like that," I told him evenly.

"Okay then, how would you put it?" He was smiling amiably.

"You'll have to avoid being such an insulting bastard, that's all."

"Ouch! All right. But I just want to say one more thing before we close out this discussion."

"Which is—?"

"Which is—and don't go ballistic on me—that I think you might have overreacted a little."

This was really too much! I started to get out of my chair as the first step in hustling this . . . this *clod* out of my apartment—and my life—once and for all.

Bruce thrust a restraining arm across my chest. "I guess I pushed my luck with that one, huh?" He looked, at this instant, like a small, mischievous boy. And I couldn't help it; I'm a pushover for that small, mischievous boy look. I felt myself beginning to turn to mush. "But on second thought," he inserted hastily, not being aware of this weakness of mine, "maybe you didn't."

"Didn't what?"

"Overreact. Jesus, Desiree! Pay attention when we're having a fight, will you!" And he laughed.

And then I laughed, too.

And a short time later we made love.

And when he left soon afterward—as he always did—I felt angry and upset—as I always did—that he didn't care to spend the night with me. Not only that, but it had been a while since he'd even taken the trouble to come up with a transparent excuse. Although maybe, in a way, that was a compliment to my intelligence. (I doubted this, but it was the most favorable spin I could put on things.)

Well, so now you know. About what an S.O.B. the guy could be, that is. Although not since our first date had he been as much of a one as on our last. Anyhow, in just a few hours I would be seeing him again. And as usual, I had this tingly feeling in the pit of my stomach, along with some other, more private places.

And if that unwelcome sensation didn't quite erase my misgivings, it was—for the moment, at any rate—certainly managing to bury them.

Chapter 6

Our date was for seven. Which judging from past performances meant I could expect Bruce about six forty-five. So I made certain I'd be ready by twenty of. And he rang the bell at six thirty.

I should have known, I grumbled, slipping on a robe to go to the door.

"You're early." I made this observation between tightly clenched teeth.

"Hey, can I help it if I found myself a cabdriver who wants to be an airline pilot?" he responded, handing me his coat.

It pained me to admit it, but he looked exceptionally attractive that night. He was wearing a dark brown suit with a white shirt and a red, brown, and cream paisley tie. Very nice with his hazel eyes. And while Bruce is not exactly tall, he carries those paltry (and yes, I'm a fine one to talk—but who cares?) five feet six or seven inches of his like a marine: shoulders back, spine ramrod-straight. You know, if you glanced at him really quickly, you might even mistake his almost-baldness for a crew cut.

But of course, he still wasn't my type. Too solidly built. Too muscular. And his manner! Much too confident for my taste—*over*confident, really. More often than not there was even something sardonic about his smile. As a matter of fact, in every way, Bruce Simon couldn't have been farther removed from the skinny, needy-looking men I find so appealing.

"I'll be with you in about ten minutes," I told him. He was taking a seat on the sofa and picking up the *Times Book Review* from the cocktail table in the same motion.

"Make it five," he suggested pleasantly as I started to head back to the bedroom.

Glaring at him over my shoulder, I walked into a chair and stubbed my big toe.

I gave him what was intended to be a really intimidating

look before attempting to stalk haughtily from the room. The
best I could manage, though, was a hobble.

We went to an opening at a small gallery in SoHo, where a
distant cousin of Bruce's was one of five exhibiting artists. I
was strolling around, having a second look at the paintings—
and feeling terribly New York and terribly, terribly chic—
when suddenly Bruce took me firmly by the arm and steered
me out of the room. And before I'd had more than two or
three sips of champagne, too.

"I was disappointed in John's work," Bruce remarked,
rubbing his empty glass of gin and tonic between his palms.
We were now seated in a booth at a pleasant little French
restaurant a couple of blocks from the gallery.

"Really? I liked his paintings," I responded, seeing in my
mind the dark country scenes—night scenes—done predominantly in deep blues and grays. "Very moody. Brooding, almost, don't you think?"

"Amateurish is what I think," Bruce snapped. "And I've
been hearing for years about what a talent this guy is, too."

"Well, I don't know a whole lot about art—"

"So why even discuss it then?" he said in a level tone. And
reaching across the table, he picked up the menu in front of
me and pressed it into my hand. "Why not concentrate on
something you do know about?"

I just sat there, holding the unopened menu. Bruce's face
was friendly now, guileless. Yet only an instant before he'd
insulted me again—or had he? Maybe I was turning paranoid. After all, there's that thing about "once bitten. . . ." He
cut short the deliberations.

"Oh, come on, now. Don't tell me *that* offended you, too!
By your own admission, you like to eat, and you're a gourmet
cook, besides." And smiling: "Which is something I can attest
to myself."

"I'm not offended," I said, only too willing to retreat from
my suspicions. "I was thinking about this new case I'm
working on, that's all."

The rest of the evening was actually thoroughly enjoyable.

The dinner was excellent—my duckling crisp, just the way
I like it, the Caesar salad delicious, and the crème brûlée,
well, that was only heaven.

And Bruce was at his most charming. He asked about the case I'd referred to, responding appropriately when I outlined the particulars. Then we discussed this flaky client he had recently acquired—a portly TV comic with a vile mouth, a laissez-faire wife, and a jealous mistress. Following that, he bantered with me about a new movie that he liked and I loathed, teased me about my faculty for getting crocked on half a glass of wine (not quite true but close enough), and clarified something I'd read earlier in the week about a Mideast dispute that, for the life of me, I wasn't able to make any sense of. (Did I mention how intelligent and informed he is?) And somewhere in the midst of all this, he even got around to paying me a rare compliment about my appearance.

"That's a very good-looking outfit you have on tonight," he said.

Now, for Bruce, this was practically rhapsodic. So never mind that the dress was five years old, and I'd never been too fond of it to begin with. (I'd only put it on because it was black and, I thought, appropriate for the occasion.) And forget that he hadn't said a word that last time about the stunning little celadon number I'd worn and for which I had practically put my soul in hock.

The *this old thing?* in my head exited my lips as "Why, thank you very much." I've learned to take my compliments when I can get them.

As soon as we left the restaurant, we spotted what looked like a nice cozy bar directly across the street and stopped off for an amaretto. And then later when we got to my place, Bruce stopped off for what he usually stopped off for.

But for once, when he left at two a.m., it didn't bother me that much. It had turned out to be a lovely evening. And Bruce had really been so attentive, such good company. For the most part, anyway.

And after all, no relationship is perfect, is it?

Chapter 7

On Monday morning I woke up at six-thirty and stayed up. Although not, I assure you, from choice.

When I arrived at the office at eight forty-five, Jackie, my secretary, was already at her desk, phone pasted to her ear. She waved a greeting before glancing at her watch, at which point her jaw went completely slack. Seeing me at work before nine like this may very well have disoriented her for the entire morning.

I operate out of this little cubbyhole that I rent from the law firm of Gilbert and Sullivan. (Really. Could I make up something like that?) It's a very good deal for me, too, since I get to share the services of merely the best secretary in New York—as well as quite likely the bossiest. Plus Elliot Gilbert and Pat Sullivan are both extremely pleasant people. And besides, they throw work my way as often as they possibly can.

Anyway, after I took off my coat, had a second cup of coffee, and then engaged in a few time-wasting tactics (sharpening pencils, straightening my desk, and reddening my already too-red lips), I made a concerted effort to focus on this case I'd been occupied with for the last week or so. It was an accident investigation that I'd basically wrapped up that past Thursday. In fact, the only thing left to be done was to type up a short report. The problem, however, was Bruce. I couldn't seem to stop thinking about him.

And while I am once again on the subject of Bruce, can you believe it was only recently that I'd told my niece Ellen—who's also my very dear friend and confidante—that I'd been dating him all these months? (And she did not react with particularly good grace to my withholding such vital information from her, either.) But the thing is, for a long time I'd considered him my own guilty little secret. I suppose, in a way, I still did. Which was also evidenced by the fact I

hadn't yet mentioned our seeing one another to my oft-
married (although not as oft as the dead woman) friend Pat
Martucci. And this, despite the fact that Pat was presently
cohabiting with Bruce's cousin Burton and, even more to the
point, that she was the one who quite some time ago had introduced me to Bruce in the first place.

The truth is, I was embarrassed about maintaining a relationship with the man, given that there was so much about
him that troubled me. And I'm not only talking about all
those things I mentioned to you before, either.

I think one of the areas of greatest concern to me was that
he was so damn secretive. I mean, for quite a while he'd
made certain our conversations were pretty much restricted
to an exchange of clever repartee—until the night I finally
put some very direct questions to him. And with all the
subtlety of an interrogator at the Spanish Inquisition, I'm
afraid. Which resulted in my not only being ashamed of my
own behavior but very resentful of Bruce for making it necessary. After all, my less blatant attempts to induce him to
talk about anything even the least bit personal had only revealed his talent for changing the subject. So, really, what
else could I do?

At any rate, as a result of my heightened efforts, I finally
learned that he'd been married for almost seven years, had
no children, and that it had been nine years since the marriage broke up.

And then he told me something I found really disturbing.
According to Bruce, the split with his wife was due to a
change in feelings on *both* their parts. Yet one week after
their divorce became final, the woman committed suicide.

Well, does this make sense to you? If it was a mutual
thing, why would she take her own life? Of course, it's possible that the timing was a coincidence. But given my opinion of coincidences, I couldn't help being skeptical.

Enough, I finally told myself that morning. I wasn't going
to think about that now. Even better than that, I wasn't going to think about it from here on in. What I *was* going to do
was keep my expectations to a minimum and, for however
long it lasted, just enjoy whatever it was Bruce and I had together (or maybe not enjoy it, since almost half the time that
seemed to be the case).

Anyway, shunting Bruce aside, I turned on my Mac. It
shouldn't take more than fifteen minutes to put together the

report on that accident case, I figured. But then with my fingers on the keyboard, Luella Pressman made an appearance.

I pictured again that lovely face—the almond eyes, those cavernous dimples. I recalled her friendliness, her talent, the dinner we'd shared. I conjured up that beautiful town house, remembering somewhat contritely how I'd coveted it. Then with a smile, I thought about that nervous energy of hers, the cause—most probably—of all that disorganization and nonstop chatter and—most certainly—of a head of salt and pepper hair that took off in at least half a dozen different directions.

But immediately after this, I replayed in my mind some snatches of my conversation with Kevin, and the smile disappeared. It saddened me to think about how Luella had neglected her stepdaughters—even as I admired her for raising them. *But how obsessive, how selfish, can you be,* I wondered, *to indulge your ambition to the point where you shut out your husband—make that plural—and children?*

Well, okay. So Luella was flawed. As we all are. It was really hardly my place to judge her. Although I have to confess, that never stopped me in the past.

Right now, though, I reminded myself, the important thing was to determine just who could have been resentful or angry or greedy enough to put an end to her life.

If, in fact, anyone had.

Chapter 8

Nadine Murray lived in a sixth-floor apartment off Lexington Avenue, only a few blocks from her former home. But this shabby and neglected-looking high-rise was a far cry from the elegant town house of her girlhood.

The instant the taxi dropped me off in front of the building, I turned clammy all over. It was with a little surprise—and a great deal of relief—that I discovered there was a functioning elevator in the place.

Kevin had suggested I show up around eight, since everyone except the immediate family would be likely to have left by then. He was almost right.

When I entered the small, sparsely furnished living room at a little after eight p.m., there were two fifty-something couples sitting opposite each other on rented (most probably) folding chairs, balancing paper plates on their laps.

And across the room was Connie.

She was seated on a love seat next to a thirtyish man with shoulder-length blond hair, who was leaning toward her, speaking quietly. She appeared to be nodding automatically, an absent expression on her face. As I approached her, I decided that, physically, Connie hadn't really changed very much since I'd visited her home five years ago. In fact, if anything, she actually looked younger. There no longer seemed to be even a speck of gray on her head. Either her hair was now ingeniously arranged to conceal those unwelcome little strands (extremely doubtful) or Connie had discovered the magic of artificial hair coloring, with which I have some familiarity myself.

As soon as she spotted me, she held up her palm to the man, and he stopped talking in midsentence.

"Oh, Desiree," she said when I came up to her, "I'm glad you're here."

I took the hand extended to me. "I'm so very . . . so terribly sorry for your loss," I mumbled awkwardly. "She . . .
your sister . . . she was a lovely person."

"Yes, she was. Thank you." The hand in mine was so cold
it sent a shiver through me. And now that I was all but on
top of her, I concluded that the woman had aged some,
after all. The lines in her forehead and bracketing her mouth
were more pronounced than I remembered. The recent tragedy
was also reflected in her face, of course: There was a puf-
finess under the eyes, and she was pallid and drawn. I'm
certain the black dress didn't help, either. It's been my observation that few of us over the age of seventeen can wear
black without shoveling on the makeup. Not unless we're
anxious to look totally washed out, that is. And Connie, who
had on just a trace of pale peach lipstick, was definitely not
among that few.

The thirtyish man stood up then, and I could see how tall
he was. Six-two, minimum. And he must have weighed over
two hundred pounds. Quite a bit over. My guess, though,
was that not an ounce of this was fat—he appeared to have
a hard, exceptionally well-toned body. I imagine that if you
like robust blond hunks (which as you know, I do not), this
was a guy who might make your heart pump a little faster.
"Why don't you sit here?" he offered. "And let me have your
coat."

"Thank you, Andy," Connie said on my behalf just prior to
my getting out my own thanks. "Desiree, this is my nephew,
Andy Hough. Andy, Desiree Shapiro." We exchanged "It's
nice to meet you"s before Andy departed for wherever he intended to deposit the trench coat I'd just foisted on him.

And now Connie proceeded to present me to the others in
the room. Pasting a smile on my face, I nodded perfunctorily
at them. I was still concentrating on Andy.

Nephew? I puzzled. But as I was settling myself in his seat,
it dawned on me. *Geena's husband—the artist. His name is
Andy, isn't it?*

My confirmation arrived about three minutes later in the
form of an emaciated-looking, fair-haired girl in a loose-
fitting navy dress. She seemed to materialize out of nowhere
as soon as Andy returned. "Your scotch," she informed him
softly, handing him a double old-fashioned glass.

"Thanks, hon," he said as he relieved her of the drink.

"And say hello to Desiree Schwartz." Then to me: "My wife, Geena."

"Shapiro. Desiree Shapiro," I corrected reflexively, being occupied at that moment with speculations as to what the family had been told about me. Kevin had assured me yesterday that he'd smooth the way for my investigation of Luella's death. But he'd given me no indication as to how he planned on handling things. Most likely because he hadn't yet figured it out.

"Oh, I'm sorry," Andy was saying. "I have a problem with names."

But it was Geena who appeared to be genuinely embarrassed. Two bright pink spots adorned the pale cheeks now. "How are you, Ms. Shapiro?" she murmured.

I extended my condolences—which were acknowledged with a shy smile and a whispered thank you—and moments later Connie asked Andy to please let Kevin know I was here. Immediately after which she changed her mind. "No. On second thought, Desiree and I will tell him ourselves." She leaned forward, as if about to get up. And then in what appeared to be almost an afterthought, she turned back to me. "You will have something to eat, won't you? That's what Kevin's doing now, grabbing a bite in the kitchen. There's really tons and tons of food. Luella's death was written up in the papers, and everyone's—" She swallowed hard before going on. "Everyone's been extremely kind. There are platters from people I've never met. A few of them I've never even *heard* of."

"Thank you, but I just finished dinner. I don't think I could manage one more mouthful."

"Well . . . if you're certain."

"I am. Honestly. I'd love a cup of coffee, though, if you have some made."

"That we do. Come. Follow me."

Just inside the door of the tiny, cramped kitchen, two young women (girls, to me) were standing at the sink counter, stuffing used paper plates, plastic flatware, and Styrofoam cups into jumbo garbage disposal bags. As soon as we came in, they stopped and smiled, obviously anticipating an introduction. But Connie nudged me past them.

I only had to walk about two feet farther into the room to get to Kevin. He was sitting at a little round table that I swear was about the dimension of a medium-sized pizza. Across from him was a middle-aged woman who, even seated, left no doubt as to her very substantial size. And I mean in all directions.

Looking up to find me hovering over him, Kevin put down his coffee mug and started to rise. But I placed my hand firmly on his shoulder. "Stay there," I commanded.

Taking my instruction the way most people do, he got to his feet anyway. "Don't be silly, Desiree. Please sit down; I'm all through. Really." And he quickly gave truth to this by grabbing the small piece of cake remaining on his plate and hastily consuming it.

"I thought the three of us could have our coffee in the living room, Kevin," Connie apprised him pointedly. "But first I wanted Desiree to meet Hortense and the girls.

"This is Hortense," she informed me, indicating Kevin's very recent table mate. *She's the one who discovered Luella's body,* I reminded myself as Connie went on. "Hortense, this is Desiree Shapiro. Ms. Shapiro has been a good friend of Mr. Garvey's for many years."

Lifting her head from a plate piled high with corned beef and potato salad, the woman glanced at me, her dark eyes sharp and appraising. Then a brief smile, in answer to mine, flickered across the plain, almost homely face—which was incongruously thin for the massive rest of her.

"Hortense, here, is my salvation," Connie enthused. "She's been with us for—what? Is it ten years yet?"

Hortense shook her head. She had to take a couple of seconds to swallow so she could reply aloud, "So far, only nine."

"You're probably right," Connie conceded before gesturing toward the sink. "And these are my nieces, Desiree—Enid and Nadine."

The girls, who had been leaning with their backs against the counter since our entrance, grinned at me. "I knew she'd get around to us eventually," the small curly-haired one joked. "I'm Nadine, and this is Enid."

I was about to make some sort of response when, just then, Geena and Andy squeezed into our already impossibly crowded quarters.

And that's when Connie said to me—but for the benefit of the others, as well—"I've told my family how the police are suggesting the possibility of foul play. Which is the most ridiculous notion I've ever heard in my life! But at any rate, we all agree that it would be a good idea to have you look into things for us and put an end to that sort of speculation."

So this was supposed to be the reason I'd been called in to investigate Luella's death: to disprove *that it was murder!*

Looking around the room now, I noted that everyone was validating Connie's words with either a nod or a mumble of some kind (except Hortense, who kept on chewing). And then right after that, Connie suggested we get our coffee and make our exit. For which I was extremely grateful, since exhaling in that kitchen had become a major challenge.

Anyway, in less than three minutes, Connie, Kevin, and I, cups in hand, were elbowing our way out of there.

We had no sooner walked into the living room when those two couples—you know, the folks with the plates on their laps—began saying their good-byes.

And now it was time to start doing what I'd come here to do.

"I had to tell them that—about the police. It was the only thing I could think of," Connie confided, as she and I resumed our places on the love seat.

Kevin remained standing for a few moments, obviously embarrassed. "I was really agonizing, Desiree, over what might be the best way to explain your involvement in all of this. I finally decided it would probably be wise to let Connie handle it." That said, he pulled over one of the not-too-substantial folding chairs, arranged it to face us, and gingerly set his large frame on it. "I think she came up with a good idea there, too. Don't you?"

"You mean the police didn't actually mention anything about suspecting murder?" I asked Connie.

"No. They did a lot of poking around on Saturday. And they did want to know what Luella had eaten that day; they even collected some food samples for testing. But one of the detectives told me they were only being thorough, that he didn't really expect anything to come of it."

"And what was it that Luella ate?"

"Just orange juice, a cup of coffee, and a piece of the cranberry nut loaf I'd baked a week ago—there was some in the freezer. But Luella and I had breakfast together, and I ate the same things she did."

"Exactly?"

"Exactly. Except that I take my coffee with milk and sugar,

and she takes it—" Here, Connie interrupted herself to smile sadly. "That is to say, she *took* it—black. No sugar."

"What time was breakfast? Do you remember?"

"Around seven-thirty." And now Connie folded her hands in her lap. "You know, Desiree," she stated emphatically, "the detective told me that it's not uncommon for people, even people much younger than Luella, to unexpectedly die of natural causes—heart, usually. And with no indication that anything at all was wrong with them." She was sounding just like one of my old high school teachers. But, of course, she came by it honestly.

Kevin opened his mouth, but Connie anticipated the protest. "It's true. It does happen. And more often than you might think."

He had no opportunity to debate this, because Nadine put in an appearance just then, carrying a platter of brownies. The girl didn't so much walk over to us as bounce over. (Kevin's description of her as "bouncy" couldn't have been more on the mark.) She was a very perky young woman, this Nadine, I thought. But not so perky as to make you want to gag, if you know what I mean. And she was cute, too. Small, with a nicely rounded figure, short, curly dark brown hair that fell in ringlets onto a wide forehead, and large brown eyes, lively in spite of the blue circles under them. In fact, even the severe, dark-colored dress (I couldn't determine if it was black or very deep navy)—its somberness barely relieved by the bit of lip gloss and touch of mascara she wore—couldn't obscure her wholesome good looks.

Nadine set down her offering on the narrow wooden cocktail table in front of us, shoving aside the Sunday *Times Magazine* section sitting smack in the middle of it. "More coffee, anyone?" she asked. We all declined. And now she focused her attention on me. "Aunt Connie made these brownies," she said, casting an affectionate glance at the older woman. "They are absolutely my favorite thing. She brought them over early Saturday morning, because she thought maybe I'd like one or two with my coffee." The girl smiled widely then and in a faux whisper confessed, "I had five of them." Not more than a second afterward, however, a frown creased the smooth brow. "Who would have thought that that same morning Luella would . . . Luella would—" Her voice cracking, she left it at that.

Out of the corner of my eye, I saw Connie part her lips to

say something, probably something consoling, but Nadine forced a smile. "You really have to try these, Ms. Shapiro."

"Oh, I will. I *am*," I amended, reaching for the first of what it took a remarkable amount of willpower to restrict to only two brownies. "And call me Desiree."

"All right. Desiree," the girl agreed, accompanying the words with what I think may have been a sniffle. Before I could be sure, though, she turned and hurried back to the kitchen.

Mmm. Nadine was right; Connie's brownies really were special. And I said as much. This led to Kevin's speaking wistfully about the first time he'd ever had dinner at the town house, and then he and Connie promptly embarked on some further reminiscences. It was quickly apparent that their conversation had nothing at all to do with the investigation, so I tuned it out, my thoughts drifting back to Nadine.

If Luella Pressman had been murdered by one of her stepdaughters, it was hard to believe it could have been this one. She had such a refreshing, open quality about her. Plus she seemed genuinely affected by her stepmother's death. And just look at how gamely she'd attempted to conceal her grief.

For maybe a fraction of a minute my trio of suspects had, for all intents and purposes, narrowed to a pair. But then I recalled a few instances where other unlikely perpetrators— with their truly Oscar-worthy performances—had waltzed me down the garden path. So before I'd even polished off my second brownie, all three names were firmly entrenched on my suspect list again.

Connie and Kevin seemed to be winding down a little now, so as soon as I could get the words in, I asked—mostly to bring them back to the present—"How long will you be sitting shiva?"

Connie was the one to reply. "Only through Wednesday. I'm moving back home then, too. Kevin did tell you I've been staying here since Saturday night, didn't he?" There was no time to answer. "I just couldn't bring myself to sleep in that house," she went on. "Not yet. And Nadine's roommate has been out in California for the last three weeks, so there's a spare bed in the apartment. Nadine swore she didn't mind. She even tried convincing me that she welcomed the company. She has *such* a good heart, doesn't she, Kevin?"

"I always *thought* so, anyway," he said.

Connie bristled. "I still think so. Nadine didn't—she

couldn't have been responsible for . . . for anything." And to me: "She *does* have a good heart, Desiree. And you can't imagine how bright that girl is, either. Enid's supposed to be the brainy one, but I'm not so sure Nadine doesn't have her beat. Wait. Let me show you something. Hand me that magazine, will you?"

I obediently passed her the Sunday *Times Magazine*, and she flipped it open to the crossword page. "Nadine is always able to work these out—even the most difficult ones. And in no time, too," she said proudly, tapping on the completed puzzle with her finger. "She did this last night—she couldn't sleep."

Glancing down at all those filled-in blanks, I shook my head in what was intended to be both admiration and wonder. And I wasn't faking it that much, either.

"Ohh, I just realized," Connie said then, surprise in her tone. "Will you look at that."

"What?"

"Ink. She worked the puzzle in ink. She never used to do that."

Now, all this while we'd been speaking in hushed tones—except for when Nadine made her brief visit, that is. But at this point Connie's voice dropped so low that Kevin drew his chair even closer, and I had to practically sit in her lap to make out what she was saying. "Maybe what we have here is an indication that she's finally gaining a little more confidence. That's the one thing Nadine's always lacked. Confidence."

"Although you'd never guess it just to meet her," Kevin put in.

Connie nodded in agreement. And then, fixing her eyes on me, she elaborated. "Nadine's so gregarious, so upbeat— under normal circumstances, of course—that people get the impression she's very sure of herself. Very much in control. But anyone who really knows her can tell you that she has a great many self-doubts. It's Enid who's the confident one. Even with having to start her career all over again a few years back—she had some awful problems with the man she used to work for—Enid's never questioned her own ability. She's always been convinced she'll eventually be a success."

"And Geena?" I wanted to know. "Is *she* sure of herself?" From the little I'd seen of Geena, a "yes" would have floored me.

"Not at all. In fact, just the opposite," Kevin answered.

"But it isn't that she's not capable—or bright," Connie hurriedly interjected. "It's just that she's so shy. Ever since she was a child, she's been like that."

"Let's face it, though, Connie," Kevin told her. "Geena was never as quick as the other two."

For an instant Connie's eyes blazed. Then she retorted tartly, "Maybe not. But she has other redeeming qualities. A lot of them."

"I was wondering," I put to her then, "if there'd been any trouble recently between your sister and any of your nieces. I'm not necessarily talking about something major, you understand. I'm talking about even a minor dispute of some sort." And now I immediately added, "Not that that kind of thing would necessarily mean anything; it would just be an area I should look into."

"There was nothing like that," Connie responded with a vehement shake of the head. And then, very evenly, she said, "You know, Desiree, I'm beginning to realize that it was a foolish idea—your investigating Luella's death. The more I think about it, the more convinced I am that there wasn't any crime committed here. She . . . well, she just died, that's all." Suddenly the tears began to flow freely down her cheeks. And burying her head in her palms, Connie sobbed softly.

In between awkward pats on her shoulder, I glanced over at Kevin. He, too, seemed close to tears. And to tell the truth—being the biggest blob of mush I know—I wasn't that far away from them, either. But Connie took her hands from her face before I had the opportunity to make an idiot of myself.

Fumbling around in the pocket of her dress now, she got out a crumpled lace-trimmed handkerchief and dabbed at the wet cheeks. After which she daintily blew her nose a couple of times. And then, drawing herself up in her seat, she reiterated the words she'd uttered previously—but with a new conviction in her voice. "She just *died*, that's all," she proclaimed. And a moment later: "My poor little sister just *died*."

Chapter 9

Well, Connie could be right. It was entirely possible Luella had died a natural death. I supposed it really did make sense to hold off on my investigation until the autopsy report came in and we learned exactly what was what.

On the other hand, though, Kevin's point was valid, too—I mean, about the consequences of waiting until the trail got cold. Of course, according to statistics, most homicides are solved within the first couple of days—if they're going to be solved at all, that is. And we could already forget about that. But certainly the sooner I started checking things out, the better everyone's memory of events would be and the greater my chances of finding the perpetrator.

Still, considering the way Connie felt . . .

What about how Kevin felt, though?

But then again, not having any idea of the autopsy findings . . .

I was seesawing back and forth like that when the whole thing suddenly became moot.

And it took just a single word: "Connie." Kevin said it softly, yet so wrenchingly that it was impossible to ignore.

His former sister-in-law looked at his grief-etched face and sighed resignedly. "All right, you win," she murmured. And now she put her hand on my arm. "Forget what I just told you, Desiree. Go ahead, and do whatever it is you have to do."

"Well, if you're certain . . ."

"I am." Then came the grudging admission: "To be honest, maybe I'm not as sure in my mind about everything as I wish I were. And I owe it to Luella to find out the truth—whatever it is." I followed the course of a single tear as it left a corner of her eye and made its way slowly down to her chin.

It was a couple of minutes later that I asked if it would be okay if I talked to Hortense before I left that night.

"Yes, of course," Connie responded, making a not-altogether-successful attempt at a smile. "You might as well get started, I guess."

I decided to question the housekeeper in the bedroom, where we'd be assured of some privacy. Hortense, however, immediately complained that she felt claustrophobic in here. I didn't comment, but I understood exactly what she meant.

The kitchen seemed almost spacious compared to the bedroom Nadine shared with her absent roommate. Maybe because there was so much furniture jammed into such a limited area: twin beds (one of which barely cleared the door), an armoire, a dresser, a night table, a parsons table, and a desk chair. Walking space in the room—which couldn't have been much more than ten feet square—was definitely at a premium. Going from the entrance to the windows, for example, was practically like maneuvering your way through an obstacle course. And adding to the congestion was the fact that Nadine was every bit as disorganized—make that *sloppy*—as her stepmother had been.

The extra-long parsons table—which fit right under the windows and was undoubtedly custom-made—functioned as a desk, hosting a computer, a printer, and a fax machine, along with so much in the way of papers and books and writing paraphernalia that only a couple of inches of the table's white laminated surface were visible. The tops of the other furniture were similarly utilized, serving as repositories for everything from a telephone and a clock radio to a jewelry box, cosmetics, perfumes, pictures, stuffed animals—even a collection of baseball caps. And while the beds were neatly covered (probably thanks to Connie), one of them was strewn with magazines, a pair of chinos, a Monopoly game (in its box, at least), and a full laundry basket. The only part of the room that had not been pressed into multiple service was the second bed, on which there was just a small closed suitcase with the initials C.N. Looking at the bed, I instantly thought of sanctuary in a storm.

Anyway, Hortense had been looming over me, giving me neck strain, and I was anxious to put us both on the same plane—more or less. Her hand was now resting proprietarily on the back of the desk chair that stood up against the parsons table. So I quickly deposited myself on the edge of the Connie bed, which was right opposite the table and only about two and a half feet away from it. Following my lead, Hortense pulled out the chair, displacing its current residents (two porcelain-headed dolls who joined me on the bed). And then after turning it around so we'd be facing each other, she sat down heavily, a sizable portion of her bottom hanging over the seat.

She took a few moments to smooth the skirt of her deep purple shirtwaist and pat her sparse, close-to-black hair, which she wore pulled straight back into an extremely unflattering bun. And now studying me with her dark eyes—a near-match to the hair—she said in a quiet, almost expressionless voice, "So you're a private detective, are you?" And when I nodded: "That's an interesting job, I suppose. Sounds like it, anyway. Well, okay. What is it I can tell you?"

"Tell me about the day Mrs. Pressman died."

The housekeeper's next words had nothing at all to do with the question. "Look, I want you to know something. I worked for Ms. Pressman for nine years, and I liked her. I liked her a lot. But the thing is, I don't cry. Not for nobody. I just can't."

I sat there expectantly, waiting for an "and" or maybe a "but." Eventually it registered that this was all there was and that some sort of response was probably in order. "I understand," I said.

"I feel it in here, though," she continued then, pounding her more-than-ample bosom with her fist a couple of times.

"I'm sure you do."

"I didn't even cry when my husband died, God rest his soul." She hastily crossed herself before adding, "There's some cry crocodile tears, and some cry for real. In the heart." Another thump to the bosom.

I had to wonder if the woman was just speaking in general about that crocodile tears thing or if she had someone specific in mind. I attempted to find out. "Oh, you're so right. I've been thinking myself that maybe not everyone here is as upset as they appear to be."

Hortense frowned. "I wasn't referring to no one here." And then without taking a breath, she at last got around to the question I'd almost forgotten asking. "Anyways, I come in around eleven-thirty that morning, and I—"

"Excuse me for interrupting, but I just want to be sure I have all my facts straight. Is that the time you normally arrive for work there?"

"On Saturdays, it is. I only go in for a half a day then."

"All right, thanks. Please, continue."

"Well, first off I went into the laundry room like always and threw some things in the machine. And then I went upstairs to make the beds and dust and vacuum and such."

"Did you see Mrs. Pressman before you went up?"

"No. Alls I saw was that her door was closed like always—the office one, I mean. You have to pass it on the way upstairs."

"What about Mrs. Neiman—was she at home?"

Hortense wasted no time in setting me straight. "You mean, *Miss* Neiman—her not ever being married—or like most everyone says nowadays, *Ms.*" I had the distinct impression I was being viewed as a walking, talking anachronism. And by someone who probably had quite a few years on me, too.

"Was she at home?" I repeated.

"She was in her own office—it's on the second floor—doin' some paperwork."

"You saw her?"

"I vacuumed in there. Besides, I seen her when I first come up. She had the door open."

"What time was it when you finished upstairs?"

"I never did finish. Ms. Pressman usually has her lunch at one, unless she's real caught up in her work, that is. So at quarter of, I took a little break so's I could prepare somethin' for her. At least, that's what I thought it would be: a little break."

"And you passed her office again when you went downstairs."

"That's right. Couldn't help but pass it."

"I don't suppose you heard anything."

"Only that cat of hers—Beatrix. Crazy name for a boy cat, isn't it?"

"A boy cat?"

"That's what I said. Ms. Pressman could be a little peculiar sometimes, much as I thought so highly of her. It didn't matter to *her* what sex the animal was. She wanted to call it after some author she was fond of, somebody else who wrote children's books. Dead lady, I think."

"Beatrix *Potter*?"

Hortense nodded. "That's the one."

I really can't say why I was surprised. I mean, if Luella wanted to grace her male cat with the name of a woman who was famous for her books about rabbits—well, why not? (I didn't learn until much later on that Potter wrote at least one cat story, too.) Anyhow, I was willing to bet that Beatrix—the cat, that is—wasn't bothered at all by the fact he'd been stuck with a girl's moniker.

"You were saying the cat was making some noise?"

"Well, not *noise* exactly. Clawin' at the door and meowing a lot."

"Did that seem strange to you?"

"The fact of it is, I didn't really pay it much mind." You could see the housekeeper was none too comfortable with her response. It was made reluctantly, with downcast eyes.

"Did he ever do anything like that before?"

"Sometimes, I suppose. Although it was generally pretty well behaved. For a cat, that is."

"I wonder if he was in the office with her all that morning."

I hadn't realized I'd speculated aloud until Hortense answered.

"Prob'ly. Wherever Ms. Pressman was, there was that cat. Most times, at least."

"Was he also making a fuss when you passed Ms. Pressman's office on your way up?" (Well, what the hell. Actually, I probably use the P.C. term more often than not—when addressing someone directly, anyhow. Hey, I've even been known to utter that silly word "waitperson." But rarely, I admit, since for the life of me, I can't figure out what the beef is against "waiter" or "waitress.")

"I think maybe so, only not as much. But I'm not really sure. If you want the truth, I try to tune the thing out whenever I can."

It was apparent that Hortense, here, was no cat lover. A bias that even extended to this particular cat (who, as I could attest from experience, was so sweet and affectionate that her lack of fondness for him was hard for me to understand). At any rate, she suddenly confronted me—more, I knew, out of a sense of guilt than anger. "Listen," she put to me, eyes narrowing and nostrils widening now, "you're not sayin', are you, that if I'da gone and looked in on Ms. Pressman earlier, she'd still be with us?"

No, I wasn't saying it, but the possibility had certainly occurred to me. Nevertheless, I wanted to reassure her. After all, how could the woman have had any idea that behind that door her employer was dying? If she wasn't already dead. "No, of course not," I responded firmly. "It was probably already too late by the time you got to work."

She nodded, satisfied. Or so I thought. Evidently, though, I hadn't been that successful in easing her mind, because almost immediately she was justifying herself. "The cat did act up some every so often, come to think of it. Playin' mostly, I suppose, the way animals do. I remember it real clear now. There was times Ms. Pressman even useta shoo it out, it would get to be such a nuisance."

"Look, Hortense, I doubt if anyone else would have tumbled to something being wrong in there, either. I'm certain I wouldn't."

This seemed to do it, because the housekeeper's features finally relaxed.

"What happened after you came downstairs?" I asked.

"I went into the kitchen and put up water for spaghetti, and then I started heatin' some of the marinara sauce I cooked on Wednesday. And I fixed a nice little salad, too. Ms. Pressman liked salads."

"Miss Neiman wasn't having lunch?" (Perversely, I refused to go with a *Ms.* on this one.)

"Ms. Neiman said not to bother about her; she said she was busy, and she'd make herself a bite later on."

"All right. What did you do then?"

"As soon as I was through preparin' her lunch, I went to check if she—Ms. Pressman—wanted to come into the kitchen to eat or if she wanted me to bring a tray in there, to her office. You never knew. As soon as I got near, though, this funny feeling took ahold of me. Like maybe things wasn't quite right, if you understand me. The cat, see, it was screechin' somethin' awful by that time." Hortense took a deep, slow breath now. "Well, anyways, I opened the door, and there was Ms. Pressman—lyin' on the floor near her desk. My first thought was she fainted. And so I tried callin' to her and patting her hand and everything. But, of course, it didn't do no good. And all the meanwhile the damn cat was runnin' around in circles and scratching at my legs. It was a terrible scene. I'm still all marked up around the ankles, too." To illustrate, she stuck out a heavy leg with an unusually thick ankle at the end of it. But her hose being opaque, I couldn't comment on the wounds.

Nonetheless, I clucked sympathetically before my next question. "What did you do then?"

"I screamed out for Ms. Neiman, and she come runnin' downstairs and said for me to go into the hall and call 911. Which I did, naturally. But she—Ms. Pressman—was gone, poor dear, by the time the emergency people come." And once again, Hortense crossed herself.

I was trying to visualize Luella's desk then, trying to remember if I'd seen a phone on it. "There's no telephone in Mrs. Pressman's office?" I asked.

Hortense shook her head. "She didn't want everyone callin' all the time and interruptin' her while she was writing."

At this juncture the housekeeper pursed her lips for a second, and when she spoke again, her tone was lower, more confidential. "I've been doin' a lot of thinking, you know. And the way I see it, Ms. Pressman's sickness, whatever it was, come on her sudden, and she was prob'ly tryin' to get to the hall to dial 911 herself. Or maybe to holler for help. But the poor little thing didn't have the strength to make it. And that's how come I found her on the floor like I did."

"Tell me, how did the family take Mrs. Pressman's death?"

"Well, Ms. Neiman carried on just awful until the paramedics come. And even worse when they couldn't do nothing for Ms. Pressman. And who could blame her, I'd like to know. It hurt my heart to see Ms. Neiman like that. Them two was just devoted to each other. The girls took it real hard, too. I was over here early this morning, before the funeral, to straighten the place up a little for when the people started comin'." She interrupted her narrative just long enough to dispel any misapprehension I might be under. "Ms. Neiman said not to bother with this room, though. As you can plainly see. But what I started to tell you is that they was standin' in the kitchen, the three of them, just cryin' their eyes out. And forget about Mr. Garvey—who's like family even today. When he walked into that house on Saturday, his face was the color of ashes. I was afraid of him havin' a stroke right then and there. And that's the truth of it." Then taking a quick glance around the room as if to make certain there was no one to overhear her, Hortense whispered, "He still cared for her—Ms. Pressman, I mean. You can take my word for that."

"I see." My tone was thoughtful, so as to give sufficient

weight to this disclosure. And then I said, "Ms. Neiman asked you to call Mr. Garvey?"

"No, she wasn't in no condition to do any askin'. But I knew she'd want him to know right away—right after the girls. Like I told you, Mr. Garvey's family. Or as good as."

"Did you contact anyone else?" I was attempting to learn what others might have played an important part in the dead woman's life.

"This new fella Ms. Pressman was goin' out with—somebody Massi. Bill or Bob, I think it might be. Ms. Neiman was worried he might not of been notified. That was a few hours later, though, when she was calmed down a bit."

"And that's it?"

"Mostly. The girls did the rest of the phonin'."

"What do you mean by 'mostly'?"

"Well, the other things wasn't that important. I canceled Ms. Pressman's beauty parlor appointment—she was supposed to get her hair done at four. Had a standing Saturday appointment, Ms. Pressman did. Imagine this even enterin' my mind at a time like that—which I still don't see how it did," Hortense mused wonderingly. "And I also remembered to call Ms. Neiman's chiropractor. She's been goin' to him every week since she threw out her back doin' some silly exercise. And why she bothers with that kind of thing, I can't hope to say. It's not as though she's got some man, and he's after her to get skinny for him. Although even if you *have* got yourself a man, you're crazy to let him do that to you. Am I right? I useta say to my John, may he rest in peace"— she crossed herself without missing a beat—" 'If you don't like the merchandise, then just keep away from the counter.' Believe me, there's no man could ever make me change what God seen fit to give me." To embellish this point, she leaned forward in her chair, raising her body just enough to administer a sound slap to her very expansive buttocks.

I was definitely expected to say something now, so I did. "I agree with you completely," I mumbled.

For the first time since we'd been closeted in here, Hortense flashed me a smile. A conspiratorial sort of smile. "Oh, I knew you was too sensible for that type of foolishness. Same as me."

Then a few seconds later, while occupying herself with a brief inventory of my person, she added solemnly, "Any fool can see that."

Chapter 10

Hortense was right, of course. I'm not exactly into fitness. In fact, the only exercise I enjoy is walking from the refrigerator to the table.

Still, I'm not crazy about having the results of my aversion to a lot of mindless huffing and puffing driven home to me like that. Especially when it comes from a woman in much worse shape (believe me) than I am.

But anyway, having pretty much wrapped up my questioning of the housekeeper at this point, I went back into the kitchen. Luella's stepdaughters were still gathered there, and I set up appointments with the three of them for once the shiva period was over. And then a few minutes after that I called it a night.

At eight o'clock Tuesday morning I was to meet Kevin in front of the Forty-ninth Street town house. On the way over in the cab, I had my fingers crossed he'd get there ahead of me. It was a bitingly cold day, and I didn't relish the thought of standing outside and shivering until he showed with the keys. But when the taxi pulled up, Kevin—bless him—was leaning against the wrought-iron gate waiting for me.

As soon as I walked over to him, he took a key ring from his pocket, jiggling it in front of me for a second. "Luella insisted I keep these after I moved out," he said, quickly unlocking the gate. "She wanted me to have them in case of an emergency."

Moments later—before my toes even had time to get numb—he let us into the house.

I followed close behind as Kevin led the way down the narrow hall, almost bumping into him when he stopped abruptly before the door to what—if I recalled correctly—would be Luella's office.

"This door has a lock, although nobody ever locked it.

Fortunately, though, Connie knew exactly where I could find this," he told me, singling out a large key on the ring. "I secured the room about an hour after you and I talked on Sunday." He was just sort of lingering there, key in hand, looking at me. Then he said, "Listen, Desiree, I'm interested in what your thoughts are. Regarding last night, I mean."

"It's too soon yet to have any thoughts." I felt a little apologetic.

"Yes, you're right. Of course it is." There was a pause before he asked, "Did Hortense have anything important to contribute?"

"Not that I can see just now. But you never know."

Anxiety pressed him forward. "How about the girls? I'm aware that you didn't get much of a chance to speak to them, but I had the idea that maybe . . . What I'm asking is, were you able to form any sort of an impression of them?"

"I'm afraid not. I didn't even exchange two words with Enid. And only slightly more than that with Nadine and Geena. But I've arranged to meet with them, and no doubt I'll have some kind of opinion—right or wrong—once I do."

"You'll keep me posted, I'm sure." But there was a question mark in his voice.

"You know I will. Only we won't be able to determine anything for certain until we learn the autopsy findings. You realize that, don't you?"

"Naturally."

But I wasn't at all convinced he meant it. Not on an emotional level, I mean.

At any rate, Kevin opened the door then and stepped aside for me to enter the room. *It looks exactly as it did five years ago,* I decided, taking in the incredibly messy desk, littered as before with pencils and books and pads and papers and still more papers—along with all the rest of Luella's familiar tools. There was the same ancient Royal, too, which even the last time I saw it appeared to be a candidate for typewriter heaven. I turned to make a comment to Kevin, expecting him to be somewhere in my immediate vicinity. But he had remained on the doorsill, his complexion chalk white now. "I'll wait for you in the living room, if that's all right," he said hoarsely. I told him it would be fine.

I slipped on a pair of rubber gloves, and for the next couple of hours I examined the contents of nine overstuffed drawers. I riffled through over half a dozen books. And I scanned every last piece of paper—even the crumpled-up pages on the floor. I had no idea what it was I was searching for. At some point or other I even speculated that I might come across a suicide note. Which, I'm sure, would have stunned and horrified everyone, including me. Happily, none surfaced.

When I'd finally done all I could think of to do, I went into the living room to join Kevin. And my heart contracted.

Although, basically, the room was as beautiful as ever, the subtle changes brought about in here by Luella's death made the tragedy seem far more real than it had only moments before. The curtains were drawn tightly together. And there was only the most meager illumination—from one small table lamp—which left all but a very confined area in semi-darkness and cast eerie shadows on the wall. (The eerie part might have been mainly in my imagination, though.) I glanced around me. Every flower in every vase was dead now, and brown-edged petals were strewn on the tables and the handsome bone carpet. And while the house was far from warm, today there was no blazing fire to relieve the chill.

Kevin was standing a couple of feet from the fireplace, his back to me. He seemed to be staring down at the unlit logs.

"Hi," I said softly as I approached him.

He started and in almost the same motion whirled around. "My nerves ain't what they used to be," he joked, embarrassed. "Good thing I'd already polished this off"—he was indicating the tumbler in his hand—"otherwise Connie's rug would have been soaking up some truly superior scotch whiskey."

"I'm sorry. I guess I kind of sneaked up on you."

"Don't be silly. It's not your fault, Desiree. It's . . . I was just remembering." He smiled then—an effort, I knew. "But what can I get you?" he asked, tapping the empty tumbler.

"Water would be fine."

We headed for the kitchen. And it was when I was leaning against the table there, swallowing the last mouthful of Evian Kevin had poured for me, that I noticed the empty bowl on the floor. *Where was Beatrix?*

I posed the question aloud.

"It's a big house," Kevin reminded me. "He could be on the second floor or on top of one of the cabinets—anywhere."

"Maybe I'll bump into him when I'm upstairs." (Which, incidentally, I didn't.) And then it occurred to me. "With Connie at Nadine's, who's taking care of him?"

"Nadine's been running over here to feed him and tend to his litter box."

"Well anyway," I said, rinsing out my glass, "I think I should tackle Luella's room now. Are you ready? You'll have to point it out to me."

Standing outside the dead woman's bedroom a short time afterward, I realized that a tour guide had hardly been necessary. A large piece of white paper with thick red letters was taped to the door. DO NOT ENTER, Kevin's message proclaimed.

"There was no lock," he told me, looking uneasy.

Actually, I'd been mainly concerned about the office, since that was the scene of Luella's death. And fortunately, no one had had access to that. Not since Sunday afternoon, at any rate. "It's okay," I assured him. "Don't worry about it." But I was curious. "Do you know whether either of Luella's other stepdaughters has been to the house in the last couple of days? Other than Nadine, that is."

"Not that I'm aware of, but all three of them have keys, so . . ." He shrugged, but he was plainly troubled by the thought.

"Well, the really important thing was to keep everyone out of the office," I advised him philosophically, going for the doorknob.

"Wait a second," he commanded, his tone sharp enough to arrest my a hand in midmotion. And now he reached about four feet above the knob, taking hold of a strand of beige thread that was wedged between the door and the frame. "See this?" I nodded. "I set that up on Sunday, and it's still in place. Nobody's been in there." (Doubtless, Kevin's been watching the same detective shows I have.)

"Good thinking," I remarked, grinning.

Having now satisfied himself that his former wife's bedroom had been undisturbed, Kevin once again retreated to more neutral ground, while I poked around in the dead woman's personal effects. The sort of chore I've never been very comfortable with.

I spent the better part of an hour holed up in there, not really expecting to uncover anything but feeling the compulsion to give the place at least a halfway decent look-through, regardless.

When I was finished, I went back downstairs and shared a Coke with Kevin. And less than ten minutes later we left the house together, neither of us surprised at the result of this morning's search but both of us disappointed, nevertheless.

If Luella's home held any clue to her death, I could only hope the police had found it. I knew I hadn't.

Chapter 11

Kevin had been anxious to join the family at Nadine's. And so after promising to keep him current on things, I left him and headed for the office, intending to grab a bite at my desk—which the arctic weather had convinced me was the only rational course. It was just past twelve when I arrived.

Now, on Monday afternoon I had finally gotten around to completing my report on that accident case I mentioned before. And right after that I'd typed up what I'd learned during Sunday's visit from Kevin. So today there was just one thing on my agenda: transcribing my notes about last night at Nadine's.

I sat down at the computer and worked for maybe fifteen minutes. Then I decided to take a break and order some lunch. But I couldn't bring myself to dial. You see, there was the notice I'd seen yesterday, posted in the window of this little boutique a couple of blocks from the office: They were having an earring sale, starting today.

Screw the temperature, I decided abruptly, grabbing for my coat.

The instant I hit the pavement, though, I almost regretted my heroics. Almost. It actually seemed to have gotten colder in the last quarter hour. By the time I'd walked just half a block, my teeth were chattering a mile a minute, plus I was certain that any second now my nose would break off.

Moving purposefully (an earring sale is maybe the one thing that can motivate me to take bigger steps), I buried my chin deep—almost up to my cheekbones, actually—into the cashmere Burberry scarf Ellen and Mike had gotten me for my birthday. Yes, they were even giving joint gifts these days. And I don't have to tell you what that means.

Smiling now, I reminded myself of the beginning of my acquaintanceship with Ellen's almost-fiancé. There I was, not even conscious. Stretched out in a dead faint in the lobby of his apartment building as the result of this truly horrifying encounter with a vicious killer. But that's another story. Anyhow, practically as soon as I opened my eyes and the attractive young doctor who was ministering to me came into focus, I earmarked him for my niece. Who, incidentally, is my niece by marriage. But the important thing, really, is that we're friends by choice. As I was saying, though, don't think it was easy getting them together. It took all of my persuasive powers to convince the two of them to meet. But my perseverance paid off. Any day I expected that—

"Hey! Watch where you're going, lady!" some obnoxious teenager hollered as he bumped into me, almost knocking me off the crowded sidewalk.

Well, why didn't he do some watching himself? How was I supposed to see every little thing when I had to keep my head down to prevent icicles from forming on my face? I glanced behind me to give him a dirty look. And that's when I was blindsided by some skinny girl with electric blue hair and a skirt up to her navel. This time, however, I remained firmly grounded, and the girl wound up practically at the curb, struggling to keep her balance. "I'm sorry, ma'am," she was polite enough to say nonetheless. (Although I could have lived without the "ma'am," which never fails to make me check myself out in the mirror to count the wrinkles.)

And what were all these people doing out this afternoon, anyhow? This was definitely an eat-in kind of day. Unless you had something very important to do on your lunch hour, I mean.

Uh-oh. Maybe a good many of the women I was presently sharing Lexington Avenue with were headed where I was— to Chez Lisa's. And maybe one of them would get there before me and snatch up a pair of earrings that I would have died for.

The thought sent my normally underachieving legs into overdrive.

It was almost three when I returned to the office, a brown paper bag in my fist and two pairs of earrings in my purse.

I'd started out for the shop thinking I'd treat myself to a single pair, but I just kept vacillating between these silver-and-turquoise hoops and a large 14-karat gold triangular drop. Both pairs cost a lot more, even on sale, than I'd had any intention of spending. But they *were* a terrific buy—considering the original prices, that is. And the thing is, the earrings were so completely different from each other than it was really impossible to compare them. In fact, the pressure I was putting on myself to make a choice was, I feared, placing me in imminent danger of a migraine. (At least, I supposed that was what this pounding in my head could lead to, having, fortunately, never experienced a migraine in my life.) At any rate, I finally had my fill of the reflection that showed me taking off one pair and putting on the second pair and then taking those off and. . . The sensible thing to do, I now concluded, would be to spring for both. For health reasons.

Glancing up from her desk as I came in, Jackie handed me a pink telephone slip. On it was a message from Ellen, and she wanted me to call her back as soon as possible. She'd mentioned the other day that she had Tuesday off—Ellen's a buyer at Macy's—so I dialed her home number, managing this feat at more or less the same time I got out of my coat and removed a sandwich and a container of coffee from the paper bag. (At some point between my purchase and the office it had dawned on me that hunger might be at the root of this damn headache. At least partially.)

"Hi, it's me," I announced, just prior to taking a bite of the sandwich.

"Oh, Aunt Dez. I was wondering if you could come over for dinner tonight." I suspected Ellen must be feeling lonely. Mike's a resident at St. Gregory's, and he'd been spending most nights at the hospital these last couple of weeks.

"What time do you want me?" I answered obligingly.

Ellen served her specialty that evening: Chinese takeout. In fact, the menu was exactly the same as the one we'd opted for a few weeks before (and I don't know how many takeouts before that)—dim sum, barbecued spare ribs, and egg roll to start off with and then for our entrees, lemon chicken and shrimp with black bean sauce. I brought the dessert. Häagen-Dazs—what else? Belgian chocolate, Ellen's favorite, and macadamia brittle, the most major of my many major weaknesses.

All in all, it was a terrific meal. And between us we more than did justice to it. I really have no idea how Ellen managed her part, though, since the way those faded jeans fit her reed-thin, no-hips figure, there hadn't seemed to be room for so much as an olive pit.

Mike—as expected—figured very prominently in our dinner conversation. Ellen was so proud of him. He'd extended his residency in order to work under this top cardiovascular surgeon—a physician he greatly admired. And the other day after Mike had assisted in a particularly difficult operation, the man spoke very enthusiastically to him about the abilities he was consistently demonstrating. If she'd had any buttons to pop, Ellen would have popped them all as she repeated the complimentary words.

Eventually I told her about my new case, which—also as expected—she was not exactly thrilled to hear about.

"Why can't you just stick to the kind of stuff you always handled before?" Ellen demanded somewhat belligerently, referring to a caseload that until a few years ago had consisted mainly of divorce and insurance investigations, with a smattering of missing persons, child custody, and similarly harmless miscellaneous assignments to add some variety to the mix. "Remember when you found that old lady's cat for her and how happy you made her?" she threw at me, making it sound as though until my forays into murder, I'd practically been a public service institution. Then she crinkled her forehead. "What was that cat's name, anyhow?"

"Tabitha. An inspired choice," I retorted in a voice dripping with sarcasm. "And while you're at it, don't forget Elvin Blaustein's pet boa constrictor. Now, *that* was a heartwarming piece of business. Challenging, too."

"Well, at least you didn't have to worry about getting your head blown off."

"You're right. I didn't even have much occasion to *use* my head."

But it wasn't long before I regretted my snappishness. Ellen's disapproval, after all, stemmed from her concern for my safety. "It's not that I'm gung ho to live on the edge or anything," I explained. "I was perfectly content with the kind of work I was getting. It's just that all of a sudden these murder cases started to come in and— Look, Ellen, it's very possible we may find that Luella died of natural causes. But at any rate, I couldn't very well turn Kevin down, could I? He's an old friend who's in a lot of pain, and he needs my help."

She shot back with, "You could have recommended someone else, if you wanted to." But then after a few moments, she relented. "Okay. You're not going to listen to me, anyway. But just swear you'll be careful."

And I swore.

Now Ellen and I were finishing our coffee (which we both agree goes perfectly fine with Chinese food). And I was thinking about what a difference Mike's feelings for her had made in my Nervous Nellie-of-a-niece. I mean, she hadn't even been thrown by that milestone birthday a couple of months ago—her thirtieth. And Ellen's been known to fuss so much over one measly gray hair that she undoubtedly worries her way into producing another one.

Don't get me wrong, though. She still wasn't exactly handling life with equanimity. But that was okay. I mean, Ellen wouldn't be Ellen if she didn't agonize over whether Mike was getting the sleep he needed. Or her neighbor's Shih Tzu had enough milk to feed the new puppies. Or, as you've seen, whether my next case would be the death of me. And you could always depend on some other little something cropping up every so often that would cause her to drive herself—and everyone else—crazy. The most recent such source of angst being finding the right dress for her friend Ginger's wedding in two months.

But lately there weren't nearly as many of these crises as there used to be. Like I said, Ellen was taking a lot more in stride since Mike. I think he even had a positive affect on her physical appearance. Not that she needed much help in that department with the way she resembles Audrey Hepburn. Nevertheless, these days her cheeks seemed to be a little rosier and her eyes more sparkly. She smiled more, too. And Ellen has *such* a lovely smile.

"I don't suppose there's been time for you to hear from Bruce again," she was saying as she attempted to scrounge up one last drop of Häagen-Dazs from a dish that obviously had nothing more to offer.

I scoffed at the question. "Don't be ridiculous. I only saw him Sunday; his year isn't up yet."

Now, Ellen doesn't laugh; she giggles. And she giggled then. But just to be polite, I think. And right after that she put to me timidly, "Any chance of my meeting this guy, Aunt Dez? Maybe we could go out one night—the four of us."

The suggestion wasn't one I particularly welcomed. The thing is, my relationship with Bruce was so tenuous that I wasn't at all sure I was ready to bring another element into it. And I have no idea whether my concern was about how Bruce would relate to Ellen and Mike. Or about what *they'd* think of *him*. Or whether I was just afraid of upsetting the status quo—even as unsatisfying as I considered it to be. But at any rate, while I've always been able to level with Ellen, this time when I went to tell her I'd prefer to wait awhile, "Let me talk to Bruce" came out instead.

My lack of enthusiasm must have showed, however, because she mumbled uncertainly, "But if you'd rather not . . ."

"No, no. I'll mention it the next time I speak to him. Assuming, of course, that I'll be speaking to him again."

"Listen, don't feel you have to say something. Not unless you really want to. We can always do it later on—in the future."

"I'd *like* for the four of us to get together. Really. I'll ask Bruce about it when he calls."

But in that instant I knew I wouldn't be asking him anything of the sort.

Chapter 12

It was on Thursday evening that I had my first meeting with one of Luella's stepdaughters—Geena Holmes, now Hough.

I was none too happy about the Houghs' living accommodations: a fifth-floor walk-up on Prince Street. I mean, the only aspect of my profession that I consider almost as hazardous as staring down the barrel of a gun is negotiating five flights of stairs. And there have been times when I actually wondered if I had the order reversed.

This was one of those times.

Kevin's having forewarned me about the climb (which in my mind loomed almost to the challenge of a Mount Everest), I had allowed myself an extra quarter of an hour. I wound up using every last second of it, too.

Reaching even the second floor was no picnic. I mean, you have never seen so many stairs to a single flight in your life!

By the time I got to the third floor I was panting as though I'd just engaged in a half hour of aerobics, God forbid.

I only made it up to four by stopping to rest after practically every step I took. And even so, I had to sink down on the landing for a couple of minutes to catch my breath. At this point I decided that the whole thing wasn't worth it. I didn't care anymore who killed or didn't kill Luella Pressman. Or that, at this very moment, I might be only one floor removed from her murderer. And so what if Kevin and Connie needed answers. The truth is, just then it would have taken precious little prompting to induce me to tear up my P.I. license. If I could summon the energy, that is.

When I reached the fifth floor at last, my heart was beating like a tom-tom. *I hope Kevin at least has the decency to send a nice floral arrangement to the funeral parlor,* I groused as I staggered out of the stairwell and into the hall.

* * *

It was Geena who opened the door to the apartment. She seemed to blanch at the sight of me. "Are you all right, Ms. Shapiro?" she demanded in a tone I already knew to be uncharacteristically sharp.

Conserving the pitifully little strength I had, I nodded.

"Wait. Don't move." She dashed across the room and, grabbing a wooden chair, dragged it over to where I was standing—just this side of the threshold. She all but pushed me into it.

Now, I'd certainly had more comfortable seats in my life—few, in fact, had been tougher on my tender derriere—but this one had a feature for which I was extremely grateful: It was *there*.

Geena stood over me for a few seconds, frowning, apparently still doubtful as to my prognosis. Then she spoke in the shy voice that I remembered from our previous meeting. "Why don't I make us some tea—would you like that?"

I answered with another nod, and she scurried away. I looked around me.

The room, I thought appreciatively, was a very decent size. And it was only minimally furnished, which probably exaggerated its actual dimensions. As to the few pieces it did contain, they were hardly in the best of condition.

Hugging one wall, sitting atop a nondescript hooked rug, was an oversized sofa slipcovered in a faded floral chintz. On either side of the sofa were a couple of beat-up end tables and, facing it, two small unmatched club chairs—one upholstered in a rust and olive stripe, the other in a badly worn blue velvet. And then against the opposite wall, under the floor-to-ceiling triple window, there was a decrepit-looking trestle table, alongside of which was the sister chair to the one presently saving my life.

Actually, I glanced at all of these things pretty perfunctorily. It was the walls themselves that held my attention—they were covered with maybe two dozen vividly colored abstract paintings. I can't tell you if the artist—Andy, almost certainly—had any talent or not. In fact, my knowledge of art being what it is, even after examining the paintings more closely later in the evening, I had no idea how most of them could possibly be about what Geena told me they were about. Or for that matter, whether they were acrylics or oils.

Anyhow, when she returned, Geena was toting one of those handy stack tables that I, personally, would be lost without.

She set it alongside me, smiled tentatively, and then went back to the kitchen. Seconds later she carried in a fairly large metal tray containing our tea and all sorts of accompaniments (including lemon, cream, honey, *two* kinds of sugar, and a sugar substitute). There was even a chipped white plateful of what I instantly recognized to be Aunt Connie's brownies. Putting the tray down on the stack table—which was barely able to accommodate it—she schlepped over my chair's twin sister and placed it opposite me.

"Are you okay?" she asked just before taking a seat. We were almost knee-to-knee now.

"It seems that I am. Or anyhow, I will be." This was attested to by the fact that I'd actually managed to get those few words out without struggling for breath.

I couldn't help thinking, however, that Geena herself did not look so okay. Her almost painful thinness was accentuated by the dark green ankle-length dress she wore, which was made of some sort of flimsy rayon material and hung on her like a sack. And she should definitely do something about that hair of hers. In my opinion, anyway. Long—it reached all the way down to the center of her back—and curly to the point of kinky, it overpowered the small oval face. What's more, the girl was so pale as to be almost wraithlike. At that moment, I had a strong desire to haul her home with me so I could force-feed her.

"You look a lot better than Kevin did when he visited," she remarked, obviously trying to be encouraging. Then, as I took my first sip of tea: "This one time, we were really afraid he might have a heart attack."

"Yes, he told me something like that."

"And he's in very good shape, too." Here, she blushed crimson. "Oh, I didn't mean that you're not, Ms. Shapiro," she hastily inserted. "I only meant . . . umm . . . that he . . . well—"

I broke in to put her out of her misery. "No offense taken," I informed her with a smile. "And call me Desiree."

She raised her teacup and drank, mostly, I think, to cover her discomfort. "Have an Aunt Connie brownie, Desiree," she said after a few seconds, pushing the plate an inch or two closer to me.

I didn't have to be coaxed. But I noticed that Geena refrained from partaking herself.

"I thought maybe Andy should be here tonight, too," she

brought up then, "but he figured if you wanted to talk to him, you would have said so. And he normally works out at the gym on Thursday nights."

Somehow she made this information sound like a question, so I told her, "No problem. I can always contact him another time."

"That's just what Andy said."

It was immediately following this that we got down to business.

"There were some things I wanted to ask you about," I began. And when Geena looked at me expectantly: "I'd like you to tell me about your relationship with Luella."

"We had a wonderful relationship. She was like my real mother," the girl responded promptly.

"You never felt she neglected you? When you were younger, I mean."

"No, I can't say that I did. Oh, she was very busy with her work, but I understood that. She was an extremely successful author, you know."

"Yes, that's what I heard."

"I was so proud of her. Her books are just charming. Have you read any of them?"

"No, I haven't." The confession made me ashamed. Which was ridiculous, since it had been a couple of centuries now since I was ten years old. Or anywhere in that vicinity.

"Actually, when she and my dad first got married," Geena went on, "my mother took a lot of time off from her writing to devote to her family. That was when I really needed her the most, too, when we were all getting adjusted as a family."

"You weren't troubled when things changed and she wasn't that accessible to you anymore?"

"You have to realize that Mother was never *in*accessible. I could always go to her—with anything at all. Maybe not that second. But soon enough. She usually had dinner with us—unless she was faced with a really tight deadline or had an important meeting. If for some reason she couldn't eat with us, though, I'd talk to her the next morning, at breakfast." I made no comment to this, so Geena added defensively, "Look, whatever time she was able to spare for me was *good* time; I loved being with her. I felt very fortunate in having her for my mother."

"She did have a pretty short fuse, though, didn't she? That must have been a little frightening to a child."

Geena didn't answer immediately. "Well, a little, I suppose," she finally conceded. "But whenever she lost her temper, she'd always apologize later on and hug me and everything would be all right again."

Here, as a delaying tactic (although maybe not strictly), I helped myself to another brownie. While I munched, I could ponder my next question. I was entering a really sensitive area, you see, and I didn't want to just blurt something out. But the tactful phraseology I was hunting for eluded me, so in the end I blurted anyway. "You didn't blame Luella at all for your father's suicide?" My tone, at least, was sympathetic—I hoped.

"No, of course not," Geena informed me evenly. "My father killed himself because he lost a fortune, and he just couldn't deal with that."

"But during a period when he was so despondent over his finances, when he obviously needed her bolstering, your mother was too busy with her career to be very supportive. Or at any rate, so I've been told."

"Whoever said that was being unfair," Geena retorted, the small, thin voice slightly harsher now. "Mother had no idea of the extent of my father's depression. And what about me? I didn't help him, either. Maybe if I'd sat down and really talked to him, gotten him to open up about his feelings . . ." She shook her head sadly. "Oh, I don't know, maybe I could have done *something*."

"That's foolish," I said, trying to dispel the guilt that I couldn't have been more surprised to find here. "You were just a child."

"I was sixteen when my father died. That's not what you'd call a baby. Anyhow, let's not go into *that*."

"Were you and he close?" I inquired gently.

"I loved him very much."

"It must have been a terrible blow to lose him that way, especially after the tragedy with your mother—your natural mother, I'm referring to."

"Yes, it was." The words came out in a whisper.

"Did you—were you there when she was killed?"

"I was in the house, but I was upstairs sleeping, and my mother was murdered in the living room. I didn't know anything had happened until Daddy discovered her early the next morning. He had just come home from a business trip."

You could almost hear the lump in her throat now, and so I switched gears. "How did Luella feel about your husband?"

Geena regarded me warily. "Feel?"

"Did she like him?"

"More or less."

"You're not exactly being straight with me, are you?" I chided mildly.

"Wel-l-l, I guess Mother wasn't crazy about him." And then very quickly: "But she didn't hate him, either."

"Do you have any idea what she had against him?"

"No, and neither did she. He just made her uneasy for some reason. She couldn't even explain why."

"I don't imagine she was very pleased about the marriage," I pressed.

"I can't say that she was." This admission was made so softly that it took me a couple of seconds to figure out what I'd just heard. Then a moment later Geena looked at me very directly, and her voice was clear and emphatic. "But when I convinced her that Andy and I were really in love, she didn't do anything to try and stop us from marrying. In fact, Mother was absolutely wonderful about everything. Besides giving us a lovely wedding and a very generous gift, she treated us to a honeymoon in Europe."

"And you kept in close touch with your mother until her death?"

"I called her almost every day. And if she was busy working or if she wasn't home, I left a message with Aunt Connie or on the machine to let her know I was thinking about her."

"When was the last time you actually spoke to her?"

"On Friday morning."

"She seemed okay? I mean, did you notice anything different about her manner, anything at all?"

"No, she was the same as she always was."

"And you last saw her—when?"

"The previous Friday. The whole family was over there for dinner."

"I have just one more question for you," I said, this being something I frequently stick in after a while, mostly to give the questionee a glimpse of the light at the end of the tunnel. (And just about then, I suspected that Geena needed to be assured there *was* an end of the tunnel.) Occasionally there's even truth to this "just one more question" business, by the way. But not—unfortunately for Geena—at present. "How did you feel when Luella married Kevin?" I asked.

"Fine. I liked him a lot, right from the beginning. Of course, I was grown up and out of the house when they started seeing each other."

"I understand that someone new had come into her life recently."

"You mean Bud Massi."

"Yes. What do you think of him?"

"I don't really know him that well, but he seems like a nice person, very bright, very personable. He appeared to be pretty crazy about Mother, too."

"You wouldn't have objected if she had married him?"

"Why should I object if that's what she wanted to do? If it made her happy, that was the important thing."

"You didn't consider it inadvisable in view of her track record?"

Geena grinned. "Probably. But who knows? This time maybe it would have worked out."

"Look," I put to her now, "your mother was a wealthy woman. And there was always the possibility that if she married this Massi, you and your sisters could lose out on a substantial inheritance. Didn't that cause you any concern?"

"My mother swore she had no intention of marrying again. Anyhow, it was her money. Besides—and you probably won't believe me—I never gave the money that much thought. Mother was such a youthful, vital person that her death seemed far, far away—in the distant future sometime. I just never imagined . . . none of us ever imagined . . ." She stopped speaking, her eyes filled to overflowing. "Would you excuse me, please?" she gulped, fleeing from the room before I could answer.

She returned a few minutes later clenching a fistful of tissues. "Sorry." And then, as she sat back down again, she glanced at my empty cup. "Oh, more tea?" she offered with forced brightness.

"No, but thank you. It seems to have rejuvenated me. Uh, I hear you're in real estate," I said at this juncture, settling on the most benign topic that occurred to me.

"That's right."

"Like it?"

Geena made a face. "Well, I wouldn't say I *like* it exactly. I'm not much of a salesperson."

"What made you go into something like that, then?"

"This close friend of mine has been very successful at it, and she offered me a job—she has her own real estate firm. And since I really wasn't trained for anything and it *can* be pretty lucrative . . ." She smiled ruefully. "So I took a short course, and here I am. I even make some sales once in a while—in spite of myself."

"There was something else I wanted to ask you."

"Go ahead." She was looking at me warily again.

"Did your sisters react the same way that you did to your mother's negl—busy schedule?"

"They understood. Just like I did."

"Neither of them ever complained about it?"

"No," she answered in a way that defied me to dispute this. I decided not to. I mean, what for?

"Just one other thing," I said then. "Would you mind telling me where you were on Saturday morning?"

Now, if Luella *had* been murdered, I had—as you're aware—no idea at this point how and when this had been accomplished. For all I knew, she could have been given a slow-acting poison days—or even weeks—earlier. Still, I figured the question should be put to everyone involved in the case.

Geena's eyes were wide with fear. "You can't possibly believe . . . Aunt Connie said you were going to prove my mother died a natural death." And before I could respond: "You don't think I actually killed my own mother." And then very, very timidly: "Do you?"

"No, I don't. I don't even believe there was a crime committed here. But I have to check into every possibility. That's what I was hired to do."

Geena nodded, apparently at least somewhat mollified.

"Uh, you haven't answered my question," I reminded her.

"I forgot about it for a minute." She was actually smiling, even if a bit sheepishly. "I had an appointment to show this property on West Twenty-second Street at twelve-thirty. I was right here until—I guess it was almost twelve."

"Alone?"

"Well, Andy was in, too—painting; his studio is in the back. But his door was closed, so we really didn't have any contact."

"Did you get any phone calls that morning? See any neighbors or anything?"

She thought for a moment. "No. Not that I remember."

"How about when you were leaving the house? Did you tell Andy you were going?"

"No, he doesn't like to be disturbed." Shifting around in her chair now, an obviously nervous Geena moistened her lips. "The only person who can swear I was home that morning," she said unhappily, "is me."

I told her that was usually the case. And then, to put her even more at ease, I inquired as to whether she enjoyed living in SoHo. From here we segued into how she and Andy had met and how long they had known each other before things got serious. All of which seemed to relax her considerably.

I spent the last five or ten minutes at Geena's enthusing over Andy's paintings (well, they *were* colorful). And then I finally worked myself up to dealing with the stairs again.

It was a lot easier going down than up, of course.

Still, I'd rather spend an entire week Häagen-Dazs-less than tackle five flights like that. In *either* direction.

Chapter 13

Once, when Ellen's elevator was on the blink, I had to make it all the way up to 14-A under my own steam. And that, of course, was a *real* killer.

Still, when I woke up on Friday morning my legs were so charley-horsed that just getting out of bed was a challenge. If I hadn't had an acute attack of caffeine withdrawal, I might have remained under the covers until the cows came home. But as it was, I got up, paid a brief visit to the bathroom, and then dragged myself into the kitchen for some coffee and corn flakes. At nine o'clock I called Jackie.

"Desiree Shapiro's office," she announced in her cool and efficient phone-answering voice. Well, I had no illusions about how long this posture would last, and I steeled myself for what many such telephone calls had taught me loomed on the horizon.

"Uh, Jackie, I won't be coming to work today. I'm a little under the weather."

"What's wrong?" I could picture her gripping the phone a little more tightly now.

I'm sorry, but I really couldn't admit that climbing those stairs had knocked me for a loop like this. I knew as surely as I know my own name that if I did, Jackie would be bent on either shipping me off to a health club or a doctor—if possible, before we even hung up. "Nothing, really," I answered. "I feel as if I'm coming down with a cold, and I figured it would probably be best if I stayed in and tried to ward it off."

Her response followed the script in my head to a T. "Are you being straight with me?" she demanded, her voice having risen about an octave.

"Of course I am."

"There isn't anything you're not telling me, is there?"

I really had no idea what sort of thing she suspected me of

keeping from her. Did she imagine I was suffering from a terminal disease and being an extremely considerate person was attempting to spare her? Or did she think it was something else—like maybe I was leading a secret life? At any rate, I wanted to say that, okay, I'd level with her: Robert Redford had reserved a suite for us at the Plaza for a full twelve hours of unbridled passion. But I resisted the temptation and, making a supreme effort to keep my annoyance in check, substituted, "No, there is nothing I'm not telling you."

"Look, I could hop a cab at lunchtime and bring you some food and whatever else you need," she offered.

Damn! As usual, Jackie had succeeded in stirring up these conflicting emotions in me. I was very touched by her solicitude. I mean, she was a really good, caring friend. But on the other hand, her refusal to accept the truth (or at least what was close enough to the truth) was making me crazy. And I had to go through this with her every time I decided to skip work, too. But the only alternative was to just not show up—which, believe me, no sane person with Jackie for a secretary would even contemplate.

"That's really sweet of you," I responded warmly, "and I appreciate it, honestly. But I've got everything I need right here in the apartment."

"Okay, if you change your mind, though, you have the phone number. And don't be a martyr."

"Thanks, but—and please take my word for it, Jackie— I'm not exactly at death's door."

"You're positive you're okay?"

"There is no doubt in my mind." Now, when I'm trying to resist the urge to scream, I speak very softly. And, while I know this sounds ungrateful, right then I was close to whispering. "Listen, I'll see you on Monday. And have a wonderful weekend."

I clicked off before she could push me completely over the edge.

For the rest of the day, I did nothing. (Unless you regard taking a bubble bath and then watching soap operas and talk shows as *something*.) One thing I was proud of, though. True to the promise I'd made to myself earlier that week, there were no inner struggles over Bruce. In fact, as soon as he entered my head—which I admit he did a couple of times—I pushed him the hell out.

Saturday was practically a carbon copy of Friday, with me planting myself in front of the TV for another entire afternoon. The only difference was that instead of *All My Children, One Life to Live*, and Geraldo, Sally, and Montel, I had to settle for an old western I ended up hating and a recent mystery I hated more. (I'm still trying to figure out how the detective doped out who the killer was when all he seemed to be doing throughout the picture was hopping from bed to bed.) The one bright spot in my day was that my legs were supporting the rest of me a whole lot better now. Even though, obviously, I had no inclination to take advantage of this.

I slept until nearly twelve on Sunday. And then right after my very late breakfast, I was once again a total cipher, spending hour after hour sprawled out on the sofa, staring unblinkingly at the television screen.

You know, originally I'd been concerned that neither Enid nor Nadine was able to see me until the following week—Nadine because she was leaving for Florida right after shiva to shoot a soft drink commercial and Enid because she was headed for the West Coast to work on a corporate acquisition. The way things turned out, though, I was making the most—if you can consider it that—of their unavailability. I really can't tell you what had gotten into me, either. There's a good possibility that what had begun as sore muscles quickly evolved into an excuse to just drop out of life for a little while. And I proved to be pretty good at it, too, I guess, managing for three whole days to block out sudden death and an old friend's grief, along with the phone call I didn't get.

I did receive a few other calls that weekend, though. One on Saturday from Ellen, who wanted to find out how the case was going and then tell me how much she and Mike had enjoyed the theater the night before. And three from Jackie spaced out over the three days, in which, each time, she inquired anxiously as to the state of my health.

Shortly after her last call—on Sunday at around five o'clock—my stomach began to remind me loudly that a person has to eat. But it took close to an hour for me to seriously ponder tearing myself away from the sofa—to which I seemed to be attached by Velcro. Before I actually made the move, however, the phone rang again.

My new portable telephone was on the cocktail table in front of me, and I could reach it by merely stretching out my arm. "Hello?" I said, simultaneously muting the TV with the remote in my lap.

"Hi, Dez," said a voice I recognized as being the property of my neighbor Harriet. "I sent Steve to pick up some Chinese food a little while ago," she went on without preamble. " 'Whatever you feel like,' I told him. Well, you should see what he just walked in with. There must be enough here to feed half of Manhattan! You'd think I'd know better, too, after being married to that crazy person for all these years." A sigh. "I swear, I must be in my dotage, giving him carte blanche like that. I'm afraid if we don't get some help, we'll wind up eating the stuff into the next century. So please say you haven't got any plans tonight and that you'll come over and pitch in."

Well, it had now been five days since my Chinese feast at Ellen's (and besides, over in China they don't seem to mind eating nothing *but* Chinese food). What's more, dinner at Harriet and Steve's sure beat the alternative of scrounging around in my refrigerator for leftovers. And, of course, it wasn't as though it would take much of an effort to get to their place—they only live across the hall.

Still, there was another, more compelling reason I accepted the invitation—and very gratefully, too.

After close to seventy-two hours of virtual solitude, I concluded that the Goulds' company—their retarded Pekingese, Baby, notwithstanding—would certainly be preferable to any more of my own.

It took me until the following morning to recognize that even a prodding with a red-hot poker was too good for me. I mean, here time was such an important factor in the investigation, and I'd put everything on hold since Friday, allowing myself to turn into something one step removed from a vegetable. It pained me to even think of the things I should have been taking care of. Well, all I could do now was to try and catch up.

I got to my office at around nine-thirty and immediately telephoned Connie at the town house.

She tensed up as soon as I mentioned my name. "Is there— have you found out anything?"

"No, it's nothing like that. I need some phone numbers from you. But first, how are you feeling?"

"All right—considering. I'm still uncomfortable in this

place—I moved back Thursday morning, you know. It feels
so . . . so eerie living alone here now. But I suppose that
sooner or later I'll get used to it."

"I'm sure you will. It just takes a while."

"Uh, listen, Desiree, I was going to get in touch with you
if I didn't hear from you soon. There's something I'm anxious to clarify. I understand that Kevin told you there were
times Luella wouldn't be too attentive to the girls—I'm referring to when they were young, of course. He's been concerned that you might have misinterpreted what he said. And
so have I. Maybe we're both being silly, because really, what
does it matter now? Still, I'd hate for you to have the wrong
impression of my sister. Those girls were very important to
her. Always. It was only that sometimes she got so caught up
in her writing she forgot there was even a world out there."

"I can appreciate that," I responded without meaning it.

It's possible Connie caught the insincerity in my tone, because she hurriedly put in, "Look, my sister was a very high-
strung person, Desiree. Very nervous. Well, you met her. It
was pretty hard to miss. Did you happen to notice her fingernails?"

"As a matter of fact, I did."

"There was nothing left of them—true? And when she
wasn't biting her nails or chewing on pencils she was all but
pulling her hair out.

"She just put herself under so much pressure," Connie
went on. "She was constantly afraid she wouldn't make her
deadlines or be able to come up with any more fresh ideas or
that her publisher would drop her—there was never a time
she wasn't on edge about *something*. That was another reason she spent so much time working. She was just so worried
about that series of hers.

"But still, she made certain she saw to the girls' needs.
Even if she didn't drop everything right then and there to do
it. Luella loved her stepdaughters a great deal—all three of
them," Connie insisted. "And it was reciprocated. That's
why I find it so difficult to go along with Kevin's theory that
one of them harmed her."

"It's premature for you to concern yourself with that. It's
very likely Kevin's mistaken and that *no one* harmed her."

"You're right. I'm certain that's what we'll learn eventually. But anyway, I did want you to know how it was—with
Luella and the girls." And now in an apparent effort to lighten

things up a bit, Connie remarked, a smile in her voice, "Actually, it was incumbent upon Luella to be a good mother. After all, she was born under the sign of motherhood."

"I had no idea there *was* a sign of motherhood."

"Oh, yes," I was informed with a chuckle. "Cancer. Of course, if she'd arrived a couple of hours earlier, she'd have been a Gemini. Which would have let her off the hook nurturing-wise, I suppose." And now brusquely: "But enough of my nonsense. You called about phone numbers. Tell me which ones you want."

"Bud Massi's, to begin with. And his address, too, if possible."

"No problem."

"Actually, I thought I might even meet him at Nadine's last Monday night," I commented.

"You just missed him. Bud left ten or fifteen minutes before you arrived. Whom else did you want to contact?"

"Well, I was wondering if Luella had any close friends."

"Only her agent and her editor. She was with them both for many years."

I was surprised. Having been so impressed with the dead woman myself, I'd been poised to take down a slew of names.

"My sister really didn't have the time to make friends. Not close ones, at any rate. She met a great many people through her organizations and all that, but they were only acquaintances. Anyhow, let me look up her agent and editor for you, too."

"Oh, and I'd also like the name and number of your sister's doctor—the one who gave her that physical exam a couple of weeks ago."

"Certainly. That's our family physician—Dr. Vanetti."

I was put on hold for maybe two minutes, after which Connie was back on the line with the information I'd requested. "Is there anything else I can help with?" she asked.

"Well, I did want to check out some facts with you, so I was wondering if we could get together for about an hour. I know this is a difficult time for you, but I think it would make sense if we talked while everything is still fresh in your mind."

"I understand. How's Saturday? It *is* all right to wait until then, isn't it?"

"Until Saturday?" I responded, somewhat taken aback. I'd been hoping to hotfoot it over there immediately.

"Yes. I'm leaving for Connecticut today. Very shortly, in fact. A friend of mine is convinced that it would be good for me to get away for a while, and she invited me out to her place in Wilton. To be honest, I was glad to take her up on it. As I told you, I just don't feel easy in this house, so—" Connie broke off for a second or two, and then she said earnestly, a tremor in her voice, "Look, I know that I'm only postponing the inevitable. But still, I welcome the reprieve."

"I hope it helps; I think it will," I murmured.

"Anyway, I'll be back Friday night," she informed me in a more level tone. "Rhonda—my friend—is expecting her daughter and son-in-law in from Virginia for the weekend, and I'm not feeling terribly sociable these days." She hesitated. "You do think it will be all right to wait until Saturday to have our talk, don't you?" she asked again.

For a moment I toyed with the idea of offering to drive up to Wilton to see her. But then I realized that would pretty much defeat her purpose in going there. So I said, "Of course." There really didn't seem to be anything else *to* say.

Chapter 14

Tuesday was cold and wet.

I had an awful job getting a taxi to Nadine's that night, but being a New Yorker for a lot of years now, I'd anticipated running into trouble and had planned accordingly. So at precisely 9:03 I was ringing Nadine's bell—right on time for our nine o'clock appointment. (I think you'd have to be anal retentive to count that lousy three minutes as showing up late, don't you?)

Luella's youngest stepdaughter came to the door looking very pert in slim black jeans and an oversized white shirt. Standing this close to the girl, I marveled at her complexion, which was creamy, pink-cheeked, and blemish-free. It's not very often you see skin like that on anyone past high-chair age. "Hi. C'mon in," she invited enthusiastically, indicating the living room behind her with a wave of the hand.

She escorted me over to the love seat, which—in the absence of last week's folding chairs—was now the only seating accommodation in the room. "Make yourself comfortable. Just sit anywhere." Naturally, she was smiling playfully when she said it.

I sank down into the familiar cushions, and then Nadine excused herself. "Be right with you," she told me.

Moments later she returned with a small black and rose needlepoint footstool.

Plunking the stool down a few feet in front of me, she carefully lowered herself onto it. An accomplishment only her diminutive dimensions made possible. "Sandi—that's my roommate—and I sent our living-room chairs out to be reupholstered over six weeks ago," she explained. "And would you believe the guy still hasn't brought them back? Every week that rotten liar keeps saying, 'Next week, I promise.'"

"I know how that is," I commiserated. "I once had a sofa

reupholstered, and it got to the point where I doubted I'd ever see the thing again."

"That's pretty much how I've been feeling lately. Anyhow, I thought it would be easier to talk if we faced each other like this. Oh, what can I get you?" Nadine inquired then. "I have soft drinks and not-so-soft drinks. Also, coffee, tea, milk . . ."

Now, I find that it often helps to ask your questions over a beverage of some kind. It seems to make the atmosphere a little more companionable. "I'd love some coffee, if you don't mind."

"Sure. And I can offer you a piece of this absolutely luscious lemon meringue pie, too," she informed me seductively.

With that, a vision of the generous portion of Sara Lee cheesecake I'd allotted myself less than two hours earlier danced in front of my eyes. An unnecessary reminder, believe me. There wasn't room inside me for another crumb. "Thanks, but regretfully, I'll have to pass. I had a huge dinner."

Nadine took my coffee order (milk, one sugar) and in her energetic style bounded out of the room. Within three or four minutes she was standing over me, a mug in each hand, one of which I immediately relieved her of. And now positioning herself on the stool again, she said, "Okay. So what do you want to know?"

"Well, let's start with how you got along with your stepmother."

"Do the police *really* think somebody killed her?"

I sampled the coffee before addressing her question. (*Not great,* was the verdict. *But certainly better than my own.*) And then I responded carefully, "I haven't spoken to them. But they can't exclude anything like that. Not until they get the autopsy report."

"Mmm. I suppose that makes sense." She took a few sips of coffee herself before murmuring thoughtfully, "Aunt Connie says that could take more than a month, though. Is that right?"

"Easily. It could wind up taking six or eight weeks. Maybe even longer." By now there was a good chance that Nadine had forgotten what I'd asked her—I was barely able to remember myself. I tried again. "About how you and your stepmother got along . . ."

"Just wonderful. Really."

"And when you were a child?"

"I used to drive her crazy. I craved attention—plus I think I might have been bordering on hyper as a kid—so I was always trying to barge into her office and interrupt her when she was writing." The girl smiled impishly. "In other words, I was a real pain in the ass."

"You must have resented her for shutting herself away so much of the time."

"Sure I did. Off and on, anyway. But young as I was, on some level I think I understood that it was something she had to do. And then when Geena came into the family, I had myself a brand-new sister, a special friend of my very own. So I started to mind Luella's work schedule a lot less."

"You and Geena really hit it off, huh?"

"Oh, yes. We were great pals right from the start." And now Nadine hurriedly added, "But don't think Enid and I weren't close, too. It's just that she was older and away at school for most of the time I was growing up."

"Your sisters—how did they react to Luella's being so frequently unavailable?"

"Well, as I said, Enid was practically an adult by the time my dad married Luella. She told me it used to bother her, especially after her father skipped out on them. But she worked things through. And as for Geena, she pretty much took Luella's routine in her stride, just sort of accepting it as something that *was*."

And here I decided to throw out—to see where it would take me: "Umm, I understand the police think it's at least conceivable that one of you might have been harboring a grudge against your stepmother all these years."

The pink cheeks instantly darkened into an angry red, and Nadine's voice had a sharp edge to it now. "They have to be out of their minds! How could they believe one of *us* killed Luella? And for *that*—for being so hardworking!"

"Look, I'm truly sorry if I'm upsetting you, and I can't say what the motivation is supposed to have been. But your Aunt Connie mentioned that they considered it a possibility—although a remote one, I would imagine—so I did feel I should go over it with you."

"Yes, of course. And I'm sorry, too—for blowing a fuse like that. But the thing is, Luella was very kind to us. She treated us like her own flesh and blood, and we all loved her for it."

I wouldn't allow myself to let up yet. "According to my

information, though, she could be pretty quick-tempered."
(Well, at least I stuck to the truth that time.)

Surprisingly, Nadine grinned. "Luella was really a pussy-cat compared to my friend Vicki's mother. Compared to Mimi's mother, too." And now she bent to her coffee for a couple of seconds. After which she looked up, put her elbows on her knees, and, leaning forward, spoke in this mock confidential tone. "Whenever Mimi's mother had a couple of drinks, she'd curse like a drill sergeant and take off all her clothes. And Vicki's mother was worse. The woman threw things. She even threw a VCR at her brother-in-law once."

"I guess it all depends on your frame of reference," I responded, laughing. "But now let's talk about how things were more recently. From what I hear, you and Luella kept in frequent touch after you moved out and got your own apartment. Is that right?"

"I called her three or four times a week."

"When was the last time you spoke to her?"

"The Wednesday before she died. I also tried to get her that . . . that Saturday. Close to nine o'clock, it was. I thought I might catch her before she started work, but she didn't pick up. Aunt Connie was on her way here by then—to bring over the brownies. So I just left a message on the machine."

"Did Luella seem at all disturbed when you talked to her on Wednesday? Different in any way?"

"No. Luella was . . . Luella," Nadine answered, her tone hushed.

"When did you see your stepmother last?"

"Two weeks ago this past Friday. We all—my sisters and I—went there for dinner. Andy, too, of course." And then a moment later she said hesitantly, "When I phoned her on Saturday? Well, maybe she was already gone—do you think so?"

"Could be she was just in her office, writing." And now I saw how troubled the girl looked. Well, it was time for a change of subject, anyway. "Uh, I understand you're an assistant producer," I said, electing to switch to something innocuous for a while. "I know almost nothing about that kind of thing. What exactly is it you do?" And for the next few minutes she told me. I could see then what Connie meant about a lack of self-confidence. Nadine certainly downplayed her own talent and capabilities. Of course, if it hadn't been for Connie's take on her niece, I'd probably have just attributed this to modesty.

Anyway, after the job description, I felt I could chance more sensitive topics again. "You must have been terribly broken up when your father was killed," I murmured in the most gentle voice I own.

"Well, yes, and no," Nadine admitted somewhat grudgingly. "To be honest, my father and I were never that close. The thing is, though, after the plane crash, I started to obsess about death. I remember how scared I was for a while that Luella might die, too. And Aunt Connie right after her. And then Deirdre, my nanny. I used to think, *What if something happens to all of them? I'll be left alone.* But eventually I decided that Enid would take care of me, and I convinced myself she was too young to die."

"Uh, your natural mother, I understand, was in an . . . "—I couldn't bring myself to say "institution," so there was a brief, awkward silence here while I searched my brain for a suitable synonym of some kind—"a medical facility," I finally came up with.

"My mother was in a mental institution," Nadine politely corrected. "It's nothing I'm ashamed of. She was a paranoid schizophrenic. It wasn't her fault or my fault. It wasn't anyone's fault."

"How old were you when she went away?" I asked softly.

"Three." Then frowning: "Listen, I don't want to be rude, Ms. Shapiro—"

"Desiree, remember?"

"Desiree, then. But what does all this about my mother and father have to do with Luella's death?"

"Most likely nothing," I conceded. "When I'm conducting an investigation, though, I try to gather as many facts as I can. And at some future point whatever doesn't tie in, I'll toss out. But look, Nadine, if this is too painful for you . . ."

"No, go ahead," she said. Which is what I was counting on her to say. "Actually, it doesn't really bother me that much. The truth is, I hardly knew my mother."

"They died within a year of each other—your parents—didn't they?"

Her expression was impassive. "That's right."

"Just one more question." (There was—as I'm sure you suspect—no truth whatever to this assurance.) "The morning your stepmother died, Connie got here—when?"

"About nine."

"And you had coffee together?"

"Uh-uh. Aunt Connie'd already had two cups at home."

"So she just dropped off the brownies and left?"

"No, she sat in the kitchen with me for a while, watching me stuff my face. And then she reminded herself about a phone call she had to make, so she went into the bedroom." I must have been wearing my inquiring expression now, because Nadine went on to say, "Aunt Connie does a little tutoring, and there was this boy she was supposed to get in touch with that morning."

"How long would you say the call took?"

"Probably around ten minutes. They were going over a book report the kid had written."

"Connie left here right after she was finished with the conversation?"

"Pretty much. She said she had some paperwork to do."

"And that was what time?"

"Nine-thirty, quarter of ten. I'm not really sure. Aunt Connie might be able to tell you."

"You seem to be pretty fond of your aunt," I remarked now.

"Oh, I am. Very." Nadine had responded quickly. *Too quickly?* I wondered. In that instant I'd gotten the impression, for some reason, that maybe Nadine wasn't quite as attached to her Aunt Connie as she would have liked me to believe. "She helped raise me; she helped raise the three of us," she declared, presumably as a clincher.

"Yes, I know."

"Poor Aunt Connie."

"Why 'poor Aunt Connie'? You mean because of Luella's death?"

She nodded. "This has been terrible for all of us," she mumbled, digging into the pocket of her jeans. "For me, my sisters, Kevin . . . Bud Massi, too—he's the man Luella had been going with recently." Extracting a tissue now, she proceeded to dab at her eyes and swipe at the wetness that had just found its way to her cheeks. This seen to, she sniffled a couple of times and then continued. "With Aunt Connie, though, well, throughout their whole lives those two had been best friends. They shared the house, meals, thoughts, feelings—everything. Even during the times Luella was married, it was like that. Aunt Connie's really lost without her. Like Beatrix."

"Beatrix?" But in a flash I figured it out for myself, and the words "Oh, *that* Beatrix" were poised to roll from my tongue. Nadine preempted me, however.

"Beatrix is our—was Luella's cat. And you can't imagine how he's changed since her death," she said sadly. "It's really strange. You don't know him, but—"

"There's where you're wrong. Beatrix and I met years ago. In fact, we pretty much bonded. But you were saying—?"

"Only that he used to have the sweetest, most loving nature. Luella brought him home when he was less than two weeks old—we had to feed him with an eye dropper." She smiled fondly at the memory. "Anyway, that was a long time ago, right after Geena's father died. I think Luella got a kitten mostly for Geena's sake. But it turned out that Geena didn't really take to him that much. Me, on the other hand, well, I was crazy about him the second I looked at him. Did you ever see a more beautiful face in your life? Did you notice he has dancing eyes?" And before I could respond, she went on with a shake of the dark brown curls, "It's like he's a different pers—I mean, a different cat now." A shamefaced grin followed the slip. "I can't help it; he's always been like a furry person to me."

"Luella was pretty attached to him, too, wasn't she?"

"*Pretty* attached? She adored him. Luella was wound sort of tight and—" Nadine cut herself short. "What am I saying? Luella was a nervous wreck! And yet most of the time it didn't bother her at all that Beatrix would jump in her lap or roam all over her desk when she was working."

"And just how has Beatrix changed?"

"Well, for starters, he used to be so friendly, and now he runs away from everyone—even me. When Aunt Connie was staying here last week, I went over to the house every day to feed him. And I couldn't believe it! He wouldn't let me near him. He even hissed at me once. And after that, he took off like a bat and jumped up on the top of the kitchen cabinet. That's what he does now. Perches on top of a cabinet or on one of the bookcases or an armoire—anything tall—sometimes thumping his tail in this really agitated way. But what *really* gets me is that when you least expect it, he's liable to swoop down on you. He did that to me last night. Came out of nowhere and leapt onto my shoulder. I was so startled, I almost fainted. Aunt Connie doesn't know what to do with him. I'm absolutely petrified she'll decide to get rid of him."

"Have you considered taking him yourself?"

"I wish I could, but I travel so much in my job that I don't see how I can. It's not unusual for me to be away for two or three weeks at a clip. Besides that, though, my roommate's allergic to cats."

"And you think Luella's death is what caused such a drastic difference in Beatrix?" I asked.

Nadine shrugged. "Maybe it was being shut up with her when she was dying. Or it could be he's just grieving for her. I can't really say. But I'll tell you this much: It's weird. *Really* weird."

"Uh, just one thing more." I thought I detected a knowing smile on Nadine's face when I said that, but she didn't comment. "What do you think of Bud Massi?" I put to her.

"I could have gone for Bud myself, but Luella had dibs on him." She checked me for a reaction—which wasn't supplied—and then she chuckled. "Just kidding. About being interested in him, that is. I used to tease Luella about that, too. I'd tell her that if she didn't grab him, I would. But in all seriousness, he does seem like a great guy."

"Have you spent much time in his company?"

"Well, not really. Luella and Aunt Connie had us all to dinner a couple of times when Bud was there. And then Luella brought him to a little birthday party Geena threw for Andy. Oh, and I saw him this one other time. That's about it."

"You mean you saw him . . . alone?"

Nadine laughed. "Yes, alone. I *was* just kidding before, Desiree. I'm not romantically interested in Bud Massi. Not even a little bit." Her right hand shot up. "I swear."

I don't think I looked skeptical, but then again, maybe I did. Because Nadine apparently decided I needed convincing. "The fact of the matter is, I went to talk to him about Luella."

"Why? Was something wrong?"

"Yes, since you're asking. He and Luella had broken up the week before, and she was positively miserable over it. But she wouldn't even consider picking up a phone and trying to straighten things out."

"So you decided to do the straightening for her."

"Well, *somebody* had to. You know," Nadine mused, "I'm glad the women of my generation don't have this hang-up about making the first move." And now suddenly struck by the accumulation of birthday candles I'm obviously required to blow out, she hastily tried for some damage control. "Of course, it has more to do with attitude than age—the hang-up, I mean. Some older women—" Breaking off, she glanced at me apologetically before proceeding slowly. "What I've been trying to say in my own bungling way is that at her core—and in spite of all those husbands—Luella was really pretty old-fashioned." At this juncture the girl looked as though she'd just picked her way across a minefield.

"So you paid a visit to this Massi?" I asked. And my voice was extra-friendly to let her know she hadn't hit a nerve.

"Yes. I went to see him at the lounge—Bud entertains at this lounge on Third Avenue a couple of nights a week. And—"

"Just a minute. I understood he was in software."

"He is. But he's also a musician—he plays the piano and sings. And he's good, too. He's been working at Emil's—that's the name of the place—for years now. Which is how he and Luella met. She and Aunt Connie stopped in for an after-dinner drink one night."

"And the rest is history," I commented with a smile.

"Well, not quite. Luella had to drag Aunt Connie back there four or five times before Bud got around to asking her out. Of course, she *said* she only went for the music."

"What was the reason Luella and Bud split up?"

"It was really so silly. Luella wouldn't see him more than once a week, because she was afraid they'd get too involved. But she didn't want to admit this to Bud—it wasn't as if he'd said he was serious about her or anything—so she blamed her writing schedule. That *was* pretty confining, as you know, but not as much as she wanted Bud to believe.

"Now, for his part, Bud didn't buy that Luella was working all of those nights. He got the notion she was spending some of her free time with another man—namely, Kevin. Well, Luella tried convincing Bud that she didn't see Kevin that often and that, besides, they were only good friends. But she didn't get anywhere. There was still the fact of her limiting her dates with *him*, you see."

Tilting her head then, Nadine grinned at me. "That's pretty much the gist of it."

"And you reunited the two of them."

"I did," she agreed with obvious pride.

"All right, let me in on it. How did you manage to do it?"

"Actually, by telling the truth. Once he knew what was what, Bud was willing to accept the status quo for awhile." She laughed. "But I had to make him promise on his vocal chords that he'd never let on to Luella that I'd been meddling in her love life."

"Sneaky little thing, aren't you?" I observed admiringly. And right after that: "Listen, Nadine, I know you won't like this, but I have to ask it. Weren't you at all concerned about how bringing Massi and your stepmother back together again could affect her finances—and maybe yours eventually?"

"You mean because she was putting money into Bud's company? Believe me, it didn't bother me one little bit."

"There was also the chance they might marry one day," I pointed out.

"I suppose." She said this almost disinterestedly. And now very earnestly: "Look, Desiree, if you think I was concerned about losing out on any inheritance, you couldn't be farther off base. When my father died I came into some money, which Aunt Connie very prudently invested for me. I haven't exactly accumulated a fortune, but I'll tell you this: If things keep going the way they have, in a few years I might even feel I'm solvent enough to try and start my own production company."

Then abruptly Nadine made a face. "This stool is murder on the spine after a while," she grumbled. And getting to her feet, she set her coffee mug on the cocktail table and stretched elaborately, slowly arching her back. "You know, Desiree," she declared, "I just decided that I'm going to make a voodoo doll of Mr. Whittaker and jab pins in all the appropriate places— Mr. Whittaker's that lying S.O.B. of an upholsterer."

"Come and sit here," I suggested, patting the cushion next to me.

"It's okay, I'm better off standing for a few minutes."

Now, that wouldn't exactly make conversation easy. And I strongly suspected that this was Nadine's clever little way of encouraging me to terminate my visit.

But it was a wasted effort. I'd been about to get up myself.

Chapter 15

It was almost noon when the phone rang on Wednesday. If it had been five minutes later, I might already have left for lunch and been spared—at least temporarily—the earsplitting tirade that awaited me.

"*You* are a dirty, rotten, miserable skunk."

I identified the voice immediately. "Uh, how are you, Pat?" I meekly inquired of my friend Pat Martucci, formerly Green, for a while Altmann, and once upon a time Anderson. I couldn't really fault her for lacing into me like this. If the situation had been reversed, I—also being too sensitive for my own good at times—would undoubtedly have reacted in much the same way. (Although Pat, I decided, had been blessed with the stronger vocal chords.)

"Never mind my health! Ask me how I feel about your not telling me you've been going with Bruce Simon." (It registered almost subliminally that, anyway, she'd at last gotten his name straight.)

"Look, Pat, I'm not *going* with Bruce. I've just had a few dates with him, that's all. I was concerned that when you found out you might be angry I hadn't said anything, but—"

"I'm not angry," she informed me with deceptive calm. And then with plenty of gusto: "I'm furious! After all, Burton and I were the ones who introduced the two of you to begin with, if you recall. And you've had more than a few dates, too, so stop B.S.ing me."

"Umm, you heard about . . . about this from Bruce?"

"Why should you be surprised? I speak to him quite often now that Burton and I are living together. Didn't you figure it would come out eventually? What's that expression?"—and her next words were accorded a deservedly dramatic reading—" 'Murder will out.' "

Now, under other circumstances I know I wouldn't have been able to refrain from laughing at this ridiculous analogy, but just then I couldn't chance so much as a titter. Besides, I was feeling much too guilty about keeping Pat in the dark for so long. "Uh, Shakespeare," I mumbled because I didn't know what else to say. (And maybe also to demonstrate that while I might be a stinker, I wasn't a Philistine, too.)

"Chaucer," Pat snapped.

I was not about to argue. (Also, she could be right.)

There was a silence now, and I realized I'd have to be the one to fill it. "Honestly, Pat, I planned on telling you myself, but—"

" 'But' what?"

"Uh, listen, I think it would probably be better if we held off on this discussion until I can explain in person."

"Fine. Meet me at the Hyatt for lunch. That restaurant overlooking Forty-second Street; the one with all the windows. The Sun something-or-other, it's called. I can be there in half an hour."

"Today?"

"Of course not," Pat retorted icily. "A year from next Easter."

"Well—"

"If you can't make it, though . . ."

"No, no. I'll see you then."

To avoid any added source of friction, I made every effort to get to the Sun Garden before Pat did. But we wound up arriving at the entrance to the hotel simultaneously. Which was okay, too. At least I didn't keep her waiting.

Now, Pat presents a formidable figure. Close to six feet tall, she has shoulders the size of a linebacker's and a bosom that extends all the way out to tomorrow. "Hi, Pat," I said shyly. And standing on tiptoe, I strained to buss her cheek, which gesture she elected to tolerate, even bending down to accommodate me. She did not, however, reciprocate or favor me with so much as a charitable little hug.

"Hello, Desiree." The accompanying smile was so fleet and faint as to be gone in the blink of an eye. Literally.

As soon as we were seated upstairs, we both asked the waitress (I'm afraid I still have trouble with *waitperson*) for a glass of chardonnay. In my case, it was mainly for fortification.

"I love your hair," I commented a few moments afterward, eyeing Pat appreciatively. Her blond hair was longer now than it had been and coiled into an elegant French twist. "In

fact, I've never seen you with a more becoming style. And
not only that," I waxed on, "it's just so shiny, so . . . so
healthy-looking."

"It's a wig," she announced dryly.

Ouch!

The wine arrived almost at once—and just in time. I immediately took a couple of healthy gulps.

The two of us ordered this Oriental chicken dish, and the
instant the waitress walked away, Pat had two words for me:
"I'm listening." And then before I could open my mouth, she
was telling me how she'd always thought we were such good
friends and how much she cared about me and how she'd
been hinting to Bruce for months that he get in touch with
me. And here she suggested that I just imagine what a fool
she felt like when he mentioned my lemon soufflé—tipping
her to the fact that we'd been seeing each other all along.
"I'm very, very hurt you didn't see fit to confide in me," she
said. And I noticed, to my horror, that her eyes were moist.

"My God, Pat, you're taking this all wrong. Of course
we're good friends, very good friends."

"If that's tr—"

But going on the offensive now, I cut her off at the pass. "I
really shouldn't have to tell you that." I even managed a hint
of disapproval in my tone.

Pat's lips parted as if to dispute this assertion, but I bar-
reled on. "The only reason I didn't say anything to you about
Bruce was because I'm really not that comfortable about being in the relationship—if you can call it a relationship, that
is. To tell the truth, a good part of the time I'm disgusted
with myself for being interested in him."

Her attitude softened a bit. "Why? What's wrong?"

"I'm not sure that I can explain it. For one thing, the whole
situation has me constantly on edge. I never even know if
he's going to call again—sometimes I don't hear from him
for weeks on end. And then when he does call, he's likely to
ask me out for that same night. It's as if he expects me to just
be available whenever he decides he's ready to see me. Do
you know what I mean?"

A nod. "Do I!"

"And as you've already seen, he can also be pretty damned
insulting and boorish and— Honestly, Pat, I can't even go
into it all. I guess what it actually boils down to, though, is
that the man isn't the least bit considerate of my feelings,

and I'm not very proud of being attracted to someone like that."

Our food appeared at this moment, and there was a brief intermission while we oohed over the attractive presentation. Then, as she cut into a piece of chicken, Pat said, "Maybe I'm being thickheaded, but I want to get this straight. What you're saying is that you didn't tell me about seeing Bruce because you're ashamed of it?"

"That's right. Only to be more accurate, it's really myself I'm ashamed of—for letting my hormones overrule my head."

"Listen, I was *born* with galloping hormones," my friend told me, grasping my hand (the non fork-holding one) for a second in sisterhood.

"Well, then you can understand."

"Why you've been keeping this a secret? Of course not. I've admitted a lot worse things to you over the years about *my* often demeaning—when not out-and-out pathetic—love life. Before Burton, of course." And immediately after this she made a wry face—and a concession. "But we're all different, I suppose." About a minute passed before she added, "Just remember, though, that if you should ever feel like talking, well, I'm here for you. And don't worry. It would only be between us. I don't tell Burton *everything,* you know."

And then smiling mischievously, but with a kind of semi-urgency in her voice, she said, "Anyway, right now it might be a good idea if we started to really concentrate on lunch. I told my boss I was only running out to the drugstore."

Chapter 16

I may do it for one reason or another, but the truth is, I've never been comfortable keeping secrets from the people I'm close to. And by that, I'm referring to keeping my own secrets; I'm fine when it comes to other people's. Anyhow, it was a relief to finally come clean with Pat. And even more of a relief to discover that I hadn't irreparably damaged our friendship.

Now, I'd spent that morning on paperwork, so when I returned to the office, I concentrated on making telephone calls. The first person I contacted was Dr. Leon Vanetti, Luella's physician. He agreed to see me at eight o'clock Thursday morning.

After that, I tried Willie Smart, Luella's agent.

"I'm sorry, Willie's with a client," the receptionist or secretary or whoever informed me. "Can you tell me what this is in reference to?"

I explained that I was investigating Luella Pressman's death and would like to stop by for a few minutes.

The receptionist (or whoever) clicked off for a moment, then got back on the line to ask if I could make it late that afternoon—at five-thirty. I said I'd be there.

Next I dialed Libby MacLean, Luella's editor. She could see me today at four. Which worked out just fine, since it was doubtful I'd be spending more than an hour with her, and her office and the agent's were both located downtown, not that far from each other.

After that, I figured I'd better phone Kevin. I hadn't spoken to him since our visit to the town house. And considering how unstrung he was over the tragedy, I knew I should have touched base with him before now. But, well, the time had just slipped away from me, owing in part to that best-forgotten weekend. And besides, I didn't really have anything to tell him.

Still, I should at least reassure him that I was working on things.

Kevin wasn't at home when I tried him, but I left a message on his machine. He rang back not ten minutes later.

"Anything new?" he asked eagerly.

"Nothing yet, Kevin. But I did want you to know what I've been up to lately."

"I'm glad you called. I've been pretty anxious about how the investigation is progressing. It's a week now since we've had any kind of contact—a week and a day, actually—and I've had all I could do to keep from calling *you*." I thought I detected a hint of reproach in the pleasant baritone voice. If so, it was understandable. "As a matter of fact, I started to dial your number two or three times. But then I'd convince myself I would have heard from you if there'd been any developments."

"Of course you would have. I'm afraid there's really nothing new—which is why you haven't. But anyhow, let me fill you in on what little has been happening.

"I've been to see Geena and Nadine, but if either of them told me anything that would help us, I haven't doped it out yet. Maybe I'll do better tomorrow night—I'll be talking to Enid then. And in the meantime I'm going to be meeting with Luella's editor and her agent, who I understand were also her good friends. That's later today. And I'm paying a visit to her physician—a Dr. Vanetti—tomorrow morning. I've only got Bud Massi's home number, so I'll try reaching him tonight. And oh, yes, on Saturday I'll be having another talk with Connie."

"Good."

"Now, tell me, how have you been holding up?"

"Okay, I suppose. I've taken on a new client who keeps me hopping—at least during the day. And I'm extremely grateful for that. But at night, when I have time to think . . . Well, the nights can be long, Desiree."

"Yes, they can be," I said quietly.

Kevin spoke before I could come out with my remedies for insomnia. (Which remedies I've never personally tried, but every time I lie there staring at a black ceiling or else toss all over the bed for two or three hours, I promise myself I'll bear them in mind for the next time.) "At any rate," he brought up, "now that you've had an opportunity to spend some time with them, what do you think of Nadine and Geena?"

I answered reluctantly, knowing I couldn't tell him what he wanted to hear. "Well, uh, they both seem very nice," I had to admit.

"Don't they." It was a simple, flat statement. "That was always my opinion of them, too. And I felt the same way about Enid. That's the hell of it, Desiree. Because one of them . . ." He broke off here, but his meaning was evident.

"I'd like for us to get together some time early next week to go over everything, if that's okay with you," I said then.

"Are you serious? Certainly it's okay."

"I'll give you a ring. And by the way, Kevin, how do you feel about hot chocolate?"

"Hot chocolate?"

"It's supposed to help you sleep. And wine's good, too. So's a hot bath."

"Given the choice, maybe I'll try the wine," he responded with a little chortle. And then very soberly: "But the thing that would really get me through the night is knowing who killed my—knowing who killed Luella."

"I'm trying to find out what happened there. I'm trying hard."

"I don't doubt that for a second, Desiree. And thank you."

I won't go into the details of my visit with Luella's editor, since it proved to be entirely fruitless. I spent more than an hour at the publishing house. Almost thirty minutes of it in the waiting room and the balance sitting alongside Libby MacLean's desk, where every few minutes I managed to grab the woman's attention for a few seconds between her incessant—and extended—telephone calls. The gist of this fractured interview was that the deceased had been a dear friend, as well as a talented and delightful person whose untimely passing was a devastating loss for millions of children and *their* children and *their* children. Also, Luella appeared to be in perfect health when the editor had dinner with her on the Tuesday before her demise. What's more, Ms. MacLean seriously doubted if Luella Pressman had had an enemy in the world.

None of this exactly a revelation.

Thanks to all the time I'd wasted with the phone-happy MacLean, I just about made my five-thirty appointment with

Luella's agent. But anyhow, during my thirteen-minute stop there, I discovered that Willie Smart was a woman. (Naturally, I thought of Beatrix immediately.) Other than that, though, I learned absolutely nothing—the one good thing being that it took very little time to learn it.

That night, after finishing a skimpy supper and its cleanup, I dialed Bud Massi's apartment. He picked up about ten seconds after his answering machine did—while I was right in the middle of my spiel. He sounded breathless.

"Hi. I just walked in," he explained. "You wanted to talk to me about Luella?" And when I replied that I did: "Yes, well, Connie said you'd be in touch. And naturally, I'll be glad to meet with you, but I really don't see how I can help."

Which is pretty much the response I receive from nine out of ten people. And you'd be surprised how many of them know things they don't know they know. If you follow me.

At any rate, Massi had a pretty busy schedule, so he suggested I drop by Emil's on Friday night. He'd be performing there then, and we could talk between sets. I told him I'd be in around nine.

Once that was arranged, I took a quick shower, got into my robe, and then settled down on the sofa with this Tom Savage thriller I'd heard about. That was when the phone rang.

Bruce's voice was cheery. "How's my favorite gumshoe?"

"Not bad," I answered noncommittally, while attempting to decide whether to give in to my irritation that he hadn't called any too recently or just let myself be pleased about his calling now.

"That great, huh?" He was laughing softly. "So how much have you missed me?"

"You wouldn't believe me if I told you," I bantered back, trying for light and airy but conscious I was making this strange sound that comes from your mouth going bone dry on you.

I'm not certain what Bruce said after that, because I was busy checking my watch—which read eight-ten—and telling myself he couldn't possibly intend asking me to dinner for this same night. Immediately following which I cautioned myself that, knowing the man, there was always that chance.

The next thing I heard was an impatient "Well?"

Apparently, a question had just been posed. Only I couldn't even guess what it was. "I'm sorry, Bruce, but my neighbor's here—in the kitchen—and she just called out to me. I'm afraid I didn't get what you said."

"I wanted to know what you were doing tomorrow night."

I smiled. This was progress. He was actually asking me out in advance. Maybe not a whole lot in advance, but still, this wasn't a drop-everything-I'm-now-ready-to-see-you phone call, either. And then it occurred to me he might be inviting himself over for dinner again. But an instant later I dismissed the thought. Whenever that was the case, he was thoughtful enough to give me sufficient notice so I could take care of the shopping and do-ahead cooking. (And yes, this is being said sarcastically.)

Of course, the whole thing was academic, anyway, since I was meeting with Enid Pressman Thursday evening. "I'm sorry, but I'm busy tomorrow night," I told him, regret in my tone. The truth is, though, I was my usual ambiguous self where Bruce was concerned—happy I had a legitimate reason for turning him down (something I didn't otherwise seem able to do) and at the same time, not happy at all that I wouldn't be with him.

"Change your plans" was the succinct response.

"I'm afraid I—"

"Look, you mentioned wanting to see *Sunset Boulevard*, and so I went out and picked up two tickets."

"I would have loved to go, too. I'm really disappointed that I can't make it."

"What's the problem, Dez? This horny husband—or whoever it is you're out to nail—won't destroy the city if he's on the loose for another twenty-four hours. Just postpone things a day, for Christ's sake."

Well, good old Bruce had managed to score a double-header here. Besides trivializing my work, which was galling enough, he had made the assumption in the first place that I'd been referring to a business commitment. And really! How dared he think there was no other man in my life—just because there wasn't? "I can't do that," I said.

"Would you mind telling me why not?"

For a moment I thought of pretending I had another date—a man-type date, I mean. But it didn't seem worth the effort. "I've waited for a week to meet with this woman, and it's critical to my investigation that I talk to her. But I appreciate the thought, Bruce, honestly." And then I asked a very rational question. "If you got those tickets to please me, though, why didn't you check on my schedule first?"

"I suppose this is what I get for wanting to surprise you," Bruce shot back. "But in all fairness to myself, I didn't expect you'd have plans that were etched in stone. There's very little likelihood the woman will drop dead the next morning, you know, so why can't you see her on Friday?"

"I'm sorry, but I intend to keep that appointment." My voice was terse, and my jaw ached now from gnashing my teeth. "I'm dealing with a very busy woman here, and I have no idea when she'll be available next. And incidentally," I added—sounding childish, I knew—"for your information, this isn't about any 'horny husband.' Somebody's already *dead* in this case, and the longer I wait, the harder it's going to be to find the killer."

There was a long pause before Bruce's retort. "Okay. Fine. You just go right on playing Ms. Gung Ho Gumshoe, if you want to. But I'll tell you one thing. You won't have anyone to play with when the lights are out. Not anymore." And with that, he was gone.

I sat there and stared at the mute receiver in my hand. And then I slammed it down. Hard.

I was seething with anger. The man was impossible. Even when he made a nice gesture like getting those tickets, he managed to louse things up with his attitude—which should be spelled with a capital "A." And you know something else? I'd never expressed an interest in seeing *Sunset Boulevard;* of this, I was positive. Not that I wouldn't have enjoyed it, I'm sure, but it was definitely not on the top of my list. If you ask me, somebody probably gave Bruce those tickets. Or else he bought them because he wanted to see the show himself.

I have no idea how long I sat there cursing him—and, of course, allotting an equal portion of my venom to myself.

How had I ever let this S.O.B. into my life? I should never have ignored my first impression of him. I mean, would anyone else have gone out with him again after that hellish blind date? Not if they had any more sense than you could fit into a thimble, they wouldn't.

And then slowly, the doubts crept in.

It was conceivable, wasn't it, that Bruce's intentions *had* been good? So what if I hadn't actually mentioned the show? Go shoot the guy for wanting to take me to the theater. I was starting to see where he might have been justified in blowing up at me, too. Things aren't always that cut and dried, you know. I'd really been totally inflexible. He had suggested that Enid and I get together on Friday, which really wasn't that unreasonable. Of course, I was seeing Bud Massi Friday night, but I supposed that at the very least I could have checked with her to find out if something else could be set up soon before turning Bruce down like that. After all, what difference would another day or two have made in a meeting that should have taken place a week ago?

I eyed the phone. I was going to call him back. No, on second thought, maybe I should call Enid first and *then* call him back.

But as I was contemplating these alternatives, reason intervened. I'd finally shown a little backbone with Bruce, yet here I was, thinking like a victim again, ready to blame myself. I had to be crazy to even consider picking up that telephone. I mean, it had apparently never so much as crossed this man's mind that I might have made other arrangements. Or if it had, he was pretty damn confident I'd cancel them. Well, he was wrong. And what's more, I couldn't—I *wouldn't*—continue to see someone who regarded me as cavalierly as Bruce Simon obviously did.

It was over. Through. Finis. Bruce had done what I'd been too chicken to do: broken off this thoroughly aggravating and pointless relationship. And I was going to leave it like that. In fact, I felt an enormous sense of relief.

Right before I broke down and bawled.

Chapter 17

It's funny. When I go to bed feeling really depressed, either I don't close my eyes until dawn or else I fall asleep instantly. I'm convinced I have this little built-in escape mechanism that activates itself at whim—but unfortunately, not nearly often enough. Thankfully, however, this turned out to be one of those times it was in operation.

I had spent a great deal of what was left of that evening reveling in self-pity. And I'm not really sure why. Most of me was glad Bruce was gone. That's the truth. Still and all . . .

Could be the reason I was so miserable was that I hadn't been quite ready to wind things up yet myself. Or maybe it was because there was no one waiting on deck to take Bruce's place. It's also possible that breakups by their very nature are *supposed* to be painful. (My memory fails me on this point, though. Until Bruce, it had been a long time since I'd even had anyone to break up *with*.)

At any rate, I'd called it a night at just after eleven—which is when I normally start coming to life again. And the next thing I knew, the alarm was ringing at the ungodly hour of six to wake me for Thursday morning's meeting.

Dr. Leon Vanetti's address was on Sixty-eighth and Park. And while the neighborhood and the building were definitely posh, the doctor's waiting room was definitely not. The chairs were shabby and discolored, the small end tables badly scarred, and the carpeting had seen better days. And quite a while ago, too.

The receptionist was sitting at a desk behind a curved, chest-high (on me) partition, and I had to say "excuse me" twice before she deigned to glance up from her paperwork and acknowledge me. She was, if anything, even less attractive than the decor. A big-boned, blowzy woman who appeared to be in her late fifties, she was heavily—almost garishly—made-up. What's more, her short-sleeved pink cotton dress—the kind most of us pack away until June— was adorned with orangy splashes that looked suspiciously like spaghetti sauce. And topping everything off was this sparse bright orange hair (an excellent match for the sauce stains), which was worn Buster Brown-style and was complete with prominent gray roots.

It was slovenly souls like this, I thought irritably, who gave other full-figured women—like me—a lousy rap. I mean, while some people may call me fat (the ones with absolutely no class), I've always taken great pains to assure that no one has cause to call me fat and sloppy. And this can also be said of most of the larger ladies of my acquaintance.

Anyhow, having finally gained the receptionist's attention, I introduced myself. "Have a seat," she told me perfunctorily, jerking her thumb to her left toward the empty waiting room. Then she bent to her paperwork again. Before I could follow instructions, though, she surrendered to the amenities. "Doctor will be with you shortly," she informed me, looking up just long enough to flash a quick, frosty smile.

I decided this must be Mrs. Vanetti. She really had to be either the doctor's wife or his mother—the only explanation, other than blackmail, that would account for her presence here.

It was about five minutes after I'd settled down with a *People* magazine dating back more than six months—which I rated as the best the end tables had to offer—that I was advised in a voice close to a shout that "Doctor will see you now."

Dr. Vanetti was thin and bald, a little gnome of a man probably well up in his seventies. He was sitting in a large leather swivel chair behind a huge cherry desk, the two oversized pieces conspiring to shrink him even farther. He rose and leaned all the way across the desk to shake hands when I came in, then gestured toward the pair of straight-backed chairs opposite him.

"You're here about Luella Pressman," he said once we were both seated and I'd finished thanking him for taking the time to see me.

"I understand she was a patient of yours, Doctor."

He shook his head somberly, and for a moment I thought

he was going to deny it. But then he murmured, "Poor Luella. I still find it hard to believe."

"Had you been her physician for a long time?"

"Since she was only a little tiny thing. Connie, too. I knew their father, incidentally. A wonderful person. I was very fond of that girl, Ms. Shapiro. So was my wife." And now he offered by way of explanation, "Clara works here in the office with me."

Aha!

"I was informed that you examined Mrs. Pressman a week or two before her death," I told him.

"That's right. I was so pleased with the results of all her tests, too." And shaking his head slowly from side to side again, he muttered, "A terrible tragedy. Just terrible."

"Her passing was quite a surprise to you, then."

"A shock would be more like it."

"The cause of death still hasn't been determined, you know. But I suppose you're aware of that."

"Yes, the police came to see me right after it happened."

"Do you think, in light of how her physical turned out, that it's likely Mrs. Pressman died of natural causes?"

"I wouldn't rule that out. Look, Ms. Shapiro, I gave Luella— uh, Ms. Pressman—a very thorough examination. But sometimes problems and abnormalities don't show up in the tests. And remember that while it happens rarely, test results can be incorrect, too. Have you ever heard of a false positive?" I wasn't sure whether this was a rhetorical question or not, but I nodded anyway. "It's also conceivable that Luella died of something she wasn't even checked for," he added. "A 'complete' physical is a misnomer. We don't go over every inch of the body; we can't."

"So what you're saying is that it's possible Luella did die of natural causes." I realize that's pretty much what the man had just taken the pains to explain, but I wanted to be absolutely certain there was no misunderstanding here. I mean, this was really important.

Dr. Vanetti smiled sadly. "By the time you get to be as old as I am, Ms. Shapiro, you'll have discovered that just about anything is possible."

The meeting with the doctor had taken my mind off Bruce. Temporarily, at least. But once I was in my own little cubicle with nothing to do that couldn't wait, I had the opportunity to just sit around feeling sorry for myself. And I took full advantage of it, too, until eleven-thirty, when Jackie buzzed me.

"Got any plans for lunch?" she wanted to know.

"I think I'll eat in. It's pretty cold out today."

"It's winter, for God's sake!" I was reminded shrilly.

"I'm aware of that, but I just don't feel like having my buns frozen off. I prefer having a bite at my desk."

"Something's wrong," Jackie pronounced then.

"Not really."

"Don't give me that. Listen, I'll order for us, and we'll *both* eat at your desk."

"Look, Jackie, please don't misunderstand, but—"

"It'll do you good to talk about it, believe me. Now, what do you feel like for lunch?"

Jackie and the food showed up in my office about twelve-forty. She let me finish my sandwich in peace and even allowed me to have most of my coffee before getting down to brass tacks.

"All right. What's bothering you?" she demanded at last.

Well, I could have told her it was none of her business— expressing it more politely than that, of course. ("I'd rather not go into it right now" was just one option.) But no matter how I phrased it, I'd have wound up offending a good friend and putting the best secretary in New York's nose out of joint at the same time. And the thing was, as usual when Jackie's being a terrific pain in the butt, she was only trying to help. Besides, I suspect that on some level I might actually have been anxious to unload.

"Well," I began, "for the past four months or so I was seeing this man . . ."

"You never said one word to me about the guy!" Jackie scolded when I was through. Her tone couldn't have been more accusatory. But she immediately tempered her reaction. "Let's forget about that for now, though. You're obviously feeling bad enough as it is." And then she looked at me piercingly. "Well? Do you want to know what I think?" But my response was evidently not really a consideration, because she went right on to tell me. "You're better off without that creep."

"Oh, I agree. But that doesn't mean I'm not upset."

"Of course you are. It's only natural. But in your heart you must realize that it wouldn't have gone anywhere. The man is totally egocentric. He obviously didn't give a damn about your feelings—what with those once-in-a-blue-moon phone calls and humiliating you in front of his friends and—"

"He wasn't that bad. He did some nice things, too," I protested weakly. I mean, the worse Jackie painted him, the more foolish it made me seem.

"Like what?" she challenged.

"There *were* the theater tickets."

"Which someone most likely gave him as a gift," she sniffed. A thought that was not new to me. "But look, the best thing for you to do would be to get right back on the horse."

"What horse?"

"I'm speaking figuratively, Dez." She was eyeing me now as if I were a trifle dim-witted. "There's this wonderful fellow I know that—"

"I'm not ready for any blind dates yet, Jackie. Maybe in a couple of months. But not now."

"Don't be silly. Now is the perfect time. What would you do otherwise—sit home and feel sorry for yourself?" I didn't get the chance to counter this. "But about Al," Jackie plowed on. "He's Derwin's dentist, also his friend—they play golf together. I met him once, and he's really a doll—bright, nice-looking, funny. Anyhow, not being privy to your relationship with what's-his-name"—it was a jab she would have found impossible to resist—"I've been after Derwin to talk to Al about you for over six months. Ever since he and his wife spit up. But you know Derwin."

That I did, Derwin being Jackie's beau for quite some time now. A gentleman of advanced years, Derwin was most noteworthy for his taciturn demeanor, his thrift (you've never seen anyone's arms get paralyzed with such regularity whenever the check comes), and his striking silver hair—a product of the thickest and most obvious toupee you can imagine. I glanced at Jackie's face. She was determined.

"All I'm asking is that you hold off awhile, Jackie." There may even have been a pleading note in my voice.

It was as if I hadn't spoken. "What it is with Derwin is he hates to get involved because he's afraid things might not work out. But when I tell him how depressed you are, I'm sure it'll make a difference. He's really very fond of you, Desiree."

This was news to me. But that was beside the point. "Hear me, Jackie," I said calmly (although I was itching to shake her). "Don't bother saying anything to Derwin, because I'm not going out with his friend. At least, not for some time. I'm just not up for that kind of thing right now." And then I reminded myself. "But I do appreciate your trying to help. Honestly."

"Well, all right," Jackie muttered, miffed. "I still think it would be the best thing for you, though." And then getting to her feet, she said magnanimously, "But I'll leave it on the back burner until you change your mind. After all, you're the boss."

But I had no illusions as to how much significance she placed in *that*.

Chapter 18

I know I'm always bitching about the cold. But the temperature was well below freezing Thursday night, plus the wind showed no mercy. I kept asking myself why, out of every taxi in New York, I had to hail this one.

No heat. Also, one of the rear windows wouldn't close all the way, leaving a good two or three inches for the bone-chilling air to come whooshing in. And to really clinch things, the ride was endless. The driver—R. R. Margolies, according to the license posted in the front—should have taken the FDR Drive, usually the fastest way to get from my apartment to the East Twenties, where Enid Pressman lived. But he didn't. Which is how come we were stuck for over ten minutes on Sixty-fifth and Second, where there'd apparently been a recent accident of some kind.

While we were tied up in traffic, R. R. Margolies turned around and apologized for the condition of his vehicle. "Sorry, lady," he told me, not sounding sorry at all. "The window just jammed up a few minutes ago, and then—wouldn't you know it?—the radiator broke down on me right after that. But what can you do, huh? These things happen," he philosophized cheerfully.

Now, I normally turn blue as soon as winter sets in, and I don't thaw out before mid-July, either. Just then, however, I didn't think I'd ever defrost.

At long last we pulled up in front of a small apartment house on Twenty-fifth Street. And believe me, making it from the cab to the lobby was as close as I'll ever come to sprinting.

While I was standing at the intercom shivering and waiting for E. PRESSMAN to answer my buzz, I observed that the newish building, although hardly in the luxury category—no doorman, no marble floor, no fancy fixtures—nevertheless appeared to be well kept and in really good condition.

Enid had a second-floor studio. She greeted me cordially enough, but still, I got the feeling that a visit from the IRS might have been preferable.

We walked down a very short hall, which opened into a large foyer. From here I could take in most of the apartment at a single glance. And I don't mind telling you, I was impressed. Everything was so bold, so vibrant.

Occupying one entire wall of the foyer was a shiny black Formica modular unit that extended almost to the ceiling and must have been seven or eight feet long. In front of the short wall was a small chrome portable bar, over which hung a good-sized modern painting that was predominantly done in shades of red and had Andy Hough's technique stamped all over it. Also in the foyer area, standing on a red and gray geometric rug, was a handsome black lacquer dining table, a crystal bowl filled with red silk flowers at its center, and two black lacquer chairs with gray and white striped vinyl seats positioned at either end. The table was flush against a wrought-iron railing and overlooked a sunken living room—something I've decided I *will* have before I die.

Enid held out her hand for my coat. "I'd like to k-keep it on for a few minutes, if that's okay," I told her. I wasn't about to fork over a single piece of clothing until my teeth stopped clicking together and I could feel my toes again.

She preceded me down the two steps to the living room, which was furnished in the same red, black, and gray—a striking contrast to the two chalk-white walls. But it was the gray brick wall opposite the sofa I was focused on. Right in the middle was a real fireplace—with a real fire! The sight made me so grateful I could have cried.

I made a beeline for the gray wall. "Do you m-mind if I stay here for a few minutes?"

Enid smiled indulgently. "Of course not. And take your time—you look frozen. I'll make some hot coffee meanwhile."

"That would be wonderful."

I stood there facing the flames, my hands outstretched, as the warmth slowly began to chase the ice from my veins. In a little while, I was even up to peeling off my outerwear, one item at a time, at maybe two-minute intervals. First came the gloves, which I shoved into my pocket. After that, I shucked my Ellen and Mike Burberry scarf. This went into the other pocket. And then a pair of earmuffs a former client had sent me last Christmas joined the gloves. It took close to ten minutes, I'll bet, before I finally relinquished my coat to a waiting and, I think, bemused Enid.

We sat side-by-side on the lipstick-red sofa. Set on the small rectangular table in front of us was a wooden tray containing coffee, milk, sugar, and a plate of assorted cookies. Pepperidge Farm, I believe. At the insistence of my hostess—and not wanting to appear rude—I did a bit of sampling, my first selection being a little chocolate confection sprinkled with nuts. While nibbling, I mentioned how attractive I found the apartment.

Enid seemed to preen a bit. "Thanks. My last place was about three times the size," she confided, "but I decided I'd regard it as a challenge to really make something of a space this small."

"Well, you certainly succeeded."

She put her cup to her lips now, and for a brief time neither of us said anything. It occurred to me then how at odds Enid herself was with these surroundings. There was just no . . . no *flair* to her. Not that I could see, anyway. Medium-tall—maybe five-six or -seven—and substantially built, she was dressed in loose-fitting chinos, a high-collared, long-sleeved white cotton blouse, and brown low-heeled oxfords. Her shoulder-length auburn hair—which was really lovely and for which I would even have traded my gorgeous new rainy-day wig—was drawn back into a tortoiseshell clip, where it could hardly fail to go unappreciated. (Except by someone who's redhead-focused the way I am, that is.) I remembered she'd worn it this same way at her stepmother's shiva, but at least she'd had on a little makeup then. Not tonight, though. Tonight there was nothing to soften her too-square jaw or enhance the long-lashed brown eyes or enliven a rather sallow complexion. And this totally sensible, no-nonsense persona of hers wasn't just about how she put herself together, either. Reinforcing it was her rigid straight-backed, chin-up posture and a direct, almost abrupt way of speaking.

I mentally scratched my head. It was hard to believe that the young woman next to me had designed a place like this, challenge or no challenge. And even harder to figure out how she could be comfortable calling it home. The truth is, as much as I admired the decor, I had real doubts about being able to face that dramatic a color palette on a daily basis. I

mean, it was scarcely soothing. Chances are, I'd have wound
up with a tic. Or at best, an occasional nightmare.

Enid turned to me with an expression that informed me I'd
just finished relaxing. I quickly got in a last swallow of coffee, then set my cup on the glass-topped table.

"I'm sorry I had to delay things like this," I said. "With the
fireplace business, I mean." And I explained about the condition of the taxi and the Second Avenue traffic tie-up and not
having any blood and all that. "I know you're a busy woman,
though, so I'll try not to keep you too long."

"Thank you. I didn't get home until late last night, and I'm
really bushed."

"Your trip—how was it?" After all, since she'd brought it
up, this seemed to me only good manners.

"Fine. It's nice of you to ask." Her clipped tone was my
clue to forget the amenities and just get on with it.

"Well, uh, why don't we talk about your stepmother for a
few minutes," I mumbled hastily. "To start with, I'd like to
know how the two of you got along."

Enid's answers to this question and the ones immediately
following it were in keeping with the family line. In fact,
plug in a different voice, and I might have been talking to
Nadine or Geena.

She and Luella got along beautifully, the girl informed me.
They spoke to each other frequently on the phone, and the
family gathered at the town house regularly for dinner.

"Then as a rule you saw Luella at her home."

"Usually."

"I assume you did other things together, too, though," I
pressed, trying to get a picture of the relationship.

"Every once in a while we'd all go out to a nice restaurant."

I waited for her to say more, so she reluctantly added,
"And occasionally—for example, when Luella had just turned
a manuscript in to her publisher or her work was proceeding
ahead of schedule—we'd celebrate with shopping or a movie."

"Just the two of you?"

"Sometimes. And sometimes with Aunt Connie or one of
my sisters."

"So you'd say you and Luella were fairly close?"

"Definitely," Enid responded, and her tone was emphatic.

"But things were a little different when you were a child,
weren't they? You resented all that time she spent writing, I
understand."

"I had a lot of problems in those days—emotional problems. As you're no doubt already aware."

"I'd prefer that you tell me about it, though, if you don't mind."

She almost smiled. "Do I have a choice?" The almost-smile disappeared at once. "All right. My father walked out on us. I was very depressed, very resentful. And I got the idea Luella should dedicate herself to me completely in order to make up for my being abandoned. Naturally, I never stopped to consider that she'd been abandoned as well. At any rate, when my expectations weren't met—or at least not to the extent I had in mind—I put in a strong bid for her attention by getting into trouble. But I'm sure you know that, too."

"I heard about it," I admitted. "I also heard that Luella saw to it you received counseling."

"Fortunately. That's what helped me realize how off base I'd been."

"You no longer felt she was giving you short shrift?"

"I came to appreciate that while she didn't devote every waking moment to me, I could always depend on Luella for support when it really counted. Eventually, it even got through to me how grateful I should be to her for bringing me up in the first place."

"It must have taken quite a lot of adjusting on your part, though, when you had to share your stepmother not only with her work, but with her subsequent husbands and their daughters."

"It wasn't like that. By the time Luella married Nadine's father, I was already seventeen years old. And as for my sisters, they were like a bonus to me."

"Speaking of your sisters, did *they* resent Luella for being as busy as she was?"

"Not nearly as much as I once did. Listen, Ms. Shapiro—"

"Desiree."

"Listen, Desiree, we all felt the same way about her—we loved her. And besides, where would we have been—the three of us—if it weren't for Luella?"

"When was the last time you saw her?" I asked then.

"A week before she passed away. On a Friday."

"That's the night the whole family was there for dinner?"

"That's right."

"Were you in touch with her after that?"

"I spoke to her the following Thursday—two days before she died."

"She seemed pretty much as usual?"

"To me, she did."

"She was cheerful?"

Enid mulled over the question for a second or two. "I wouldn't say *cheerful*. She'd just finished eight or nine hours of work, and she was tired. The way she normally was—the way most people would be—after putting in a full day of writing like that. Look, if you're thinking there's even a remote chance that Luella committed suicide, I—"

"I'm not thinking anything right now, believe me. I'm just trying to get a fix on things."

Enid nodded, satisfied. "I got the idea from the detectives who came to see me that they weren't discarding the possibility she might have taken her own life. And I'll tell you something. While I don't for one second believe Luella was murdered, even that would be easier to accept than her killing herself."

"Why do you say that? Any specific reason?"

"My stepmother was a totally fulfilled person. She had a devoted family. A rewarding career. And she was seeing a man she showed every indication of being in love with—although she never admitted to it. She even felt as though she was making a little headway lately on this historical novel she'd been slaving over for years." Enid produced a little grin before tagging on, "And years and years."

And now I took a minute to steel myself for the impact I anticipated my next words would have on her. "Um, do you remember just where you were the morning your stepmother died?"

A scowl let me know that Enid was none too pleased with the question.

"I have to ask," I added hastily.

"I was at the office from eight-fifteen until close to two in the afternoon."

"And that's—where?"

"Endicott and Leahy. It's on Seventy-first and Madison."

"Do you normally work on Saturdays?"

"I do when I have to put figures together for a client on an important acquisition."

"Did anyone else come in to work that morning?"

"My boss was already crunching numbers by the time I

arrived. He'd been at it since a quarter to eight, he told me. And his secretary got in when I did—we met at the elevator. Do you want their names?" she asked testily, holding out her palm for pen and paper.

"I'd appreciate it." I lost no time in equipping her.

Enid scrawled down the names, together with the office phone number—all of which, by the way, I later found to be practically illegible (a result of her being so ticked off, I'm sure). When she looked up, her eyes were blazing. "Listen, I must tell you that I really resent your asking for my whereabouts. I didn't kill Luella. None of us did. Wasn't that what you were hired to establish?"

"Let me put it this way," I said, not answering the question directly. "You're convinced that your stepmother died of natural causes, and I'm hoping that's where we'll eventually wind up. But still, I *am* conducting an investigation here, so it's essential I have all the facts. And I can't get them if certain questions are declared off-limits."

"You're right, I suppose," Enid conceded. "But Luella wasn't murdered. Not unless some lunatic, some deranged *fiend* did it. And since there weren't any signs of a break-in . . ." For a few seconds she left it at that. And then in a strong, clear voice she pronounced, "No. Luella died because a vital organ simply gave out. In all likelihood, her heart."

"I tend to agree with you."

Now Enid put her hand to her mouth, attempting to stifle a yawn. (But I'm not at all sure the attempt was in earnest.)

"I have just one more question," I said.

"Okay. *Did I hear a sigh?* "What is it you'd like to know?"

"How did you feel about Bud Massi?"

"Nice guy, from what I've seen of him."

"You had no reservations about your stepmother's involvement with him?"

"It was none of my business."

"Granted, but you must have had some reaction to the romance."

"I didn't. If that's what she wanted . . ." Enid hunched her shoulders.

"What did you think about her investing in his company?"

"It was entirely her own decision."

"I would imagine you'd have an opinion, though, considering your profession."

"Wrong. If Luella had asked me to check into Bud's company for her, I would have. But she didn't. So *I* didn't."

"But what if she'd married him?"

"What if she had?" Enid threw back at me.

"I'm sure you realize that this could have affected your inheritance."

"Ms. Shapiro—"

"Desiree," I had to remind her a second time.

"Desiree, you don't know me. But I'm a very ambitious woman and—at the risk of sounding conceited—a capable one. And while the inheritance will certainly come in handy, the only money I'm really interested in is the money I intend making on my own."

And now she said almost meekly, "I don't want to seem inhospitable, Desiree, but I'm really wiped out from my trip." And she got to her feet.

Which was okay. I'd run out of questions, anyway.

But I would have *loved* another cup of coffee before venturing outdoors again. I didn't get one, though.

Also okay. I didn't really expect one.

Chapter 19

Sometimes I think that the stickiest aftermath of a breakup is having to tell people that it happened. An opinion that had been reinforced only yesterday.

Still, there was no way I was going to be able to escape going through it again—and yet again after that. So on Friday I phoned Ellen at the store. "Can you talk?" I asked.

"Sure. I'm on my lunch."

I glanced at my watch; it was close to four. *Now?*

"Well, it's been a hectic day." I just knew there was a shrug accompanying this. "What's up?"

"Nothing that can't wait a few hours," I assured her. "Would you rather we talked tonight?"

"Not if you don't mind chicken salad in your ear. I'm really starved." And then with a sudden sharpness: 'Nothing's wrong, is it?"

"No, something's probably *right*. And for the first time in months, too." I proceeded to give her a rundown of Wednesday night's conversation with Bruce and the resultant parting of the ways.

Predictably, Ellen was incensed. "The nerve! That bastard!" The slightest bit shriller and her voice would have been out of human hearing range.

"Anyway, that ends that," I said. "There won't be any more Bruce around, and I just wanted to tell you." I was now prepared to hang up."

"I'm so sorry you've been hurt," Ellen murmured. And then a moment later she added hesitantly, "But, well, do you want to know something, Aunt Dez? I didn't trust that man."

A reminder appeared to be in order. "You never met him."

"I didn't have to. It isn't always necessary to come face-to-face with someone to know them."

"It helps," I responded dryly.

"What about Hitler?" she put to me, crunching noisily (no

doubt working on a pickle just then). "Or Al Capone? Or Ted Bundy? I never met those three sicknesses, either, but I still have a pretty good idea of the kind of people they were."

She had a point there. What's more, once I'd finally clued her in to the fact I'd been seeing him, I continued to supply her with enough material on the woes of the romance—if you can call it that—to offer plenty of insight into the less attractive aspects of Bruce's character.

"I didn't say anything before," Ellen went on, "because there was always the possibility I was wrong." Her voice dropped. "I wanted so much to be. You know that."

"Of course. But it's okay." And then I slipped in the appropriate cliché—two of them, actually. "These things happen. And anyhow, it's probably all for the best."

"I'm glad you realize that. The second you told me you'd split up, I was worried that you'd start blaming yourself."

I'm sure it was only because I'd already been a little guilty of this that I found myself bristling at the remark. "What makes you say something like that?"

"Probably because that's what *I* always used to do. But just remember how he's been acting all these months."

"I promise to keep it in mind."

Apparently not taking me at my word, Ellen found it necessary to add, "You were never really that happy in the relationship."

"I admit it had its ups and downs, but I did enjoy Bruce's company," I retorted, feeling the need to justify myself now—much as I had with Jackie. "He can be very charming, Ellen, as I'm sure I've told you many times. And he's certainly intelligent. He has a sense of humor, too. A good one. The truth is, he was a lot of fun to be with."

Ellen pounced. "*Fun*. That was part of the problem."

"I don't get you."

"All he did was joke around. Am I right?" And before I could give her a yes or no: "Which is fine some of the time, but were you ever able to hold a serious conversation with him?"

"Of course I was," I answered irritably.

"I don't mean a discussion about politics or religion or anything like that. Did you ever have a serious *personal* conversation with him?"

"Yes, as a matter of fact." (Of course, to keep this from

being an out-and-out lie, I had to count this one evening that I'd pinned him to the wall and practically forced him to tell me something about himself.)

"How many times?"

"Oh, Ellen, puleeze!"

"He kept things light for the same reason he always had you wondering whether you'd ever hear from him again."

"And just what do you figure was his motive?"

"He had to prevent you from getting too close, from feeling any sense of security with him," expounded my niece Ms. Freud. "This is a man who goes out of his way to avoid any type of commitment. And I mean any type at all. Think about it. He wouldn't even commit himself to the next date."

Embarrassed now, Ellen giggled. "I'm sounding like an awful blowhard, aren't I? But I'm pretty positive that I'm right about him—I've been thinking about the two of you a lot—and I just don't want you to have second thoughts about this. If it hadn't ended over the theater tickets, it would have been something else. And besides, you deserve someone a lot nicer than that *Bruce*." She spat out the name. "You deserve someone really terrific."

I laughed. "I agree. But anyhow, now that I've filled you in on the latest in my young life, let's talk about something a little more pleasant. How's Mike?"

And following another one of those pickle sounds, Ellen was happy to tell me.

Pat Martucci seemed surprised to hear from me.

"This is a coincidence. I was going to get in touch with *you* tonight." she informed me. "Burton and I would like you and Bruce to come over to our place for dinner a week from—"

"Uh, Bruce is the reason I'm calling. We aren't seeing each other anymore. I wanted you to hear it from me." *So I wouldn't be on your shit list again,* I added silently.

Pat was taken aback. "Oh." And after a rather lengthy pause: "Since when?"

"Wednesday night. On the phone."

"That explains it. I mentioned something to Bruce only the other day about having you both to dinner, and he was fine with it. That was on Monday, though, as I recall. Or it could have been—" She interrupted herself. "But tell me what happened."

I gave her a brief summary.

"May-be," Pat said slowly, "he was . . . you know . . . just upset after spending all that money for the tickets." And now she put in hurriedly, "And before you jump down my throat, I'm not saying he did the right thing—he definitely should have checked with you first—but I think he probably did mean well."

"It never even occurred to him I might have made plans of my own," I pointed out.

Pat sighed extravagantly. "I know. Men can be so stupid sometimes."

Can you believe it? She's turning this into an indictment of the male sex in general—and giving Bruce absolution in the process. I shook my head in disgust. She might just as well have clicked her tongue a few times and said that boys will be boys. "Listen, I—"

"Maybe if Burton spoke to him. You know, laid it right out there about how he behaved like a real jerk and everything. What do you think?"

"No, Pat. Let's just leave things as they are."

"Burton could—"

"Thanks for wanting to help, but there really isn't anything worth salvaging here. Honestly."

"All right, if that's what you want . . ."

"Yes, it is."

"Dez?"

"What?"

"Bruce was stupid and thoughtless and insensitive. I realize that. I suppose I was alibiing him because . . . because, well, I want you to be happy. I mean, *with* someone. I was kind of hoping that things could still work out between the two of you. But I guess not, huh? After all, you had your problems with him long before this, didn't you? Yes, of course you did."

And now her tone changed completely, and there was an earnestness in her voice as she told me softly, "Anyhow, I just want to make sure you know that I'm on your side, that I care about you."

By the time Pat and I had finished our conversation a minute or two later, my throat was tight and my eyes stung. Now, I can't say for certain whether this was because I

was so touched by those warm words of friendship or because I still hadn't completely come to terms with the end of
my relationship with Bruce.

I suspect it was a combination of both.

Chapter 20

Emil's fit my definition of "cozy" to a T. Not only was it a small place and dark, but the tables here were packed so close together that you could easily play kneesies with your neighbor if you wanted to. The room was less than a quarter filled when I arrived—in spite of the fact that it wouldn't have taken too many bodies to fill it. But I suppose nine p.m. is kind of early for the cocktail lounge crowd.

A slight man with light hair and small, regular features was at the piano now. I didn't have to wonder whether or not it was Bud Massi, since he was Emil's only entertainment. At my request, I was shown to a corner table in the back. I decided to go all out and treat myself to a champagne cocktail while I waited for him to finish his set.

It was, I thought after a couple of minutes, just delightful relaxing here is my well-padded armchair, sipping champagne and listening to this man. Massi had a very pleasant tenor voice and was at least well versed enough on the piano to accompany himself without hitting a bunch of sour notes. Plus I loved his repertoire. He did the really old standards, songs by Cole Porter and Jerome Kern and George Gershwin—people like that. And interspersed with these were more recent show tunes, including two of my favorites—"The Music of the Night" from *Phantom* and "What I Did for Love" from *A Chorus Line*. I was almost sorry when it came time for him to take his break and join me.

As soon as he left the piano—and before I could signal to him—Massi was stopped by a middle-aged couple who'd just come in. While they were chatting, I bent to my drink. When I lifted my head, he was standing over me. He opened with, "You must be Ms. Shapiro." And then noting my expression, he laughed. "Don't look so puzzled. There are only two people in the room that I don't know, at least by sight. And the other one has a beard. I suppose it's okay if I sit down," he said, smiling and settling into a chair. Almost immediately a waiter materialized and placed a drink in front of him.

Seeing him face-to-face like this, I realized that Bud Massi was quite a bit younger than I'd imagined he would be. I estimated he was in his late thirties. Forty, at the outside—but only if he'd been blessed with outstanding genes or had been leading a really immaculate life. Luella, on the other hand, must have been near fifty when she died.

Now, ordinarily, I wouldn't have been too surprised by Massi's comparative youth. I mean, over the last few years these older woman/younger man relationships seem to have become more and more acceptable. (And about time, I say. After all, the older man/younger woman thing has been going on practically forever—and without any raised eyebrows, either.) But what was throwing me at the moment was that no one had even mentioned the disparity in the ages of the dead woman and this beau of hers. And that included Kevin. You'd think—wouldn't you?—that he might have said something about it when he first told me there *was* a Bud Massi.

"So what would you like to ask me?" Massie inquired softly.

"Well, first, I want to tell you that I'm very sorry for your loss. I understand you and Luella Pressman were going—uh, were close."

"Yes, we were."

"When was it you last saw her?"

"Two weeks ago tonight—the night before she died. She and Connie had gone to a play and they stopped in here afterward, around eleven-thirty."

"And they were here until when?"

"Until one, when we closed."

"Did you leave with them?"

"Yes, but I was really exhausted that evening, so I put them in a cab, and that was that." There was a muscle twitching in Massi's cheek now, and the hand resting on the table had clenched into a fist. "If I'd known it was my last chance to be with her ever again . . . God, if I'd only known! I—" He broke off with something like a sob.

"I'm so sorry," I mumbled, reaching over and self-consciously patting his forearm—the part of him that was most accessible to me at the moment.

"Thank you, Desiree." And then in an obvious attempt to regain his composure, he sat up a little straighter and said with a faint smile, "It *is* permissible to call you Desiree, isn't it?"

"You can even call me Dez, if you like."

"If you don't mind, I'll stick to Desiree. It's classier." He smiled more broadly. He had a nice manner. A nice face. I could see where Luella would have found him attractive.

"Umm . . . I hear that you and Luella had broken up for a while," I brought up at this point. Reasoning that, under the circumstances, this could be a very sensitive area, I was anxious to get it over with.

"That's right. I had a fit because she refused to see me as often as I wanted her to." A second later in a voice filled with self-disgust, Massi elaborated. "Never mind that she was an extremely busy woman who was really committed to her career. Or that she might also have had legitimate personal reasons for requiring some space."

"You also objected to her spending time with her ex-husband, I was told."

"That, too. I acted like a jealous imbecile. I resented her friendship with Kevin, her writing—everything. Listen, for a while there I wasn't even crazy about sharing her with her family. And they couldn't be nicer, either—Connie and the girls. How are they, by the way? Do you know?"

"They seem to be getting along. I'm sure this is still extremely painful for them, though. Connie, in particular."

Massi nodded. "I'll give her a call tomorrow. She's been up in Connecticut this week, as you've probably heard. But she was due back today."

"Yes, she mentioned that she'd be going."

"Actually, if it weren't for her family, I'm not sure if Luella and I would ever have gotten together again. They're the ones who set me straight. Of course, I like to think that eventually I'd have come to my senses on my own. But you never know. I can be amazingly pigheaded sometimes."

"Did you say 'they' set you straight? I thought it was Nadine who persuaded you to see the light."

"Well, that's true. Connie gave it a shot, too, though. Only without much success."

"Oh, I wasn't aware of that." I grinned at him. "You're right, Bud." (I decided to make the first-name business unanimous.) "About the pigheaded, I mean."

Chuckling, he glanced at his watch now. "Listen," he told

me, rising, "it's time for me to wow the public again." And he made a sweeping gesture that took in the room—which had suddenly gotten very crowded. "Can you stick around until I finish this set? We can talk some more then."

"Actually, I'll be only too glad to stay. I didn't get a chance to say so before, but you're good. Damn good."

He smiled and thanked me. "It's something I really love doing. Of course, I'll never be a Sinatra, but then neither will anyone else."

I spent the next half hour or so enjoying Bud's musical talents once more. In a moment of happy abandon, I even ordered a second champagne cocktail—a foolish decision in view of the fact that I have a very limited capacity for alcohol. To my dubious credit, though, I only took a couple of sips before admonishing myself to stay clearheaded. At least until I was finished questioning the man.

"Something wrong with the drink?" Bud asked when he sat down with me again. In order to safeguard my good intentions, I'd pushed the glass away from me, almost to the edge of the table.

"No. With the drinker. Experience has taught me that one should definitely be my limit."

He acknowledged the explanation with a slight tilt of the head, then leaned back in his chair: "Okay, now, where were we?"

"I was about to ask how Luella seemed to you on that Friday night. Was she happy? Depressed? Nervous? What?"

"She was happy. We were happy *together*. Believe me, the last thing on Luella's mind was suicide, if that's the reason for the question."

"Just how serious were the two of you?"

"All I know is that Luella was a special person—warm and smart and funny and talented. And to top it off, she was beautiful, too."

If he thought I was going to let it go at that, he was a pathetically misguided optimist. "Do you feel there might have been a marriage in the future?" I persisted.

"I don't really have the answer to that. Luella had once mentioned in passing that she'd never marry again. And there's no way of finding out if she would ever have changed her mind, is there?" His lips curved in a brief poignant smile. "We'd never discussed anything like that as it pertained to us personally, though. It was too soon. Besides, I have a marital history myself—although a short one and almost ten years back. Still, it was pretty much of a disaster, and it left me damn skittish. But I can tell you one thing: I cared for Luella deeply." With this, he picked up the highball that had been standing untouched in that same spot since he'd sat down with me initially. And now he drained a good portion of the liquor with his first swallow.

Bud's grief was so close to the surface at this point that I restrained myself from intruding on it, letting him finish the drink in silence. Which is how I became aware of the couple at the table to my left.

The boy couldn't have been much over twenty-one, and his date was most likely a year or two younger. (Although she really didn't look more than twelve.) I had to wonder at those two even coming to a place like this. I mean, it wouldn't have surprised me if their *mothers* were too young to appreciate Bud's kind of music. The boy was arguing spiritedly, while the girl kept brushing at her eyes with the back of her hand. Since I was practically in their laps anyway, I hardly had to lean over at all to eavesdrop.

This shallow little cad was spouting that recycled-ad-infinitum garbage about "If you loved me you would." Remembering back to my own pre-Ed Shapiro experiences, I grimaced. *When will they finally come up with something fresh?*

Well, at least now I could figure out why they were here: That little creep must have brought her in just to get her in the mood. (Which was, in a way, a real tribute to Bud.) Anyhow, I was waiting anxiously to find out how the poor girl would handle things—I'd have loved to see her dump her wine in his lap, but I knew this was expecting too much—when at that moment I was reminded of why I myself was here.

"Who am I kidding?" Bud murmured. I promptly removed my nose from the next table's business. "*Cared* for her? The truth is, I loved her. That was tough for me to say: *love*," he confessed sheepishly. "I'm kind of allergic to the word."

"It's hard to admit sometimes, especially to yourself." I allowed a decent interval—a good five or six seconds—to go by before hitting him with, "Uh, Luella was planning to invest in your company, wasn't she?"

"Yes, but that had nothing to do with *us*. That is, with our relationship," Bud protested. "Except, of course, that it was

through me she found out about my company to begin with."
The fleeting grin accompanying this was, I suspect, inadvertent. "But I assure you, I never pressured her for so much as a dime. Luella's decision to put money into the company was strictly business. She thought the investment could earn her a nice profit. And it would have, too."

And now I posed what was usually my least appreciated question. "I have to ask this," I prefaced. "Where were you that Saturday morning Luella died?"

"You don't think I had anything to do with her death, do you?" Bud demanded, a black look momentarily crossing the pleasant face.

I gave him the same response I'd been giving everyone else: No, I didn't, but I had to examine every possibility.

"Look," he challenged, "why would I want Luella dead? Even if you're not convinced I'm sincere about my feelings for her, you have to see that with Luella gone, I'm under a great deal of pressure financially. She intended investing quite a lot of money in my company. Money I'll have to find somewhere else if I'm ever going to get this enterprise off the ground."

He was certainly making sense. But still . . . "I can't see where you had a motive," I conceded. "I *would* like to know your whereabouts that morning, anyway, though. Just for the record."

"All right." While the expression on his face was somewhat less than friendly now, Bud's tone was non-committal. "I worked at home on Saturday until maybe eleven-thirty. And then I went out and did a little grocery shopping. I was back at the apartment by . . . I'd say about twelve forty-five. Could have been even later, though."

"Before the shopping, did anyone phone? Or stop by?"

"No to both."

"What about when you left the building? Is there anyone who could verify the time?"

"I doubt it. I don't have a doorman, and I don't remember any of the neighbors being around just then."

"Let me ask you one thing more." (And believe it or not, I meant it.) "How do *you* think Luella died?"

Bud responded almost before I got the words out. Which was hardly a surprise. Almost certainly he'd been struggling with this same question ever since the tragedy. "I wish I knew! God, I wish I knew! She seemed to be in good health, but I guess you really can't tell about something like that. I suppose that all we can do is wait for the autopsy report."

And now, eyes boring into mine, he said firmly, "But there *is* something I'm absolutely positive of, Desiree."

He waited for my "Which is?"

"That Luella *did not* commit suicide."

Well, I hadn't come across a single soul who'd argue with him on that.

In the taxi on the way home, I briefly reviewed the evening's meeting. I could add Bud's name to the list of people who had no proof of their whereabouts that fateful morning. But it scarcely seemed worth the bother.

From everything I'd learned, of all the people without an alibi, Bud Massi was, I decided, the least likely to need one.

Chapter 21

You want to know how crazy I am? Practically the first thing that popped into my head when I got up the next morning was how I hoped that little girl at Emil's had stuck to her guns. I opted to think that she had.

Connie called at just after ten.

"How was Connecticut?" I asked warily. We had an appointment for two o'clock that afternoon, and I was concerned she was phoning to break it.

"All right, I guess. My friend's place is certainly beautiful. Lovely old house, gorgeous grounds, a tennis court, a stable of horses . . . They even built a heated indoor swimming pool last year."

"Sounds pretty posh."

"It was—*is*. But I'm glad to be home, where I can hang around in bare feet and a bathrobe that's almost in shreds and cry for my sister whenever I want to."

"I was hoping it would help to get away," I told her softly.

"It did—at first. Although I suppose the truth is that right now my surroundings don't really make that much difference. It still feels so strange here without Luella that by tomorrow I'll probably wish I were back in Wilton.

"But the reason I called: I was wondering if it would be possible for you to make it a little earlier today—around one, say. I thought maybe you could come for lunch."

"That would be very nice, if you're sure you want to bother."

"I didn't sleep too well last night, Desiree—sometimes I don't think I ever will again. At least, not in this house. The point is, though, I got out of bed at five-thirty this morning and did a little cooking and baking just to occupy myself. And now someone has to help me put everything to good use. So can I count on you?"

"I'd be happy to do my part," I assured her.

* * *

As soon as I stepped over the threshold, Connie hugged me, which had the effect of making me feel more uncomfortable than welcome.

I realize that sounds pretty weird. And I'm not sure I can explain it. But the thing is, this was more than an "it's nice to see you" type of hug; it was too clingy for that. And as you're aware, Connie and I weren't exactly bosom friends. Which is why I pegged it as a *dependent* kind of greeting— you know, like I was important to her. Well, I could see only one reason for that. She was pinning her hopes on me to provide the answer to Luella's death—the *right* answer, I'm talking about. The one that would exonerate those three nieces she was so fond of. Maybe she had even come to believe her own story about hiring me so I could prove that Luella's demise was the result of natural causes. At any rate, you can appreciate my being a little ill at ease—considering. After all, who knew how the case would finally be resolved?

Anyway, I followed Connie into the living room, and she offered me a drink—which I declined—and then we seated ourselves across from one another. It struck me now how much better she was looking than when I'd seen her last— the night of the funeral. The drab black dress she'd been wearing that evening had been replaced by a pale beige sweater and coordinating beige tweed skirt. And she had on just enough makeup today to add color to her cheeks and emphasize the almond-shaped eyes that were indisputably her best feature. Even her skin seemed smoother, the lines less deeply etched.

"You're looking well, Desiree," she said.

"You are, too—in spite of everything. I was just about to tell you that."

"It's wonderful—the power of a dab of rouge and a touch of mascara—isn't it? Rhonda—my friend in Wilton—insisted it would cheer me up a bit if I spent a few minutes on my appearance. She wasn't completely wrong, either. It *is* easier to face yourself in the mirror after you've gotten a hand from Estée Lauder.

"But never mind about that. Help yourself to a little pre-lunch snack." And so saying, she indicated the coffee table between us, which was presently enhanced by two plates that, of course, I was already well aware of. On one of them was an assortment of artfully arranged crudités—carrots, cauliflower, zucchini, olives, and red, yellow, and green peppers—with a small glass bowl in the center of the platter holding a dip of some sort. The second dish was compartmentalized and contained red lumpfish caviar, chopped onion, and sour cream. Alongside it was a tiny basket with crackers and party pumpernickel bread.

"I love fresh veggies," Connie stated, as I dunked a piece of red pepper in the dip. "Hortense couldn't come in today—she flew out to Missouri early this morning to visit her sister. But I got home last night to find a very well-stocked kitchen. You're sure I can't get you something to drink, though?"

"Thanks, but I'll pass. You're not having anything yourself?"

Connie shook her head. "I've been imbibing a little more than I should since Luella's been gone. So I'm passing, too." She piled a generous dollop of caviar together with the trimmings on a slice of pumpernickel.

We chatted for a while now. I reported seeing Bud at the lounge the previous evening and mentioned that he planned to call her. And Connie seemed to brighten for an instant. "He's a very thoughtful person," she said.

"Attractive, too. He was, uh, younger than I'd expected."

I was promptly rebuked. "I don't happen to think age should be a factor in whether two people choose to enter into a relationship. And after all," she reminded me, nostrils flaring, "it wasn't as though Luella were robbing the cradle."

"Oh, I agree. Totally. It was an observation, not a criticism."

"Sorry. I guess I overreacted," Connie murmured, embarrassed. "It's just that I believe it's what a man and woman have to offer each other that's important."

This conversation ended, we moved on to her Wilton hosts, with Connie telling me how only a few years back they had struck it very, very rich. First Leo—the husband—had done extremely well in some risky real estate deal. And then Rhonda—the wife—had taken a chunk of the money he'd raked in and invested it in the stock market, with phenomenal results. "And she's a woman who had absolutely no head for finance—or so everyone thought." Connie concluded with a chuckle that seemed to express both wonder and pleasure at her friend's success.

Right after this, I began a really innocuous question. I got as far as "Listen, have you—" when she broke in.

"Would you mind very much if we waited to talk about . . . what happened until we're through with lunch?"

"I'd prefer we did it that way. I was only about to ask if you'd been in touch with Kevin this past week."

There was a quiet "Oh." Then Connie told me that they'd spoken twice while she was in Connecticut and that just a couple of hours ago she'd heard from him again. "Which reminds me, he says hello."

"Is he okay? I owe him a call."

"I don't think I know what 'okay' is anymore," she answered sadly.

And seconds later she excused herself to see to lunch.

Alone now, I automatically reached for a carrot stick, glancing around me at the same time. In contrast to my last visit, no shriveled remains of dead flowers lay piled up on the tables and scattered over the thickly carpeted floor. The room was well lit today, too, so there weren't any shadows on the walls to play on the nerves of wimpy, overly imaginative P.I.'s. Still, just as before, a feeling of sadness swept over me. Every one of the many vases was sitting there empty. *All gone*, I thought, visualizing the colorful bouquets that had once added so much warmth and life here. *Gone. Like Luella.*

It was shortly after this, as I was sampling the caviar, that I remembered about Beatrix. Jumping to my feet, I circled the entire living room, standing back from the taller pieces on tiptoe, so I could see on top of them. But once again, the cat was nowhere in sight.

I was about to resettle myself on the sofa when, just then, Connie appeared and announced that our meal was ready.

The round wooden table in the kitchen was covered with a pale pink linen cloth and set with pretty floral china.

"I thought we'd eat in here. When there are only two people, the dining room can feel like a mausoleum," Connie explained, placing a bowl of pale orange soup in front of me. "I hope you like butternut squash."

The soup—it was a bisque, really—was delicious. As I knew it would be, since I had extremely fond memories of the exquisite dinner I'd been served here five years earlier. The bisque was followed by a tangy Caesar salad and a wonderful quiche with an incredibly light, flaky crust and a delectable mushroom filling. But it was the finale to the meal that I absolutely *had* to have the recipe for. A dense chocolate loaf sprinkled with pecans and accompanied by a rum-

laced custard sauce, it was one of the most decadent and irre-
sistible concoctions I'd ever tasted.

Now, when it comes to my own expertise in the kitchen, I
have no modesty whatsoever. (I'm good—*really* good—
even if you do have to hear it from me.) Still and all, this
woman could put me to shame.

Well, on second thought, that's probably going too far.
But her culinary talents were definitely impressive.

At any rate, we were through with lunch and I was just
turning away from the sink after depositing our dessert plates
(mine was virtually spotless), when the elusive Beatrix materialized at last. He was sitting on the end of the counter (I
swear he hadn't been there two minutes ago), as handsome
as ever. Forgetting about the purported transformation in his
character and ignoring the agitated twitching of his tail, I
rushed over to say hello to my old buddy.

But as I leaned forward to lavish him with affection—he
spat at me!

I immediately pulled the upper part of me back, but I was
so stunned, I seemed to be rooted to the floor. I just stood
there, my jaw dropped almost to my chest, and watched
Beatrix get up on all fours and stealthily inch a little closer to
me. Maybe he was going to try to make amends, I speculated
naively. Suddenly he arched his back and, looking me squarely
in the eye, repeated his singularly unfriendly greeting. After
which he promptly leapt to the top of the adjacent refrigerator and from there to the cabinet above it.

My hostess, being in the powder room at the time, was unaware of this little encounter. And I quickly made up my
mind not to enlighten her. Nadine was fearful that her aunt
might already be contemplating getting rid of the cat. And I
had no desire to supply yet another reason for showing him
the door. Regardless of what a little bastard he'd become.

"All right," Connie said as soon as she was sitting at the
table again. "Why don't you just fire away."

I smiled. "Okay, you asked for it." And then losing the
smile, I began with, "I'd appreciate it if you could go over
for me again exactly what you did that Saturday morning."

"Well, Luella and I had breakfast together. That was about
seven-thirty, as I told you before. And a half hour or so after
we'd finished—I didn't check the time—I left for Nadine's
to deliver some of the brownies I'd baked."

"She was expecting you?"

"Yes, I had called on Friday to let her know I'd be dropping them off."

"Do you have any idea when you got to the apartment?" I put to her, wanting to verify the information Nadine had given me.

"It was probably around nine. Maybe a little earlier. Or it could even have been a few minutes later. I'm not really certain. It isn't important, is it?" Connie inquired anxiously.

"I very much doubt it. What time did you leave Nadine's?"

"Somewhere close to ten. Again, I'm afraid I can't be any more precise than that."

"So you were at her place for almost an hour?"

"Actually, I don't think it was quite that long. Although I suppose it could have been."

"What did you do while you were there?"

"Do?"

"Did you have coffee together—or what?"

"I just kept Nadine company while she ate breakfast. I'd already had my fill at home."

"That was it?"

"What do you mean?" Connie looked perplexed.

"Your niece mentioned something about your making a telephone call."

Now Connie looked even more perplexed, the frown lines on either side of her nose becoming deep parallel ridges. But after a moment or two, her mouth formed an "O," and the ridges smoothed out. "Harry Chan," she proclaimed. "I forgot all about that. Harry's this little boy I tutor. I was supposed to get in touch with him that morning to go over an assignment. And I wanted to be certain I didn't miss him, so I phoned him from Nadine's. We must have spoken for five or ten minutes."

"Did you spend any more time with Nadine after you were through with your call?"

"Practically none. I had a lot of paperwork waiting for me at home, and I was anxious to get started."

"You came straight back to the house?"

Connie nodded. Then she correctly anticipated my next question. "The walk took me ten to fifteen minutes, I would guess."

"What did you do after you got here?"

"I went directly up to my office."

"Did you pass Luella's office?"

"Yes, I had to. I'd used the back entrance."

"Did you hear any sounds coming from there? Anything at all?"

"Nothing. I know that Beatrix made a terrible fuss later on, but everything was quiet when I went by."

"You didn't go down again, by any chance, did you?"

"Not until . . . not until Hortense began to scream." Her voice quivered now, and I was very much afraid that a serious crying jag might be just around the corner. But I had to proceed.

"Tell me what happened next," I prodded gently.

"I rushed downstairs. The door to Luella's office was open, and she was lying there on the floor—completely still. At first I thought she'd fainted. Or maybe I hoped that was all it was." Sighing, Connie shook her head slowly from side to side. "At any rate," she continued, "Hortense seemed to be frozen to the spot, so I shook her and told her to run out in the hall and call 911—there's no phone in the office. And then I knelt down and patted my sister's hands and touched her cheek and probably did a half-dozen other useless things that I can't even remember."

"Beatrix was still in the room at the time?" I was trying to fix a complete picture of the scene in my mind.

"No. He dashed past me just as I was going in."

"Continue. Please."

"Well, when Hortense came back, she pulled me to my feet, and we stood over Luella like two goddamn zombies until the paramedics arrived a few minutes later." At this point, Connie covered her face with her hands. "She was dead. My little sister was dead," said the muffled, tremulous voice. And the woman's shoulders heaved with silent sobs.

When at last she was all cried out, she sat up and revealed a face that was streaked with tears mingled with mascara. "Excuse me for just a minute while I wash up," Connie murmured.

She returned to the kitchen a short time afterward, her face wearing the unmistakable red blotches you get with a good, hard scrubbing. "I look a mess, but there's nothing I can do about it," she told me lightly.

"You look fine. But are you okay?"

She managed a game little smile. "More or less, but mostly more." And then meekly: "I'm very sorry about this, Desiree."

"Please. You have nothing to apologize for."

"What else would you like to ask me? And don't worry, I can handle it. I want to do whatever I can to help."

"All right. Tell me this: Who has keys to the house? I know that Kevin does. The girls do, too, don't they?"

"Of course. It was once their home, remember."

"What about Andy?"

"Uh-Uh."

"How do you feel about Andy, by the way? Do you like him?"

"I think he's a charming young man. Talented, too. I could never understand what it was about him that bothered my sister like that."

"And Bud Massi, did he have a key?"

"No. I'm certain he didn't."

Well, that about covered it. At least for now. "You'll be glad to know you're finally getting rid of me," I announced. "I can't figure out anything else to ask you."

But Connie appeared reluctant to leave it at that. "Uh, I understand you've seen all three of my nieces."

"Yes. Enid was the last. I stopped by her apartment on Thursday night."

There was silence for what must have been close to two minutes. During this time, Connie's lips parted once or twice, then promptly came together again. I had the feeling she was working up her courage. "Well, what do you think?" she got out at last. "What I mean is, do you suspect any of them?"

"It's really too soon to ask me something like that."

Connie responded with a short, harsh laugh. "Aren't *we* the cautious one?" But almost immediately she put up her hand. "Please don't dignify that with any kind of answer. It was a dumb thing to say. It's just that I want so much for Kevin to be mistaken." And now, in a voice filled with anguish, she told me, "I honestly don't think I could stand losing someone else I love, Desiree."

I was wracking my sluggish brain trying to come up with something reassuring—yet noncommittal—but she let me off the hook. "Why am I carrying on like this, though? They didn't do it. None of them. And you'll see that I'm right, too."

"I wouldn't be a bit surprised." My tone was as sympathetic as I could make it.

"The fact is, the longer I turn things over in my mind, the more convinced I am that Kevin's just gone off half-cocked on this thing. Oh, I still want you to continue your investigation—I suppose that's the right thing to do. Besides, I *did* make a promise to Kevin. But his theories are all so much silliness. Just before I left for Connecticut, he and I were going back and forth again about his speculations. And I couldn't see where he was able to ascribe even a *semi* legitimate motive to any one of the girls."

And now Connie leaned across the table. "I can't buy that revenge business," she said earnestly. "Plus Kevin insists this fear of losing out on the inheritance brought everything to a head. But that doesn't wash, either. None of them really cares that much about money. And that's the truth. Naturally, the inheritance will make things easier for them, but they would have managed quite nicely without it, too.

"Take Enid. She's determined to get to the top of her profession. And there's no doubt in my mind that she will. She's very intelligent and extremely hard working. Driven, you might say. But the monetary rewards that come with success would be secondary to her. What really matters to her is her own ability to achieve.

"And as for Nadine, she's made plans for a cruise—an expensive cruise. She'll be sailing the Mediterranean the last two weeks in June, lucky girl." There was a slight pause to give the next words added impact. "But the point is, Nadine booked that vacation ages ago. She didn't have to wait for any inheritance to pay for it. She had more than enough money of her own, believe me. Thanks to her father's insurance policy and some sound investments, she's very decently fixed."

"And Geena?"

Connie shook her head emphatically. "Geena's completely out of the question. She always refused to take a dime from Luella. Or from me, either, for that matter. And we both offered any number of times to help out financially until she and Andy got on their feet."

Suddenly Connie's tone grew confidential, and she spoke almost reluctantly. "Look, all three of the girls loved my sister very much—in my heart, I've always been convinced of that. But Geena was . . . well . . . Geena was totally devoted to her." She sighed. "I don't think that poor thing will ever get over Luella's death." Her voice dropped to a whisper. "Any more than I will."

And now Connie placed her arms on the edge of the table and, burying her head in them, wept inconsolably.

Chapter 22

I didn't know it, but I was about to have an adventure. Of sorts, anyhow.

After I left Connie, I headed straight for Fifty-ninth and Lex—and Bloomingdale's. The repository of most of my disposal income.

I hadn't yet shopped for a Christmas/Hanukkah gift for a soul on my list. Just about every day I'd been assuring myself that there was still plenty of time. But when I looked at my newspaper that morning, for once, I actually made contact with the date. December 16. The holidays were breathing down my neck.

Now, normally, it takes me forever to pick out a present. But I had decided months ago to give Ellen a pin—a turtle pin—and that afternoon I saw exactly what I wanted in Bloomingdale's jewelry department. A darling little fellow with ruby eyes. Naturally, it took forever to get waited on— next year I'll start my shopping in August, I swear—and then the darling little fellow turned out to be a lot dearer than he looked. *I really shouldn't spend that much*, I decided. But as the saleswoman was putting him back in the glass case, I relented. Hey. He was for Ellen, wasn't he?

My next stop was the men's department, where I promptly began an inspection tour that took over an hour. I mean, I checked out practically every sweater, shirt, and tie in the place—while barely managing to avoid being squished, elbowed, or stepped on by a relentless horde of my fellow procrastinators. (I hoped all of these people didn't make up their minds to holiday-shop next August, too.) At any rate, when I finally concluded that I hadn't left a single piece of merchandise unturned, I headed back to the display table I'd started at.

Earlier, I had admired this one particular sport shirt here. It was a wide brown, white, and gray stripe in a beautiful imported cotton fabric. In fact, I'd contemplated buying it right then and there. *I'll bet Mike would like this*, was what I'd thought as soon as I spotted it. But of course, I hadn't pawed through enough merchandise yet to satisfy myself that I'd found the ultimate gift. Anyway, I was now back to pick up the size Large of this shirt, which I remembered had been sitting right on top of a neat pile of similar shirts. But by this time, the piles were no longer neat. And more to the point, the size Large was no longer in sight.

I tore through the stack it had formerly headed up. A lot of Smalls, a few Mediums, and some Extra Larges . . . Damn! *Why hadn't I asked a salesperson to hold it for me until I made up my mind*, I lamented.

Well, there were five other shirt stacks, along with a whole bunch of scattered strays. I riffled through the strays first—forget it. And then I tackled another stack. From what I could see initially, none of these shirts was even the same style. But you just never knew . . .

Now, even as intent on my task as I was, I still noticed peripherally that there was a woman alongside me engaged in a similar pursuit. She was really tiny—I mean, all five-two of me could have eaten apples off her head. If not for her jet-black beehive "do," that is, which added at least six inches to her height. But anyhow, you can see, can't you why I would hardly have felt threatened?

As we both bent to our work, the beehive struck my face a few times, but I chalked it up to one of the hazards of holiday shopping. And once or twice I felt the woman was deliberately cracking her gum in my ear, but then, I'm particularly paranoid when I'm frustrated. Besides, as we were attacking neighboring shirt piles and our hands accidentally made contact, she smiled politely at me. Proving that this was a civilized human being here.

It was in the middle of the very last pile that I found it: Mike's shirt!

I was about to walk away with my prize when the beehive woman took a firm hold of my arm. "Hey, what have you got there? Izzat a size L?"

"That's right."

"Then it's mine," she informed me.

"What do you mean—yours?"

"I was all ready to buy it before you even showed up here."

"Why didn't you, then?" I inquired reasonably.

"I put that shirt down so's I could get out my charge card. And right away some big idiot goes plowin' through everything, and he dumps all this other stuff on top of it. And then I couldn't find it no more, that's why."

"Well, I'm sorry, but—"

"Hey, *can* the sorry. I don't want no sorry; I want my shirt." And releasing my arm, she grabbed the garment with both hands and gave it a good hard yank.

I was almost expecting to see half the shirt in her fists, but to my surprise, I still retained sole custody.

The woman's eyes narrowed. "You're not gonna gimme it?" she inquired in a voice that was suspiciously soft.

I summoned up my courage. "No, I'm not." Just then I became aware that this elderly couple who had come over to the table only a minute or two before had begun backing away. What's more, we had, by now, attracted a small group of onlookers.

"Well, don't say I didn't try to be nice about this," Beehive mumbled, mostly to herself, as one of her heels—a four-inch spike—came crashing down on my instep.

Hopping around on one foot and yelping with pain, I involuntarily loosened my grasp on the shirt. And that's when she made her move, snatching it away and attempting to escape through the crowd with her ill-gotten booty.

"Stop her!" I hollered before I had time to censor myself. "Stop that woman!"

A new addition to our little audience quickly latched on to the perpetrator. "Don't worry. She's not goin' no place. What happened? She take your wallet, lady?"

But before I had to provide the answer—which had just become an embarrassment to me—a security guard hurried over. Taking Beehive gently—but firmly—by the arm, he led her to where I was standing on my one good foot.

"What's going on here?" he wanted to know.

"She stole my shirt," I said. Since I was now able to appreciate how ridiculous this whole thing was going to sound, I at least had the sense to make the accusation quietly.

Obviously the beehive woman didn't have as much sense as I did. "It's *my* shirt," she contested in a loud, high-pitched voice, clutching the garment to her bosom.

"Either of you ladies got a receipt?" the guard inquired.

Shaking our heads in unison, we simultaneously started to babble our explanations.

The man actually seemed to get the gist of the dispute. "Hold it for a second," he commanded politely, interrupting the heated claims and counterclaims. (Which did not include mention of my damaged appendage, since it was really a whole other matter—and one I had no desire to take the time to pursue.) "Let me have that, please," he said to Beehive. She surrendered the shirt with extreme reluctance. "I suppose you ladies checked with a salesperson to find out if there are any more of these in the back?"

Feeling myself flush, I murmured, "Well, not specifically, I guess." *Whatever that was supposed to mean.*

"I had it first; it was up to *her* to check," my adversary asserted with a vicious snap of her gum.

Raising himself up on the balls of his feet now, the guard lifted his arm over his head. "Mr. Filippone!" he called out. Moments later a young salesman had elbowed his way through our audience, which had expanded considerably.

Handing the salesman the contested merchandise, the guard explained. "These customers are having a little disagreement about which one of 'em gets to buy this shirt here. Appears to be the only Large on the table. Would you happen to have any others in stock?"

"I don't know offhand. Let me look."

For a few minutes Beehive and I stood there glaring malevolently at one another, the guard between us. And then Filippone returned—carrying *two* shirts. Flashing a happy-I-could-be-of-service smile, he presented the original shirt to Beehive. I got the one from stock—the unpicked over, untugged at, uncrumpled one.

As I hobbled away to pay for my purchase, I heard this strident whine. "How come she gets the good shirt? Huh? Just tell me that!"

Between the foot and the rest of the trauma, I couldn't handle another minute of shopping that day. Fortunately, as soon as I stepped outside the store, I came face-to-face with an empty cab. Which, considering the holiday crowds, was probably as close to a miracle as I'm ever likely to encounter.

Anyway, the first thing that occurred to me on the way home was, *Suppose that, after all this, Mike doesn't even like the shirt?*

No, he'll like it. I pressed my lips together tightly. *Or I'll strangle him with the damn thing.*

Chapter 23

It was definitely a mercy invitation.

And I wanted to set the record straight.

"If you think I'm sitting here agonizing over Bruce, you couldn't be more wrong," I informed Ellen, who had called not even five minute after I got home from Bloomingdale's.

"Bruce has zero to do with our asking you to come to dinner with us. Honestly," she insisted.

I still wasn't convinced.

"We've been planning to ask you for weeks now," she went on, "but you know Mike's schedule. Look, you're always preparing these terrific meals for us, and we like to reciprocate once in a while. It isn't even polite not to let us do that."

Not polite? Well, leave it to Ellen to come up with an argument like that. "Come on, Ellen. How many times have you had *me* over for dinner?"

"Yeah. For Chinese takeout," she scoffed. "You know, you are really making this difficult. What's the matter with you today, anyway?" And then, concern in her voice: "You're not sick or anything?"

I didn't dare mention my foot, which was throbbing worse than ever at that moment. If I knew Ellen, she'd have called the paramedics immediately. Or worse yet, insisted on coming over herself to play Florence Nightingale. (Trust me, if there's anyone who can outmother Jackie, it's Ellen.) Besides, the foot had nothing to do with my being so perverse.

Anyway, I relented then. I *was* acting extremely ungracious. "I'm sorry, Ellen. I'm a little tired, that's all. I'd really love to have dinner with you and Mike tomorrow."

"Good." There was such genuine pleasure in her voice that I could have kicked myself for turning this nice, thoughtful invitation into a debate. "Is Chinese all right?" she said.

"Fine."

Ellen giggled. "Just kidding. We were thinking of Italian food, if that's okay with you. Mike and I went to this lovely Italian restaurant in Chelsea a couple of weeks ago. I think you'll like it."

"I'm sure I will."

We made arrangements to meet at the restaurant at seven-thirty the following evening.

The first thing I did after Ellen and I hung up was to pull off my panty hose so I could have a good look at my instep, which I discovered was a magnificent shade of purple. I took a couple of Extra-strength Tylenols for the pain and then deliberated for ten minutes about whether it would be better to soak the foot in hot water or ice water. Finally deciding to split the difference, I settled on lukewarm.

As I sat there with my foot in a basin, I gave vent to the self-pity that had been building up in me for the last half hour or so. My second acute attack of this indulgence in a week.

The breakup with Bruce still hurt a lot, much as I denied it. Even to myself, most of the time.

Plus investigating the death of Luella Pressman was an exercise in the bizarre. And it was getting me crazy. How was I supposed to do my job, I groused, without the facts on how the woman had died? Kevin was the only one crying murder here. And he might very well be as off base as Connie maintained that he was.

And now this lousy foot.

That woman was definitely a menace. *You should have told the guard about the attack,* I chastised myself.

I had the retort all ready. *Sure, and then you'd have had to press charges and waste who-knows-how-much time in court.* Seconds later, I juiced things up a bit, for good measure. *Besides, maybe her family's even crazier than she is. And who's to say they wouldn't come after you with blood in their eyes for turning her in like that?* (Hardly what you'd call a fearless P.I., am I?)

Just then a sharp pain emanated from my instep and shot halfway up my leg. *My God! I may have to go to dinner on crutches tomorrow!*

It suddenly occurred to me that I was like that character in Li'l Abner. The one with a black cloud over his head—what was his name?

Another sharp pain followed the first. "That psycho beehive woman," I muttered aloud. "She'd better not have broken anything." Although what I would do in that event, I hadn't figured out yet.

By the next morning, a lot of the purple had turned this kind of yellowish color you get when a bruise is healing. The instep felt considerably better. And so did I—mentally, I mean.

It was maybe ten of twelve when I phoned Kevin, who—without saying anything of the sort—managed to convey how slow I'd been to contact him again and how anxiously he'd been awaiting my call. Actually, it was only four days since we'd last spoken. But I could appreciate how long those four days had been for him. At any rate, we set up a meeting for Monday at nine forty-five in my office.

A short while later I had a light lunch, following which I got busy typing up some of my notes. And then at around five-fifteen I had to begin dressing for that seven-thirty dinner with Ellen and Mike, since when it comes to getting myself together, I'm probably three paces behind a snail.

After a leisurely bubble bath and a few liberal spritzes of Ivoire, I took my celadon wool A-line out of the closet. This was the little number I'd run out and bought practically the instant Bruce invited me to that cocktail party in TriBeCa. You know, the party at which he'd so thoroughly humiliated me. I stood there for a moment, staring at the dress with revisited anger mixed with determination. I loved that dress. It had wonderful lines, plus the color couldn't have been more flattering. Well, I thought, slipping it off the hanger, I certainly didn't need a Bruce Simon in my life to make use of the damn thing.

I put on my clothes, then started to apply my makeup. I was doing such a professional-looking job that I was ready to congratulate myself—when the mascara wand somehow wound up in my eye. It took four handfuls of cold water to reassure me that I wouldn't go blind.

And now it was time to tackle the really tough stuff.

The humidity had been way down today, so I was hardly expecting a particularly fierce battle from my absolutely impossible hair. Still, that's what I got. And after a couple of minutes of tugging and teasing and teeth-grinding, I gave up and dragged out my wig. Which is an exact replica of my natural hair, only a lot better behaved. My neighbor Barbara recently dubbed it my "rainy-day" wig, because I have to

press it into service whenever the rain turns my glorious hennaed coif into a hideous, frizzed-up mess. As it invariably
does. But that "rainy-day" tag also applies in the figurative
sense. What I mean is, I rely on the wig in time of need. And
that can occur even if there isn't a cloud in the sky or a drop
of moisture in the air. Like now.

At any rate, thanks to my spare head of hair, I managed to
make it down to Chelsea on time.

The minute I walked into Vito's—and, happily, without a
limp—I was impressed with the restaurant's ambiance. It
was a quiet, pretty place with soft lights, pastel paintings,
and pale lavender tablecloths. In fact, it was intimate enough
to elicit surprise that a very much in love, practically engaged couple would invite a third party—an aunt, of all
things—to join them here. Unless it was *this* couple, that is.

They were sitting at a table toward the back. I hadn't set
eyes on Mike in over a month, and in spite of the terrible
hours he'd been putting in at the hospital, he looked really
fine. As attractive—and tall—as ever. Rising, he had to practically fold himself in half to kiss my cheek. (Ellen managed
the same demonstration of affection by just bending her
knees a little.)

As soon as I sat down Mike ordered a bottle of Chianti.
And right after that, I took two packages from my shopping
bag. "Happy Hanukkah and Merry Christmas—just in case I
don't see you again before the holidays," I explained, dis-
pensing the gifts.

Ellen loved the pin. "How did you *know*?" she squealed.

And Mike *said* he loved the shirt. Maybe the squint-eyed
stare I fastened on him as he was unwrapping it was his clue
that he'd *better* love it.

They'd no sooner finished with their "thank you"s when
Ellen reached into her pocketbook and produced a small
green box tied with a bright red ribbon. "This is 'just in
case,' too. Merry Christmas from Mike and me, Aunt Dez."

Like Ellen, I acknowledged my present with a squeal. "It's
beautiful. Really, *really* beautiful!" I exclaimed, slipping on
the silver cuff bracelet and then extending my arm so Ellen
and Mike could admire it on me. "But you shouldn't have
gotten anything so extravagant."

Ellen's response was delivered with a bone-crushing hug.
"Neither should you," she said.

* * *

The food was excellent. But I probably derived as much pleasure out of watching Ellen and Mike together as I did from the meal. They were just so perfect for each other.

Okay, I thought for maybe the thousandth time. *So he's still a poorly paid resident. But who says you have to be a Park Avenue specialist to get married? After all, look at the money they'd save by living in only one apartment and sharing expenses.* (I would not, however, be overjoyed if they opted to merely cohabit. Uh-uh. I intended to be the matron of honor here or bust.) But for now, I'd settle for at least seeing them officially engaged.

Naturally, I didn't attempt to discuss their future at dinner. It's something I wouldn't dream of bringing up in front of Mike. I mean, give me credit for that much intelligence, anyway. In fact, I'd been seriously considering never again mentioning the word "marriage" to Ellen, either. It seemed that every time I *had* gotten up the nerve to question her, she'd shut down the conversation with some vague, totally unsatisfactory answer. Well, I decided at that moment, from now on, if I *did* broach the subject with her—and I never said definitely that I wouldn't—I'd try a more roundabout approach.

At any rate, table talk that evening hopped around from Mike's career—he was really thrilled to be working with that guru of his—to Ellen's friend Lois—who was divorcing her husband to marry her mailman—to Ellen's Uncle Sam (on her father's side)—who at seventy-plus had just gotten himself a face-lift. And then right after we disposed of Uncle Sam, Mike asked how my new case was coming along.

"Ellen told me about it. It must be pretty tough investigating the woman's death if you don't know what killed her," he commiserated.

My thoughts exactly. "You bet it is," I grumbled. "All I can do at this point is gather information and then cross my fingers I'll be able to make some sense of the whole mess later."

"You know, Aunt Dez," Ellen said slowly, apparently thinking things through as she spoke, "this case isn't really that different from your last murder case."

And before I had a chance to say, "What in God's name are you talking about?" she went on.

"Or even the one before that. Oh, maybe you *did* have an autopsy report in those two instances, but there wasn't any clear indication a crime had been committed either time. Remember? You were really unbelievable, though," my one-member fan club enthused. "You had no trouble at all in uncovering the killers."

Damned if she wasn't right! I *had* been in similar situations—well, somewhat similar, anyhow. And I *had* done the job. Although that "no trouble at all" was such a gross exaggeration as to almost qualify as an out-and-out lie. Nevertheless, for the first time since I'd begun looking into Luella Pressman's death, I felt a little encouraged.

And now Ellen abruptly returned to the present. "What are they like—the stepdaughters?"

"They *seem* nice enough. But who knows?"

"Are they pretty?"

"Nadine's very cute. Geena—she's the married one—is kind of fragile, waiflike. But I suppose some people would consider that sort of quality appealing. And Enid—well, I found her to be the least attractive of the three, the least personable, too. Not that she's rude or anything. It's just that her manner's a little brusque."

"How did they take their stepmother's death?"

"Again, they all *seem* to be shaken up about it."

It was Mike's turn. "She was a very wealthy woman, I understand. Did any of the three have a pressing need for money?" And then he put in quickly, "I realize, of course, that need isn't always a criterion."

"You're right. Still, Geena and her husband Andy, who's an artist, could certainly use some funding. Although Connie—the girls' stepaunt, I guess you'd call her—claims that Geena is too independent to accept any help. Both Luella and Connie had been offering her money all along, which Geena consistently turned down.

"Now, from what I know of Enid—"

Ellen broke in. "Enid's the snotty one?"

I smiled. "She's not exactly snotty. Anyhow, Enid could benefit from a little financial assistance, too. She lost her job a while ago and had to take a much lower-paying one." And then recalling Enid's words about moving to the studio from a considerably larger apartment, I added, "And naturally, that meant altering her very comfortable lifestyle, too. But Connie insists that Enid is hell-bent on succeeding on her own."

"You don't believe her?" Ellen asked.

"Well, it's probably true. But with Connie as overprotective of those girls as she is, I'm not sure I can regard every word she says about them as gospel."

"And the third stepdaughter?" Ellen demanded.

"Nadine appears to have some money of her own. Her father left her well provided for."

"But that doesn't necessarily let her out."

"Of course not," I agreed. "Some people never have enough. "Besides, we don't know how much of a part animosity toward the dead woman might have played in this thing." I turned to Mike. "As I've explained to Ellen, Kevin feels that's an essential element in the motive."

"When do you suppose you'll get the results of the autopsy report?" Mike inquired.

I thought of all the additional weeks I could conceivably spend fumbling around in the dark. "Not soon enough," I told him regretfully. "Not nearly soon enough."

Believe me, I hadn't planned to.

But it was a few minutes to ten when I came home that evening—way earlier than my normal bedtime. And there wasn't anything in the apartment to read. Nothing on television, either—nothing that didn't make me want to gag, that is. So before I was even aware I was doing it, I fished out my notes on the case.

I read them through very carefully. But like I keep saying (okay, *bitching*), I had no idea what it was I was looking for.

Which in retrospect is, I guess, the most charitable explanation of why I didn't find anything.

Chapter 24

"I never meant to lose touch with you—you've always been one of my favorite people. But the time just got away from me somehow." Kevin's voice grew husky then. "Who could ever have anticipated it would take Luella's death to bring us together again?"

"I know," I said, because I had no idea what else to say. And I reached over and grasped his hand for a moment.

"It's all right. I'm okay," he assured me with a sad smile.

"Are you up to a few questions now?"

"I'm up to as many as you want to ask me."

"I'd like you to tell me a little more about Luella's step-daughters. I mean, about their personal lives. Is Nadine or Enid romantically involved?" It was a factor that I though could conceivably impact on any decision to commit murder.

"Not that I'm aware of," Kevin answered. "Although Nadine was dating someone pretty regularly last year."

"It's over?"

"According to Luella, Nadine claimed he was too wishy-washy. Something like that."

"But she's not seeing anyone at present."

"She goes out. I can't say how often, but I'm fairly sure there's no one special."

"What about Enid?"

"Enid doesn't really have time for a social life. She's consumed with her work. She may date once in a while, but the last time she had a regular boyfriend—that I know of, at least—was back in college."

"I see." There was nothing here I could pursue, so I moved on. "I understand you had a discussion with Connie about motives before she left for Wilton."

"Yep." Kevin grinned. "And she strongly disagreed with every word I uttered. But, of course, she has a great deal of ambivalence about looking into Luella's death to begin with."

"I still can't get over the fact that she got the idea to bring me into this originally, before you could even broach the subject yourself, I mean."

"Well, once I talked to her about my conviction that Luella had been murdered, I think her own nebulous fears came to the surface. And then she felt we had no choice but to hire someone like you."

"Why no choice?"

"I expressed my concern that the police wouldn't conduct a very thorough investigation until they had the results of the autopsy—at which point it might well be too late. However—and I'm sure I mentioned this before—when Connie suggested I hire you, she insisted it was just to allay *my* suspicions. She wouldn't admit to having any herself. And as you're aware, she's been on the fence about your involvement ever since.

"I'll tell you one more thing. When we have these heated arguments regarding Luella's death, Connie is mainly fighting to put down her own doubts. I'm certain of it."

I decided this was very perceptive of Kevin. (Most probably because it was about the same as my take on things.) "Just what was the gist of this conversation you two had?" I asked now.

"It was primarily about motive, which is something I think about a great deal. In fact, there isn't much else I think about these days. At any rate, I've developed some theories as to the specific reason each of Luella's stepdaughters might have been carrying around this deep-seated hatred of her. And when Connie and I spoke last week, I spelled them out for her."

It didn't require any prompting for Kevin to spell out these same theories for me.

"Let's take Geena," he began. "No matter what the girl claims, I can't believe she wasn't deeply affected when her adored new stepmother suddenly started rationing their time together. Geena has always been very shy, very vulnerable, and in her eyes, it must have seemed like a kind of abandonment. You have to bear in mind that it hadn't been that many years since the murder of her natural mother, who by dying had, in a way, also abandoned her. And remember, too, that later on there was a third 'abandonment,' which was her father's suicide."

"I see you've been playing shrink again," I accused jokingly.

Kevin acknowledged the remark with a sheepish smile. And

then he continued, his manner intense now. "Listen, I don't think it's the least bit farfetched to assume that Geena might never have gotten over the idea that she'd been deserted by the people closest to her. Or that based on two of these instances, she was extremely bitter toward her stepmother."

"Two of the instances?"

"I'm not at all sure Geena didn't hold Luella partially, if not completely responsible for Fred's killing himself."

And clearing his throat now, Kevin waited for my reaction.

I had to admit the whole thing was plausible. And I said so. He seemed really heartened—grateful, almost—at the support.

"Now, as for Enid," he put forth next, "by her own admission, she resented her stepmother a great deal for not smothering her with affection when Walter—that's her father—ran out on them. Enid went through therapy, as you know, and she appears to be level-headed enough today. But from all I've heard, she was a very angry young girl. And it's possible she still harbors the same feelings toward Luella that she did as a teenager. What I'm trying to say is, who can be certain she didn't fool her psychiatrist and everyone else into believing the treatment had helped her? Could be she's a much more talented actress than anyone is aware of."

"Enid's not a terribly warm person, is she?" I threw in at this juncture.

"She thaws out with people she knows well. To be honest, I always admired that young woman. She seemed very forthright and aboveboard to me. I liked her sense of humor, too—she has the ability to laugh at herself. And, of course, I've never met anyone so committed to her goals."

And now our focus switched to the remaining stepdaughter. "What's your theory about Nadine?" I asked.

"Now, I *still* think her motive would be the same as her stepsisters'. More or less, anyway." His tone was almost combative. "Nadine must have seen herself as neglected, too. But, well," he continued, "there is something else to consider in her case. In fact, Connie called me about it early this morning. I'd told her I would be seeing you today, and she wanted me to promise not to reveal certain information concerning Nadine. But I couldn't go along with her. First of all, I believe I may already have passed the basic fact on to you. If not, though, I should definitely rectify that omission so that you're aware of how it might have impacted on the girl.

But I have to stress that we're only considering a possibility here. And if you want my opinion, an outside possibility, at that."

"Just what is it Connie asked you to keep from me?" I put in quickly, concerned he might go on elaborating without providing even a clue as to the subject matter.

"That Nadine's mother had been in a mental institution."

I felt a little let down. "I already knew about that. To be frank, though, I never considered the mother's condition in relation to Nadine. Of course, I'm not that familiar with schizophrenia." And then I added grudgingly, "But I'll look into it."

"No need to. Connie and I already have. Connie has a friend who's a psychiatrist, and we had dinner with him yesterday evening. Supposedly it was just a social thing. But I think Connie's been worried all along about Nadine's inheriting the disease. Of course, Connie never told me this, but I'm certain that was the real purpose of the dinner."

"But Nadine seems—she seems perfectly normal."

"I agree. But at any rate, Connie got this Dr. Schaffer— Bill Schaffer—to talk about paranoid schizophrenia. And eventually she mentioned Nadine. The doctor said to relax. If Nadine had developed the disease, it would be readily apparent," he said.

"That's what I thought," I responded smugly. "So why didn't Connie want you to tell me about the mother?"

"Because there's more. According to Bill, there still might be some predisposition to mental illness there. And he asked some probing questions about Nadine's personality. When he heard that she's always lacked confidence, he said it was possible her mother's confinement had traumatized Nadine more than anyone realized. He told us her insecurity could stem from a deep-seated fear that she herself might be institutionalized some day. And this insecurity could very well have been intensified when her father died. After that, it seems, she was terribly afraid that everyone else she was close to would die, too, and there'd be no one left to look after her."

"Getting back to her mother's confinement for a second," I put in, "I broached that topic with Nadine myself, and she didn't appear particularly disturbed by it. On the contrary, really."

"That's just it, though. According to the doctor, she may

have been burying her fear all these years. It's something he
called post-traumatic stress disorder."

"But what does all this have to do with Luella's death?" I
interjected impatiently.

"Well, it could be that some chance remark Luella made
about the mother's illness or some remark someone else *attributed* to Luella brought everything to a head, triggering an
episode of acute paranoia in Nadine. And the interesting
thing is," Kevin went on, "if Nadine did murder Luella under
those circumstances, it's possible she has no recollection of
it at all. She may have completely blocked it from memory."

Now, my initial reaction was to pooh-pooh everything I'd
just heard. I mean, *post-traumatic stress disorder—Nadine?*
Besides, just as Kevin had pointed out, what we were dealing
with here were only a lot of "possible"s and "could be"s and
"may have"s. But I supposed I shouldn't completely disre-
gard Dr. Schaffer's speculations; after all, the man *was* a
qualified psychiatrist. And so at the same time that I told
Kevin I couldn't quite buy into any of this, I instructed myself to keep it all in the back of my mind somewhere. "How
did Connie react to what her friend had to say?" I asked then.

"Not particularly well, as you might imagine. I don't think
she gave very much weight to Nadine's having that post-
traumatic stress thing, either. But I know she'd been hoping for total reassurance as to the girl's mental health. And
this not being the case, she insisted—after we left him, of
course—that Dr. Schaffer was getting senile. Which is typi-
cal of Connie, really. She can't bear to hear anything even
the least bit troubling about any of those girls. We got into
quite a hassle about that last night." A pause. "But I can
never really stay angry at her."

"You're very fond of Connie, aren't you?"

"That I am." A warm smile played on his lips. "I developed a real affinity for her from the time she helped me put
out the first of those fires I set in cooking class."

I thought of something then. "Now, this is just to satisfy
my curiosity. But why, in heaven's name, did Connie need
instruction in cooking? She could be *giving* it, for crying out
loud."

"I think Connie was just desperate for something to do at
the time. Luella was working every night during that period
to meet the deadline for her latest book. And then right after
that, she was scheduled to go on an extended cross-country

tour to promote another book—the one that had just been published. Which would have left Connie pretty much at loose ends."

I proceeded timidly now. "Was there . . . umm . . . were you and Connie ever . . . was there ever any kind of romantic feeling between you? Of course," I rushed to clarify, "I'm referring to right at the beginning, before you and Luella met."

"Kevin's response was matter-of-fact. "Oh, no. We've never been anything but very good friends. Like the two of *us*." And he wiggled his finger back and forth at me.

"The girls—how do they feel about Connie?" I was thinking about the impression I'd gotten when talking to Nadine. I mean, that maybe she wasn't quite as crazy about this aunt of hers as she maintained. (But then, I don't exactly have a great track record when it comes to picking up on people's vibes.)

"Those girls are very attached to Connie. They really love her."

"All three of them?"

"Yes, why do you ask?"

"I'm not even sure why."

"Look, Connie was the one who shouldered most of the responsibility when it came to raising them. She had to give up her teaching for a long time in order to do it, too. And she was always very loving, very generous with them. She constantly bought them expensive gifts and took them on trips—to Disneyland, Hoover Dam, Fisherman's Wharf, Yellowstone Park, everywhere. She even took Nadine and Geena on a vacation in Europe. But that little jaunt was mostly because Connie decided that Luella and I should be alone in the house for a while—it was immediately after we got married. We had to have a chance to settle into marriage, she said."

"That was very thoughtful," I commented.

"Connie's like that."

"But by then, Geena was no longer living at home, was she?"

"No, she already had a place of her own. But Connie wouldn't just restrict the invitation to Nadine; she'd have been concerned the others might feel left out," Kevin explained.

"Enid didn't care to join them, though?"

"She didn't want to spend that much time away from work. And besides, Enid had a business trip to Europe scheduled for the following month."

Discussing the love Connie had been lavishing on those girls all these years prompted me to wonder why she'd never married and had children of her own. (A husband, I was sure, being a prerequisite for motherhood where Connie was concerned.) But, of course, it was possible she *had* been married at one time. I questioned Kevin about it.

"No," he said. "She was close to engaged many, many years ago, but the fellow broke it off. And after that, she was determined not to put herself in the position of getting hurt again. In fact, for a long time, Luella kept trying to introduce her to suitable men, but Connie wouldn't hear of it. And so eventually Luella just gave up."

"The two sisters were very close, weren't they." It was really more of an observation than a question.

"Extremely close. There wasn't that much difference in age, but in some ways, Connie was like a mother to Luella. She was devoted to her. They were devoted to each other, actually."

"Does Connie have may friends?"

"Not too many, a few—other teachers, mainly. Aside from her work, Connie's life has been centered almost entirely around Luella and the girls. Although about three months back—to the astonishment of just about everyone—she finally seemed to be ready for something more. Luella had just begun seeing Bud Massi, I remember. And Connie enrolled in this basic computer course. It was time she caught up with her seven-year-olds, was how she put it—Connie teaches second grade. And then she bought herself a whole new wardrobe and even colored her hair."

"Do you think this might had had anything to do with a man?"

Kevin shook his head. "No, there wasn't any man. This latest relationship of Luella's—the involvement with Massi— evidently woke her up. It's conceivable it occurred to her that her sister might even marry again. Anyway, at long last she was through sitting on the sidelines; she was out there trying to meet some people herself."

"How did Luella feel about this? The change in Connie, I mean."

"She was delighted. She'd been urging her to get some

outside interests for years." There was a long pause before Kevin said sadly, "I'm afraid, though, that the new Connie may have died with Luella." And then he added softly, "But I hope not."

"I've been wondering about something for a while now, Kevin," I brought up here.

"What's that?"

"Just how was Connie able to convince three intelligent girls that it would be to their advantage to have me on the case? Didn't they expect the autopsy report to reveal whether or not their stepmother's death had been a homicide?"

"Connie, being one extremely bright lady, sold them quite a bill of goods," Kevin responded, grinning. "She told them the findings aren't always conclusive." *Well, as I'd learned the hard way, this was true enough.* "And then she planted the seed that when it comes to the death of a well-known person, there's always the possibility the police might get over-zealous. She was worried, she said, that without substantial evidence to the contrary, the detectives on the case could decide to see foul play where there really wasn't any. Particularly if one of them should be looking to make a name for himself. I also believe Connie mentioned the obvious ambition—she *claimed*—of a certain Sergeant Blake, who is in charge of the investigation.

"And she backed up all of this by alleging that Blake had already mentioned murder to her a few times. Which is what really clinched things."

My surprise at the woman's ingenuity must have showed. (Bulging eyes are a dead giveaway, I suppose.)

"There's more," Kevin informed me, his grin covering half his face now. "She even tossed into the mix that you have some very good connections in the police department that could prove helpful down the line."

"Well, how do you like that!" She'd thought of everything, it seemed.

"Connie may have her qualms about allowing you to investigate," Kevin said, pride in his voice, "but as long as we'd agreed to bring you on board, she presented you as a virtual necessity."

What a devious woman, I remarked to myself. I mean, she was positively Machiavellian.

I was very impressed.

Chapter 25

"I've been keeping a pretty tight rein on myself so far, don't you agree?" Kevin was leaning forward, elbow on my desk, chin resting on his knuckles.

I had absolutely no idea what he was talking about, and I wouldn't have been surprised if my face was as blank as my brain.

He chuckled for a moment, which reinforced that feeling about my face. After which he said almost defensively, "Look, let me first make it clear that I already know what you're going to tell me, and I have no doubt that you're right. Nevertheless, I have to ask. Okay?"

For a second or two, I was still sitting there in the dark. And then all of a sudden, I realized exactly what was on his mind. "Go ahead," I said anyway. I mean, I had to let him get it out of his system.

"Do you have any idea at this point who might have killed Luella?"

I reminded myself about patience being a virtue. (And after all, he *had* managed to contain himself for the better part of an hour.) "Listen, I—"

But Kevin, determined to cut me off at the pass, broke in before I could once again point out the obvious. "I'm aware that you can't be certain of anything until we learn the results of the autopsy"—he had almost literally taken the words right out of my mouth—"but I was hoping, well, that you might have come across *something* that seemed suspicious to you."

"No. I can't say that I did." His expression was so dejected that I added, "But I didn't expect that I would yet. At present, I'm only trying to gather information. When we find out how Luella died, I'll be in a position to start piecing the facts together." Now, if this sounds as familiar to you as it did to my own ears just then, it's because I'd made more or less the same explanation at dinner only the night before—and who knows how many times before that.

"There isn't one of the girls who said something a little questionable or strange or . . . or anything?" Kevin finished lamely.

I shook my head. "Not that I picked up on."

"Oh."

"Don't worry. We'll get to the bottom of this before long," I stated firmly. It was an attempt to not only reassure Kevin, but myself, as well.

And Kevin's response was similarly motivated. "Oh, I know that. I'm confident you'll work it out," he said—for both our benefits, I'm sure. And then he pushed back his chair. "Well, if there's nothing else I can tell you . . ." He was prepared, I could see, to get to his feet.

Actually, there *was* something more he could tell me. The trouble was, I had some qualms about bringing it up. I mean, it was really none of my business. But then giving myself the benefit of the doubt, I decided that I wasn't being nosy at all; I was being professional. What I learned could provide some further insight into the dead woman's character, I informed myself.

Still, I prefaced my question to Kevin with an almost interminable preamble. "I hope you won't mind my asking you this, Kevin, but I think it might help me to understand Luella better. Which could certainly prove of value in determining why anyone would want her to die." And then I quickly interjected, "Naturally, I'm not discarding the theories you've already developed. They seem to me to be very valid. Really perceptive. It's possible, though, that what you have to say would give them additional weight."

Understandably, a puzzled expression had, by now, taken up residence on Kevin's handsome face. And let me assure you that at sixty-five years of age or thereabouts, the man was still handsome. (Which really shouldn't be that big a shocker. I mean, a lot of women found Cary Grant sexy when he was past eighty. Although I, personally, wouldn't go quite that far.)

"I'm not sure if I've made myself clear," I went on. "What I—"

Breaking in, Kevin looked amused. "Why don't you just ask your question, Desiree, *please*." The tone was one of mock despair.

"Well, I was wondering how come—That is, I just can't help wondering why you and Luella divorced . . . uh, considering that you remained such close friends."

Kevin frowned. But it seemed to be more a matter of concentration than anger or even annoyance. His next words confirmed this. "I'm not certain I can explain that to you. There are times when I'm going over it in my mind that I'm not entirely clear about it myself."

"Maybe you could just tell me a little more about what she was like," I suggested, figuring he'd probably work his way around to the divorce anyhow.

"Well, I'm not sure what else you'd like to know. But all right," he agreed, sighing resignedly. "I'll do my best. Now, where to start . . ." He sucked in his cheeks and then absently loosened his tie as he pondered that.

And after a brief interval, he began.

"As you've seen for yourself, Luella was a charming and beautiful woman. The most desirable woman I've ever met. And wonderful, stimulating company. She was a very generous and warmhearted person, too. On the other hand, though—" Kevin stopped abruptly. "God! This is tough. I know you expect me to be completely forthright, and I certainly want to be. But I'm concerned that anything even the least bit critical will sound disloyal. And not so much because you might regard it as such, but because *I* will." And pulling a handkerchief from the pants pocket of his immaculately tailored gray suit, he mopped his brow.

I was ready to tell him to forget I'd ever posed the question. I mean, on second thought, the chances were I wouldn't learn anything, anyway. Not anything meaningful. But I suppose it was seeing the unhappiness on Kevin's face that really prompted this change of heart. However, he was able to continue before my better nature could kick into gear.

"Look Luella wasn't perfect. Like everyone else, she had her faults. In fact," he said, trying for a little levity, "you'll probably dispute this, but I have one or two of those things myself. At any rate, while she possessed a great many terrific qualities, Luella also had some traits that were . . . that were less admirable." He hesitated before going on. "I guess I'd have to say that she was somewhat self-involved. But you already know this. She was strong-willed, too—Luella certainly wasn't one for compromises. And as I've already told you, she had quite a temper. But a good part of that was due to her nerves and the pressure she put on herself."

"Still, she can't have been very easy to live with," I commiserated.

It was a few moments before Kevin responded, and when he did, there was something like wonder in his voice. "It's strange," he murmured. "And I've never considered it until this instant. But I don't really think that what happened between Luella and me—my decision to leave—had as much to do with her shortcomings as with her attributes."

Huh? "I'm afraid you'll have to clarify that for us dummies," I told him.

"Well, you see, I loved being with Luella—a couple of hassles every so often notwithstanding. She had a marvelous, off-beat sense of humor. And you may not have been able to tell from just that one evening with her, but she was extremely knowledgeable, too." And then he said almost guiltily, his face turning redder with every word, "She was also a very sensual, passionate woman." He hurried on. "And she was a bit of an eccentric, as well, which I found delightful. I even enjoyed her nonstop chatter.

"That was the *real* problem, I realize now. The fact that I cared about her as much as I did and that she had so few hours to dole out to me. The longer we lived together, the more stingy she became with her time, too. I suppose that was only natural—the demands of her career coming to the forefront again once she'd settled into the marriage. But at any rate, she would often spend evening after evening holed up in her office. Of course, knowing her history, I should have been prepared for it. I wasn't, though. I felt deprived. I missed talking with her and laughing with her—even just sitting around and doing nothing with her. It got to the point where I had an almost constant ache—when I wasn't angry or disgusted, that is. And in the end I guess I decided it was just too . . . *lonely* being Luella's husband."

And now Kevin said apologetically, "I don't suppose I've been making much sense."

He barely waited for my "Of course you have."

"The truth is that as much as she wanted it to, marriage just didn't fit very well into Luella's schedule."

"Yet you think there was a chance she would have tried it again with Bud Massi?"

"It's entirely possible. Although she denied it even to

herself, she was in love with the man. And given her strict moral code . . ." He shrugged. "Besides, Luella was forever optimistic. She always fooled herself into thinking she could make it work *this* time."

Which reminded me. "Did you know about her other three husbands before you and Luella married?" (I'm afraid I may have emphasized the *three*.)

"Certainly I did." He sounded offended. "Luella was a very truthful person. But just as she thought things would be different with us, I did, too." And here Kevin's eyes began to fill up. "We were both wrong," he murmured.

There was a box of Kleenex on my desk, and I used my elbow to casually inch it in Kevin's direction—just in case.

He smiled—actually, he only managed to turn up one side of his mouth—and mumbled his thanks. After which he availed himself of the Kleenex, pressing a few firmly against his eyes.

I grabbed a bunch of tissues, too, and applied them to my own eyes, which were suddenly overflowing.

It was a minute or two before Kevin was able to rein in his emotions. (And a minute longer for me to get mine under control.) And then he said, "I suppose you want to know how Luella and I could have remained so close after the divorce."

Well, I felt rotten enough about putting him through the wringer like this in the first place. And it didn't appear as though that sort of information could be of help in the investigation, anyhow. "I can understand it. You don't have to explain."

But he had such a distant expression just then that I wouldn't swear he even heard me.

"Once we began living apart, I discovered that I couldn't stand being away from her. And as for Luella, she didn't blame me for leaving her. She said she probably would have done the same thing if the situation had been reversed and I'd neglected *her* like that. So there wasn't any animosity there, you see. And the thing is, we really *mattered* to each other."

"The two of you never considered remarrying?"

"We agreed that it didn't make too much sense. I was less resentful this way, and I doubt if we were together much more as husband and wife than we were as *ex* husband and wife. And that was what was important to me—being with her."

For a brief while, neither of us said anything. And then

Kevin spoke, very softly this time. "There are still moments in the day when I forget that she's gone, Desiree. I've even reached for the phone to dial her number." A pause. "It took me most of my life to find that woman, you know. And now—" He broke off, unable to continue.

Oh, Kevin! Watching him, I almost started bawling all over again. And then a thought struck me. *Suppose Luella had lived to marry Bud Massi? How would Kevin have felt then?*

It was more or less a rhetorical question. (After all, how *could* he feel?) But as he so often did, Kevin seemed to peek into my head. "I never anticipated Luella's falling in love with somebody else," he admitted. "And, incidentally, I don't believe that she was completely happy about it, either—she didn't want to hurt me. Besides, it complicated things for her; it upset the status quo she'd established once I moved out."

And here Kevin cleared his throat, and when he continued his voice had this husky quality it can get when you're trying to keep a lid on your emotions. "For a time," he said quietly, "I thought that the worst thing that could possibly happen to me would be for Luella to marry Bud Massi.

"But now I realize how much worse it is that she can't."

Chapter 26

I've heard people say that every once in a while they like to take in a really sad movie so they can have themselves a good cry. But me, I don't need a movie. Clients can be every bit as useful in the blubbering department. What's more, many a suspect has moved me to tears. And there have even been occasions when a murderer has managed to do the job. (Although that's something I probably shouldn't admit to.)

At any rate, after Kevin left, I used up what remained of my Kleenex supply. I was pretty much cried out, though, when Jackie poked her head in my office. But she did manage to catch the tail end of my last series of sniffles.

"What's wrong?" she demanded.

"It's Kevin, Jackie. He's so . . . so grief-stricken that I feel just awful for him."

"You really can't put yourself through this every time you take on a new case," Jackie admonished. "You're going to burn yourself out."

"I don't react this way with other cases"—I ignored her gratuitous smirk—"but Kevin's not just a client; he's an old friend. Remember?"

"I'm aware of that, but— Hold it a minute." She was now looking at me through narrowed, suspicious eyes. "Listen, you're sure that's what prompted this crying business—and not the rotten creep you were going out with?"

"Bruce? Definitely not. I just *told* you what got me so upset, didn't I?"

"All right. But I hope you're leveling with me. I'd hate to think you were still pining for that miserable lowlife. But listen, the reason I made this trip all the way down the hall is to ask if you're free for lunch."

"Thanks, Jackie, but I think I'm going to order in. I have a lot of notes to transcribe, and then I have a couple of phone calls to take care of."

"Okay. It's a shame, though: it's a beautiful day. And there's a one-third off sale on leather goods at that new little shop over on Thirty-eighth. I figured maybe we could find ourselves a bargain and afterward grab something at that burger place you like so much." She waited just long enough to see if I'd take the carrot. And when she realized that I'd summoned up the willpower to resist, she finished up with "But if you can't, you can't." Her departing glance, however, let me know what she thought of this decision.

Well, no matter. I had work to do.

Now, common sense told me Enid would never have brought her boss into the picture unless she was certain he'd verify her Saturday morning alibi. Still, I'd have felt remiss if I didn't follow through. So after a quick glance at my watch—which notified me that it was twenty to twelve and that the man most likely hadn't gone to lunch yet—I dialed the number Enid had scribbled down for me.

Stephen Endicott, as anticipated, confirmed that Enid had gotten to work at eight-fifteen on the morning of her stepmother's death. He was able to give me the exact time, he said, because he'd just glanced at the clock on his desk, wondering when she would be coming in.

Well, that had been more than two weeks ago, and I was impressed that he'd recall something like looking at his clock. "You have a very good memory," I observed.

"No," Endicott corrected arrogantly, "I have an *excellent* memory."

Well, talk about attitude! Nevertheless, my thank you was almost saccharine. But I couldn't keep myself from slamming down the phone—just a little.

Okay. I'd established that Enid had been at her office on the morning of her stepmother's death. (I didn't bother checking this out with Endicott's secretary, too; I was already positive she'd provide further corroboration.) Of course, the downside to verifying an alibi in this case was that I had no way of knowing whether or not it would turn out to have any significance. I mean, a slow-acting poison, and it wouldn't be worth beans.

But as you're already aware, I'm not one to complain.

I went on to the other person on my agenda now: Andy Hough. And talked to the answering machine. I told it I'd like to set up an appointment with Andy and requested he get back to me, leaving both my office and home numbers.

The third time I spoke into the phone—which was all of ten seconds later—I ordered lunch.

While I was waiting for delivery, I began typing up my notes on the meetings I'd had with both Connie and Kevin. Connie was first. I was only about a quarter finished with her, though, when my food arrived—a turkey and brie with honey-mustard dressing.

And that was as much as I accomplished that day—notes-wise, I mean. Because just as I swallowed the last bite of my sandwich, Elliot Gilbert—you know, of Gilbert and Sullivan—rapped on my door.

"Can you spare me a couple of minutes?" he asked in this polite, soft-spoken way he has.

"Sure. C'mon in."

Taking the two or three steps required to get to the chair next to my desk (which, in the closet of an office I occupy, is all the way across the room), he perched on the edge of the seat. "I hope you're not too busy for a small assignment," he said. "I don't think it should require much of your time, and I would be very grateful if you could fit it into your schedule."

Now wasn't that just like Elliot! I mean, here he was, giving *me* work and making it sound like I'd be doing *him* a favor by accepting it.

"I suppose I can make some space for it on my crowded calendar," I responded, grinning. "What's it about?"

"A hit-and-run." For a moment, a cloud seemed to cross Elliot's round, pleasant face. "The woman was seriously injured, too. Although, thank God, she appears to have made a complete recovery. But at any rate, there was a witness at the scene, and he managed to get the license number of the vehicle. It was traced to a nineteen-year-old boy—who is now my client. But Rob swears he didn't use the car that day, that he lent it to a friend."

"Who, I gather, denies this?"

Elliot nodded. "And he has an alibi. A young lady. The accident occurred in Queens one night last year, at about six-thirty p.m. This friend—a fellow named Shorty Meister—claims he took the subway into Manhattan to visit his girlfriend that evening. According to Meister's statement, he got there at six o'clock and didn't leave until the following morning. And the girl's given a statement confirming his story."

"And you want me to—?"

"Talk to the girlfriend."

"All right."

Elliot leaned forward now, his expression reflecting the tension he was feeling. "Look, Desiree. I've known Rob Dimitri since he was seven years old. The family used to live next door to us in Ozone Park—they still live there. And you've never met a nicer family—a nicer *kid*. I can't conceive of that boy leaving a woman to possibly bleed to death in the street like that. But even if Rob did panic and drive off—and I would have a very big problem believing that—he certainly wouldn't implicate a friend. So see what you can find out. Okay?" And he slid a small piece of paper across the desk.

"Okay." I picked up the paper. "Is this the girl's work number?"

Elliot shook his head. "She doesn't work. She has young children to look after. Uh, listen, I just took over the case. A nephew of Wally's—that's Rob's father—had been handling it. But, well, rightly or wrongly, Wally was convinced the nephew had been giving it short shrift. Anyhow, we go to trial in less than a month, so, uh, I was wondering how soon—"

"I'll call her right away," I said. To Elliot's very obvious relief.

Chapter 27

Shanna Vincent—alibi of Shorty Meister—lived all the way uptown. Just a couple of blocks from the Bronx, in fact. It is not a neighborhood I would like to wander around in after the sun goes down. But, fortunately, the girl had been willing to see me right away.

Although hardly more than a baby herself, Shanna was the harassed mother of a couple of very active little boys: one two years old, the other not yet three. It wore me out just to watch them keep running back and forth across the tiny living room—when they weren't jumping all over the furniture, that is.

Anyway, I had prepared this whole long spiel about how not telling the truth could ruin the life of a very fine young man and about how important it is to set the right kind of example for your children, et cetera and et cetera. But Shanna preempted me as soon as the words "About that accident" came out of my mouth. She wanted to change her story.

It bothered her conscience, she said, that she'd told the police Shorty was here that night. The only reason she had agreed to lie for him in the first place was because he was her baby's father (the two-year-old baby's, that is). But now she found that she couldn't go through with it, after all. She came from a decent and religious home, she let me know. And her mother had raised her to be truthful.

My praise of Shanna's admirable character—and that of her mother, too, while I was at it—must have lasted a good two or three minutes, and all the while Shanna sat there preening, a smile stretching almost to her earlobes.

It wasn't until I was getting into my coat that I learned the *real* reason Shorty was about to bite the dust.

"I have to leave in about a half hour myself. As soon as my sister shows up to watch the kids," Shanna began offhandedly. "I'm meeting my boyfriend for supper tonight—

my *new* boyfriend." And then almost, but not quite suppressing her excitement: "I think he may be moving in soon."

Well, who cared about the girl's motive, anyway? I can't tell you how exhilarating it was just to have an assignment turn out so positively. To say nothing of being able to wind it up one-two-three like this.

I could hardly wait to talk to Elliot. But don't think spreading the good news was that easy. First, I had to find a working pay phone. I finally lucked out four blocks away from Shanna's. On my sixth try.

Elliot was extremely relieved when I filled him in. He thanked me warmly, then complimented me effusively on my ability and persuasive skills. He even threw in my all-around goodness. None of which had anything at all to do with the outcome of my meeting with Shanna. But for a minute there I felt just like Kathie Lee Gifford.

The stores were impossible that night. But I'd barely made a dent in my shopping list so far, and this was already the first day of Hanukkah, with Christmas only a week away.

I found a couple of really beautiful scarves—one for my sister-in-law Margot (Ellen's mother) and the other for Jackie. Ellen's father would be getting a pale yellow cotton sweater this year—perfect, I thought, for those balmy Florida evenings. And I bought a book—a biography—for my neighbor Barbara.

That was it, though. Between running around for two and a half hours and dealing with three different stores' worth of desperate holiday shoppers and all of that weighty decision-making, I wasn't worth a damn anymore. Besides, I'd accomplished a lot more than I normally do in that amount of time. So I treated myself to a nice supper at Lord & Taylor's and then headed for home.

It was a few minutes to ten when I walked in, and my answering machine was winking at me. There was one message.

"Hello, Desiree," the voice said. "This is Andy Hough. You wanted to get together. How's tomorrow morning at nine? Geena told me you had some trouble with our stairs—a lot of people do—so why don't we meet at the coffee shop around the corner from my apartment." He gave me the address. "You don't have to call if you're okay with that. But let me know if you have a problem."

Well, there was no need to get back to him. Those arrangements suited me fine.

In fact, at that moment I was probably in the best mood I'd been in for days. Shanna Vincent had recanted her statement. Plus I'd crossed four more names off my gift list. And now Andy Hough had readily agreed to see me—something you can never really be sure of—and had set up a meeting for the very next morning, too.

But my mood was soon to change.

The telephone rang when I was in the bedroom, about to step out of my dress.

"It's all right, I forgive you" was the cheerful response to my hello. There was even a low chuckle that went along with that.

My throat tightened. And the hand holding the phone began to tremble so badly that I had to call on the other hand to support it. I had every intention of hanging up—but then I didn't.

"What is it, Bruce? What do you want?" I got out, hoping my voice didn't sound as shaky as I was sure it must.

"Oops! I see that humor wasn't the way to go here." Abruptly his tone turned sober. "I don't blame you for being angry, Dez. I behaved kind of stupidly last week. My only excuse—and it's a piss-poor one—is that I thought you'd be pleased about the theater tickets, and I was disappointed when you didn't jump up and down. Besides, I was anxious to see you; I missed you—a lot. But I realize now that I handled the ticket thing badly from the beginning, and I apologize. I promise you, nothing like that will happen again."

"You're right, Bruce. It won't." And then slowly, carefully, I put the receiver back in its cradle.

After which I had my third cry of the day.

I'm not sure how long I lay sprawled across my bed, the tears seemingly endless, as my thoughts bounced back and forth between pride and uncertainty.

I'd done the right thing. And it was very satisfying to me that I'd had the guts to do it, too.

But then again, Bruce did sound genuinely contrite. Maybe things *would have* improved if I'd been willing to give him another chance.

Do you actually believe that? I demanded of myself disgustedly.

Well, I guess not. But who can be absolutely sure?
Honestly. You should know better after all these months.
People do change, though. . . .
And on and on it went.

Finally, after close to an hour, the tears and the angst and the second-guessing had exhausted me enough so that I abandoned all three.

I finished undressing and climbed into a warm, comforting bubble bath, clutching the new courtroom mystery I'd picked up the other day. I soaked and read for the longest time, while first all of the fragrant bubbles disappeared. And a little later my eyelids started to droop. And at last the print began to skitter around on the page.

Then I went to bed. And immediately dropped off to sleep.

Chapter 28

It had to be the world's tiniest coffee shop. A single stool, presently empty, stood in front of the counter—which was probably less than four feet long. And while all of the tables were occupied, there were only three of them in the place. With Andy Hough and me sipping coffee and munching donuts at one of them. Even seated, Andy's hulky presence seemed to further shrink the miniature eatery.

He'd just verified that on the day Luella died he had been closed up in his studio—at the back of his apartment—from about seven-thirty a.m. until almost one. Which meant Geena could have left at any time that morning without his knowledge. Conversely, when Geena was in the kitchen or the bathroom, Andy had had the opportunity to sneak out himself. All he needed to do was shut the door to the studio, and his wife wouldn't even realize he was gone.

"I can't vouch for Geena's whereabouts, and she can't vouch for mine," Andy said now. "But then, why would either of us require an alibi? I don't see how anyone can claim Luella was murdered. There's nothing whatsoever that would indicate a thing like that. Not as far as I know, anyway."

"Not as far as I know, either," I conceded.

"And I doubt there ever will be."

"Listen, Andy, I'm not saying you're wrong, but—"

"Believe me, Geena and her sisters were on very good terms with their stepmother. Nobody wanted her dead—and Geena, least of all. To her, Luella was like flesh and blood. I think there were times Geena even forgot that Luella wasn't her natural mother. And what could her motive have possibly been?"

Now, I didn't see questioning the girl's affection for the deceased—à la Kevin—as being at all productive here. So I restricted my theorizing to recent developments. "Well," I said carefully, "the motive *could have been* money. Luella was planning to put some of it into Bud Massi's company, wasn't she? Maybe even a lot of it. And if the business failed—as so many do—that would have cut back on Geena's inheritance."

"My wife couldn't have cared less about Luella's money. We were managing okay. More important, Geena's always been confident that eventually I'll be able to support us very nicely with my painting. But setting those things aside, even if Luella had sunk a bundle into that company, she'd have had a bundle left over, I assure you."

"But what if she'd lived to marry Massi? Under those circumstances, it's conceivable she would have changed her will and made him her sole heir."

"I don't know if anyone's told you this, Desiree, but as soon as Geena and I got married, Luella offered to help us out financially. And Connie's offered, too. But we always refused to accept anything from either of them. So why would Geena have suddenly become that greedy now?"

"It's possible—and I'm merely speculating—" I was quick to assure Andy, "that she didn't feel it was worth humbling herself for a few thousand. But a few million is something else again."

The sound coming from Andy's throat could, I guess, best be described as a guffaw.

"Or maybe success has been slower in coming to you than Geena originally anticipated." And before he could counter this: "Also . . . umm . . . I don't know quite how to phrase this tactfully, but Geena's not accepting help from Luella might have had something to do with how she—Luella, that is—felt about you. You're aware, I suppose, that your mother-in-law—your stepmother-in-law, to be accurate—wasn't too fond of you."

Andy's expression was impassive. "Of course I'm aware of it."

"You have no idea why that was?"

"None at all. And neither did Luella herself. She admitted as much to Geena. But tell me, why would Luella's dislike for me have precluded Geena's accepting the money?"

"Could be your wife was concerned that your being willing to let her do that would only reinforce Luella's negative opinion of you."

Making one of those I-can't-believe-I'm-hearing-this-junk kind of faces, Andy rolled his eyes heavenward. A moment later he said, "I imagine all of this speculating you're doing as to Geena's motive would apply to me as well.

"Yes, I suppose it would."

"Maybe even more than to Geena, right? Considering that there were certainly no warm fuzzies between Luella and me."

I couldn't say the point he was making had never occurred to me. "That's true, too. It must have been difficult for you to even be in Luella's company. And I understand you had to see her frequently."

"Do you want to know something? I was usually able to put Luella's prejudice against me out of my mind. That's something I did for Geena's sake. But it really wasn't as hard as you might think. Luella was always polite enough to me. Actually, if I hadn't known how she felt, I probably wouldn't have *known* how she felt. If you take my meaning." And he grinned. "Besides, I've always gotten along just fine with Geena's sisters and with Connie—I'm very fond of all of them—and for the most part, I'd spend my time at our family get-togethers talking to them."

"Still, you couldn't have been too kindly disposed toward the woman."

"I wasn't. But, believe it or not, I didn't hate her, either. And incidentally, there's something I should probably clear up for you. It wasn't Geena who made the decision not to take advantage of her stepmother's largesse. Geena left it up to me; I was the one who turned thumbs down."

"Geena wanted to accept Luella's help?"

"On the contrary, she was very pleased that I took the position I did. And, of course—and this is something you should keep in mind—if Geena had been that anxious to get her hands on the money, she wouldn't even have consulted me. She would have said yes to Luella herself. Okay, maybe I wouldn't have been too thrilled about that, but Geena knows me well enough to realize I wouldn't have kicked up too much of a fuss, either. After all, I couldn't deny that the money would have made life a little easier for her."

"Umm, just one more question," I murmured as our coffee cups were being refilled by the elderly waitress. "Did you have a key to Luella's house?"

"No, certainly not." For the first time, Andy was plainly irritated. (Most likely I'd just applied that final straw to the camel's back.)

Nevertheless, having broached the subject, I couldn't merely leave it at that. "But you're aware, aren't you," I put to him rhetorically, "that your wife had one?"

"That's two questions," he snapped.

"Well, uh, they're tied together. So it's really more like one and a half."

The plaintive note in my voice and the guilty little smile on my face combined to more or less break the tension. "You're a pistol, you know that?" Andy responded with a grudging laugh. "But I think I'll keep you honest by not answering your extra half a question." Then he purposefully set his cup down in its saucer. "Listen, I do have to get some work done this morning."

And he signaled for the check.

During the cab ride over to my office, I thought about that business with the key. Why on earth had I brought up something like that? What difference did it make whether Andy had a key of his own to the town house? As long as Geena had one (and according to Connie, all the girls did), Andy would have had access to the place. He could have borrowed his wife's key at any time—with or without her knowledge—and had a duplicate made. Or he could even have slipped the key off her key ring the morning of Luella's death.

What I'm saying is that while there are instances where in attempting to get at the facts you have no choice but to rile someone up, this very definitely had not been one of them.

Still, Andy's antagonism toward me had been pretty short-lived. Actually, he seemed to me to be a very amiable man. So what was it about him that could possibly have affected the dead woman so adversely, I wondered.

Almost immediately, though, I realized what a boob I had to be to think I might come up with the answer that had eluded Luella herself. I mean, who said your feelings have to be based on reason, anyway?

And suddenly an old poem that I'd learned all the way back in grammar school popped into my head:

> I do not love thee, Doctor Fell,
> The reason why I cannot tell;
> But this alone I know full well,
> I do not love thee, Doctor Fell.

Chapter 29

It was my second lunch-at-the-desk day in a row.

As soon as I arrived at work, I began to diligently transcribe the rest of my notes on that visit with Connie. The only time I allowed myself even a short break being for some much-needed sustenance. Which, by the way, was nicely supplied by a cheeseburger and an order of really crispy fries.

Once I'd disposed of Connie (so to speak), I moved on to Kevin. It took me a long while to polish off my old friend. Frequently, I found myself so moved by his words that it tended to slow me down. (However, since my Kleenex supply had not yet been replenished, it was fortunate I had the self-control to hold back on the tears, at any rate.)

There was also something else that reduced my progress to tortoise speed. When I was close to wrapping things up, I started to ruminate on whether Luella and Kevin had been sleeping together after the divorce. Prior to her involvement with Massi, that is. I finally decided that the woman's strict moral code hadn't applied to ex-husbands. I mean, it was impossible to imagine Kevin's being that satisfied with the status quo unless there'd been at least an occasional locking of limbs. But, of course, it was doubtful I'd ever find out for certain.

Now, if you're trying to figure out what this could possibly have to do with the investigation, the answer is nothing at all. The only thing it did have to do with was my being nosy as hell. Thanks to going off on tangents like that, though, I didn't finish typing up my notes until well after six.

As I was getting ready to leave for home, I realized with both surprise and satisfaction that not once during this entire long afternoon had I devoted even five straight minutes to Bruce. (Although I admit that every so often there *was* a stray minute or two when I succumbed.)

Anyway, right after I'd retrieved my coat from its hanger

on the back of the door, I got this really strange visit from Jackie.

"Dez?" She was standing hesitantly outside my office.

"You still here, Jackie?" I asked intelligently.

"I had to type up a brief for Pat. And, uh, I just wanted to say good night."

Well, Jackie has never, that I can recall, "just wanted to say good night." So I was puzzled, maybe even a little suspicious. "What's up?"

"Nothing. I was wondering if there was anything new, that's all."

Here we go again. I was practically programmed with that damn explanation. "Not so far. Of course, we're still waiting for the autopsy report to—"

"I'm not talking about your case. I'm talking *personally.*"

Taken aback for a second, I was barely able to manage an "Oh." And then since I definitely did not want to get into a discussion about Bruce's phone call right now, I quickly followed up with a question of my own. "Could you tell me, please, what sort of thing you're referring to?"

"If I knew, I wouldn't be asking. But I guess it's been pretty quiet lately, huh?" Jackie's cheeks were actually flushed at this point, and I noted that she was averting her eyes. Which made me very curious as to what, specifically, was on her mind.

Before I could get out another syllable, however, she turned around, threw me a hasty over-the-shoulder, "Well, see you tomorrow," and was gone.

The minute I left work I realized that I was in no mood to cook. Let someone else hang over the stove tonight; it had been a tiring day. In the face of a really nasty wind, I trudged downtown to this little pasta place five blocks from the office (there wasn't a single unoccupied cab in sight)—only to be greeted by a sign saying, CLOSED FOR RENOVATIONS. Which, of course, is more often that not a euphemism for GONE OUT OF BUSINESS. Anyway, I didn't feel like letting the wind have its way with me any longer. Rather than continue to get my cheeks lashed and my hair whipped into a frenzy while I hunted around for an alternative to Pasta & More Pasta, I decided to fix myself something simple at home.

A short time later, after a survey of my kitchen, I determined that I had but one option tonight: a refrigerator omelet—so named because it contains virtually every scrap that's in your refrigerator at the moment. I began to gather all the available ingredients: ham, peas, shallots, green pepper, tomato, cheddar cheese . . . I'd just uncovered a forgotten sliver of salami—which, luckily, had not yet turned green—when the phone rang.

Now, just then the entire upper half of me was buried deep inside the refrigerator. And in my haste to extricate myself, I banged my head on the water pitcher and then decorated the floor with peas.

But the instant I heard Bruce's hello, which seemed to be almost tentative this time, I forgot about my sore crown. Dry mouth had set in.

"Don't hang up," he instructed at once.

I didn't.

"Listen for a minute, okay?" And then without waiting for a response, he hurried on. "I made a mistake. I admit that. But haven't you ever made one yourself?"

"Look, Bruce, this isn't only about last week. It's about everything."

"You're right. I've been pretty insensitive all along. But things will be entirely different from now on. Honestly."

"Why?"

"What do you mean, 'why'?"

"I mean why *would* they be any different?"

"Because I care about you. And I want us to keep on seeing each other. And you've made it clear that for that to happen I'm going to have to do some reforming."

"Maybe your intentions are good, Bruce, but I have my doubts as to whether you're even capable of changing."

"Give me a chance, and let me prove it to you." And then when I was still trying to figure out what to say to this, he had a reminder for me. "Hey, it's the Christmas season. *Goodwill toward men.* Remember? Look, I'm going home to Chicago on Friday to spend the holidays with my family, but I was hoping I could convince you to have dinner with me before I leave."

Bruce went on talking—he mentioned Christmas again, I think—but my brain was in a jumble and working furiously to unscramble itself.

He sounds sincere. And maybe he is—at the moment, anyway.

But then again, maybe not.

Of course, he wouldn't have called this second time if he hadn't been really anxious to see me, would he?

Okay, this is true. But what does it prove? For all I know, I'm nothing more than a once-in-a-while diversion he wants to keep around a little longer. There's is a good chance he'll be reverting to type again as soon as he thinks he can get away with it.

". . . tonight," he wound up.

Now, although I hadn't taken in the first part of this, I thought it safe to assume that Bruce had just asked me out for that evening. (That one word in combination with his past record being pretty much a dead giveaway.)

"I'm sorry, but I already have plans," I responded. Even if I *was* inclined to take up with the man again—which was still a big "if"—I had no intention of making things that easy for him.

Suspecting me of this, he chuckled softly. "I can't say that I blame you. How would tomorrow night be?"

"I'm busy then, too." I hadn't even realized this would be my answer, and I was already thinking that perhaps I'd been hasty.

There was no laughter now. In a quiet, even tone, Bruce informed me, "I'll give it one more try. And if you're still unavailable, I'll assume that you have no interest in seeing me again." I had to wait a couple of seconds for this final invitation. "Are you free Thursday night?"

"Umm . . . yes."

To this day, I'm not certain whether that answer was prompted by my actually hoping things would be better this go-around or because I felt it was the only way I could achieve any closure. I mean, as you know, as disgusted as I was with Bruce at the time he called it quits between us, I hadn't quite reached the point where I was disgusted enough to pull the plug on the relationship.

And I'd just discovered that this was still the case.

So I really had no choice but to go out with him at least one more time, don't you see?

Chapter 30

You wouldn't believe the butterflies I had on Wednesday. Or maybe you would.

I couldn't have been in the office for more than five minutes when I thought about running right over to Woman of Substance to see if I could pick up something special for Thursday night. And then I was immediately furious with myself for even considering it. After all, it was yet to be seen whether Bruce would show himself worthy of my springing for yet another new dress on his account—even if it should happen to be on sale. The one small concession I did permit myself to make for the DATE (in my mind, it had evolved into a capital letter thing) was a beauty parlor appointment. I would be getting my glorious hennaed hair coaxed—or hammered—into obedience tomorrow at noon.

Now, since I only had one case to occupy me at present and since there really wasn't anything more I could do on it until the medical examiner's report was released, I was very much afraid I'd be at the mercy of my nerves all day. So just to keep from becoming certifiable, I picked up the file on Luella Pressman and went through it again. But I was in no state to absorb too much of what I read.

Jackie popped into my office at about eleven-thirty. "Free for lunch later?" she inquired.

It was the first time I'd had any contact with her this morning—she hadn't been at her desk when I got in—and I was still wondering about her little visit last night.

"I've got some errands to run at lunchtime," I answered, having that instant overruled my ban on shopping for tomorrow evening to allow for one small purchase: a pair of earrings. Seconds later I even managed to convince myself that I was really in dire need of a new pair, Bruce or no Bruce.

"So . . . umm . . . nothing much has been happening lately, right?" Jackie said then.

"What *is* all this about, Jackie?"

She was Ms. Injured Innocence. "My God, all I meant is that you're not working on anything but this one case at the moment—true or false? And *that's* in limbo." She inclined her head to indicate the single folder on my desk, which was now lying in the far corner, closed.

I actually apologized—for which I would eventually have reason to kick myself all the way to New Jersey. "Sorry, Jackie. But yesterday you were acting kind of"—just in time, I stopped myself from saying "peculiar"—"uh, not like yourself."

She drew herself up to her full five-seven or whatever height. "I haven't got a clue what you're talking about. All I did was poke my head in to say good night."

Well, although this in itself was definitely unusual for her, I was, of course, referring to more than that. Mostly, it was her manner. But in retrospect, maybe it hadn't really been that odd. Maybe I'd just exaggerated things in my mind. And so, like a jerk, I produced another "I'm sorry." And following a short but suspenseful pause, Jackie condescended to accept the apology.

"Forget it, " she grumbled with no grace whatsoever.

I could hardly wait to indulge my earring weakness. So right after Jackie left, I headed for this little jewelry shop on Third Avenue that had only recently moved into the neighborhood. When I passed there last week, they'd had some things in the windows that I all but salivated over. And I knew then that it was only a matter of time before I succumbed.

An hour later I was back in my office, admiring the two pairs of earrings I'd just acquired—one of which I could almost afford.

How much admiring can you do, though?

With nothing else to occupy me, I was ready to call it quits for the day at a little after two. I notified Jackie of my intention. "I think I'm going to cut out now and go see a movie," I told her. "I can't stand just sitting around and staring at all the scratches and water rings on my desk anymore. I could really use a little diversion."

For once, she didn't even question the truth of my explanation. "You can say that again," she agreed in an undertone.

* * *

I went to the Thirty-fourth Street East, which is right near my office. *Il Postino (The Postman)* was playing. Now, If you had happened to come across me leaving the theater that afternoon, you'd have gotten some idea of the extent to which I loved that movie. I mean, I just couldn't seem to stop my eyes from leaking.

And I was still making good use of what was left of a brand-new packet of tissues when I walked around the corner to Mumbles. Where I submerged my grief in a cheese steak sandwich, a glass of wine, and—why not?—a very generous slice of pecan pie.

Ellen called that evening. Mike would be working on Christmas Eve, she informed me. "If you haven't got other plans, why don't you come over for dinner?"

I presented her with a counteroffer. "Why don't *you* come here? I have some gorgeous steaks in the freezer."

"Sold," she responded, giggling. "Although they'll probably never speak to me again over at Mandarin Joy."

"Sure they will. They'd probably be bankrupt without you." But I said it absently, since at that moment I found myself wondering if I should tell Ellen I was going out with Bruce tomorrow. I hadn't intended to; I figured I'd let her know all about it on Friday. Still, in a way, I was anxious to confide in her. And as long as she was right here, on the phone . . .

But the decision quickly became a moot point. "Ooh, there's my bell!" she exclaimed just then. "It's dinner, thank goodness—I'm famished. Bye, talk to you soon."

And I was left holding a dead receiver.

I didn't sleep too well that night. I finally dropped off sometime after four—and who knows *how much* after. At any rate, I was seriously thinking about skipping work on Thursday. But then I reminded myself that my hairdresser is only a couple of blocks from the office. So since I'd be right in the vicinity anyway, I might as well go in and stare at my desk scratches some more.

It was a little past ten when I arrived. Jackie handed me a pink message slip as soon as I walked in the door. "She sounded like it was urgent."

She? I glanced at the message. It read: "Pat Martucci. Says to call her immediately." There was a double underline to emphasize the word "immediately."

Uh-oh.

As with Ellen, I hadn't planned on saying anything to Pat about Bruce until the deed was done. Apparently, she'd heard about it from *his* side, though. And she was undoubtedly having very unkind thoughts about me again—which she was all too eager to share. Unless, of course, it was coincidental that she was so intent on reaching me today. Not being big on coincidences, however, I wasn't counting on that.

I had started back to my office when Jackie called out. "Dez!" I turned around.

"It's Pat Martucci again; I put her on hold."

That got me to accelerate my pace. I mean, leaving Pat dangling on the phone was definitely not going to make it any easier for me to smooth out what must be some extremely ruffled feathers.

"Hi, Pat," I murmured timidly when I picked up. (Sometimes I really can't stand myself for being the easily intimidated creature that I am.)

"Oh, Desiree, I'm so glad you're in," said this soft, anxious voice. It was a voice I hadn't expected.

"Pat?"

"I feel so terrible, Dez," she moaned.

"About what?" I held my breath. I certainly hoped there was nothing wrong between Pat and Burton. She'd been so happy since he came into her life.

"Look, I swear I knew nothing about this. Burton never said a word to me. Not one word. He didn't feel right about betraying a confidence. Although in this case it would certainly have been justified, and I told him so."

It seemed that things were okay between Pat and Bruce's (relatively) normal cousin, at least. But a chill had gone up my spine at this mention of betraying a confidence.

"I would have called you last night," she went on, "but do you know when Burton finally worked up to spilling the beans? It was almost one-thirty in the morning."

"Spilling the beans about what, Pat?" I asked. I thought I sounded surprisingly calm, considering that every nerve in my body was now on red alert.

"Well," she said gently, "it's about Bruce. . . ."

Chapter 31

A few seconds went by before Pat fed me a little more. "He hasn't been leveling with you." And after an even longer interval: "Bruce is . . . well . . . uh . . . the bastard's engaged."

"You're kidding!"

"Oh, Dez, I wish I were."

"When did this happen?"

"Months ago. Right before that rotten, lying piece of garbage moved up from Chicago."

"The woman's from Chicago?"

"Yes. But she's a flight attendant, and she usually manages to get to New York a few times a month."

I must have been in shock. All I know is that I wasn't angry. I wasn't even really upset. Mostly, I was curious. "When's the wedding? Or haven't they set a date yet?"

"They'll probably get married in the spring. I am so-o-o sorry, Dez. I could kill Burton for going along with this. I wouldn't even talk to him this morning. And the way I feel right now, I may never talk to him again."

Well, if you want the truth, I wasn't overly pleased with the light of her life myself. Still, I didn't want to be the cause of any friction there. "You shouldn't blame Burton," I put in almost reluctantly.

"As far as I'm concerned, he's no innocent, either," Pat countered. "Although he did try to talk Bruce out of stringing you along like that. But Bruce wouldn't listen. He actually justified the whole thing with this nonsense about how, after all, it wasn't hurting anyone if the two of you went out every so often. In fact, he was showing you a good time, taking you to nice places, he told Burton. He wanted Burton to swear on his mother's grave—can you believe it?—that he wouldn't say anything to me."

"Why did Burton suddenly confess all now?"

"When he heard that you and Bruce had had that argument

last week and it looked as if you wouldn't be seeing each other anymore, Burton was very relieved. His conscience had been bothering him all along, he said, and he figured he was finally off the hook. Besides, he was getting really nervous about what would happen when I found out about Cheryl—that's the fiancée. And, of course, I was bound to learn about her sooner or later—probably sooner since Burton is supposed to be best man at that stupid wedding. But anyway, after Bruce went ahead and started things up with you all over again the other night, well, Burton had just had it by then, that's all."

I was still feeling fogbound. Completely out of it. This man I'd cared so much about (maybe even obsessed over), this man I'd laughed with and fought with and—in spite of all my reservations—slept with was, I told myself dispassionately, a total stranger. Someone I didn't know at all.

I shook my head slowly in a futile attempt to clear it.

Later, the numbness—the disbelief—would wear off, I realized, and I'd no doubt be rabid. But just then . . .

"Are you okay, Dez?" Pat asked anxiously.

"I'm stunned, of course. But otherwise, I'm okay."

"Please don't be too angry with Burton. Believe me, I could kill him right now myself, and I'm certainly not making excuses for what he did—or I should say, *didn't do*." She went on at a faster clip here, as though afraid I might interrupt. "But on the other hand, he *was* between a rock and a hard place, I suppose, considering how close he and Bruce are—the two of them grew up together. Honestly, in spite of how it must seem to you now, basically Burton's a really good person." And then she added plaintively, "It's important to me that you like him, Dez, so I hope that you'll be able to, well, get past this."

"Don't worry, Pat. I don't hold Burton responsible," I assured her. "Just see that you're not too tough on him yourself. After all, he did finally come clean."

And then I added silently, *Months and months too late.*

Chapter 32

Maybe five minutes after our conversation ended, I came to the conclusion that I had to speak to Pat again. I got her on the phone.

"Do you think Burton will say anything to Bruce?" I asked. "About having broken his word to him, that is."

"I'm sure he will. He'd feel obliged to let him know what he can expect as far as tonight goes."

"He might already have gotten in touch with him, then."

"Oh, no. I imagine Burton would want to own up to his crime in person. And besides, he's probably been too busy to deal with something like that; he has a very hectic schedule this morning. If I know my Burton, he's planning to lay it on him over lunch."

"Okay. Do me a favor, will you?"

"Name it."

"Ask Burton not to tell Bruce he's spoken to you about this. Not today, anyway. Do you think he would go along with that?"

"Maybe reluctantly, but he'll do it. Listen, before I left the apartment this morning I had him feeling so guilty he was ready to put on sackcloth and ashes. So don't worry about it. Uh, is it okay if I ask what's on your mind, though?"

"It's just that I want to take care of this my way, Pat. And I don't want Bruce to be forewarned."

"I understand. Any idea what you'll say to the little shit?"

"I haven't thought it through yet."

"You're not still planning to go out with him, though, are you?"

"I'm not even sure about that."

"Oh." Pat was obviously surprised. "Well, however you handle it, I just hope you let him have it with both barrels. Although there's no way he'll be getting what he really deserves."

Amen to that.

* * *

Bruce was supposed to be picking me up at seven-thirty. I started to prepare for the date at just past five.

Still in my numb mode, I took a half-hour-long bath, splashed on the Ivoire, and in the absence of my usual nerves, probably did the best makeup job of my life. Then I put on my most flattering dress—the celadon green A-line. After which, just from force of habit, I spent a few minutes patting my coif here and there, which actually hadn't required a thing, since Emaline—my hairdresser—had at last, after six years, exhibited the "golden hands" she always claimed to have been born with. Finally I embellished my attire with Ellen and Mike's silver cuff bracelet and the overpriced—but definitely *me*—silver disk earrings I'd acquired yesterday.

Checking myself out in the full-length mirror a little later, I smiled. I was satisfied with the image smiling back at me. No, I was more than satisfied; I was actually very pleased. I mean, almost inevitably, when it's important to you to look really special, something goes wrong, and you wind up cursing the fates or your hairdresser or the woman who sold you your dress. Not tonight, though. In my own eyes, I had suddenly turned into the short, full-figured, henna-haired version of Heather Locklear. Of course, it's also possible I'd become slightly delusional.

At five minutes of seven I sat down on the sofa to wait for Bruce, a glass of wine in hand. The wine being a backup in case the numbness should start to wear off.

I'd downed about half a glass of Beaujolais when the intercom buzzed. I buzzed back. It was ten after seven.

Bruce had arrived ahead of time, of course. As usual. Which is something else—in addition to his other, more obvious shortcomings, I mean—that had bugged me about the man. I could always count on his showing up when I wasn't quite dressed. And then in my hurry to get ready, I was almost certain to smear my mascara or put my foot through my panty hose or create some other small-scale disaster, which I would then have to deal with and which would set me back at least ten minutes more.

The apartment bell rang now, and I didn't so much pull open the door as fling it open, a welcome grin fixed on my face.

I disappeared the grin as soon as I set eyes on Bruce standing there in the hall. He was looking very dapper, by the way, in a charcoal-gray double-breasted coat. In spite of his lack of stature, he does wear clothes nicely. I'll give him that.

"Bruce?" I said to him, astonishment in my voice. "What are *you* doing here?"

"Cut it out, Shapiro," he chided, laughing.

"I don't understand. What are you doing here?" I asked again, reaching for the knob and drawing the door a few inches closer to me.

"Never mind the games." He was still laughing, but not quite as heartily. "Aren't you going to let me come in?"

I continued to block his entrance. "Oh, God, this is so embarrassing," I murmured. I could even feel myself blushing. (Listen, it's not for nothing that back in high school I was second runner-up for the part of Emily in *Our Town*.)

"What's going on, anyway?" he demanded, a full-scale scowl on his face at this point.

"You're a week early; our date was for *next* Thursday," I explained patiently, as if speaking to someone lacking a crucial few of his marbles.

"You're crazy! I won't even be in town then. I told you I was going to Chicago for the holidays." He glanced up and down the hall. "But look, can't we discuss this inside?"

"Umm, I don't think so," I responded apologetically, closing the door another couple of inches. "I have another d— I have other plans. Someone should be picking me up any minute, in fact. I'm really awfully sorry about this, Bruce, but I did say I was busy tonight. Don't you remember?"

"Like hell you did!" And then his expression changed. "Wait," he said, eyeing me suspiciously. "This wouldn't be your way of paying me back because we had that disagreement last week, would it?"

"Certainly not! How can you even think that?" I snapped, reproving him in my best how-dare-you tone. The door, meanwhile, had just closed a little more.

And here my downstairs buzzer sounded. (My neighbor Harriet, bless her, had done her part.) I knew Bruce couldn't help but hear it clearly. That thing is so piercing that I'm certain it will someday gift me with a coronary.

I glanced over my shoulder. "I have to get that," I said. "Look, it's unfortunate we had some kind of miscommunication, but I'm afraid there just isn't anything I can do about it." And with this, I shut the door completely—but not before catching a glimpse of the anger and disbelief on Bruce Simon's face.

Naturally, I knew that tomorrow—or maybe even later this evening—Bruce would be apprised of the fact his engagement was no longer a secret. And the truth about tonight would then become apparent to him.

But that was okay. For a few minutes, at least—and for the first time in our relationship—*I* had been the one pulling the strings.

Chapter 33

I wouldn't be surprised if I actually fell asleep with a smile on my face that night.

But I was definitely sans smile when I woke up at just past four. I'd finally broken through the anesthetized state I'd been in. And as predicted, I went ballistic.

That lying, low-life scum! That ferret-faced weasel! (It made no difference that the man bore no resemblance to a ferret at all.) *That conscienceless creep! That human compost heap!* And I'm just repeating the more complimentary stuff here, too.

I must have raged and cursed for a good ten minutes. Sometimes even aloud. Being me, I didn't completely spare myself, either. After all, I'd come off as a pretty pathetic judge of character, hadn't I? And look how long I'd allowed the whole sorry affair to drag on. But for once, the major portion of my wrath was directed at the appropriate target.

At any rate, I had little expectation of getting back to sleep, considering how worked up I was. And at around quarter of five I gave up on the idea completely and went into the kitchen. I made myself some coffee and toasted an English muffin. And soon after that, I relocated to the living room, stretching out on the sofa to read the newspaper. . . .

The insistent ringing shook me into consciousness. I reached out to turn off the alarm clock on the table next to the bed. But there wasn't any clock. Or even any table.

It took a little while before I realized just where I was and how I'd wound up there. In the meantime, my answering machine picked up the phone call.

"Where *are* you? It's after eleven and I haven't heard from you," Jackie scolded. "I thought you weren't going to pull this kind of junk anymore." But after an exasperated "Honestly!"

she had second thoughts. "Uh, I hope everything's all right, Dez. Please get in touch with me as soon as you can."

About three seconds after she hung up, I was dialing the number.

"I'm sorry, Jackie, but I overslept. I had a terrible night. I woke up at four, and then I couldn't fall asleep again. But apparently (HEH-HEH), I eventually managed it."

Now, I can't even imagine what other possible reasons for this morning's truancy Jackie's fertile brain might have been conjuring up just then. But my ever-trustful secretary actually had me swear to the truth of this explanation before mentioning that Pat Martucci had phoned twice—the first time when it was not yet nine. "Don't your friends know you at all?" she remarked only the slightest bit snidely.

This didn't rate a response. And it didn't get one. Instead, I wished Jackie a nice weekend and she wished me one and then we hung up. Following which I called Pat.

"I've been dying here," she said at once. "What happened last night?"

I gave her a comprehensive report.

"If it was yours truly, I think I'd have had to tell him off," she commented when I was through.

"Originally that was exactly my intention. But then I realized he'd only have come back with another lie—I doubt if he's even capable of the truth—and I'd have gone nuts and wound up screaming at him like a shrew. Which would have been lousy for my blood pressure. And what for? Nothing I said would have made a real impression on him anyway. Or left me feeling any better. But handling it like this and being able to get under *his* skin, for a change, well, it may have been childish and it certainly wasn't the big payback I'd have liked, but it was still pretty gratifying."

"Yes, I can see now where it would be," Pat murmured.

"But you know what?" I went on. "I could never have pulled it off—actually, I would never even have attempted something like that—if not for that stupor I'd been walking around in all day. I mean, I didn't stop to do any analyzing or anything. I didn't even give the idea that much thought. I was too numb to care."

"I'm curious, though," Pat said then. "This business about getting a neighbor to buzz you from the lobby—what if Bruce had stuck around to have a look at who was coming to take you out and then no one showed?"

"For all I know, that's exactly what he did. And if you want the truth, I hope so. Because then he'd have been a hundred percent certain I was dumping him. And can you imagine what *that* would have done to his ego? He'd probably have started talking to himself—until he found out what was behind the whole thing, anyway."

Pat's boss called out to her then, and we said our good-byes. But just before clicking off, she added a quick "I'm proud of you, Dez."

As it turned out, my little stunt with Bruce produced some very positive side effects. For weeks afterward, I was amazingly relaxed. Also, I couldn't remember when I'd felt so content. Yet at the same time, I was surprisingly energized.

My personal life was no longer angst-ridden. The Bruce fiasco was finally over with—for good.

And what's more, in the end, I'd been the one to pull the plug.

Chapter 34

That evening Kevin and I met for drinks.

I felt we should talk, and I had intended fixing dinner for us at my apartment—I'd even planned the menu. But Kevin's dinner schedule was pretty full for the next few days—some family things, he told me—and he suggested we get together at around five o'clock. He knew a nice Irish pub in my neighborhood.

Donahue's was comfortable and homey, all scarred wood paneling, faded maroon leather seats, and tempting kitchen aromas. We sat across from each other in a booth, me with my Beaujolais and Kevin clutching a Heineken.

After a few slow sips, Kevin set down the beer mug. "I don't suppose you wanted to see me because you have any big news." Nevertheless, he couldn't quite keep the hopeful note out of his voice.

I shook my head.

"Well, I said that I didn't suppose," he pointed out, smiling wistfully.

"I thought we should discuss the next few weeks."

Kevin's brow folded up like an accordion. "What's happening in the next few weeks?"

"Probably nothing. That's just it."

"I don't follow you."

"What I mean is, I don't imagine we can expect to find out how Luella died for quite a while yet, and until we do, there's really no way I can proceed. For now, I've gone as far as I can think of to go."

"Maybe if you spoke to everyone again . . ." he put to me tentatively.

"Uh-uh. Don't you see, I wouldn't even know what else to ask until we learn the results of the autopsy."

"Well, now that that's out of the way . . ." And looking dejected, Kevin reached for his beer.

I couldn't leave it like this. "Listen, the waiting around is driving me crazy, too, so I can imagine what it's like for you I wish something could be done to speed up the process, but I'm afraid we just have to let things take their course."

"I understand," he said, following which he took a healthy swallow of the Heineken.

"We *will* find out what happened to Luella, Kevin, I promise you. So just try to be patient."

He was able to dredge up a grin. "I'll do my best," he said.

"There's one thing more."

"Go ahead."

"You've never once mentioned Andy. As a suspect, that is. And it's kind of been puzzling me. He certainly stood to benefit from Luella's death. And besides, they were anything but fond of each other."

"That's true," Kevin conceded.

"He had access to the town house, too—he could easily have borrowed his wife's keys. And he doesn't really have an alibi for the morning Luella died, either."

"Also true."

"So—?"

"The motive—I'm referring to the underlying motive—dates back to the girls' childhood and how one of them felt about Luella then. I'm positive of it."

"How can you be so sure?" I challenged. I mean, the man was absolutely fixated on that theory of his.

"It's just something I feel, Desiree." And he placed his hand over his heart. "In here."

The following day—Saturday—the newly rejuvenated me braved the department store crush once more to wind up my holiday shopping. And about time, too, since Hanukkah was practically over and tomorrow would already be Christmas Eve.

Well, this year again UPS would have to assume the responsibility for my late-arriving gifts. I mean, who else could I blame?

Anyway, I got home from the stores in the early evening and had a quick supper. Then at eight-thirty I sat down on the sofa to watch TV for a half hour before starting the advance preparations for Sunday night's dinner with Ellen. The next thing I knew, this rejuvenated me awoke to test patterns. I barely had the energy to drag myself off to bed.

At any rate, it was actually fortunate I'd conked out like that. Because at nine o'clock the next morning Ellen called to ask if I'd done any cooking yet. She was very relieved to hear that I hadn't. "I was wondering if it would be okay if we had dinner at my place later," she said. It seems she'd taken a bad spill last night and spent until two a.m. in the emergency room with a sprained ankle and bruised kneecaps.

And so I ended up eating spare ribs and lemon chicken at Ellen's on Christmas Eve. Which was fine with me. The food was excellent. And besides, who wanted Mandarin Joy to have to file for Chapter Eleven?

As for the other red-letter days of the season . . .

On Christmas Day I trekked across the hall to Harriet and Steve's. And in view of the fact that their twenty-something son Scott (presently ensconced in his own apartment at his parents' expense) was also here to partake of Harriet's roast beef and Yorkshire pudding, I enjoyed myself a lot more than I'd anticipated I would. Scott is practically world-famous for his short fuse and sullen nature—at least partially the result of having been spoiled rotten every second since his emergence from the womb. But that afternoon he was actually pleasant company, for a change.

New Year's Eve I was at home. I had politely declined an invitation from my neighbor Barbara Gleason to join her and some of her fellow teachers for dinner. And I'd likewise turned down a party invitation from an acquaintance who had only recently split from her husband of more than twenty years. I soon realized that Frieda fully intended her singleness to be a very temporary state, however. This I figured out when she advised me that every female attending that soiree of hers was expected to do so with a male platonic friend in tow. Well, I couldn't think of a soul to throw into Frieda's pot. But even if I could, I would have passed.

I celebrated New Year's Eve the way I prefer to celebrate it since Ed died: snuggled under my down comforter with a good mystery and a pint of Häagen-Dazs macadamia brittle.

Chapter 35

After the holidays, I got a couple of cases from Pat Sullivan—nothing big, but enough to fill the hours, pay the rent, and keep a medium-size refrigerator fairly well stocked.

For weeks the Luella Pressman business was at a standstill, however. I didn't once crack open the file; in fact, I made a conscious effort not to. The closest I came to any involvement there was to check in with Kevin every so often. But not as an investigator—as a friend. I was just anxious to know how he was doing. (He was okay. Or as okay as you could expect him to be, considering.)

Also, I should mention that during that time I'd still catch Jackie looking at me strangely every now and then. Although she did stop asking me if anything was new, at least.

And, oh, yes, I no longer gave Bruce any thought to speak of. Sure, on occasion I would go back over the crap he'd pulled and allow myself to get all riled up again. But it would quickly pass. And after a while he came to mind less and less frequently.

And then not quite two months after Luella's death—at two-ten on a Wednesday afternoon—the intermission was finally over. The autopsy report had come in.

"Sodium fluoroacetate," Kevin announced. "Luella died of sodium fluoroacetate poisoning." He was so agitated that for a moment I didn't even recognize his voice. "Have you ever heard of it?"

"No, what is it?"

"A pesticide—a rat poison. Look, can you meet me at Connie's? I'm on my way over there, and she asked if you'd come, too."

"I'm leaving right now."

* * *

Connie opened the door before I'd even rung the bell. And when I stepped inside, she practically fell on me, throwing her arms around my neck.

"Oh, Desiree," she half sobbed into my hair, "I don't understand this. I don't understand it at all." And then she released me, moving back. She looked to be in terrible pain, as if the reality of the tragedy had been brought home to her all over again. "But come in. Please. Kevin's in the living room."

She took my coat, and we both joined Kevin, who was pacing in front of the fireplace, his hands clenched together, his complexion close to gray. He was as grim as I'd ever seen him. As soon as Connie and I sat down, he perched on the edge of one of the chairs opposite the sofa.

He began filling me in at once, keeping his tone dry and flat—a major effort, I was certain.

"The police paid Connie a visit a few hours ago. As I told you on the phone, they now know what killed Luella. What they don't know is how it was done. The food she ate that morning was analyzed—the juice and coffee and cranberry nut loaf—and everything was perfectly okay. Besides, Connie had exactly the same breakfast. So—"

"Except," Connie broke in, "that I had my coffee with milk and sugar, and Luella always drank hers black. But I don't see where that would have made a difference, do you?" She was addressing this to me.

"No, I'm sure it wouldn't. But tell me what you can about this sodium fluoro—" I turned to Kevin. "What did you say the name of it was?"

It was Connie who enlightened me. "Sodium fluoroacetate. It's a rodenticide. Sergeant Blake—he's the detective in charge of the investigation—says you can't even purchase it in the United States anymore; you have to buy it in Europe. It seems there were numerous instances where it accidentally got into food—Kevin did explain that it's completely tasteless and odorless, didn't he?"

"I didn't go into any of the details," Kevin answered for me.

"Well, it's an exceptionally toxic poison. In other instances, people died by just inhaling the dust."

"We're talking about a fine-textured white powder here," Kevin elaborated. "Although, unless I'm mistaken, Blake also told Connie the stuff was water soluble." He looked to Connie for confirmation.

"Yes, it is." There was a contemplative expression on her

face. And then three or four seconds later, speaking slowly
and thoughtfully, she said, "Right now you two are primarily
concerned with how Luella was given the poison. And don't
misunderstand me, I'm extremely puzzled about that, too.
But even more than the *how,* I keep coming back to the *why.*
Why would anyone want to do away with Luella?" The question became a wail. *"Why?"*

"I thought we discussed that some time ago, Con," Kevin
pointed out gently.

"Yes, we did. The girls. But I can't believe it was one of
them."

"They've all been to Europe," he reminded her. "You took
Geena and Nadine on a trip there yourself. And Enid went
abroad on business only a short time later."

"That was five years ago," Connie scoffed. "When you and
Luella got married."

"Exactly right." And now very deliberately: "When—
Luella—and—I—got—married." He let this impact on his
former sister-in-law for a few moments before adding, "Listen, Connie, the poison would have been bought at that time
for the same reason it was put to use now—to insure that
Luella didn't get to alter her will in favor of a new husband.
If it was purchased back then, though, the murderer apparently had a change of heart. Maybe whoever it was learned
that she had no intention of revising the will, after all."

"Has anyone been to Europe since then?" I asked. "Aside
from Geena and Andy," I put in, referring to the couple's
honeymooning there the year before.

"No," Connie responded. "After we came home I promised
the girls we'd do it again soon. I was anxious to return myself, but I just never got around to following through. And
Enid doesn't travel overseas on business anymore; she left
her old job maybe a month after her trip." And now Connie
murmured wistfully, "Maybe we'll all go again when this is
resolved."

"Well," I said to Kevin, "there's still that honeymoon."

He shook his head. "Luella and Massi didn't even meet
until this year. If Geena did away with Luella, it was with
fluoroacetate she got ahold of five years ago."

"I was thinking of Andy," I told him. "The man might have
been planning to speed his wife's inheritance along. But then
he chickened out. That is, until Luella became interested in

Bud Massi, and he envisioned those beautiful millions slipping through his fingers."

"I'm sorry. I just don't see Andy as being involved," Kevin pronounced stubbornly.

Nevertheless, Connie grabbed onto this alternative as if clinging to a life preserver. "Maybe it *was* Andy." She looked at me. "Oh, I've always been fond of him. Even so, though, if it wasn't the girls—and it wasn't—then I suppose it could have been Andy who . . . who did this." And reaching into the pocket of her skirt, she produced a crumpled tissue and wiped away some just-forming tears.

"Andy didn't kill Luella," Kevin reiterated, with quiet conviction now.

"Those girls would never have harmed her," Connie insisted, her moist eyes riveted on my face. "My sister gave them a good home, a real sense of belonging. She loved them dearly, always. Even when they were grown up and on their own, she saw to it that we stayed a close-knit family. Do you know why the girls and I didn't spend a longer time in Europe after her wedding to Kevin? Because Luella wanted us to be together for Thanksgiving. No matter what was happening in her life, those three were an essential part of it. That first year she and Kevin were married, Kevin thought they'd celebrate her birthday just the two of them. He made all sorts of extravagant plans, too—including arrangements for a limousine. But Luella wouldn't even hear of anything like that. Remember, Kevin?"

"I remember," he answered softly. "But listen, Connie, I've already told Desiree how family-minded Luella was. Evidently, though, it didn't have much of an impact on her stepdaughters. Or on one of them, at any rate."

"You can't convince me of that."

"Look, do you think I—"

I interrupted Kevin's retort. "I think we should concentrate now on how the poison might have been administered. It's conceivable it may enable us to discover who killed Luella and—along with that—why. The detective didn't say how fast-acting the stuff was, did he?"

"As a matter of fact, he did. He said it could take effect in minutes," Connie replied.

"Did he mention the outside time?"

She nodded. "Six hours at most is what he told me."

"Then it would seem that Luella was poisoned sometime Saturday morning," I mused.

"Yes, I know. But how could that be?" Connie demanded. "They tested her breakfast—*our* breakfast, I should say. And the results had to be accurate, too—after all, I'm still alive."

"You're overlooking something, aren't you?" I put to her.

"What's that?"

"Luella could have been given something containing the poison at any time, and she might not have gotten around to ingesting whatever it was until that morning."

Connie was skeptical. "If you're referring to candy or gum—things of that nature—Luella didn't indulge. Besides, the autopsy report would have revealed the fact she'd eaten candy, wouldn't it? And I imagine the detectives would have questioned me about a thing like that."

"Was she on any medication?"

"That's what the police wanted to know. Occasionally, when she had a severe headache, she'd take a couple of Tylenol Extra-strength Gelcaps. But that was about all. She seemed fine at breakfast, though; she certainly didn't complain of any headache. Nevertheless, the police carried off the Tylenol bottle today—plus her toothpaste, her toothbrush, her mouthwash, and I have no idea what else. But they won't find anything."

"You're sure of that?" I said.

"As far as the dental paraphernalia, I am. Look, I'm certain Luella brushed and rinsed on Friday night, too—before she went to sleep. She always did. And I know she was in bed by two. So figure it out.

"I didn't leave for Nadine's until well after eight Saturday morning. In fact, it was probably after eight-thirty. And I saw Luella as I was walking out—she was just going into her office then. Believe me, there was absolutely nothing wrong with her. If the poison had been applied to any of those items, it would have affected her by that time."

I did a rapid count on my fingers—arithmetic not being my long suit. Connie was right. Given the six-hour maximum reaction time we were dealing with here, the damage would have been done by then.

At any rate, for a brief while after this, nobody said another word. I was searching my brain for additional possibilities; I suspected we all were. "Something . . . something she'd have put in her mouth or maybe inhaled . . ." I mumbled. At that moment it hit me:

"Her fingernails! Luella was always biting her fingernails!" Kevin jumped up. "That's it!"

But almost immediately I realized that it would have been impossible to introduce the poison here without the victim's knowledge.

Kevin's face fell when I explained the flaw in my theory.

"Did she ever use nail polish, though?" I asked, knowing the answer already.

And now Kevin and Connie exchanged bemused glances. "She didn't have enough nail left for that," Connie responded.

"That's what I thought. But how about a lipstick?" I suggested. "Or face powder?"

Connie ruled these out at once. "Luella wasn't wearing makeup that day. She never wore any around the house. Not even lipstick."

Actually, I'd seen that for myself—at least, if my one meeting with the victim was any indication.

I glanced over at Kevin then. His expression, I decided, mirrored the frustration we were all feeling.

The three of us stood in the hall a short time later, and I was still struggling to come up with other viable means of administering the poison as Kevin helped me on with my coat. We were only a few feet from Luella's office, and for a split second I could picture the door swinging open and the dead woman framed in the doorway, looking as I had first seen her five long years before. . . .

"I think I've got it!" I all but shouted now. After which I grinned broadly, in recognition of my own brilliance.

The grin vanished instantly, however—and with it this inordinate pride in my deductive powers—when at that moment Kevin exclaimed, "The pencils!"

Chapter 36

Kevin was barely able to contain himself. "Somebody made a solution of the fluoroacetate and applied it to the pencils!" And now he hesitated. "That *is* what you were going to say, too, isn't it, Desiree?"

"It's exactly what I was going to say. Anyone who knew Luella would be aware that she chewed up her pencils. She even had one between her teeth the first time I set eyes on her."

"Nadine always used to be after Luella about that," Connie murmured. "She warned her she'd die of lead poisoning one day. Maybe she wasn't really that far off." And with this, a short, brittle laugh seemed to escape unbidden from her lips.

Naturally, if it *was* the pencils, I realized then, this would shoot those Saturday morning alibis to pieces. Nadine's and Enid's, I mean. And virtually at the same instant that this occurred to me, I said it aloud.

Connie was perplexed. "I'm not sure I follow your reasoning."

"I just can't envision somebody coming here that Saturday and borrowing Luella's pencils, applying the solution, then returning the pencils to her desk—and with her right there in the office all that while, too."

"So you think—?"

I laid everything out.

"Luella was writing as usual on Friday, I assume."

"Yes, she was," Connie verified.

"Which meant she no doubt chomped away on those pencils all day long. And since she was in good health until Saturday, we can be certain they hadn't yet been contaminated. On Friday night, though, as I recall, you and Luella went to the theater and afterward to see Bud Massi perform."

Connie nodded, and I thought I saw a look of understanding on her face at that moment. I glanced over at Kevin. His initial excitement having faded, he was regarding me intently, his expression impossible to read.

"Well, that," I would up, "presented the killer with the perfect opportunity."

"Of course," Connie said ruefully, tapping her forehead. "I don't know where my head could have been."

"I'm sure you're still trying to come to grips with the whole idea of the poison," I told her. (After which I was immediately aware that I'd managed to make this sound disgustingly patronizing.) I quickly followed up with the obvious question. "Nothing appeared to have been disturbed when you got home?"

"I didn't notice anything."

"Who knew the two of you were going to be out of the house then?"

"I'm not sure. I picked up the tickets a few weeks before, and it's very likely I mentioned it to the girls at some time; I really can't recall. And it's also likely Luella herself said something to them. And that one of us told Andy, too." The glance she shot Kevin with this last speculation bordered on the defiant.

"I'll have to check on where everyone was on Friday evening," I said.

Now, all this time we had remained standing there in the hall—me, still bundled up in my coat. And Connie didn't appear to be any too steady on her feet just then. "If it's all right with you," I said to her, "I'd like to stay here a few minutes longer."

"I wish you would," she responded.

I shrugged out of the coat, and the three of us went back into the living room. "How about some coffee?" I asked when the others were seated.

Connie began to get up. "I'm sorry. I should have thought of that myself."

I put a restraining hand on her arm. "No, I'll do it. Can I get you something to eat, too?"

"I couldn't, thank you. But would you like something? I made egg salad this morning, and I think there might also be some smoked salmon."

"No, nothing for me, thanks."

"Kevin?"

"Nothing for me, either, thanks, Connie."

I was about to start for the kitchen when Connie had some

advice for me. "Be careful, Desiree. The last time I checked, Beatrix was in there. And he can scare the life out of you. He jumped down on Geena's shoulder the other day and left the poor girl shaking like a leaf. And just yesterday he missed me by inches. He's been doing that more often than ever lately, too. Thank goodness Nadine's taking him off my hands next week. Frankly, I don't know how much longer I would have been able to stand it."

I couldn't blame the woman for feeling relief at the prospect of Beatrix's imminent departure. I mean, living with an attack cat like that had to play absolute havoc with your nerves. His future address, though, surprised me. "I didn't think Nadine was able to care for him," I remarked.

"Oh, we were fortunate there. Her old roommate was allergic to cats, you know. But now Sandi's decided to remain in California permanently. Although, actually, Nadine was gathering up the nerve to ask her to move, anyway, so she'd be able to have Beatrix with her. But at any rate, in looking for a replacement for Sandi, Nadine made it a priority to find someone who likes cats and doesn't do any business traveling. Someone who'd be available to Beatrix-sit when Nadine has to go off on a shoot somewhere. She—" Connie broke off, flustered. "But that's not what's important now, is it? It's Luella who matters." And on voicing her sister's name, Connie's face seemed to crumple.

Well, in spite of the fact that I was a little uncomfortable about being around Beatrix (translation: the cat terrified me), I was glad to hear that things had worked out for him. Assuming, of course, that Nadine didn't have an acquaintanceship with sodium fluoroacetate that could effect a change in her own address.

Anyway, the instant I entered the kitchen I got up on my toes to scan the cabinet tops. Nothing. Not that I could see, at least. But as I was preparing the coffee, I kept sneaking quick, anxious peeks over my shoulder. And my hands weren't as steady as they should have been, either. When I emerged from the room a short time later, however, I was unscathed. There'd been no sign of the Scourge of Catdom.

I found Connie curled up on the sofa sobbing her heart out, with Kevin endeavoring—quite ineffectually—to comfort her.

As I set the tray down on the coffee table, she glanced up at me. "Just give me a moment," she said.

"Take all the time you need."

But she immediately began wiping her eyes and blowing her nose, and within two or three minutes, she appeared reasonably composed.

We all had some coffee then, and right after that I suggested that Connie phone this Sergeant Blake to let him know about Luella's habit of putting the pencils in her mouth.

Kevin offered to make the call.

He was walking across the room toward the telephone when I stopped him. "Hold it a sec, Kevin." And then to Connie. "Have you been in Luella's office since the police left here this morning?"

"No, why?"

"I suddenly realized they might have seen the condition of those pencils and gotten the same thought Kevin and I did. Maybe they've already removed all of them for testing."

And now the three of us hurried to the office.

Connie threw open the door, and we made a beeline for the desk. "Don't touch anything!" I shouted, since I was—naturally—trailing a few feet behind the others.

The desktop, I saw, was pretty much as it had been on the day after the funeral: unbelievably messy.

"Uh, I've had Hortense under orders not to disturb things too much in here," Connie explained, embarrassed by the clutter. "I said to just do a bit of vacuuming and to dust where she could. Sooner or later I'll have to look everything over and straighten up, but, well, I haven't worked up to that yet. Anyway, it doesn't seem as though the pencil idea even occurred to the police," she pointed out.

I estimated that there were eight or nine pencils strewn over, around, and peeking out from beneath Luella's incredible jumble of papers and books. Plus there was a small additional supply in the familiar white ceramic mug, with its startling Beatrix look-alike image.

I glanced down perfunctorily at the pencils closest to me—two of them were lying on top of a pile of blank paper that was practically under my nose.

And I couldn't believe it!

I raised my eyes to look at Kevin and Connie, then quickly lowered them again to confirm that I'd actually seen what I saw.

I had.

I asked Kevin for his handkerchief. As soon as he handed it

to me, I used it to remove one of the stubs from the mug, wrapping the cloth around the eraser top. And after a cursory examination, I laid this pencil on the desk alongside the other two.

"Do you notice anything?" I focused on Kevin and Connie just long enough to put the question to them, and then I was back to staring at the desktop.

"About what?" Connie said. And following my gaze, she peered down, too, with Kevin doing the same only a split second later.

"The pencils." I could scarcely breathe now.

Kevin was the first to react. He sucked in his breath. "My God," he murmured, incredulous.

Less than a minute afterward a stunned Connie inquired of no one in particular, "They're not . . . but why in the world would somebody do this?" And lifting her head, she turned to me. "Why would anyone switch the pencils?"

Chapter 37

Yes, why?

I responded with a shrug and then still totally nonplussed, fastened my eyes on the desktop again.

Luella's pencils, you see, had been replaced with a whole different bunch! I mean, there wasn't a tooth imprint in sight.

Kevin appeared to be turning things over in his mind. "None of these pencils seems to be new, either," he said at last.

"Mmm," I responded by way of agreement. The pencils were of varying sizes, the stub I'd taken from the mug not more than a few inches in length. Plus all the erasers had apparently done their fair share of erasing. "Well, let's see what kind of shape the rest of the pencils are in—those underneath this clutter." And opening the center drawer of the desk, I got out the ruler I vaguely remembered coming across in there the last time I'd been in the office. Then with the ruler for leverage—I didn't want to get my fingerprints on any of the pencils—I systematically lifted the papers from the desk.

What I found were more pencils that also had obviously never done pacifier duty for Luella.

And now I emptied the contents of the ceramic mug on the desktop.

After a quick inspection revealed that these pencils, too, lacked the dead woman's characteristic stamp, I borrowed Kevin's handkerchief to replace them in the mug.

I had just become ninety-nine percent convinced that Luella's pencils were the instruments of her death.

Kevin, as he so often did, verbalized my thoughts. "I believe we can be fairly confident now that it was Luella's pencils that were treated with the poison. Otherwise, I can't see why anyone would bother doing something like this." There was a pause before he shot a meaningful look at Connie. "Most likely the killer wanted to insure that her aunt or one of her sisters didn't die by accident later on."

"No one else ever uses this desk," a furious Connie pointed out.

But Connie was wrong. I'd sat right here the morning I was going through her sister's papers. Suddenly I was cold all over. *My God! What if the pencils hadn't been switched yet, and I'd absentmindedly stuck one of them in my mouth?—the sort of thing that on occasion I've been known to do. I would have wound up joining Luella in the Great Beyond!*

"Are you all right, Desiree?" Kevin was asking.

I had to swallow a couple of times before I could speak. "Of course, why?"

"I was talking to you, but I don't think you heard a single word. You seem a little pale, too."

"Guess I should have gone heavier on the makeup today," I responded lightly. "Anyhow, what was it you were saying?"

"I said that the murderess probably wasn't willing to take that kind of a chance—as far as no one ever using the desk, that is. And I wanted to know if you agreed."

I thought for a moment. "Actually, I don't believe I do. If the perpetrator's concern was that someone else might be poisoned, wouldn't it have been simpler just to remove the pencils? I mean, why go to the trouble of substituting?"

"Then perhaps it was to prevent the pencils from being identified as the murder weapons," Kevin offered, but a little uncertainly.

"I suppose that must be it. But still, I'm puzzled. Say it was eventually determined that Luella died by sucking on pencils treated with sodium fluoroacetate—okay, so what? Any one of our suspects had the opportunity to both acquire the poison and apply it."

Kevin nodded. "I see what you mean." And a short while later: "At any rate, if—for whatever reason—her purpose was to conceal the exchange, the murderess was pretty clever about it. Utilizing *used* pencils was certainly less likely to call attention to the fact they were replacements."

Most probably true. Although if she—or he (I refused to dismiss Andy Hough as a suspect)—*had been* really *clever, the replacements would have had tooth indentations, too. But then few killers think of everything. And thank God for that, I say.*

"Desiree?" I glanced over at Connie. A perplexed expression was scrunching up her face. "I was just wondering. Why didn't the . . . the person who killed Luella bite down on these pencils himself? That would have made the substitution virtually impossible to detect."

"That's the—" I began.

But Connie had started to speak again at this same instant, and she unwittingly cut me short. "On second thought, though, the murderer may have been concerned that if he did, his saliva—or maybe even his teethmarks—could serve to identify him." And having supplied herself with an explanation, her features relaxed.

"Makes sense to me," I told her—a trifle grudgingly, I admit. (Although I'm absolutely positive this would have occurred to me, too. At some point or other, anyway.)

And now Kevin had a question for me. "That day you were in here checking through Luella's things, did you happen to take any notice of the pencils?"

"None at all." And once again a shiver shot through me.

The three of us stood there quietly for a brief time before Kevin observed morosely, "It appears as though we're up against it, doesn't it? How can the police have Luella's pencils tested if there are no longer any of them around?"

"Wait a minute," Connie put in then. "I just had an idea. Luella was very careless; you know that, Kevin."

"Yes, that I know," he concurred, looking at her quizzically.

"Well, maybe she dropped a pencil on the floor. Hortense—on my instructions, as I explained before—hasn't been doing a very thorough cleaning job in here. So unless the pencil was in plain sight, there's at least a chance it would still be lying there."

"Then let's see what we can find," I said, promptly getting down on all fours to comb the area around the desk. Kevin and Connie assumed similar positions, crawling off in opposite directions. Judging from *my* view of *them*, we were as ludicrous-looking a trio as you're ever likely to see. Anyway, after a few minutes, we sort of came together—empty-handed—in what was approximately the center of the room.

"I don't think we should give up just yet," I told them, a new resolve having been instilled in me by what I regarded as my own almost-murder. I struggled to get to my feet. Kevin managed to stand up first and gave me a hand. (Actually, it required both his hands.) After which he assisted Connie.

Now, since I myself often recruit pencils for bookmarks, I decided at that moment that it might be worthwhile examining Luella's books. And turning each of them upside down, I spread the pages and then rapidly thumbed through them. On my second try—with *Roget's Thesaurus*—a gnawed yellow stub dropped to the desktop.

Hallelujah!

A dog-eared almanac soon produced a similar result.

Once I was finished with the books—which yielded nothing more—I stood back and looked around the room for other possibilities. My gaze eventually returned to the desk—and Luella's relic of a Royal. Here, too, I was going by my own experience. At my request, Kevin tilted the outsized typewriter a bit, while I fished under it with the ruler. And this time I really hit paydirt, as two more chewed-up specimens reluctantly rolled out in the open.

Kevin was practically jubilant. While Connie appeared to be—well, I guess *satisfied* is as good a word as any. And it was probably the most you could expect from her, too, the way things stood. After all, any progress here could conceivably bring us closer to unmasking a perpetrator who might turn out to be her niece. So as much as she might want to discover who killed her sister, I doubted she could be feeling exactly gleeful at the moment.

At any rate, I felt I had to caution them both. "Listen, since we have no idea how long these pencils have been where we just found then, we can't assume that any of them were treated with the fluoroacetate. At this point, we can count ourselves lucky if even one of the four ended up where it did on the day Luella died. Let's keep our fingers crossed, though."

"Amen," Kevin murmured fervently. Connie's seconding nod was, understandably, a little less enthusiastic.

And now Kevin went into the hall to phone Sergeant Blake. And the minute he was out of sight, Connie leaned toward me, a conspiratorial note in her voice. "I know you don't completely agree with Kevin about who may have poisoned my sister. I—" She broke off to glance over her shoulder, continuing only after reassuring herself that Kevin wasn't back there, hovering in the doorway. "What I'm trying to say is, you do think it's at least conceivable that Andy murdered Luella, don't you?"

"I wouldn't discount him."

"Thank you, Desiree," she whispered gratefully. And she reached over and squeezed my hand.

Kevin returned soon afterward. "Sergeant Blake is gone

for the day. So is Detective Wolfson—his partner. I'll try to reach them first thing in the morning."

A short time later, as we were walking out of the office, it occurred to me that I'd leafed through Luella's books when I was here last. Had the pencils been there then? I couldn't remember. Preoccupied with searching for clues—and unaware of the possible significance of the chewed-up stubs—I probably wouldn't have paid attention to them.

I turned to Connie now. "I think it might be a good idea to lock up this room." And when she agreed: "I wouldn't be surprised if we actually have the murder weapon in here."

But this last remark, I suspect, stemmed at least partially from my desire to hear those words myself.

Chapter 38

Connie had invited Kevin and me to stay for dinner—she had a pot roast in the freezer. But I was anxious to go off by myself, away from Connie and Kevin and everyone and everything else that had anything to do with murder. Any murder. Even if only briefly.

Kevin walked outside, waiting with me for an empty taxi to come along. "I thought I should keep Connie company awhile. She's pretty unnerved by all of this," he explained. And then he smiled—a smile, I thought, that had gratification but no mirth at all in it. "Well, at any rate, it looks like we're finally getting somewhere."

I had the cabdriver drop me at Jerome's, this coffee shop not far from my apartment that I'd recently begun patronizing every now and then. It was a clean, convenient place to take sustenance when I was too bushed or lazy to provide it for myself.

The elderly gentleman who came for my order had only waited on me two or three times before. "Cheeseburger deluxe," he announced, pointing a finger at me. "Well done. Fries also well done. And you want a Coke—but not before I bring the burger." The grin that followed let me know how proud he was of his memory.

Now, it may reflect on my credibility, but I swear that this was one time I'd had every intention of settling for the tuna platter—and with the dressing on the side, too. Only I couldn't bring myself to embarrass the man.

But anyhow, while at Jerome's, I absolutely refused to think about recent developments—which, of course, were considerable. There'd be time enough later to wrestle with all of the things that had come to light today.

* * *

The telephone rang not more than ten minutes after I got home.

"Desiree?" inquired an unfamiliar male voice.

' Yes, this is Desiree."

"This is Al Bonaventure."

I waited for the man to say something further to identify himself. And then I realized he was waiting, too, evidently regarding this information as sufficient to produce a response of some sort.

He was the one to end the short silence. "We have mutual friends." His manner was tentative and maybe a little embarrassed. "Derwin? And Jackie?"

Aha! Damn that damn Jackie, anyway! "Oh, sure."

The acknowledgment seemed to make him feel somewhat more relaxed. "I understood you were expecting my call. Of course, I was under orders from Derwin—via Jackie, no doubt—to get in touch with you more than a month ago"— *No question about it; I was going to kill the woman*—"so you've probably forgotten about the whole thing by this time. Uh, Jackie did mention me, I hope."

"Yes, she mentioned you," I said, seething. And then more amicably (after all, Al, too, was an innocent victim of Jackie's machinations): "I don't think she ever told me your last name, though."

"Oh." There was an awkward pause before he went on. "Look, this is pretty difficult for me. To tell you the truth, I'm kind of a virgin at this—that's why it's taken me so long to work up the nerve to pick up the phone. But I really would like for us to meet; I've been hearing wonderful things about you."

"You can't believe anything Jackie says, even if you get it secondhand."

He laughed. "But Derwin gave you a great review, too. And he's not only an old friend, but I'm also his dentist. And believe me, Desiree, you don't want to mislead the guy who puts a drill in your mouth."

In spite of myself, I laughed, too.

"Listen, would you be available Sunday night?—to go out to dinner, that is."

"I'm really sorry, Al, but I'm in the middle of a murder investigation right now—I'm a private investigator—and I'm not going to be able to do a thing socially until I've put this case to rest."

"I understand." There was another awkward pause before he made his suggestion. "Listen, why don't I give you my number, and you can call me whenever you free up. How would that be?"

I told him it would be fine. Unthinkingly—since there was a pen and pad right by the phone—I even took down the number. And then we said good night. After which I immediately crumpled up the paper and tossed it into the garbage.

Death, I decided then, *was too good for Jackie. Unless, of course, it was very slow. And very, very painful.*

It wasn't until close to ten o'clock that I was able to browbeat myself into taking out the file on Luella Pressman.

I was just about to open it when something struck me. On first learning that Luella had been poisoned. I hadn't for a single second considered the possibility that Connie might have been the person responsible. And after all, this would have presented a very simple solution to the mystery of how the two sisters could have ostensibly eaten the exact same breakfast—and only one of them had made it through the day. (Of course, I'm talking about before we'd begun to speculate on how else the poison might have been ingested.)

I wondered for a moment if Connie had escaped my suspicion simply because Kevin had me so convinced that the motive here—or at least the immediate motive—was one of financial gain. Which, of course, would certainly have eliminated her.

But then I decided that there wasn't any other reason for Connie to do away with Luella, either. At least, not as far as I was able to determine. And going back to that breakfast business, if Connie *had* wanted to get rid of her sister, she was too smart to choose a method that would set her up as the logical suspect. But even more in Connie's favor had to be her suggesting to Kevin that he involve me in the case. I mean, why would the killer herself want someone brought in to uncover the killer?

No. Kevin hadn't brainwashed me. I'd come to my conclusion about Connie on my own. And now I felt a little better about myself.

Anyway, that settled, I began to pore over my notes, as I had so often before. But tonight there was a difference. For the first time, I was working with a piece of definite information: The dead woman had been a murder victim—more specifically, a poison victim.

I read slowly, going back over many of the sections—sometimes again and again—in an attempt to assure that I hadn't overlooked anything.

But even armed with this new knowledge, two hours later I still didn't have a single clue as to Luella Pressman's killer.

It was when I was about to get ready for bed that I remembered to take out the garbage—which now contained coffee grinds, an apple core, some grape stems, an empty container of Häagen-Dazs, and Al Bonaventure's phone number.

I was already standing at the compactor when, on an impulse, I reached into the trash bag and retrieved the phone number. Although liberally splashed with macadamia brittle, it was, I noted, nevertheless still legible.

Not that I ever intended making use of it. But I don't know, destroying it like that just didn't seem like a very nice thing to do.

Chapter 39

Kevin called at eight-thirty Thursday morning. "I've just spoken to Sergeant Blake, and he told me he'd pick up the pencils from Connie today. Somewhere around ten o'clock. And, Desiree? Now that they know what to look for, we may even have our answer by tomorrow." He sounded the way I felt at that moment: optimistic—but afraid to be.

The thing is, what if the pencils turned out *not* to be the murder weapon? We'd have to start all over again—and face the very real possibility that we might never discover how the poison had been administered. Even the thought of that made me shudder.

"Listen, I'll be heading over to Connie's in a little while," Kevin said then. "I'd like to hear for myself what the police have to say—about things in general, that is. I could swing by your apartment if you're interested in coming, too."

"I'm interested, but I'd better pass. This Sergeant Blake doesn't know me, and he might regard it as interfering on my part." *In fact,* I was thinking, *even if he knew me—or maybe especially if he knew me—he might regard it as interfering.* It has never been my experience to have a police officer jump up and down with glee when our paths crossed on a case. So far, though, I'd been keeping a low profile with this investigation. And I preferred to leave it that way, if I could.

"All right. If I learn anything worth passing on, I'll phone you later," Kevin assured me.

I left for work at just after nine. And for a brief interlude, the murder took a backseat to this other, more immediate matter I would have to deal with. By the time I arrived at the office, I was all revved up.

Jackie was sitting at her desk, diligently typing away on the computer. "Now I know why you kept asking me what was new," I said accusingly. "You were supposed to hold off having Derwin give his dentist my telephone number, remember? I *told* you I wasn't ready to meet anyone yet."

She stopped typing and swiveled around to face me. "I don't think you have any idea at all what's best for you," an unrepentant Jackie informed me. "If you did, you'd never have gotten involved with anyone like that whatever-his-name-was. And here I have an opportunity to introduce you to a man who is absolutely perfect for you, and who—" Cutting herself short, she sighed dramatically. "Okay, let me ask *you:* What sort of friend would I be if I'd waited so long to do something about Al that it gave some *bimbo* a chance to sink her claws into him?"

"But I'm really not up to doing any dating right now, Jackie. And although I'm sure you have my interests at heart—and I appreciate it, too, honestly—I wish that just once in a while you'd pay attention to what I have to say."

"Well, that's what I get for caring about you," Jackie mumbled, turning to her computer again.

"Listen, Jackie, I—"

"I don't want to talk about it anymore," she said huffily, her fingers dancing all over the keys.

And thus dismissed, I slunk off down the hall to my office.

I had a quick dinner that evening—a sandwich and a plate of soup—and then at a little before eight, I called Geena Hough.

"You know, I suppose, about the poison," she murmured when I identified myself.

"Yes."

"My mother, she— Somebody actually *murdered* her!" the girl told me tearfully. "I just can't believe it. My mother was so—" And now her voice began to fade. "She was the kindest, the most . . ." If anything further was said, I didn't hear it.

"Are you all right?" I asked gently.

"Mmff." (That's what it sounded like.) She sniffled loudly a few times before getting out any more actual words. "It's just that it's all so . . . so terrible."

"Would it be better if I called back tomorrow—or spoke to Andy?"

"No. I'm okay. And Andy's not in; he goes to the gym on Thursday nights. Have you . . . have you found out something else?"

"No, but, uh, Geena, I'd just like to know where you both

were—you and Andy—on the Friday night before Luella died."

"Home. (SNIFFLE) We were b-both home."

"All evening?"

"Yes."

"Can anyone verify that? Did you receive any phone calls or anything?"

"No, none."

This was followed by a whole procession of sniffles. But I managed to slip in my "thank you" and hang up before the thing developed into a full-fledged crying jag.

I spoke to Nadine next. And while she, too, appeared to be devastated by the fact that Luella had been poisoned, she was, at least, more in control than her sister.

When I inquired about how she'd spent that Friday evening, Nadine responded that she'd had dinner with a friend after work. She was, however, back at her place by nine and remained there all night. But no, there wasn't anyone who could attest to this.

As soon as I hung up, I dialed Enid Pressman's number. Not unexpectedly, I was greeted by her answering machine. I left a message requesting she get back to me when she came in; I wouldn't be going to bed until twelve, I said.

And now it was time to cook.

Ellen and Mike were having dinner here tomorrow night, and I wanted to do as much in the way of advance preparations as I could. Enid called—wouldn't you know it?—when I was up to my elbows in pastry dough. I picked up the telephone with sticky hands.

Initially, as we exchanged the requisite brief pleasantries, Luella's oldest stepdaughter appeared quite calm. But the moment I brought up the subject of the autopsy report, her demeanor changed. Suddenly she was totally unlike the girl I'd talked to that night in her apartment. She spoke almost ramblingly now. About how shocking the news was and how distraught Aunt Connie was and how shaken she herself was. And then just as suddenly, she stepped back into character. Her tone was somewhat terse when she asked the reason I was phoning her. And even more so when she answered my question. (Which—remembering that last time—had been very tactfully posed, I assure you.)

Like the others, Enid had no alibi for the evening before the murder. In fact, she wasn't even very definite in her response. "I can't recall exactly, but I was most likely at the office until seven-thirty or eight. I normally am. And then either I stopped off for something to eat or I went directly back to my apartment and ordered dinner in."

"You were home by—when?"

"If I ate out, I was home by nine-thirty. Quarter of ten, at the latest. Otherwise, it might have been"—and now she was plainly irritated—"oh, I don't know, eight, eight-thirty. Possibly eight forty-five."

There was a beep on the line at this juncture. "Call Waiting," Enid said curtly. "Could be business; I'd better get it."

She clicked off before I had a chance to say goodbye.

So that's how it stood. There were now four people who might have committed the murder. Assuming, of course, that the pencils would prove to be the vehicle for the poison—and, therefore, that those Saturday morning alibis had to be scratched.

And it *was* the pencils, too. I had never been more sure of anything.

But I quickly admonished myself. I mean, if only one thing surprised me since I began investigating homicides, it was how often I could be wrong.

Chapter 40

When I walked into the office on Friday, Jackie mumbled that I'd had a phone call.

She averted her eyes as she extended the message slip to me. What's more, she was handling that innocuous little piece of paper with the tips of her thumb and middle finger, as if fearful that contact might cause her to break out in blotches.

I regarded this as a fair indication that I wasn't back in her good graces. (And to think, I'd originally been under the impression that I was the one with a gripe here.)

The message was from my dentist's office, confirming an appointment for a cleaning at one o'clock that afternoon. *Ugh!* I'd been trying to forget about that for days.

Anyway, as soon as I was ensconced in my cubbyhole, I reached for the telephone. And then I drew my hand back. I really didn't want to call Kevin. There was absolutely no reason to. If there'd been any news from the police, he would have let me know immediately. Still, an instant later, I stretched my arm toward the phone again. And this time I couldn't seem to control my fingers. They lifted the receiver.

"Have you heard anything yet?" I suddenly felt as if my heart were pounding in my ears.

Kevin sounded dejected. "No, not so far. Blake promised to get in touch with Connie as soon as he knew something, but I spoke to her a few minutes ago, and she hasn't had any word yet."

"Well, I suppose we'll just have to hang in a while longer. They did pick up the pencils only yesterday," I reminded us both.

"That's precisely what I'm doing—hanging," Kevin responded with a weak little chuckle. "It doesn't appear that we have an alternative, though, does it?"

"You'll call me the minute—"

"The second," he answered.

Ellen was at my door at seven o'clock—she'd had the day off. Mike would be arriving at eight-thirty, straight from work.

"I'll come early to give you a hand," she had threatened that morning. In self-defense, I made sure I took care of everything by six-thirty. But she did help me open the chardonnay she'd brought. And between the two of us, we managed to leave at least half the cork floating around in the bottle.

We were sitting at opposite ends of the living-room sofa, sipping wine and stuffing ourselves with hors d'oeuvres—a lovely shrimp mousse and a brie that was mixed with herbs and shallots and baked in a pastry crust. Ellen looked just adorable that evening, by the way, in a forest-green turtleneck sweater, a long beige skirt, and British-tan ankle boots.

Anyhow, it took a while to work up to it—I kept trying to think of some clever, less obvious approach—but eventually I asked straight out how things were going between her and Mike. Only I think I may have unwisely used the term "progressing" instead of "going."

Ellen was immediately defensive. "We're just not rushing into anything, if that's what you want to know."

Now, I don't consider becoming engaged after dating someone exclusively for over a year as moving along at breakneck speed. But I refrained from making this observation. "It *is* serious, though?" I said, seeking reassurance.

"Well, of course it is," Ellen replied, her tone not that far from waspish. But almost at once she leaned over and patted my hand. "I'm sorry. I didn't mean for it to come out like that. Look, I promise that when it happens" (I was somewhat placated by the fact that she hadn't said, "*if* it happens") "you'll be the first one I tell. Okay?"

"It's a deal," I answered with feigned enthusiasm, managing, I think, to conceal my disappointment. I'd really been hoping for a firm date here—assuming that it wasn't in the too-distant future, of course. But I would even have been satisfied with an approximation at this point.

It was a short time after this that I finally got around to Bruce—a subject I'd figured on disposing of when Ellen and I shared Chinese takeout at her place on Christmas Eve. But I just couldn't seem to bring myself to go into it then. At any rate, it required quite a bit of backtracking now to get her current, since she had no idea I'd even had plans to see the lowlife again.

She made an awful face when I came to the part where I agreed to give him another chance. But to Ellen's credit, she contained herself until she'd heard me out.

"So that's all there is," I concluded.

"That took guts—doing what you did. I don't think I could have gone through with anything like that."

"I don't think I could have, either, if I hadn't been like a total zombie after finding out he had a fiancée. Of course, it's too bad I wasn't able to devise something a whole lot nastier. But I'm not the most creative person in the world, so it was the best I could come up with. And it gave me *some* satisfaction, at least."

For a moment, Ellen sat there quietly. And then she exploded with "That . . . that horrible man!" Which is as close to a curse as you're ever likely to hear from my niece, being that Ellen is one of the few people I've known in my life without at least one or two colorful expletives in their vocabulary. "I just wish I had him here right this minute," she fumed.

It was an effort not to smile. "Why? What would you do?"

She thought for a couple of seconds. "I'd tear out his liver and stuff it down his lying throat, that's what," she announced, more than redeeming herself for the vocabulary deficiency.

Mike arrived soon afterward, looking kind of drained but, nevertheless, very attractive in gray slacks and a red turtle-neck sweater.

While I was doing some last-minute kitchen duty, he relaxed a little with the wine and hors d'oeuvres. Ellen, who'd already skarfed down a goodly amount of food by the time he walked in, apparently continued along those lines—I could hear her talking and munching away. Once again I marveled at her capacity, considering that there is no side view to the girl. I mean, physically, she is practically two-dimensional.

At any rate, within about twenty minutes we sat down to dinner—which Mike was to pronounce my best ever. And which Ellen was somehow still able to devote herself to with relish.

We began with leek and potato soup. The entree was veal chops in a marvelous cream and mushroom sauce. And, accompanying it, new peas with mint, plus a tossed salad that included a real smorgasbord of the bounty to be found in the earth and in little glass jars. There were iceberg and romaine lettuces, cherry tomatoes, red cabbage, radishes, scallions, eggplant appetizer, marinated artichokes, black and green olives, cucumber, capers, and red and green peppers. The star of the meal, however, was indisputably its finale: Connie's chocolate loaf. (You didn't think she'd have gotten me out of her house that day without divulging that recipe, did you?)

Conversation during dinner had been easy and light. But now, as the three of us sat around with our anisettes, we talked murder. Luella Pressman's murder, to be specific.

"So somebody really did kill her," Mike said softly once I'd presented them with the facts. He seemed to be having trouble believing it.

"There's no doubt about that. I'm only hoping we can find out how it was done."

"I'll bet it *was* the pencils," Ellen told me. "You have *such* a knack for putting your finger on things." Which was certainly supportive. Only I always try to bear in mind that Ellen couldn't be any more partisan if she'd carried me around in her stomach for nine months.

"You'll keep us posted, won't you?" Mike asked.

"Of course she will," Ellen answered for me. "She always does."

And I fully intended to this time, too. But after that night, well, everything just happened so fast. . . .

Chapter 41

I'd had a late breakfast and was sorting the laundry when Kevin called at just past noon.

"You were right. It *was* the pencils," he told me excitedly.

"I gather that Connie's heard from the police."

"Blake was there this morning. A couple of forensic people, too. Connie said they did some more poking around." And then uncertainly: "I suppose this would be considered good news, wouldn't it—about the pencils?"

"Of course it would; it *is*," I assured him. "At least we have something to go on now." But to be honest, I was nowhere close to being as confident as I sounded. "Tell me, were they all contaminated?" I asked, merely out of curiosity.

"I don't know; Connie didn't say. It doesn't matter, though, does it?"

"Not one little bit."

"Well, what's next?" Kevin put to me then.

"Next I go over all my notes again and try to make sense out of what we've learned."

"You'll call me right away if—when you've got something, won't you?"

"You know you don't have to ask."

The laundry would have to wait. I took out the Luella file, along with a yellow pad and a couple of pens. And then, prepared for a lengthy siege, I settled into the sofa armed with a bowl of grapes and a Snickers bar.

And now I began to read.

I combed through page after narrow-margined page of typewritten notes, keeping one simple truth uppermost in my thoughts: *Someone had felt it necessary to replace Luella's chewed-up pencils.*

And when I closed the folder a little more than an hour later, I had a good indication of who that someone might be.

I do want to make it clear, though, that I hadn't unearthed any overwhelming motive for the substitution. Not by a long shot. But on the other hand, from what I could see, only one person had even the slightest reason for doing a thing like that.

At any rate, I took a short break after this to unwind. During which time I drank my third cup of coffee of this still-young day. Not that I had the slightest desire for any more coffee—particularly my own. But it was something to help wile away the next fifteen or twenty minutes.

And then I returned to my notes.

But now that this one suspect had been singled out, I looked at everything with an entirely different mind-set, searching for further evidence that might back up my initial impression.

I have no doubt it was being focused like this that accounted for my picking up on another piece of information that fit right in. Again, there wasn't anything definitive here—no actual proof, that is. What I'd found was a small thing, really. But nonetheless, in light of the pencils, a small *meaningful* thing.

I think the clue that really convinced me of the killer's identity, though, was something that made no impression at all until I forced myself into one final read-through:

Luella Pressman was a Cancer.

Chapter 42

I contacted Kevin immediately. Or tried to, anyway.

I wanted to scream when I got the answering machine. Nevertheless, I managed to speak calmly. "I know who killed Luella. Please get back to me as soon as you can." My hands were none too steady when I put down the phone.

A moment later I lifted the receiver again. I was well aware I should hold off until I talked to Kevin. But I couldn't help it. "Will you be in for a little while?" I asked Connie. "I'd like to drop by."

"Of course. Is— Do you have anything to tell me?"

"We'd better wait until I see you."

And now I had an update for Kevin's answering machine: "I'm going to Connie's," I said. "Meet me there."

Connie answered the door looking very chic in a knife-pleated navy skirt and a white silk blouse with navy trim. But she had a worried expression. No doubt directly related to my call.

She gestured for me to come in. "I thought Kevin would be with you," she remarked.

"I wasn't able to reach him."

"Oh." We were facing each other in the foyer now, and she was regarding me with very large eyes. (I would never have imagined almond-shaped eyes could open up that wide.) "What is it, Desiree?"

"I think it might be a good idea if we discussed this sitting down."

She nodded. "I'll put up some coffee."

When we entered the kitchen, though, I suggested that we postpone the coffee for a few minutes. It wasn't so much that I didn't feel like a fourth cup—although, God knows, I didn't— but that I could barely contain what I'd come here to say.

"All right," Connie agreed. And we sat down at the table.

Then, fastening those still-huge eyes on me, she said in a tremulous voice, "What's happened? Talk to me. Please."

Now that I had my opening, it was surprisingly difficult to get the words out. "I know . . . I just learned who mur— . . . uh, who poisoned your sister."

Connie's lips parted, and her hand went to her mouth. For what seemed like a very long time, she didn't respond. And when she did, it was with a single, hushed syllable: "Who?"

"Nadine," I answered gently. "It was Nadine."

Connie shook her head. "Oh, no, not Nadine," she whispered. "There must be some mistake." Abruptly her hand fell to her lap.

I reached over and patted it. The hand had turned to ice. "Can I get you something hot to drink? A glass of water?"

"No, nothing. I'm fine. Just tell me what makes you think it was Nadine."

She was all choked up now, and for a fleeting moment I regretted not having spoken to Kevin first, so that we could break this to her together. I mean, I'm pretty much of a bumbler when it comes to dealing with grief. Besides, being my client, Kevin really should have been notified before anyone else. Although Connie was, after all, at least partially responsible for my involvement in the investigation. And anyway, I rationalized further, Kevin would probably be showing up in a few minutes, so it didn't much matter.

But actually, all of this was moot. The truth was, nothing short of pulling out my tongue could have stopped me from sharing my discovery just then.

"Look," I explained. "There's no one I'd rather *not* have it be than Nadine. I liked her a lot. Honestly. But I'm afraid that the evidence points right to her door."

"What evidence?" Connie demanded quietly.

I took a deep breath. "All right. Why don't we start with the pencils. Nadine was always warning Luella that she could get lead poisoning from chewing on them like that." Connie's lips parted, and I could tell she was about to protest. "Oh, I'm not offering that in the way of proof," I put in hastily. "But it's obvious the killer removed Luella's pencils in order to conceal that they'd been treated with the fluoroacetate. And a smart girl like Nadine would have had to realize that her constant carping about the pencils could make her suspect if they were ever determined to be the vehicle for the poison. It would also make sense for her to assure that their absence wouldn't be cause for speculation." I stopped and took another deep breath. "The fact is, nobody else had anything to gain by making the switch—not as far as I can see. Do you understand? It wasn't primarily someone's *using* the pencils—to murder Luella, I mean—that got me to zero in on Nadine. It was the *replacing* of them."

Connie's tone was almost scornful. "And this is why you're so sure it was Nadine who murdered my sister?"

"Of course not. This is just why I took a closer look at her."

"Go on."

"Do you remember that night during shiva when you showed me the crossword puzzle Nadine had just completed?"

"I don't believe I do, to tell you the truth. If you say I showed you a puzzle, though, then I must have. But where does a crossword puzzle enter into this?"

"Nadine had worked it in ink."

Connie frowned. "And that's meaningful because—?"

"Nadine didn't normally work the *Times* puzzle in ink, did she?"

"No" was the reluctant admission.

"In fact, has she ever done it in ink before, as far as you know?"

Another reluctant "No."

"Well, the pencils that had been substituted for Luella's had obviously not been new ones. And I would have to assume they were the property of the killer."

"Your point, I take it, is that Nadine used a pen because all of her pencils were now here—in my sister's office?"

"Exactly. Oh, maybe she kept one or two and just couldn't find them then—I recall that her desk was pretty disorganized. But evidently there weren't too many around anymore."

"And just when do you figure she made this substitution?"

"Well, since she filled in that puzzle on Sunday night, my guess is that it was sometime Sunday—before Kevin secured the office, of course. You know," I pointed out, "of all of the people connected with the case, Nadine was the only one who wouldn't have had to do any fancy explaining if she should be spotted coming in here. With you staying at her place, she was at the house every day, anyway, to feed Beatrix."

"But if Nadine had replaced Luella's pencils with her own," Connie argued, "she would have bought herself new ones."

"I'm sure that's just what she did. But she was pretty busy

with arrangements for the funeral and the shiva that day. Besides, most stationery stores aren't open on Sundays. And remember, there wasn't really any big hurry. At that juncture, nobody had the slightest suspicion Luella's death was even a homicide."

"Well," Connie pronounced, "you may call Nadine's working a puzzle in ink evidence of her guilt. I call it a coincidence."

"I don't believe in coincidences, Connie," I told her flatly.

"Nevertheless, they do occur."

Sure. Once every millennium. But I didn't debate this. "There's something else," I said.

Connie bit her lower lip and waited.

"Luella always insisted on having the girls—the entire family—celebrate special occasions with her. That's right, isn't it?"

A cautious "Ye-e-s."

"And she was a Cancer, wasn't she? Born on the cusp of Gemini, as I recall. That would make her birthday—when?"

"June twenty-second."

"Nadine intends going on a cruise of the Mediterranean the last two weeks in June. And she booked those reservations months ago—before Luella died. You told me so yourself."

Connie appeared to be gathering her thoughts. "I must have misunderstood," she murmured after a few seconds. "Nadine would never have made arrangements to go away then."

"Not if she expected Luella to be alive when June twenty-second rolled around, she wouldn't."

"I'm certain I got it wrong. It was undoubtedly the *first* two weeks in June Nadine was talking about. Yes, I'm sure that's what she said." And now her voice grew stronger, and there was an edge to it. "Just consider this logically, Desiree. Why would Nadine even mention the cruise to me if it meant she'd made plans to be away at that time?"

"In all probability it just slipped out. That sort of thing happens pretty frequently." And here, in an attempt to prevent the discussion from becoming too adversarial, I injected a less serious note. "Without slips like that, those of us in the detecting business wouldn't be able to do much detecting, you know."

But Connie wasn't paying attention to me just then. "I don't understand this," she said softly, thinking aloud. "I don't

understand it at all. Nadine and Luella always got along so
beautifully."

"It could be," I suggested halfheartedly, "that Nadine isn't
as . . . uh . . . as healthy as she appears to be."

Connie looked at me warily. "What are you talking about?"

"I know about her mother and that it's possible Nadine
murdered Luella while in the throes of an episode of acute
paranoia."

"Kevin told you!" Connie exclaimed angrily. "And after I
pleaded with him not to!"

"He did what he thought was right, Connie."

I was prepared for her to dispute this. Instead, she made a
grudging concession. "I suppose."

"And besides, the paranoia thing isn't really that likely," I
added, still not able to accept that Nadine might be mentally
ill. Somehow—and don't ask me to explain—it was easier to
believe that this vivacious young woman was a cold-blooded
killer.

"Well, if Nadine did this . . . this terrible thing to Luella,
it's the only explanation I can think of." And now Connie
burst into tears.

Oh, where is that rotten Kevin? I am just so terrible at this.

I leaned toward her and mumbled something like, "It'll be
okay, Connie." Although what was going to be okay, I had
no idea.

At any rate, once the tears began to abate a little I asked
again if I could get her a drink.

She shook her head, and I sat there silently for a couple of
minutes—except for a few "there, there"s every once in a
while—until she got herself together.

"I'm so sorry," she told me then with a poignant smile. "I
always seem to be saying that to you, don't I? But I suppose
that's because I always seem to be crying."

"You've had good reasons for it."

Connie's sigh seemed to come straight from her toes. "I'm
going to pray you're wrong about this, Desiree. And I firmly
believe that to be the case," she informed me. "But for now, I
intend to put everything out of my mind and fix us something to eat. What time is it, by the way?" And glancing
quickly at her watch, she answered the question herself.
"Twenty after five. I'm afraid my refrigerator isn't as full as
I'd like it to be—I'd planned on doing some heavy-duty marketing today—but how about a sandwich?"

Well, I'd been in such a frenzy to impart my news that, for once, I'd given my stomach short shrift. So anything edible would have sounded just dandy to me at that moment. "I'd love one."

"Good," she said, rising. "I bought some lovely ham yesterday, and I have an Italian bread in the freezer. How does an open grilled ham and Swiss appeal to you?"

"That would be great."

While Connie busied herself with fetching things from the refrigerator, I offered to see to the coffee.

The instant I stood up I noticed Beatrix's empty dish on the floor. And that's when I suddenly got this strong feeling—a conviction, almost—that I'd been overlooking something. But the haze that seems to be a semipermanent fixture in my brain hadn't lifted yet. I sank back down.

Something didn't fit. Something, I was certain, was wrong with my whole damn theory. But what?

And then it came to me.

"Nadine didn't do it! She couldn't have!" I cried, springing up. Connie, who was at the counter now slicing the bread, looked over at me, astonished. "And I can prove it, too!"

I turned and hurried toward the cat's dish. I would present it to Connie (*ta-da!*) as a tangible representation of her niece's innocence. (I do have a ridiculous flair for the dramatic sometimes.) And that's when I heard this god-awful screech.

I whirled around in time to see Connie close behind me, a very vocal Beatrix just landing on her shoulder.

Off balance now, my gracious hostess fell to her knees, loosening her grip on the bread knife that had been aimed at my back.

It skittered across the floor to wind up at me feet.

Chapter 43

For the space of one or two of my pounding heartbeats, Beatrix and I both stood motionless, staring at each other. And then that sweet, darling creature leapt onto the sink and from there seemed to actually fly back to his perch atop the cabinets.

With blazing speed now (for me, anyway), I covered the short distance to an already half-prostrate Connie, supplying the kind of push needed to complete the job. And as she lay sprawled on the floor, flat on her back, I plopped myself down on her legs—and none too gently, either—while in the same motion pinning her arms to her sides.

She struggled to free her arms. But weighted down like this, the woman was hardly in top fighting form. "Get off me!" she shrieked. "You'll break all my bones, you cow!"

I ignored both the command and the insult. I was occupied with sorting things out in my mind.

It had been Connie who killed Luella, of course. I mean, it had to be. And then I realized that she'd orchestrated my entire investigation right from the beginning, targeting Nadine and doling out the clues that would eventually lead me to the girl. *Like a trail of damn bread crumbs!* I fumed.

A screaming Connie broke my concentration. "You'll be sorry! I'll sue you!" But after a couple of seconds there was a dramatic change in her tone. "Look, you're really hurting me," she said reasonably. "I don't know what you think you saw, but it wasn't like that. I can understand how you might have gotten the wrong impression, though; believe me, I can. Why don't we have some coffee. I'd like the chance to explain things to you." She was grimacing horribly now, which, all things considered, I didn't mind a bit.

An instant later I was struck by a frightening thought: *How long will I have to sit here like this, riding sidesaddle on a murderer?*

The wall phone was well out of reach. And if I were to yell for help, who would hear me—Beatrix?

Wait a minute. Where was Hortense? I recalled that the woman came on Saturdays. But at around eleven-thirty, as a rule. No, I'd have to scratch Hortense. If she'd been in at all today, she finished her work before I arrived.

Don't panic. There's still Kevin. I'd left word for him to meet me at Connie's, hadn't I? But the question was, when would he show up? And just as important, how would I even let him in?

And now another unwelcome idea forced its way into my head. *Good God! What if I have to go to the bathroom?* I ordered myself to banish this possibility from my mind immediately. But I couldn't help squirming, and I inadvertently shifted my weight a little.

Which provoked a high-pitched "Owww!" from Connie.

I actually mumbled an apology. But mostly because I'd just concluded that as long as I was stuck with her anyway—literally, you might say—maybe I could use the time productively.

"Why did you kill your sister, Connie?" I inquired politely, as she made another, even more feeble attempt to release her arms from my grasp.

"I didn't kill her. And please let me up."

"I'm sorry, but I can't do that."

"But you have no idea of the pain I'm in. And I know I can straighten out this whole misunderstanding if we could just sit down and talk."

"First, let's talk about your sister."

"No. Get off me, and then we'll discuss my sister."

I shook my head.

"You bitch!"

Which ended the conversation.

I don't know how long after this it was that the doorbell rang. It felt like hours, but in all probability it was no more than five or ten minutes.

Kevin! I would have bet on it. But what did it matter, anyway? I couldn't go to the door.

"Why don't you answer that? Maybe with someone else here you'll give me the chance to prove how mistaken you are," Connie said, moaning a little with practically every word. "You can get up; you don't have to worry about me," she cajoled. "I'd have to be crazy to do anything to you with somebody right outside the house."

I swiveled my upper torso completely around to glower at her just as the doorbell rang again. And rang. And rang . . . And when it stopped I wanted to put my head down and bang it against the floor.

Only about three minutes had passed when I thought I heard a noise inside the house, toward the front somewhere. I leaned my body in the direction of the sound, straining to listen.

Nothing.

It was only my imagination, I decided. And my eyes stung with tears.

And then I heard footsteps. And they were getting closer. . . .

Kevin stood in the doorway, gaping.

I forgot! He has the keys!

"What in the name of heaven is going on here?" he demanded.

"Connie killed Luella," I announced. And now I had to raise my voice to a shout to drown out the strident denials of his former sister-in-law. "And a while ago she attacked me with that knife over there."

"But it can't be. She—"

"Call the police," I instructed. "I'll explain everything later."

"She's crazy, Kevin," Connie insisted shrilly. "The woman should be in a straitjacket."

But Kevin went to the phone.

And within fifteen minutes I was finally able to detach my rump from Connie's thighs.

The police had arrived.

Chapter 44

Well, as you know, it was Beatrix's dish that triggered the solution to the killing—the bona fide solution, I'm talking about. Seeing that dish, I realized that there was no way Nadine could have murdered her stepmother. Not with any poisoned pencils, at least. That cat was always making himself at home on Luella's desk, sniffing, nuzzling, and/or licking everything in sight. Which, of course, meant there was a better than even chance he'd end up a casualty, too. And one thing I would swear to. Even if Nadine had been positively desperate to get rid of her stepmother—and paranoia or no paranoia—she wouldn't have risked her beloved Beatrix's life to do it.

But to get back to the aftermath of the attack . . .

Except for Kevin's last-minute change of heart, I might still, to this day, be sitting in that kitchen, crushing Connie's legs. He had hesitated about using his key, he told me. In fact, he'd even started to walk away from the door. But then he'd changed his mind. The messages I had left him said that I'd uncovered the killer and that I'd be at the town house. Well, he'd reasoned, what if the killer had shown up there, too?

At any rate, I was willing—*eager*—to press charges against Connie. But no one had actually witnessed her aborted try at canceling me. So it was her word against mine. And you should have heard her story.

She's been slicing bread for sandwiches, she informed the police, when I said I had something to show her. And so she dutifully followed behind me, not even aware she was still holding the bread knife. But then I looked around and—neurotic creature that I am—on seeing the knife in her hand, became totally unglued.

The thing is, though, it wasn't really what she said; it was her delivery. I almost believed her myself, honestly. A little training and that woman might have wound up First lady of the American Theater, for God's sake.

In spite of her stellar performance, though, Connie was detained at the station and, I understand, arraigned that night, charged with menacing and criminal possession of a weapon. But this nice young officer with the most gorgeous blue eyes cautioned me not to expect anything to come of this. In all probability, he told me, the case would be thrown out of court.

And who cared, really? As soon as I had time to think about it, I realized that even if, by some miracle, she should eventually be convicted of going after me like that, this would hardly satisfy Kevin. Or me, either, for that matter.

It turned out, however, that luck was finally on our side. As I was to learn soon afterward, a couple of crucial pieces of evidence were uncovered in the town house right around the time of my little set-to with Connie. And the prospects for her being brought to justice for the death of her sister—particularly when you also factored in the knife-wielding—suddenly became a whole lot brighter.

First, before I arrived that Saturday, a minute amount of the sodium fluoroacetate powder was found in the grooves of the spigots in the basement sink—where Connie had apparently prepared the lethal solution. Also discovered were some traces of the liquid mixture that had dripped onto the floor in front of the sink.

And then on the morning after the altercation, the police came up with something else, something that was perhaps even more damning. Two tiny, gnawed-up poisoned pencil stubs had been wrapped in a handkerchief and hidden in a hat box in the attic. And the hat box had Connie's fingerprints—and only Connie's fingerprints—all over it. Naturally, I can't be sure about her plans for these pencils, but their size suggested something to me that I'll pass on to you. Although Connie being Connie, a much more ingenious use for them had probably been devised.

For what it's worth, though, my idea is that she'd been holding the stubs in abeyance should she feel at some point that additional evidence against Nadine was required. And in that event, she would plant the stubs somewhere in the girl's apartment. For example, she might slip them into a pocketbook or a canvas tote, something like that. This way it would appear as if the bag had been used to transport the poisoned pencils from Luella's office, with Nadine, naturally, intending to dispose of the lot of them. However, these two little ones had been overlooked, concealed in the folds of the bag. But as I said, that's only one possibility.

There's another piece of information, too, that I've done a fair share of speculating about: Detective Wolfson, Sergeant Blake's partner (yes, I met them at last), confided to me that it was actually a fluke the poison was ever identified at all.

According to Wolfson, sodium fluoroacetate is not something you'd normally test for. But it seems this young toxicologist on the case happened to be discussing poisons with an uncle of his one night. And the uncle, a retired toxicologist himself, mentioned sodium fluoroacetate—which he'd encountered a couple of times in the course of his own career—going on to talk about how lethal the stuff was. Well, Wolfson didn't know whether it was an inspiration, a whim, or a last resort, but anyhow, that led to the nephew's examining Luella's organs for evidence of the fluoroacetate.

Of course, to my way of thinking, this raised an interesting question: If you wanted to frame someone for murder, would you dispose of your victim by means of a substance that might never come to light—and therefore could result in the erroneous finding that death was due to natural causes?

Uh-uh. Not knowingly, you wouldn't. I had to believe that either (a) Connie had no idea how unusual it is to check for sodium fluoroacetate or (b) Nadine was merely her ace in the hole, that she was doling out all these clues to divert suspicion away from herself *just in case* Luella's death should be ruled a homicide. And if, on the other hand, it should be determined there'd been no foul play here, then fine. No harm done. She hadn't actually supplied what could be considered hard evidence against the girl.

It was the Sunday evening following the Saturday afternoon Connie tried to murder me (or "menaced" me, if you care to accept the stupid legal designation). It would be weeks before Wolfson was to tell me of the rather esoteric nature of the poison. And more to the point, a couple of days yet before we had any inkling of the recent discoveries in the town house. This lack of knowledge regarding the latter being the reason Kevin and I were here at Nadine's, meeting with Luella's family.

I'd done some really intensive boning up on Connie since the previous night, coming across things about her in my notes that I'd managed to skip right over all the other times. A matter of focus again.

At any rate, the word was already out about the "alleged" knife attack, with the family members, understandably, totally confused. And we were determined that they have the facts. Connie had been released on her own recognizance, you see, and Kevin and I—unaware that her arrest was imminent—were afraid for the girls. After all, it was impossible to gauge the depth of the woman's animosity toward Nadine and to know whether any of that animosity spilled over to her sisters. And, actually, we both held ourselves at least somewhat accountable for any danger they could be in.

I'd not only failed to recognize the truth but, to top it off, had allowed myself to be taken in by trumped-up and/or slanted evidence. And as for Kevin, you can imagine how mortified he was. He'd been so positive that one of Luella's stepdaughters had to be the killer that he'd completely closed himself off from any other alternative.

Right now the small group was gathered in a kind of semicircle in the living room. Kevin and I took up opposite ends of the love seat, Enid and Geena occupied a couple of club chairs (the upholsterer had evidently come through at last), Andy sat cross-legged on the floor, propped up against his wife's legs, and Nadine was perched on the embroidered footstool.

I began by saying that Connie had set Nadine up as Luella's killer, which prompted expressions of shock and disbelief. A whole chorus of them.

"But why?" Nadine cried. "I loved Aunt Connie, and I thought she loved me, too." (Well, so much for my theory that the girl wasn't all that fond of her aunt—one more example of my uncanny perceptiveness.)

"I'll go into that in a few minutes," I answered. "First I want you to know just what precipitated the incident between Connie and me yesterday." And I went on to detail how, upon seeing Beatrix's bowl, I'd stumbled into the realization of Nadine's innocence—and provoked Connie's attempt on my life. This report of their aunt's murderous intent was greeted by more expressions of shock and disbelief. But Nadine beamed when I related the cat's subsequent—if unwitting—heroics. (And did I mention that, thanks to a call from Kevin, she had picked Beatrix up yesterday evening before Connie's release, and he was now in permanent residence here, where he belonged?)

"I could grab him and squeeze him," Nadine was saying. And then she smiled plaintively. "If he'd only let me, of course. And if I even knew where to lay hands on him." And here six pairs of eyes automatically—and nervously—went to the top of the bookcase, the tallest piece of furniture in the room.

There were a couple of moments of silence before Enid asked, "But even if you decided Nadine hadn't killed Luella, why would Aunt Connie go after you with a knife?"

"I think I said something about there being proof that Nadine wasn't responsible for the murder. Maybe Connie interpreted this as my having some sort of proof that *she* was. Or it could be that she was that anxious to see Nadine convicted of the crime."

"This is so bizarre," Enid responded. "Aunt Connie helped bring us up—Nadine, all of us."

"Yes, but she had her reasons for resenting Nadine. Or so she thought, at least."

Suddenly Enid was struck by the full impact of my encounter with Connie. "And you're saying that Aunt Connie killed Luella?" she gasped, horrified.

"I am."

"My God," Nadine murmured.

"Let's get back to that attack on you, for a second, Desiree," Andy put in here. "How did Connie hope to explain away your body on her kitchen floor?"

I shrugged. "She didn't really have the luxury of thinking things through, don't forget; she acted instinctively. But not to worry. Connie would probably have come up with a doozy of a solution."

"Maybe you're right," Andy conceded. Although he sounded far from convinced.

"Look, she could have claimed she'd persuaded me to stay for dinner and that she'd gone out to the store to get something for our meal. And by the time she returned, her house had been burglarized, her jewelry was missing, and poor, dear Desiree lay stone-cold dead next to the cat bowl. I give her an 'A-plus' for imagination, though. She'd no doubt have done better than that. She might even have found a way of implicating Nadine.

"And I'll tell you something else. She'd have seen to everything, taken care of every last detail to ensure that whatever scenario she decided on appeared authentic. I've learned that it's pretty much impossible to overestimate that woman."

"There's something that makes no sense to me," Enid brought up then. "It was her idea to call you in to investigate, wasn't it?"

I glanced over at Kevin now, who seemed to be absorbed in his own private thoughts. (Earlier today, though, he'd heard most of what I was relating here.) "Well, it was a joint decision," I answered. "But I was an important part of Connie's plan. While I suppose she managed to throw one or two of her so-called clues out to the police, too, her opportunities there were limited. A private investigator, of course, would be much more accessible to her. She had to be very careful, you see, that it didn't look like she was doing what she was doing—if you follow me. Which meant that she couldn't just drop all of those clues of hers one-two-three. They had to be spaced out over time in order to make it appear that the revelations were inadvertent. And incidentally, it wouldn't surprise me if she had some additional pieces of evidence ready to go in case the gems she'd already provided didn't get the appropriate response."

"It wouldn't surprise me, either," Kevin said. *He had been paying attention, after all.* "And do you know something? I'm not at all certain that, in spite of her protestations, Connie didn't somehow encourage my stance on Luella's death—my insistence that she'd been murdered, that is. She's a very clever woman. Strange that I can only fully appreciate just *how* clever now that I know she's a killer."

"I can't seem to take all of this in," Enid told me, shaking her head. "Aunt Connie and Luella—you've never met two sisters any closer."

"I believe Connie was terribly jealous of Luella," Kevin responded.

"*Murderously* jealous," I stated firmly. And about a minute later: "I suppose you're all aware by now that Luella died by chewing on her pencils,"

Four heads nodded—Andy's, the most vigorously. And then he asked, "When did Connie actually coat them with the poison—after she and Luella came home that Friday night?"

"Had to be. Once Luella went to bed, Connie must have sneaked down to the office, gathered up the pencils, and

prepared the solution. Or maybe she'd collected the pencils
earlier in the evening—say, when Luella was upstairs getting dressed—and just left the treating of them for later."

"What was it that made you suspect me?" Nadine posed
the question almost fearfully.

"Yes. Why would you believe Nadine was the killer?"
Enid demanded.

Everyone—Kevin included—was leaning toward me now.
There were even a couple of open mouths in my audience.
Well, here goes.

The first thing I did was explain that it had been Nadine's
repeated remarks about lead poisoning that served as the
cornerstone of Connie's diabolical plot to single her out as
the murderer. Following which I reminded Nadine about
Connie's visit on the morning Luella died. "Remember how
she spent all that time in your bedroom, ostensibly on the
phone with a student of hers? Well, that was her opportunity
to grab up the pencils on your desk. And she probably managed to get hold of some others around the apartment, too.
Then later that week she substituted your pencils for Luella's,
the idea behind this being that I was supposed to conclude
you'd made the switch because you were afraid your lead
poisoning comments might place you under suspicion."
There was a pause before I mumbled disgustedly, "And I was
very obliging, too."

"But wasn't Connie concerned that the police might take
Luella's pencils with them for testing right away—before
she could do any replacing?" Andy wanted to know.

"Oh, she was fairly safe there," I told him. "What reason
would there be to check out the pencils? Poison wasn't indicated at that time. Luella's death hadn't even been ruled a
homicide."

It was Enid's turn again. "Once it was established that
Luella *had* been poisoned, though, how could Aunt Connie
be sure you'd think of the pencils?"

"I don't have the slightest doubt," I answered dryly, "that
she'd have provided whatever little prod was required to as-
sist me with that."

"And she left four pencils for you to find?"

"Four that I know of. Although she most likely concealed
some in other places, too."

"Was that it?" Nadine asked, a shrillness in her tone. "Or

did my dear aunt supply still more clues that made me appear
to be a killer?" It was apparent she was dreading the answer.

"There were others, too," I had to admit. And I went into
the business about the crossword puzzle.

I drew the line, though, at mentioning Connie's bogus attempt to extract that promise from Kevin about Nadine's
mother. You know, that he wouldn't disclose the woman's
mental illness—and its possible consequences to her daughter. Connie—as I should have realized—was well aware this
would only serve to stress the importance of his sharing
these things with me. I wondered if that dinner with Connie's psychiatrist friend had also been artfully constructed
for my eventual benefit. But I decided instantly that Connie
already knew all about post-traumatic stress disorder and
that she'd steered the doctor into discussing it. And that this
why she'd invited Kevin to join them.

I glanced over at Nadine now. She was sitting there hugging herself, looking sad and hurt and bewildered, totally unlike the pert, bouncy young woman I'd met before.

No. There wasn't a reason in the world to dredge up any
of this.

Geena was reacting to her sister's body language, too. "Let
me get you some tea, Nadine," she offered quietly. I suddenly
realized it was the first time she'd spoken up tonight. "Would
you like that?"

"Yes, please," Nadine answered in a tiny little-girl voice.

Geena started to rise, but Kevin quickly jumped to his feet.
"I'll do it. I think it's important that you hear the rest of this.
Anyone else care for anything?"

We all declined politely, and then—mostly just to tie up
the one loose end—I broached the subject of Connie's remaining clue. "Uh, I understand you'll be taking a cruise,
Nadine."

She looked at me blankly. "What cruise?"

I should have known. "The one invented by your aunt," I
muttered bitterly. "She told me you'd booked a reservation a
while back—before Luella died, I mean—for the last two
weeks in June."

"I'd never have gone away at that time. Luella's birthday
was June twenty-second. We—all of us—celebrated it together." And then seconds later, she murmured, "Oh." Followed by an almost inaudible "I see."

But Geena's expression informed me that she didn't see.

And it seemed that Andy, too, had no idea of the significance of this supposed reservation. Plus I wasn't that sure about Enid, either. So I clarified for them. And then I went on to point out how this was a prime example of Connie's cunning.

"She never overplayed her hand," I said. "First, she mentioned casually one day that Luella was a Cancer on the cusp of Gemini, trusting, I guess, that I wasn't entirely unfamiliar with the astrological signs. It wasn't until weeks later that she fed me the rest of the clue—about Nadine's purported cruise."

"Tell me," Enid said now, "didn't Aunt Connie consider that you might check out something like that with Nadine?"

"Apparently this didn't faze her. It would have been easy enough for her to insist that she'd misunderstood Nadine, that she didn't know where she could have gotten such an idea. In fact, when I mentioned the trip yesterday, that's pretty much what she did say. Only she said it in such a way as to suggest that she hadn't realized the implication inherent in Nadine's making plans for then. And, of course, being a devoted aunt, she was now attempting to cover for her niece."

"This is—it's just unreal," Nadine whispered, when, at that moment, Kevin returned with the tea. Mouthing her thanks, she bent her head to the bright red ceramic mug and took a few sips.

When she raised her eyes, they glistened with tears. "But why was she so jealous of Luella? Was it the success? Her looks? All the men she'd had in her life?

"And what did I do to make Aunt Connie feel so—" And setting the cup on the floor now, she gazed at me imploringly. "What I'm asking is, why me?"

Chapter 45

First questions first.

"I have no idea how Connie felt about Luella's success," I said. "But I don't imagine that having a sister who was so talented and well known could have been much of an ego booster. And the same goes for Luella's good looks. All I know—and this is just about a certainty—is that Connie cared for two men. And Luella snagged them both."

"Two men?" an astonished Kevin parroted.

"That's right. There was Bud Massi, as I told you this afternoon. And before that, there was you."

I heard a gasp of surprise—from Geena, I think—and then Kevin protested, his face crimson now, "Oh, come on, Desiree. Connie and I were merely good friends."

It never ceases to amaze me how even the most intelligent men act like their brains are made of Jell-O when it comes to women. I responded with infinite patience. "As soon as you and Luella got married, Connie rushed off to Europe. And I don't believe it was to give you and her sister time alone with each other, either. She needed to get away because of her feelings for you.

"Look, the proof is in the poison. It was then that she bought the fluoroacetate. It had to be; she hasn't been abroad since. Now, why she didn't make use of her purchase when she came home is anybody's guess. But it's clear that she never entirely abandoned her plan to eliminate the competion because she held on to the stuff until Luella beat her out for the second time."

Kevin was still in denial. "You forget that Connie asked me over for dinner so that she could introduce me to Luella."

"That's what she claimed *after* you fell for her sister. A way of saving face. But she even told me once that she didn't put it that way when she invited you."

"I can't really recall."

"My take," I said, "is that Connie attended that cooking class to start with because she wanted to meet people—and most likely male people. Think about it. She was hardly in need of cooking lessons, Lord knows. But that, I believe, was the whole idea. It was something she was good at, something that would show her off to advantage."

"Makes sense," Andy agreed.

"The more I turn it over in my mind, the surer I am about it. But anyhow, let's fast forward five years. Connie is, apparently, over you by now, Kevin. And Bud Massi enters the picture. Well, he, too, falls for Luella, and they begin seeing each other. But Connie doesn't give up. Not this time. In fact, she goes all out to pique the man's interest. She colors her hair, buys a new wardrobe—even takes a computer course because of Bud's involvement with software. And will someone satisfy my curiosity? Hortense mentioned that Connie had hurt her back exercising. Was the exercising also a recent thing with her?"

"It was recent," Nadine answered softly. And then: "Do you think she was still hoping she'd have a chance with Bud? Once Luella was out of the way, I mean."

"Yes, I do think so."

For a moment Nadine was thoughtful. Then she frowned. "I feel so stupid. None of the things Aunt Connie did to attract him made any impression on me."

"Listen, I knew about these changes in the woman's lifestyle, too. But I didn't attribute them to an interest in Massi, either. And this is supposed to be what I do for a living—put facts like that together. At one point I even made some remark to her about the difference in age between Bud and Luella, and Connie definitely overreacted—by her own admission. I probably should have wondered why the age thing would bother her so much. But I didn't.

"And would you like to know what else I overlooked? Seemingly, Connie tried to patch up the rift between Luella and Bud. Only she got nowhere with him. Which should certainly have struck me as being a little odd. This is an unusually bright, very persuasive woman—remember how she went about selling all of you on the need for my services? Yet she wasn't able to make any headway with Massi. And we know he wasn't that unreceptive to a reconciliation, either. Because when Nadine approached him shortly afterward, she had no trouble in getting him to give the relationship another try."

Here Nadine revisited the apparently forgotten mug that had been sitting at her feet. The tea definitely had to be on the chilly side by now, but she appeared not to notice. She took four or five sips as if to fortify herself. "Is that why Aunt Connie hates me so much?" she said at last, sounding like a little girl again.

Well, we had worked our way around to that other question of hers. "I'm not sure 'hate' is the right word," I responded. "At the very least, though, her electing you to take the fall for Luella's murder leads me to believe she resents you a great deal. But at any rate, the answer is yes, I think your intervention with Bud Massi could be part of it. Or maybe she was afraid that you wanted him for yourself. You used to tease Luella about that, didn't you?"

"If Nadine had wanted Bud for herself, why would she convince him to go back to Luella?" Geena asked.

"Most likely she wouldn't. But I've been trying to look at this from Connie's perspective, Geena. Bear in mind that Connie pretended to try to set things right between the two of them. It's remotely possible that she thought Nadine's efforts were in the same vein as her own. Not being as clever as she—Connie—was, however, Nadine inadvertently succeeded."

"I think that's pretty farfetched," Enid put in here.

"So do I. I'm only offering it as a possibility. And there's also another one. And this makes a little more sense to me."

"What's that?" Nadine said anxiously.

"She might have thought that you were attempting to get Luella and Bud back together again in spite of your own interest in the man. In other words, you were being altruistic. But now, with Luella gone, you would be free to act on your feelings."

"That's not true!"

"*I* know it isn't. But maybe Connie didn't."

By this time, I'd about covered everything, and a few minutes later I was through answering questions, too. So after a final warning about their Aunt Connie's vengeful and duplicitous nature, Kevin and I said our good nights.

"Well, mission accomplished," he pronounced as we entered the elevator. "You did very well, too. I think it'll be

some time, however, before I can look those girls in the eye.
But at any rate, I'm glad it's over."

"So am I. I'm a little disappointed that I didn't get to see
Beatrix, though."

"Why on earth would you want to? Maybe it's not his fault,
but that cat's become totally insane. And a menace, besides."

"Well, he *did* save my life, you know."

"And it was completely inadvertent." Kevin looked at me
skeptically. "You do realize that, of course."

"Of course. Don't be silly."

"But?"

"It's just— Uh, nothing."

"What were you going to say?"

"Nothing, really. You're—"

And now the elevator jerked to a stop on the fourth floor.
Three people were standing there, waiting to get on. And so
the dialogue was discontinued. By the time we reached the
lobby, Kevin seemed to have forgotten all about it. Which
was just as well.

I couldn't even consider telling him what was on my mind.
I mean, if I'd so much as suggested the *possibility* of a thing
like that to Kevin, he would have thought I'd gone right over
the edge—regardless of my explaining my doubts about its
actually having happened, too. (And honestly, I really do
have doubts.)

But the truth is, just after Beatrix landed on Connie's
shoulder—you know, in that split second when we looked at
each other—I had the impression—and I'm sure I was
wrong—that he smiled at me.

Don't miss the next Desiree Shapiro mystery,
Murder Can Singe Your Old Flame

It was a familiar voice—and one I'd hoped never to hear again. "Please, Dez, don't hang up," it pleaded.

I promptly slammed down the receiver, astonished at how quickly my mouth had gone bone dry on me.

It took less than a minute for the phone to ring again. I let my answering machine handle things this time.

"I need to talk to you. Please. Just listen for a little while, okay?" For a moment I stood there mesmerized, staring at the machine. "I don't blame you for not wanting to speak to me— honestly, I don't. I behaved like a pig. Believe me, I'd never have gotten up the nerve to call you if the situation wasn't . . . well, critical. I suppose that by now Pat must have told you what happened. To my wife, I mean. It was really—" A half sob now, a second or two of silence, and then the voice went on.

"But what I'm calling about, Dez, is that I could be in trouble. Terrible trouble. I know I don't deserve it, but I was hoping that maybe I could convince you to help. It's . . ."

I reached over and, teeth clenched, turned off the machine. And then, my legs steadier than I'd have imagined, I shut off the lights and left the room.

Five minutes later I was soaking in the tub, up to my chin in fragrant, soothing bubbles.

"Well," I silently announced to myself, "you certainly showed *him*."

As soon as I got to the office the next morning, I dialed my friend Pat Martucci.

"I heard from Bruce last night," I informed her tersely.

"Yes, I know. He said he was going to call you." And before I could respond: "He's pretty desperate, Dez. He thinks the police may suspect him of murdering Cheryl."

"That would be nice."

There was a long pause before Pat said softly, "I can't really blame you for taking that attitude. But Bruce isn't a murderer. A louse, maybe." And then she amended hastily, "No. A louse, definitely. But not a murderer."

"You can't be sure of that."

"He really cared for Cheryl. I'm sure of *that*. And so is Burton," she added, referring to her live-in love, who also happened to be both Bruce Simon's cousin and close buddy.

"And Burton wouldn't be at all prejudiced, would he?" I said to her snidely.

"Maybe he is. But *I'm* certainly not. I think Bruce deserved to be . . . well . . . *stoned* for that stuff he pulled on you."

Stoned? Why not castrated? But I refrained from posing the question aloud.

"You can't really think Bruce is capable of killing someone, can you?" Pat demanded.

Actually, who could say what that man was capable of! In the months I'd dated him, Bruce had lied to me, insulted me, and humiliated me. And that was his more benign behavior. What finally provided the jolt I seemed to require in order to get my brain in gear again was his neglecting to apprise me of the fact that he had a fiancée back in Chicago. Must have slipped his mind, huh? I know it's mean-spirited of me, but my one consolation in all of this was that he hadn't been playing fair with her, either—this same Cheryl Pat was insisting he'd been so crazy about.

Still, it was hard to picture Bruce pushing his new wife— or anyone else—in front of a train. But then, it's usually hard to imagine someone you know committing a horrendous act like that.

"Well, *do* you?" Pat was saying.

"Do I what?"

"Do you really think Bruce is capable of murder?"

"If being a P.I. has taught me anything, it's never to make that kind of a judgment."

"So I, uh, gather you've decided not to help him, then."

"Listen, Pat, I'm not the only private investigator in the world. I'm sure Bruce can get someone else to look into Cheryl's death. As a matter of fact, he never had a very high opinion of my investigative skills, anyway. In his mind, all I was capable of was dogging straying husbands." (Which, in truth, was at one time the high end of my business. But that was long before Bruce Simon made his unfortunate entrance

nto my life.) "He'd be much better off finding someone he can
)ut his faith in."

"But he has faith in *you*," Pat protested. "Lots of it." And
1ow she waited for a response that didn't come. "Maybe
/ou're right, though," she said at last. "Maybe Bruce should
;et someone else." Then giving me absolution: "And no one
:an say you don't have every reason to feel the way you do,
:ither."

. didn't get any work done that day. (Not that I had all that
nuch to do.) I was too busy trying to justify myself to myself.

What did he expect, anyway, after the way he'd treated me—
hat I'd drop everything just because he was in some kind of
rouble?

The man had chutzpah; I'd give him that. But this was some-
hing I'd discovered a long time ago. Less than five minutes af-
er I met him, actually.

It wasn't that I wanted to see him get hung with a crime he
lidn't commit, you understand. (Although being a true Scor-
)io, for a while there the idea wasn't exactly repellent to me.)
The thing is, though, wouldn't it make more sense for Bruce to
1ire someone who wasn't going to be bogged down by all these
ll-feelings toward him? Of course it would.

After almost an hour of driving myself crazy, I succeeded in
vorking my way up to a five-star headache, which two Extra-
Strength Tylenols did little to alleviate. I absolutely refused to
et Bruce affect my appetite, however. So at a little past noon,
ifter rejecting the idea of venturing out into the heat of this op-
)ressive August day—a record breaker, the weatherman had
varned that morning—I had a sandwich at my desk. A ham
ind brie with honey-mustard dressing. And I thoroughly en-
oyed it, too.

Just as I was consuming the last mouthful, I received a visit
from Elliot Gilbert, one of the principals of Gilbert and Sulli-
/an, the law firm that rents me my office (read "cubbyhole")
ipace. He wanted to know if I'd finished my report on this in-
iurance case I was handling for him—a very simple task, by
he way, and the only piece of business I had at present. I was
orced to admit that I still hadn't wrapped it up and, moreover,
hat I was thinking of cutting out early today. "Would it be
)kay if you got it first thing in the morning?" I had the gall
o ask.

I was assured that this would be fine. But Elliot—one of the best-natured people you could ever meet—would have given me that same answer if I'd been working on something he needed for court in five minutes.

"Are you sure it's all right?"

This response, too, was predictable. "Absolutely."

Anyway, at around two I grabbed my attaché case—inside of which Elliot's insurance file now lay in wait for me—and vacated my office. First, though, I had to explain the reason for my early departure to Jackie. Now, this woman—whose services I can only afford because of my arrangement with the Messrs. Gilbert and Sullivan—is probably the best secretary in New York. The trouble is, though, she could also qualify as the most impossible secretary in New York—thanks to a very strict work ethic, a tough-love approach to bringing up her employers, and a genuine and often smothering concern for our well-being.

"What's the matter? Aren't you feeling well?" she demanded upon hearing of my intention.

"I'm okay. A headache, that's all."

"That's why you're leaving early?" Her tone bordered on incredulous. "Why don't you just take a couple of Tylenols?"

"I did. But apparently this isn't that kind of headache."

"What kind of headache *is* it, then?"

At that point Jackie's telephone rang, and she was forced to cut the interrogation short.

Ignoring the "wait" she mouthed, I beat it out the door.

The first thing I did when I got home was put up the coffee, which turned out to be so excruciatingly bitter it didn't even live up to my usual rock-bottom standards. And then I sat down with Elliot's insurance file. Forcing myself to concentrate, I managed to wrap up the remainder of the work fairly quickly.

And then I took some grapes from the refrigerator, switched on the TV, plopped down on the sofa, and prepared to watch a couple of deliciously lascivious talk shows.

After I was about three minutes into the first program, my jaw dropped almost to my chest, where it remained for most of the show.

Are those people for real, do you think? There they are, revealing the most intimate details of their lives to millions of people—and for reasons that make no sense at all. One woman said she was appearing on TV like this because she was pregnant with her husband's brother's child and wanted the audience's advice on whether to tell her husband the baby wasn't his. I mean, didn't it occur to this ditz that her on-air confession had taken that decision out of her hands?

Anyway, I was all caught up in the histrionics of an angst-ridden eighteen-year-old girl who admitted to carrying on with her fifty-plus stepfather while her poor mother lay in a coma—when the phone rang. It wasn't easy to tear myself away from Cindy and her newborn conscience, but I answered it.

"It's me again," Bruce Simon said timidly. "Just hear me out for a couple of minutes. Please."

"Go ahead." It's possible that close to an hour's worth of talk show had weakened my brain.

"I tried to reach you at your office before," he explained. "But they told me you'd already left. You're not sick, are you?"

"No, I'm fine. And I'm listening. So say what you have to say."

"Yes. All right. Thanks," Bruce responded hurriedly. "You know that my wife was hit by a train."

"Yes, I do know. And I'm truly sorry for your loss, but—"

"Thank you. What I wanted to tell you is that I think the police suspect Cheryl may have been murdered. And it's very likely she was. But they also think I might have been the one to push her off the platform. Why would I, though? I loved . . . that is, Cheryl and I were . . . the thing is, we—"

Apparently, he was attempting to soft-pedal his affection for his wife in the event I might find this upsetting—all this concern for my feelings a first for Bruce. I broke in to spare him any further discomfort. "It's okay. I'm not the least bit disturbed to hear that you loved your wife."

"Oh, I didn't mean— What I'm trying to make clear is that there was no reason for me to want Cheryl dead. I swear there wasn't. You do believe me, don't you?"

"I don't know if I do or not. But, for the moment, anyway, I'm willing to give you the benefit of the doubt."

"Will you investigate her death for me, then?"

"Why me, Bruce? I'm hardly your advocate. In fact, if you want the truth, I'm afraid that I have very little use for you. Why not bring in someone who's at least neutral, who doesn't already recognize you for the snake you are?"

Now, if you think that I was being unnecessarily harsh with this man in view of the tragedy he was coping with, I can only tell you that in deference to this tragedy, I actually swallowed most of what was on my tongue.

Bruce had to have had some reaction to my words, but he didn't let it show. "I'd like you to look into this because I trust you, Dez," he answered, his tone even. "And because you're smart. Plus I know you to be a fair person. I'm certain that you won't let what went on between us—the crap I pulled—affect your doing your job."

Well, he'd never complimented either my intelligence or my ethics before. Another measure of his desperation.

"Look, let me give you the names of a couple of colleagues of mine. Also smart. And also fair. They'd—"

"No, please. I have a very strong feeling—a *sense,* you might call it—that you're the only one who can help me."

Naturally, I protested, maintaining that he was being foolish. After which Bruce protested my protest, insisting I was his sole hope. Well, the windup was that I finally agreed to look into Cheryl Simon's death. Sucker that I am.

But then I suppose I'd known that I would—on some level, at any rate—from the very beginning.

SIGNET

Selma Eichler

"A highly entertaining series."
–Carolyn Hart

"Finally there's a private eye we can embrace..." –*Joan Hess*

Also Available:

❑ **MURDER CAN SPOOK YOUR CAT**   0-451-19217-6/$5.99

❑ **MURDER CAN WRECK YOUR REUNION**   0-451-18521-8/$5.99

❑ **MURDER CAN STUNT YOUR GROWTH**   0-451-18514-5/$5.99

❑ **MURDER CAN RUIN YOUR LOOKS**   0-451-18384-3/$5.99

❑ **MURDER CAN KILL YOUR SOCIAL LIFE** 0-451-18139-5/$5.99

❑ **MURDER CAN SINGE YOUR OLD FLAME** 0-451-19218-4/$5.99